Also by Rebecca Chance

Divas
Bad Girls
Bad Sisters
Killer Heels
Bad Angels
Rebecca Chance's Naughty Bits

KILLER QUEENS

Rebecca
CHANCE

**SIMON &
SCHUSTER**

London · New York · Sydney · Toronto · New Delhi

A CBS COMPANY

First published in Great Britain by Simon and Schuster, 2013
A CBS Company

1 3 5 7 9 10 8 6 4 2

Simon & Schuster UK Ltd
1st Floor
222 Gray's Inn Road
London
WC1X 8HB

www.simonandschuster.co.uk

Simon & Schuster Australia, Sydney
Simon & Schuster India, New Delhi

A CIP catalogue record for this book is available from the British Library

Paperback ISBN 978-1-47110-169-4
Trade Paperback ISBN 978-1-47110-168-7
eBook ISBN 978-1-47110-170-0

Typeset by Hewer Text UK Ltd, Edinburgh
Printed and bound in Great Britain by CPI Group UK Ltd, Croydon CR0 4YY

For everyone at Thomson TUI, the Karisma hotel group and the staff of the El Dorado/Casitas Royale on the Mexican Riviera, for the amazing stay they organized for me while I was writing this book – it was the trip of a lifetime!

Acknowledgements

Huge thanks to:

At Simon and Schuster: Maxine Hitchcock, my always-superb editrix, plus Clare Hey and Carla Josephson, who've worked like Trojans alongside Maxine to get this book into print on a very tight deadline. Sara-Jade Virtue and the amazing marketing team – Alice Murphy, Dawn Burnett, Ally Grant – who work just as hard promoting the books. Dominic Brendon, James Horobin, Gill Richardson, Rumana Haider and Rhedd Lewis in sales are raising my sales with every book, and I'm incredibly grateful. Hannah Corbett in publicity has been brilliantly efficient and very generous with the bubbles!

At Simon and Schuster in Australia: a big thank you to Kate Cubitt, Carol Warwick and the whole team.

At David Higham: Anthony Goff, my ever-wonderful agent. Marigold Atkey has been helpful and efficient way beyond the call of duty, and Tine Nielsen, Chiara Natalucci and Stella Giatrakou in foreign rights do a fantastic job of selling Rebecca Chance overseas.

Emma Draude and Sophie Goodfellow at Emma Draude PR, who are getting reams of fabulous coverage for my books! Lucky me!

Garry Wilson, Fiona Jennings, Lisa Jones, Emma Lee, Katie Badger and everyone at Thomson TUI who helped to organize my trip to Mexico so that I could set part of the book in the most fabulous resort imaginable. Thanks so much for your superb skills in organizing the trip and the competition – it's been a really fun and delightful collaboration, I hope the first of many! Special thanks to Sharon Johnstone in Cancun, killer heels and all, who put together so many great excursions for me to write about and let me pick her brains over a delicious lunch at the stunning El Dorado Maroma hotel.

Everyone at the Karisma hotel group for hosting me so generously when I visited the El Dorado Royale and the Casitas Royale (the resort featured in the book). Their hospitality to me as I simultaneously researched and wrote the Mexico sections of this book was simply outstanding, absolutely world-class. Jose Carlos Vasquez gave me a fascinating tour of the resort, and introduced me to Pancho and Maria, the resident alligators; Flor Rodriguez very sweetly let me ask her lots of questions about the hotel in the glamorous Martini Bar; Francisco Jorge oversaw everything with superb efficiency, and our butlers, Pablo, Liliana and Elizabeth not only seemed to know what I wanted before I did myself, but were utterly charming. I must have been a considerable nuisance with all my queries, but they kept smiling their lovely smiles and never let me know it! Jesus, Irving and Alejandro kept the strawberry Popsicles coming (not a euphemism). Thanks also to Andrew and Alan, who also got roped into question-answering, and to our waiter Innocencio at Jojo's restaurant, who made me a grasshopper out of palm leaves and brought me dessert cocktails, just as he did for Lori. It really was the most amazing stay and I could cry right now thinking of how lovely the swim-up suite was, the gourmet food, the drink, the luxury – truly, if they gave six stars to resorts, the El Dorado and the Casitas would be first in line. Thanks also to Martina at the Maroma and to Lucero at the Azul Sensatori, who gave me tours round their stunning hotels, and to Jonatán Gómez-Luna and his team at Le Chique for a twenty-eight course dinner that was one of the best I've ever had in my life. Roll on the Michelin star!

Matt Bates, my beloved partner in the worship of Eleanor Burford and her many pseudonyms.

The Royal Navy Commander (who wishes to remain anonymous) who let me pick his/her brains about navy ties, destroyers etc for Hugo. And the person married to the Commander, who provided me with a lot of nicknames from their time at the University Royal Navy Unit.

The utterly charming Sujata Naik of GiGi London Medical Aesthetics, who's also a dab hand with the salt microdermabrasion gun . . .

Sarika Patel of Clarity Colonics, who really is as nice and gentle as her description in the book!

Colin Butts, my man in Ibiza, who knew *exactly* where the young royals would go to party with off-duty ladies of the night . . .

My new intern, Lydia Laws-Wall, who does a killer Power Point presentation: really looking forward to working together!

As with BAD ANGELS, I honestly don't think I could have written this book in a very short amount of time without the Rebecca Chance fanfriends on Facebook to cheer me up, distract me and express naked envy at my amazing photos of Mexico! Angela Collings, Dawn Hamblett, Tim Hughes, Jason Ellis, Tony Wood, Melanie Hearse, Jen Sheehan, Helen Smith, Ilana Bergsagel, Katherine Everett, Julian Corkle, Robin Greene, Diane Jolly, Adam Pietrowski, John Soper, Gary Jordan, Louise Bell, Travis Pagel, Lisa Respers France, Stella Duffy, Shelley Silas, Serena Mackesy, John Holt, Tim Daly, Lev Raphael, Joy T Chance, Lori Smith Jennaway, Alex Marwood, Sallie Dorsett, Alice Taylor, Marjorie Tucker, Teresa Wilson, Jason Ellis, Margery Flax, Clinton Reed, Valerie Laws, Simon-Peter Trimarco, and Bryan Quertermous, my lone straight male reader (bless). Plus Paul Burston, the Brandon Flowers of Polari, and his loyal crew – Alex Hopkins, Ange Chan, Sian Pepper, Enda Guinan, Belinda Davies, John Southgate, Paul Brown, James Watts, Ian Sinclair Romanis and Jon Clarke. Plus the ineffable sisters Dolores Feletia von Flap, Phyliss du Boire and Ida May Stroke. If I've left anyone out, please, please, send me a furious message and I will correct it in the next book!

Modified thanks to Laura Lippman for introducing me to the torture that is Pure Barre – as with Belinda, it's so much nicer when we sweat through the DVDs together!

The adorable McKenna Jordan and John Kwiatkowski, for bringing my smut to Texas.

And as always – thanks to the Board.

Oukaïmeden, the Atlas Mountains

Twenty years ago

The paparazzo's cold fingers were slow to move on his Nikon. He had been waiting for nearly an hour in the freezing cold, pacing up and down, ducking behind the primitive hut that was the only possible place of concealment every time the cables of the chair lift started to whir, indicating that a skier was on their way up to the top of Jebel Attar. Twice he had been on standby, expecting to see Her step off the rickety, slow-moving lift with Her usual grace, and twice he had been disappointed. Both sets of arrivals had been locals, lean Moroccan-looking men who were clearly familiar with the pistes; they had wasted no time heading for the approach to Grande Combe, the bumpy descent known as a mogul field, for experienced skiers only.

Still, he would keep waiting. If there had been a Paparazzo's Paparazzo award, a sculpture of a camera lens, whisky bottle and brimming ashtray, Nigel Slyme would have been consistently in the top three finalists. It was his life. He didn't mind heat, cold, wading through waist-high water carrying his precious camera above his head, or spending fortunes on the latest telephoto lenses, as long as he snatched that precious shot of a British princess getting her toes sucked by her American lover as she reclined on a sun lounger, or an internationally famous pop star nipping out onto the private balcony of her five-star hotel suite for a furtive joint, topless and looking as rough as a badger's brush after a hard night partying. The chase was everything. Once he'd captured the shot, sent it off to his agency, he felt nothing but a depressing comedown. He suspected his colleagues of sharing exactly the same sensations once they had filed; why else did they all smoke like chimneys and drink like fish?

The wife who had left Nigel years ago had been a shopping addict, silly mare. Went out and spent a fortune on things she didn't need, then let the bags pile up around the flat, never even bothering to take out the contents and put them away. Once she'd gone on the hunt down Oxford Street and dropped the dosh, she couldn't have cared less about her purchases. Looking back, though, Nigel understood his ex in a way he hadn't when he'd been kicking those bags across the lounge and yelling at her about racking up the credit card bills. It was all in the anticipation. That was what made your blood run hotter, your heart beat faster, as you heard the cables singing overhead and wondered if this time, it would be Her arriving for Her early-morning ski.

Nigel's ex-wife had said sourly, many times, that Nigel thought more about Her than he ever had about the then-Mrs Slyme, and she had been absolutely right: Nigel couldn't deny it. His nerve-endings were tingling as he pulled off his gloves and blew on his hands to warm them up, slapping them together. He had to have bare fingers to operate the delicate focusing ring of the Nikon; minor frostbite would be nothing if he managed to get these photos.

He saw the long legs first, a second or two before the rest of Her body came into view, and his heart soared. It was the closest Nigel Slyme had ever been to falling in love. And if you had asked him if love, to him, meant hiding out to capture photographs of his obsession when She thought She was alone, take Her private moments and plaster them all over the tabloids, Nigel would honestly have been baffled at the question. She courted the press, didn't She? Worked it like She was born to it. Posed like a pro. And he always made Her look gorgeous. Mind you, that wasn't hard, was it, with that face and figure?

Besides, how would he have known that She was making a habit of sneaking up here to Jebel Attar to go skiing by herself at the crack of dawn, if he hadn't been tipped off by someone in Her entourage? Oh, She was in it with him, every step of the way.

Nigel drew in his breath as he saw Her jump down lightly from the chair lift, the tight blue ski suit flattering Her lean body. On the crown of Her head were silver goggles, propped on top of the white cashmere pull-on hat which framed Her lightly tanned face. Her skin glowed, Her cheeks were flushed from the cold morning air thousands of feet above sea level, Her lips shiny with protective balm.

Nigel had been expecting Her to look exhilarated at the impending exercise, and the rare treat, for Her, of solitude in a public place. But Her expression, as She looked around the mountaintop, glancing at the faded old signs which barely did the job of indicating the pistes, was ... *thoughtful*, he decided. *Like She was making a big decision. And sad.*

Like She knew what was coming, he would say afterwards to the myriad journalists who all wanted to talk to him, the last person to see Her on that fateful morning. *It sounds mental, but that's what it was like. She was beautiful and sad and sort of resigned. Like She really did know what was coming.*

Of course, it wasn't just Nigel's words that conveyed how Princess Belinda had seemed at daybreak in the Atlas Mountains. Once Belinda had surveyed the small, snowy plateau, she didn't glance again at the ramshackle hut. Nigel was able to inch up, place the lens of the Nikon on its roof, and start to shoot. The light, gusting wind covered any noise of the camera shutter as it clicked away, capturing every fleeting expression that passed across one of the best-known faces in the world. The long straight nose, the straight dark brows over the big hazel eyes, the Cupid's bow lips which made her smile so entrancing; from the moment it had been clear that Prince Oliver, heir to the British throne, was seriously considering the young Lady Belinda Lindsey-Crofter as a potential bride, her Disney-princess smile had been flashed around the globe, creating such excitement that the world had held its breath waiting for the Prince to finally propose.

Her silky straight dark hair fanned out over her shoulders below the white pull-on hat, those strong athlete's shoulders which, combined with her height and her lean hips, made her a perfect clotheshorse. Her small breasts rose and fell as she drew in a deep breath, staring over the stunning, snow-covered landscape below, the Piste des Mouflons, scattered with boulders and stone outcroppings that looked terrifying to Nigel. He found himself devoutly praying that Belinda wouldn't choose that route, and sighed in relief as she turned towards where the earlier skiers had headed that morning, the Grande Combe.

It all happened so fast. She pulled down her goggles and pushed off, the swift, skilled strokes of her poles signifying her expertise at the sport; commentators had said that Belinda was gifted enough to have been picked for the British ski team, that Prince Oliver's gain was a loss for the sport at an international level. She schussed off on a straight run down the start of the hill, flying along, her hair whipped by the wind, her posture perfect, barely using the poles at all. Nigel dashed out to the edge of the plateau, no longer needing to be concerned that she might become aware of his presence, switching for the telephoto shots to the Canon which also hung round his neck, capturing her as she sped down the piste, imagining with glee how much the agency would eat up this photo sequence of Belinda all alone in the expanse of white.

The ink was barely dry on her divorce from Prince Oliver. She was still Princess Belinda, but no longer Her Royal Highness, a small but crucial distinction. She shared custody of her son and daughter with Prince Oliver, and the children were with him at Sandringham now for the winter holidays as Belinda took her first getaway as a single woman, away from it all in one of the most obscure ski resorts in the world, high in the Atlas Mountains above Morocco. Only Nigel Slyme had tracked her down here, and the elation pumping through his veins was near-orgasmic as he frantically found an angle to snap the Princess as she shot away, heading for a stand of tall Spanish fir trees, covered in snow, disappearing from view for twenty seconds; he used the time to readjust the focus, preparing for her to emerge on the other side.

And there she came, flashing out from behind the last tree, her blue figure angled forward, poles tucked in, as she headed along the base of an overhanging ridge. It was the most stunning image: the slim blue shape bright against the white snow, dark firs behind her, the ridge rearing above her, piles of snow-covered boulders stacked dramatically along its slope.

It really did happen so fast.

From one second to the next, the world changed. Nigel didn't know if he'd felt the shudder of the impact first, heard the dull roar, or saw the first boulders beginning to topple as the cliff exploded before his eyes. Only the instincts drilled into him by decades of his work kept his finger on the shutter; you kept shooting, no matter what happened, until someone hit you or put a gun to your head. So he captured everything, that split-second where the blue figure was still visible, still in its skier's crouch, either unaware of the avalanche or trying desperately to outrun it; and then the moment where it disappeared forever, buried under the mass of boulders pouring down to cover the piste entirely, the entire ridge, shockingly, horrifyingly, disappearing in a single blast, as if blown up in a puff of smoke.

And there *was* smoke, in a way. A cloud of snow, obscuring the blue sky, hanging there for a long, suspended moment before drifting down to land on what had been a cliff and was now a flattened heap of rocks and stones, like a gigantic cairn that marked the final resting place of one of the most famous, beautiful, unhappy women in the world. The woman who had once been Her Royal Highness, Princess Belinda, before turning her back on the prospect of ever being Queen.

Nigel Slyme kept clicking on the shutter release, again and again and again, until finally it would no longer move; he had run out of film. Lowering the Canon, he stared blankly at the scene in front of him, the chaos left by the avalanche. The occasional stone was still falling, rolling slowly down the mountainside until it ran out of momentum and settled. The snow, too, had settled now, masking the ugly debris, softening its lines.

He would never see Her again.

Nigel's face was icy cold and stingingly painful. It was only when he raised one frozen hand to his cheek that he realized that his skin was wet with icy tears.

London

Present day

Chloe Rose was sitting on one of the curved suede banquettes at Pirate's Cove, Mayfair's latest go-to club for the young, rich and titled party set. She was smiling. Nowadays, whenever she was out in public – even in the dimly lit basement of Pirate's Cove – Chloe always smiled. It wasn't a big, fake, beauty-queen smile; she was careful never, ever to flash one of those, because in the beginning she had, a couple of times, and the photographs had not only looked horribly fake, but had revealed that her teeth weren't completely even.

She'd thought she had an idea of the level of scrutiny she would be subjected to, when the news emerged that she was dating Prince Hugo. She knew that she was fairly slim, had regular features, dressed smartly, and, best of all, was highly photogenic, which wasn't at all the same thing as being pretty. Not being arrogant, Chloe was perfectly well aware that she was nice-looking, but not a beauty: nothing to rival Hugo's dead mother, the famously stunning Princess Belinda.

But she had told herself that she was fine with that, and she meant it.

What she hadn't anticipated was being torn to pieces by the media for every tiny little flaw in her appearance, every single choice of clothing, every accidental smudge of mascara, every stray wisp of hair. As if she'd been a model or an actress, someone who set herself up as a beauty icon, not just a young woman who worked for a charity and whose job merely required her to look groomed and professional.

Chloe could have listed then and there every single thing that she had been told was wrong with her physically. And while she did so, she would have kept smiling, a small, seemingly contented smile that she had perfected through extensive practice in front of the mirror. Not smug, not a smirk, just a happy little smile. She caught sight of herself now in the mirrored wall facing the banquette, and nodded, confirming that it was perfect. As was her hair, as was her makeup. Her judgement was perfect too; she'd allowed herself one cocktail all evening, sipping from it slowly, letting the ice dilute the rum even more as time passed. Prince Hugo's girlfriend could not ever be seen to lose control in a public setting.

What was sauce for the goose, however, wasn't sauce for the gander. She glanced over to Hugo, who was enthusiastically rocking back and forward on the small dance floor to a reggae remix, the kind of music very much favoured by rich white drunk posh boys, as it didn't require any actual dancing abilities. You just stood there and rocked happily, pretending you were much cooler and blacker than you actually were, occasionally saying 'Yah, mon!' in what you thought was a Rasta accent as you waved your beer bottle around in time to the beat. Hugo wasn't a big drinker, but he certainly liked to take the edge off, something Chloe only allowed herself at strictly private parties.

As she watched, a rake-thin girl, with the cascading blonde hair that the British aristocracy seemed to have specifically interbred to grow thicker and lusher and blonder than that of commoners, gyrated up to Hugo, turned round, and shoved her almost non-existent bottom into his crotch, giggling hysterically. She circled it around, managing to toss her hair repeatedly at the same time, her hands straight out in front of her in a parody of a video vixen that the men on the dance floor greeted with whoops of encouragement.

The women, on the other hand, glanced immediately over to Chloe, who was sitting by herself on the banquette; the rest of her party was dancing or out the back smoking. Chloe could almost hear what people were thinking: 'Lonely Chlo', the nickname the meaner tabloids had given her. 'Lonely Chlo', who had to wait for long periods of time in London for her boyfriend to come back on shore leave from his Navy post, but had to avoid looking miserable, upset or, God forbid, scruffy, whenever she left the house. 'Lonely Chlo', because she didn't fit in with the posh Pirate Cove crew, with their titles and their trust funds and their infantile nicknames – 'Squishy', 'Pug', 'Eggy', 'Boo-Boo', which they all maintained to demonstrate to outsiders that they would never truly be insiders, no matter how hard they tried.

'Lonely Chlo', a nickname which Chloe was sure had been given to her by her nemesis, Princess Sophie, Hugo's absolutely horrible sister . . .

'Whoo! Sexy! Go Minty!' cried a cut-glass, utterly triumphant voice, and Chloe looked round to see Sophie herself, theatrically throwing back her own stunning blonde mane, applauding her friend, who was now wrapped around Hugo, apparently attempting to execute a series of pole-dance moves using Hugo as the pole.

'Chlo! Babes, come and dance!'

A hand grabbed hers, pulling her to her feet. She looked up at Prince Toby, Hugo's cousin, the biggest slut in London, and the nicest. Chloe knew perfectly well that Toby had come to rescue her from an embarrassing moment, and gratitude flooded through her. The rest of their group were Hugo's friends, not hers. It was sink or swim for Chloe, as far as they were concerned, and if she were drowning they would never have raised a finger to help her out.

'Thanks, Tobes,' she said, her smile widening into one that was entirely genuine. 'Top mate.'

'Don't give it a thought,' Toby said, winking. 'Always happy to rescue a damsel in distress.'

He wheeled her across the dance floor, to the far side, blocking her view of Minty, who was winding her slender limbs around Hugo like a boa constrictor.

'She doesn't stand a chance with old Huge, you know,' Toby said with his usual endearing frankness. 'No way could Minters ever be a princess. She's shagged half of Eton and half of Sandhurst – and not one at a time, either. Nothing wrong with that, of course, but the stories chaps could tell! God, one night we were all off our faces, and Minty climbed on the billiards table stark naked and started trying to put the cue ball into her—'

'Stop!' Chloe shrieked in his ear. They were swaying back and forth in the traditional Sloane mating dance, her arms around his neck, his around her waist, so it was easy for the two of them to talk without anyone else hearing them over the music.

Toby rolled his eyes.

'Forgot you were a nice girl from suburbia,' he said, but in such a friendly way that Chloe didn't take offence. 'It was pretty bloody hilarious, I can tell you. She lay back and started screaming: "Pot me! Pot me!" So we all did. Jolly good time all round.'

As so very often with Toby, Chloe was rendered speechless. She hadn't expected to discover that a certain section of the upper classes were so sexually uninhibited, and some of their anecdotes literally made her toes curl. Fortunately, Hugo was cut from the same cloth as her; he might be happy to dance with Minty – aka the Honourable Araminta Farquhar-Featherstonehaugh – but if she had stripped off in front of several men, stretched out on a billiards table and started doing something suggestive with a cue ball, Hugo would have shot out of the room faster than you could say: 'Time for a nice cup of tea, I think.'

Toby, however, was Hugo's polar opposite in the sexual mores stakes. And that was exactly the right way to put it: Toby always wanted more. More girls, more booze, more noise, more fun. To be fair, Toby did not rely on his privileged status to get laid; he exuded a natural charm and a red-blooded enthusiasm for all of life's simple pleasures that made everyone he met want to be his friend, fuck him, or both. A tall, strapping redhead with wide shoulders, a hard body from polo-playing, and a faceful of freckles, he was like a winning combination of a Cabbage Patch Kid and Action Man.

'And it's not just chaps telling stories, either,' Toby went on. 'There must be photos of Minty *en deshabille* on half the mobiles in London.'

Chloe allowed herself an ironic smile. The Palace set had a tendency to assume that they knew everyone, or rather, everyone who mattered; they would regularly say 'all of London', or 'all of Scotland', when what they really meant was 'the handful of families we grew up with'. 'The *gratin*, as Hugo's father, Prince Oliver, called it, meaning 'the upper crust'.

'And videos, too,' Toby added as they shuffled round. '*Lots* of videos. I've got one of her and Nacho Montes after a polo match – top stuff! Honestly wouldn't have thought it possible. Nacho's really pretty damn impressive. Huge thighs, you know. Helps for balance, I suppose, when you're shagging a girl on top of a horse.'

Chloe was giggling now, her head on his shoulder. Toby always managed to cheer her up when she was feeling down.

'Thank you, Tobes,' she murmured in heartfelt tones into his handmade Savile Row shirt. 'You do know how to make me feel better.'

Toby pulled back a little and looked down at her, his handsome face unexpectedly serious.

'You're the one for old Huge, Chlo,' he said. 'Really, you are. He's got a big old job to do, and it's heavy on his shoulders. You're just the girl to help him carry the weight. Nothing against Uncle Olly, but he hasn't exactly been much use in the father department. He should have married again, really. Given Huge and Soph another mama. And Great-uncle and Great-aunt' – this was how Toby referred to King Stephen and Queen Alexandra – 'are all terribly stiff-upper-lip and buck-up-and-play-the-game, you know? Doesn't suit Hugo. He's a lover, not a fighter.'

Chloe had never been more grateful for her ability to keep a natural smile plastered to her face. As she stared up at Toby, letting the full weight of his words sink in, no one around them would have realized the importance of what he had just said. Toby had endorsed her as Hugo's future wife. This was truly momentous. Her feet kept moving, following Toby's shuffle, her body swayed gently, but her brain was processing what he had just said with a mixture of excitement and disbelief.

Chloe and Hugo had been a couple, on and off, for five years. Long enough for Chloe to be absolutely sure that she was in love with Hugo, the person, and not Prince Hugo, the heir to the British throne. Long enough for Chloe to fully understand the level of scrutiny to which she would be subjected for the rest of her life, if she were given the opportunity to marry him, and to accept that that would be the price to be paid. Long enough for any normal young couple to decide that they were ready to get engaged: Chloe was twenty-seven, Hugo twenty-nine.

And more than long enough for the nickname 'Lonely Chlo' to burn its reluctant owner, every time she heard it, as if it were a dash of acid over her bare skin.

Chloe knew that she was by no means the bride that the Royal Family would have chosen for Hugo. To be fair, neither was the Honourable Araminta Farquhar-Featherstonehaugh (surname pronounced Farker-Fanshawe, in what Chloe considered a deliberate attempt to make common people look stupid when they got it wrong). The King and Queen would have preferred a nice, quiet, not-very-bright girl from the ranks of the aristocracy, one who had been born into the *gratin* knowing every unspoken rule, who had her own silly nickname – 'Wonky', or 'Flaps', perhaps.

She felt her chin raise in defiance of Hugo's snobbish grandparents and icily distant father.

Toby's absolutely right, she thought proudly. *I am the girl to help Hugo carry the weight of being King one day. I love him and he loves me. I may not be posh, but I'm not a chav either. And frankly, the Royal Family could do with a bit of common blood in it. Hugo's mum was really posh, and that marriage was a complete disaster – Prince Oliver and the King and Queen won't even hear her name mentioned!*

'Darling!' Hugo came up, throwing his arm around her shoulder. 'Tobes, unhand my lady! Whatever he was whispering in your ear, Chlo,' he said, grinning at his cousin, 'you should just bloody well ignore. You know what a dirty bird he is.'

'Toby was actually saying really lovely things,' Chloe answered pertly. 'Not a rude word to be heard.'

'Oh my God! It's worse than I thought!' Hugo pulled her away from Toby. 'He's trying to seduce you! Toby, this one's off-limits!'

Chloe was giggling with happiness. One of the things she loved most about Hugo was that he never tried to be cool, to make her jealous, to play games at all. The Mintys of his social circle might try to dirty-dance with him, or corner him for a full-on flirting session, but their advances all went over Hugo's head: he just thought they were jolly friendly girls.

'You know what you'd be getting into with that one,' he said, glancing at his cousin. 'He's an utter freak show.' Lowering his head to Chloe's, he hissed loudly:

'Ginger pubes! Absolute bush of 'em, too! Chaps never wanted to use the shower at school after he'd been in there! Soap was plastered with 'em, and the drain—'

Toby was sniggering.

'I *do* have a big bush,' he said, complacently cupping the crotch of his jeans. 'Apart from my huge cock, I'm practically a woman.'

Some parts of being posh Chloe would never understand if she lived to be a hundred.

'Should we be going?' she said, turning to Hugo. 'It's past midnight, and I have to be up for work . . .'

'Of course! Sorry, darling!' He bent to kiss her. 'We're off, chaps!' he announced.

Chloe sighed. Just once, she'd like to slip off with her boyfriend, just the two of them – well, plus his security officers, of course – avoiding the procession that always fell in behind them. Everyone wanted to be seen with the heir to the throne, and since photos were strictly prohibited inside Pirate's Cove, being snapped by the paps waiting outside was the ideal way to secure that trophy. A group clustered around them, and in the bustle at the cloakroom Chloe and Hugo were separated. She was pulling on her Reiss coat – bought on sale, and still at the absolute limit of her budget – as she heard Sophie say to Minty, in that clear, cutting voice which was lowered, but still pitched to carry perfectly to her intended victim:

'Darling, have you *heard* the latest thing they're calling Lonely Chlo? Dog Rose! Because she's *such* a social climber! Awfully clever, don't you think?'

Minty, more than a little tipsy and not Britain's Brainiest at the best of times, slurred: 'Sorry, darl, don't get it . . .'

'Her surname's Rose! Dog Rose! Honestly, you *are* as thick as a brick, Minters,' Sophie snapped impatiently at her drunken friend.

'*Oh!*' Minty could be heard saying as they turned to leave, Sophie glancing back swiftly at her victim to ensure that her words had hit the bull's eye.

And they had. Chloe was frozen to the spot, her hands at her belt, which she had just finished buckling and pulling smooth. She wanted, very badly, either to cry or to slap Sophie in the face, but she couldn't do either. She couldn't do anything but keep smiling. This was the true price of being with Hugo – the slights and slurs visited on her by his spiteful sister and her coterie, a level of sheer, snobbish nastiness which spread all too quickly to the press, and was picked up by a large section of the public. Chloe was resented by women who were desperate to be in her place, the girlfriend of a prince in line to be king. Those women would have accepted Hugo being with one of his own kind, but were driven to heights of jealousy specifically because Chloe, the daughter of a suburban retired engineer and a housewife, wasn't remotely posh. She was just a normal middle-class girl. Like them.

And if a normal middle-class girl could have a chance with Prince Hugo, why not me? envious women thought, looking at the latest photographs of Chloe and Hugo together at a charity event or a polo match, Chloe pretty and well-groomed, her light brown hair streaked with blonde, her figure trim but not skinny, her subtle green mascara bringing out the emerald lights in her hazel-grey eyes; an attractive girl, but not a model or an actress or an aristocrat. Just a very nice example of the girl next door.

So why her and not me? women thought resentfully. *What does she have that I don't?*

Sadly, Chloe had been made all too familiar with that mentality. The upper classes thought she was an upstart, and the middle and lower ones resented her for exactly the same reason.

Poor Cinderella must have had a really miserable time after the fairy tale ended, Chloe thought bitterly. *I wonder if Prince Charming had a sister who spent her life making up increasingly nasty nicknames for Cinderella . . .*

Everyone was leaving. For a split second, Chloe was tempted to hide out in the loos for a good cry. Finally letting go, letting it all out. She always carried spare makeup: she'd be able to repair any damage before she eventually emerged. That vicious phrase, 'Dog Rose', was already causing the tears to well up. It would catch on immediately, of course: Sophie had a twisted genius for insults. She should be writing for late-night Channel 4 comedians.

But if I hide out, there'll be a huge scene. Hugo will come back to find me, Sophie will put out the story that I'm crying because I heard someone saying 'Dog Rose', and that'll not only make the nickname spread even further, it'll show that it has the power to upset me.

And I can't let that happen. If it does, I'm lost for good. You can't be a princess and show that you're affected by nasty gossip. You have to be above it all, or you're not fit to be a princess in the first place . . .

The awful thing was that it felt as if Sophie won either way. And Sophie had planned everything meticulously. The insult had halted Chloe in her tracks for long enough that, by the time she emerged onto Piccadilly, the rest of the party was already walking towards their waiting cars. Minty had wound her arm through Hugo's and was telling him something '*terrifically* funny', laughing up into his face for the benefit of the paps, looking to all the world as if *she* were his date for the evening, not Chloe. Flashes were going off, rough male voices calling all of their names as familiarly as if they were friends: Chloe was used to it by now, but this time it rankled as never before. And it wasn't just her name they were calling: she could hear 'Lonely Chlo!' being shouted to provoke a reaction.

Next time it'll be 'Dog Rose'. She shuddered at the prospect.

Minty was hanging off Hugo's arm, dressed in her designer shaggy Mongolian fur coat, dyed neon green, short enough to show off not only her long bare legs, but, by implication, that she was rich enough to never really need to worry about the cold, because she was never outside long enough to feel it. If Chloe, a size 12 to Minty's 8, had tried to wear that coat, she would have looked like a joke, a Big Bird who waddled rather than tripped lightly in the six-inch heels Minty was sporting.

And Sophie had pushed her way forward to follow Hugo. Being royalty, next heir to the throne after her older brother,

Sophie didn't need to hang on his coat-tails for press attention: in fact, as a pretty princess, she naturally commanded more. But she had twined her arm through Toby's, was giggling and smiling for the cameras just like Minty, and the impression given was of two handsome, perfectly matched, aristocratic couples who had been out together as a foursome.

With me tailing behind like a fifth wheel, Chloe recognized with a sinking heart.

'Chloe!' To her great relief, her boyfriend turned round, looking for her, dropping Minty's arm. 'Darling, we completely lost you there! Terrible crush – I should have waited for you. *So* sorry.'

He strode back towards her, capturing her hand, tucking it familiarly over his elbow, patting it reassuringly.

'Let's get you home for some sleep,' he said. 'My Chloe has a proper job, not like you three layabouts.'

Warmth flooded through Chloe. The tears were back, prickling at the corners of her eyes, and when they were safely ensconced in the car, curled on the back seat, she let them fall. The security officers were in the front, one at the wheel, one beside him, but she knew them to be totally trustworthy.

'Darling!' Hugo said again, pulling her even closer. 'What's up? I thought we had a lovely night out!'

Oh Hugo, you are so sodding blind, she thought with immense irritation. But that one, at least, she couldn't blame on him being royal. Hugo was a typical man; he had no idea of the evil machinations of which women were capable, nor did he want to know. Chloe knew better than to complain to him about his sister or Minty: that would just put his back up. And she couldn't mention the Dog Rose thing either. Talking about class made Hugo incredibly uncomfortable;

like all posh people, he did his best to pretend that it didn't exist.

'We did have a lovely night,' Chloe agreed, sniffing back the tears. 'I'm just knack— *tired*, I suppose.' She really was tired if she'd even let the word 'knackered' half-slip from her lips; usually she was so careful to posh up her vocabulary. 'It's a lot to go out dancing after a long day at work.'

This was exactly the right line to take. Hugo was hugely proud of the fact that Chloe worked for Rescue Children as the deputy head of fundraising: she was a serious girl, with a grown-up job doing something socially worthy, a total contrast to Toby and Sophie's crowd of party animals. Hugo, a Royal Navy Lieutenant, was much the same, having risen through the ranks not entirely due to his royal status but also to his capacity for hard work.

'I won't drag you out during the week any more,' he vowed. 'Or at least, we won't stay so late.'

'I feel better now I'm alone with you,' Chloe said, reaching up to kiss him; she had long got over her embarrassment at making out with security officers nearby. Hugo kissed her back with great enthusiasm, reaching down and pulling her legs across his lap: she could feel his erection swelling beneath her thighs. One of the positive sides to his absences on board ship was that when he was on post-deployment leave, he was always keen to make up for lost time.

'Can't wait to get you back to mine,' he muttered against her lips, sliding his hand up her body to stroke one breast, making her moan. 'I've got a lovely bunch of bananas in the fridge, just waiting for us . . .'

Hugo might not be as wild as many of the Sloanes in his set, not cut out for group sex on billiards tables or filming Minty shagging a polo player on his horse, but he had one very specific sexual preference, involving bananas, that, very luckily, Chloe enjoyed too. And it meant that Hugo wasn't *completely* vanilla, always a good quality when you were planning to have sex with only one man for the rest of your life . . .

'I can't wait either,' she whispered. Some things were too private even for the highly discreet security officers. 'Will they be nice and cold by now?'

The hand on her breast slid higher, caressed her neck, reached her lips: he slid his thumb into her mouth, and she sucked on it eagerly.

'As cold as you're all lovely and wet and hot,' he sighed into her ear. 'Jesus, Chlo, I can't wait, I've got the most massive stiffie—'

'Mmn,' she observed enthusiastically, reaching down to stroke it. 'It really *is* massive—'

The car turned onto Palace Green, slowing down, and came to a halt outside Kensington Palace, where Hugo had his London quarters. From Piccadilly, around Hyde Park Corner down South Carriage Drive, along Hyde Park Gate took a bare ten minutes. The driver tapped on the partition, and Chloe slid her legs off Hugo's lap, taking her time, giving him a few moments to calm his breathing and settle down the royal erection before she reached for the door handle. This was the protocol that had evolved for this kind of situation. Chloe didn't actually open the door herself, but the movement of the handle was the signal that the security officer waiting outside could open the car door without exposing the Prince and his girlfriend *in flagrante delicto*.

Kensington Palace, despite its name, was actually a series of large, interconnected houses arranged around several wide courtyards; Hugo, as a bachelor, occupied a suite of rooms that did not, unfortunately, have its own front door, as many of the houses did. Usually, Chloe secretly lamented this arrangement, which meant that she and Hugo could never have a makeout session coming home, work themselves up to a happy heated state, then tumble out, unlock a front door, shut it behind them and fall to the hallway carpet to fuck each other's brains out.

Instead, they had to bid goodnight to the security team, greet the waiting footman, exchange a polite few words, walk down miles of corridor and up two flights of stairs to Hugo's suite of rooms, greet the second footman waiting there for them, go through the same routine ... it might have been specifically designed as a very effective passion-killer. Hugo's erection, she could tell at a glance at his crotch, was long gone.

It wouldn't take long to get it back. Not at all. But that wasn't actually what Chloe wanted, not quite yet ...

'Toby's such a sweetheart,' she observed as the footman left. She sank down onto one of the two chintz sofas that faced each other, very conventionally, in the living room. You would never know that a young man lived here. The apartment was decorated in classic Sloane style, from the yellow walls hung with gilt-framed oil paintings to the Chinoiserie vases on the mantelpiece and the unavoidable Colefax and Fowler fabric prints of oversized red and pink flowers called plumbagos exploding all over the cream background of every sofa, armchair, cushion and window treatment.

It was about as manly as a bikini wax, and Chloe had been taken aback by the décor on her first visit, imagining that Hugo must feel suffocated by it. All her male friends wanted stripped-down lines, modular sofas, dark wood, stripy sheets. But then, her male friends had to buy their own furniture. Aristocrats inherited, they didn't buy. And Hugo was perfectly comfy and cosy in this chintzy nest, because it signified something much more important than masculinity: it said that People Like Us lived here.

'I do love him madly,' Chloe added, watching Hugo's reaction as she praised Toby.

As she had learned, this was standard upper-class terminology for 'I like him a lot', but it was enough to get Hugo – who had always been a little jealous of his more handsome, more charming cousin – on edge.

'Ginger pubes, remember?' he said sharply, perching on the arm of the sofa. 'They match his freckles *exactly*. He looks bloody ridiculous naked.'

Chloe giggled, just as she was supposed to.

'That *does* sound awful!' she said, smiling at him sweetly. Actually, she thought Toby's Titian hair was very attractive, a fire burning warm and lively, a perfect reflection of his personality. But Hugo was the one she loved, the one she wanted to be with for the rest of her life, and if she had to tell a few white lies to make him feel secure – well, she'd want him to do exactly the same for her.

'So—' Hugo bent to kiss her. 'Shall I go and get the bananas? I'm feeling *very* randy.'

'Yes . . .' Chloe said, with just the right touch of hesitation in her voice. 'Yes, that'd be lovely.'

Hugo frowned. He was clearly torn: she had given him the go-ahead with her words, but not with her tone, and Hugo was not only a well-brought-up young man, but genuinely sweet-natured. With obvious reluctance, he said: 'Darling, is something wrong?'

'Oh, not really . . .' Chloe sighed. 'It's those horrible paps, I suppose. They do really get me down. It wasn't just tonight – they were outside my work again at lunchtime, yelling things. You know what they shout. The name they call me.'

'They're just trying to get a reaction,' Hugo said uncomfortably, his erection, which had shot up as soon as he mentioned the word 'bananas', diminishing for the second time this evening.

'I couldn't go and get a coffee, even,' she said sadly. 'Lauren had to get one for me. It's like being under house arrest. I'm in that office all day and I can't even pop out for some fresh air at lunchtime.'

'I don't know how you do it, working in an office all day,' Hugo said sympathetically, still hoping that he could soothe her quickly and get on with the business in hand. He stroked her hair, his hand slipping down to caress her neck in a way he knew she loved. 'Those horrible light strips overhead! I'm damn lucky to be out on a destroyer, you know. Most of the time it's so much fun it doesn't even feel like work.'

Chloe bit her lip; she was going to have to push harder. But after Toby's supportive words, coupled with Sophie's 'Dog Rose' comment, she was determined not to be distracted by Hugo's attempts to move matters from the conversational to the physical.

You've got to get on with it, she told herself firmly. *Just tell him how you feel. It's decision time. Lauren says that you should tell him if he doesn't propose in six months, you'll leave him.*

Lauren, Chloe's best friend and work colleague, was tough as nails, and pretty much always right. *Don't think of it as becoming a princess – that's always what messes with your head*, Lauren had advised. *Just think of it as getting your man.*

And she thought, too, of her last visit home, and what her mother had said to her when her father was out in the garden: 'Men all need a push, love, princes or not. I needed to give your dad a big old nudge to get him to go down on one knee, believe you me.'

Mum and Lauren together have to be right. Chloe took a deep breath and said as winsomely as she could manage:

'You know the weird thing? It's not even being able to pop out to the *coffee shop* that really upsets me. Every time I go in there it makes me smile, because it reminds me of how we met.'

This made Hugo sentimental, just as she had known it would. It was one of his favourite memories, because it proved to him all over again how genuine Chloe's feelings for him were. Even someone with as open and friendly a personality as Hugo couldn't have helped but be aware, when he was single, how much his title might influence a young woman's view of his other attractions. So it was always hugely reassuring to him that Chloe hadn't had the faintest idea of the identity of the young man in jeans and stripy rugby shirt and sunglasses who had been ahead of her in Freedom of Espresso, fumbling in his pocket for enough change for his coffee, five years ago . . .

'God, I'm so sorry!' Hugo had said to Carmen, the Romanian girl behind the counter, his cheeks flushing pink with embarrassment. 'I'm just back from, um, overseas, and I don't quite seem to have enough dosh – can I cancel the order?'

'No, I already make the cappuccino!' Carmen had said firmly, plonking it down in front of him. 'You need to pay.'

'How much are you short?' Chloe said quickly to the young man. 'I've got tons of change.'

'Two quid,' he said, turning to look at her. 'But I really can't—'

'No, it's fine,' Chloe said, reaching in her bag for her purse. 'Carmen's made your coffee now, you might as well have it. And my purse is stuffed, honestly. I'll be glad to lighten it.'

'Thanks, Chloe,' Carmen said gratefully as Chloe handed her the coins.

'This is awfully nice of you,' Hugo said, taking his cup.

Chloe smiled up at him under her lashes; she hadn't seen his face initially, so she hadn't realized how good-looking he was, even with the sunglasses on. Just her type – tall, fair and, if not exactly handsome, then with nice solid features and that posh-boy blush, which suffused not only his cheeks, but went right up to the tips of his ears. She had always fancied the Sloane boys, with their butter-blond silky hair and pinky-white skin; this one had Cupid's bow lips that were the colour of dark red roses. Very kissable.

'No problem,' she said. 'It's easy to get caught short.'

He started to say something, cut himself off, and then, grinning at her a little inanely, turned away from the counter. Chloe hoped he would wait for her, ask for her number; he had the perfect excuse, because he could offer to pay her back. But to her disappointment, she heard the doorbell clang as he left the shop.

'He likes you, I think,' Carmen said, making Chloe's skinny cappuccino with chocolate topping without needing to be told what she wanted.

Chloe pulled a face: *well, why didn't he ask me out, then?* She sighed; she'd definitely felt chemistry between them. *He must have a girlfriend*, she told herself to avoid feeling rejected. He was exactly what she'd hoped she'd meet when she was hired for Rescue Children, whose head office was in Fulham; the area was packed with just the kind of young men she liked. But so far, very disappointingly, they seemed to travel in packs with girls of their own class.

She paid Carmen and went out into the street, holding the hot coffee carefully.

'Um, hi!' said a voice behind her, and she jumped and nearly dropped the cup.

'Sorry!' he said as she turned round; he had gone pink all over again. 'I sort of guessed which way you'd go, and I got it wrong.'

'My office is down there,' she said, nodding to the unpromising modern block at the end of the short street.

'Oh, right! Well, I mustn't keep you,' he said. 'It's just – it was very nice of you, but I can't possibly take money from a girl . . .'

'That sounds a bit sexist,' Chloe said, her flirtatious smile making it clear that she was teasing him.

'Oh! Gosh! I didn't mean – Oh, I see!' He grinned at her. 'Nice one. So, um, I was wondering if I could maybe buy you a drink later on? To say thank you? Obviously,' he added hurriedly, 'I'd have some money by then.'

They stood there on the pavement, smiling at each other, for a long, happy moment; a nanny tried to push a Bugaboo past them, and Hugo jumped aside politely to give her room.

'So you'll come for a drink?' he said hopefully. 'Are you around later?'

Chloe debated whether she should play it cool, make him ring her for a date, and then decided that she'd been reading too many magazine articles about playing hard to get.

'I *am*, actually,' she said, though she did try to infuse a note of surprise into her voice that this was the case.

'Oh, wonderful!' he said enthusiastically. 'What a piece of luck! Look, shall I meet you when you finish work? What time is that?'

'Six, usually,' she said.

'Six it is. Um, just one thing.' He rubbed the back of his head. 'I won't actually be alone. Completely.'

Chloe frowned. 'I don't understand.'

She didn't like this, either. He had seemed so nice and normal; now things had taken a weird turn. She was bracing herself for him telling her that his girlfriend would be joining them; he looked awkward enough, suddenly, for something that outlandish. And his blush had by now spread to his neck. She took a little step back.

'Oh look, it's nothing *freaky*!' he blurted out, seeing her back away. 'You really don't understand, do you?'

She shook her head.

'I might just go,' she said. 'It was nice talking to you.'

'Please don't!' He flapped his arms like an agitated swan. 'Whatever you're thinking, it's not that! Look—' He pointed down to the far corner of the street, to where a man was standing with his back to a shop front, dressed in jeans and a sweater, lean and fit, his eyes on Hugo and Chloe. 'I know it sounds silly, but that's my bodyguard. There's another one, too. They sort of have to be around. But at a distance! They won't hear anything we say.'

Chloe's frown deepened as she wondered for a second if this young man were an escaped mental patient. But they *were* in Fulham, an area of London inhabited by some of the richest people in the world . . . people who might well need a bodyguard or two . . .

'You don't *sound* like an oligarch,' she said frankly. 'Or a footballer.'

He laughed, looking ridiculously happy: it was only later that Chloe realized why, that this was a further demonstration that she really did have no idea who he was. And she didn't. Maybe in a different context, she might have had an inkling, but here in Fulham there were so many Sloaney young men that looked like him . . . and he still had the sunglasses on . . .

'Can I tell you later?' he said. 'Over a drink?'

'I'd rather know now who I'm going for a drink with,' she said honestly.

'You have to *promise* to come if I do,' he said nervously.

'All right,' she said. *How bad can it be?* she thought. *It's just a drink! And I don't see anyone else asking me out right now* . . .

Hugo bent down and whispered his name in her ear.

It took all she had not to drop her cappuccino all down her Boden dress. But as soon as he'd told her, she knew it was the truth: she could see the press photos of him, slot the face looking down at her above the Navy dress uniform or polo outfit in which he was usually pictured. You just never thought you would bump into a royal prince in Freedom of Espresso; how could she possibly have anticipated this?

She was goggling at him. Briefly, he pushed his sunglasses up, showing her his face, just in case she had any doubt about his identity. His entire face by now was bright red with embarrassment and doubt as to her response.

'You *will* still come?' he asked, his voice just as anxious as his expression.

She nodded wordlessly and turned away in the direction of her office.

'See you at six!' he called after her, pushing down his sunglasses to the bridge of his nose again.

She nodded again and kept going blindly; she didn't remember anything about the rest of the day at all. Not a single thing. Until about five, when she went on a panicked rampage round the office scavenging for makeup, dry shampoo, hair straighteners, earrings to borrow; she was scared of popping out to buy anything in case he'd turned up early and was waiting outside. Who knew if his bodyguards had insisted on sweeping the area beforehand, or whatever it was they did?

'I never even drank that cappuccino,' Chloe said to him now. 'I told you that, didn't I? It sat there on my desk all afternoon till it went stone cold.'

'I honestly think I fell in love with you outside the coffee shop,' Hugo said simply. 'You were so pretty and funny and lively, and meeting you like that felt so . . . *normal*. It was just like – what *normal* people do.' He looked abashed. 'You know what I mean.'

'I do,' she said, stroking his leg.

That he used the 'love' word was no surprise: they had already said they loved each other, after a split four years ago when Chloe had been struggling with not only the attention that came with dating a prince, but a prince who went away on seven-month deployments off the coast of Somalia, chasing pirates. No matter how much Hugo assured her that, as a Captain of the Watch, all he did was 'drive the ship' and that the Royal Marines did all the daredevil stuff like boarding pirate boats, Chloe worried about him constantly, missed him horribly. And the drip-drip torture of paparazzi photos combined with the nasty little captions the tabloid press slapped on them had driven her to distraction. She had told him as soon as he came back on post-deployment leave that she couldn't bear it; they had broken up, then got back together on his last day of leave in floods of tears and declarations of love.

But Chloe couldn't wait any longer for the next stage.

'Sometimes,' she said brilliantly, 'I *so* miss being normal.'

'Oh Chloe!' Hugo enfolded her in his arms. 'That's the one thing I can't give you – I'd give you anything I could, but I can never ever give you that—'

'I want *you*,' she said, hugging him back tightly. 'I've always wanted you, from the moment I saw you in that coffee shop.'

'You don't know how grateful I've been ever since that I barely had any dosh on me!'

'I love you so much, Hugo!'

'I love you! *So* much!'

She thought swiftly.

'I'm going to get a lovely cold banana now,' she said, pulling away a little. 'I'll be right back.'

Hugo drew in his breath in excitement, settling back on the sofa in anticipation. Chloe returned almost immediately with a nicely firm banana, and he exhaled with a long, deep sigh of sexual anticipation.

'God, all those times at school,' he said with deep contentment as she started to unpeel it, his erection tenting his jeans for the third time that night. 'All those times I used to get a cold banana out of the fridge in my room and mush it up in my hand and go at myself with it . . . I used to dream of a lovely girl doing that for me, a lovely girl who looked just like you . . . I used to come and come and just feel lonely afterwards . . .' He reached out his hand for her. 'Ladies first.'

Their sexual life had settled into a very happy pattern by now. The banana was definitely for special occasions, rather than being a necessary fetish, but although Hugo had initiated it, shyly, years ago, Chloe had taken to it with great enthusiasm. The usual pattern was that the peeled banana would first be drawn down Chloe's naked body and slipped slowly inside her, alternating with Hugo enthusiastically eating her out; once she had come a satisfactory number of times, Hugo would replace the banana with his cock, and when things were getting close to the point of no return, he would pull out, Chloe would quickly chew up some banana and finish him off in her mouth.

But now Chloe shook her head.

'Darling, I'm pretty shattered,' she said, a phrase she would never have used before meeting Hugo. 'I'm just going to do you.'

'Are you *sure*?' Hugo said, to be polite, but he was already unzipping his jeans and shifting his bottom to pull them and his boxers down in one go.

'Totally,' Chloe said, hiking up her skirt to make it easier for her to kneel down on the carpet. 'I love sucking you off.'

'You do it the *best*,' Hugo sighed ecstatically, closing his eyes, throwing out his arms, letting himself go completely in anticipation, his royal penis, sprung free of its coverings, large, red, inflamed, and clearly in need of urgent attention. '*No one* does banana blowjobs like you.'

It was the opening Chloe had been waiting for. She gasped so loudly that Hugo's eyes snapped open again in time to see her throwing the banana down to the coffee table. He whined like a dog in protest.

'How many girls have given you banana blowjobs?' she shouted furiously. '*Honestly*, Hugo, you're so bloody insensitive! I'm being stalked by paps all day and all night shouting horrible things at me, you barely danced with me all evening – *Toby* danced with me more than you, *and* he said nicer things to me as well! – and I offer to suck you off even though I'm knackered, because I love doing it and I can tell you're absolutely gagging for it, and then you go and make me feel that I'm just one in a long line of your girls! God, I could scream!'

Poor Hugo, blindsided by this sudden stream of consciousness, stared at her, his rose-pink lips flapping goldfish-like without making a sound.

'I'm going home,' she declared. 'I don't care how late it is. I just want to cry and be alone – maybe they're *right* to call me Lonely Chlo! It's *just* how I feel at the moment!'

Too much? she wondered frantically as she turned away and strode across the room.

But behind her she heard Hugo tumbling off the sofa and staggering towards her, hopping along as he struggled to pull up his jeans.

'Chloe, wait! Don't go! Darling, don't be like this! What's wrong?'

'I just *told* you what was wrong!' she wailed. 'You made me feel like—'

'You're *not* one in a long line! Not at all!'

Hugo had caught up with her. She thought of something else her mum had said: clever women run away and let men catch them. He grabbed her shoulder with the one hand he had free; the other was bunched around his jeans, his engorged cock still bobbing in the air.

'I love you!' he shouted. 'You're the only one for me, the only one ever! You're the *last* one in line! I mean—'

He caught himself, desperately searching for better words, but Chloe was already reacting in a way he hadn't expected; she threw himself against him, kissing him so passionately that both his hands rose to tangle in her hair and kiss her back.

'You mean it?' she was saying between kisses. 'You really mean it? You want me to marry you? I'm the only one ever? Really, you want me to *marry* you?'

The rest of Hugo's body briefly imitated his cock and went stiff as a pole. This was it, the moment of truth. Now or never. Shit or get off the pot, as Lauren had said pithily to Chloe just a few days ago. He pulled back, looked down at Chloe's tearful face, opened his mouth and said, simply: 'Yes.'

It wasn't the most romantic proposal in the world, but Chloe was light years past caring about how it had happened; all that mattered was that it *had*. Hugo loved her, and she loved him, and she was the right girl for him. Even Toby had told her that. And now she was no longer, would never again be Lonely Chlo.

Bliss flooded through her. Still kissing her brand-new fiancé, she backed him up until his thighs hit an armchair, and then she pushed him down to sit. The banana on the coffee table wasn't as cold as he'd like it, but sod that, his cock must be so desperate by now that it'd be past caring about anything but getting off.

'Oh *yes*!' Hugo repeated, now on a groan of infinite relief as Chloe took a bite of banana, chewed it up and sank her mouth over the bulging head of his cock. Hot wet mouth, cold squishy banana. He was, to his great surprise, in heaven, and not just because he was finally getting his cock sucked. He had finally committed, finally done what he knew he had been putting off longer than he should. Chloe had been The One for years, the one he would get around to proposing to one day. The girl who had fallen for him without knowing who he was, who had looked up at him, outside that coffee shop, with that particular dancing brightness in her eyes. Not Prince Hugo, second in line to the throne. Just him.

It was just that, before he'd done it, proposing had seemed so . . . final. Prison doors closing behind the growing boy, like a poem they'd made him learn at school. As if all the fun would be over, and now they'd have to be seriously married people. No more larks, no more . . . fun.

Well, that was pretty thick of me, he thought, gripping onto the padded arms of the chair, throwing his head back, groaning even louder as his fiancée sucked him off with a snug tight grip of her lips that frankly – though obviously he wouldn't dream of telling her that – no other girl he'd been with before her had ever come close to achieving. Chloe pulled back, swallowed the banana in her mouth, took another bite, chewed it and resumed sucking Hugo off. Every time her lips left him, he moaned in anticipation, waiting eagerly for the resumption of activity; every time she sank back onto him, the immediate contrast of colder banana and warm wet tongue made him groan even louder.

I ask her to marry me and I get one of the best b-js I've ever had in my life! I'm a bloody idiot! Why didn't I do this before?

Hugo had already convinced himself that the proposal had been his own idea. He was the man; *he* was the one to decide.

That was how it worked when you asked a woman to marry you. Prince Hugo, Earl of Albion, Baron Llantrisant, Knight of the Garter, etc etc, had made his own decision, had not been swayed by the media or his family, had waited until he was ready, and had eventually, triumphantly, proposed to his long-term girlfriend, sure that she could cope with the demands of being the Countess of Albion and then a Royal Princess and then a Queen, confident that—

'*Aaah!*' he groaned, his brain switching off completely as his cock swelled and butted even further inside his fiancée's mouth, teased and excited beyond endurance. He wanted to hold out for ever, to stay in the sheer ecstasy of this moment, the suspended anticipation of extreme pleasure; but as soon as he told himself not to come yet, his cock let go, shooting a hot stream to the back of Chloe's throat.

She swallowed it down happily. The banana technique made giving blowjobs fantastically pleasurable for her too; she'd always enjoyed them, but the pauses that taking fresh bites of banana afforded her spun out the experience, stopped her jaw locking, and the groans of delight every time she took Hugo's cock in her mouth again were fantastically satisfying. Plus, Hugo, being rich enough to afford it, ate a great deal of asparagus, which made his come taste of it, and Chloe really didn't like asparagus; the banana, however, masked it with great success.

She raised her head, licking the last traces of banana from her lips and smiling at him with starry eyes.

'God,' Hugo sighed, 'I do love you so *very* much, Chloe!'

'Oh darling,' she said, filled with triumph and royal sperm, 'I love you too!'

Lori

Present day

Has Joachim actually ever told me he loves me?

Lori Makarwicz, fiancée of King Joachim of Herzoslovakia, stood on a dressmaker's stool, three Herzoslovakian seamstresses kneeling around her and pinning the hem of her duchesse satin wedding dress. She had been told to hold herself absolutely still, but since, as an Olympic athlete, she had perfect muscle control, this wasn't hard. Every so often Frau Klertzner, the principal seamstress, would pat her approvingly on the waist and mutter something in Herzoslovakian that Lori thought meant 'good girl'; Lori's waist was about as high as little old Frau Klertzner could reach, as Lori was five foot ten in her bare feet, and with her two-inch heels and the extra height from the stool, she towered like a blonde Juno over the little Herzoslovakian women.

He must have done.

Lori tried to play back his proposal in her head. It had been so unexpected, so breathtaking, so romantic, that it was hard to remember every single moment, every word Joachim had said: she knew that she had kept repeating: 'This is so sudden!' like some dumb heroine from an operetta or one of those really old movies her grandmother had grown up on – Jeanette MacDonald and Nelson Eddy, him trying to hold her hands and her singing straight to camera about love and moonlight and being a Ruritanian queen or something.

Which she was about to be. She really wished her grandmother was in good enough health to travel for the wedding. But there was no way Olga would be able to leave the nursing home, let alone take two planes, crossing the Atlantic for the first time in her life – she didn't even have a passport! – land in Austria, and take a helicopter to Valtzers, the capital of Herzoslovakia, to see her granddaughter becoming its Queen.

Me, a Queen! It's like I'm in some crazy fairy tale! Lori shook her head in disbelief, but since this didn't interfere with the dressmakers – who were now dragging step stools over so they could climb up and work on the upper reaches of the dress, like Lilliputians doing tailoring work on Gulliver's fiancée – they didn't bother to tell her to be still.

Just a few months ago, I was competing in London at the Olympics. Playing beach volleyball for the US. Spiking hard in the British rain with 'California Girls' playing in the background. A few months ago I hadn't even met Joachim.

I honestly can't believe how fast my life has changed for ever.

Lori shook her head again. *I couldn't imagine anything more exciting could happen to me in 2012 than competing for the US at the London Olympics! It was the biggest thing ever to happen to me and Shameeka. We were over the moon to have been selected. If anyone had told me that something even bigger would happen to me this year, I'd've thought they were insane . . .*

But one could not have happened without the other. It was the Olympics which had set things in motion, brought

Lori and Joachim together at a routine meet and greet after the second heat, when they'd crushed the Chinese team two sets to nil. Lori and Shameeka had been escorted to the Corinthia Hotel, just five minutes from Horse Guards Parade, where the beach volleyball sand court had been set up for the duration of the Games; their sponsors and the US officials were all beaming with pleasure at their decisive win.

'We even have royalty to meet you!' one young eager-beaver cultural attaché from the US Embassy had said, leading the girls through the crowded hospitality suite, smiling faces on all sides raising glasses to their triumph.

'OMG, is it Prince Toby?' Shameeka, who had a huge crush on the redheaded bad boy of British royalty, had nudged Lori in high excitement. 'That would be *beyond* awesome!'

However, though the man waiting on the balcony of the Corinthia Hotel's penthouse suite was shorter, chubbier, and distinctly more formally dressed than Prince Toby would have been, he was also of a higher rank: not a prince, but a king. A king who clicked his heels on greeting the girls, nodding his head at each of them as he took their hands to kiss, one after the other. His navy suit was so perfectly tailored that Lori was utterly embarrassed by the ugly grey tracksuit jacket, unflatteringly baggy black trousers, and glaring lime-green trainers that were the US team's official post-competition wear. It was the trainers she particularly hated. Tall as she was, she had feet in proportion to her height, and the neon colour made them look the size of canoes.

'King Joachim!' the eager beaver proudly announced, his eyes shining like stars: Lori couldn't help smiling at his excitement.

Nothing like republican Americans for going nuts about royalty, she thought.

'Congratulations, young ladies!' King Joachim said, as Shameeka giggled.

'Wow, do all kings kiss your hand?' she asked, never backward at being forward. 'That is *beyond* cool! I'm gonna tell everyone back home I got my hand kissed by a real king! Hey, do you know Prince Toby?'

'We meet at State weddings and funerals,' King Joachim responded politely. Lori had thought this was very funny. It was only later that she had realized Joachim hadn't been joking.

'King Joachim is the ruling monarch of Herzoslovakia,' the young attaché added.

'Herz – what? Is that even a *country*?' Shameeka blurted out, but Lori, used to having to deal with her teammate's tendency to impulsiveness on and off court, dived in to remedy the impending disaster.

'It's a real pleasure to meet you, Your Majesty,' she said, bobbing a curtsey as best she could in the tracksuit. 'Did you watch our heat just now?'

Joachim swivelled to face her, his round blue eyes fully focusing on her. 'I certainly did,' he said with much enthusiasm. 'I am a great admirer of sport, but I am not familiar until now with beach volleyball. I found much skill and athletic ability in your performance today.'

'Oh! Thank you!' Lori blurted out, seeing that he was quite serious. She and Shameeka, used as they were to competing in sports bras and skimpy bikini bottoms, were equally used to male spectators goggling at them while they competed, and praising their 'outfits' afterwards in considerable detail; April Ross, another US female basketball player, said in interviews that people were often drawn in by the women's uniform but stayed for the sport. Lori, however, could have done without it. Competing on the beach at the University of Miami, which she'd attended on a volleyball scholarship, was one thing: everyone in Miami lived in tight skimpy clothing, and no way could you ever be as sexy as the hot, hip-wriggling Cubans there.

Outside of Miami, however, it was a different story. Leching everywhere. Lori would have loved to compete in shorts, even really tiny ones; anything not to have most of her ass on display. But sex sold, and a guy who met you straight after a heat and talked about your athletic ability instead of making coded references to your tits and ass was a prince, metaphorically speaking.

And this one's a king! Even better!

She was positively beaming at him.

'Thank you so much!' she repeated. 'Are you coming to any more heats? We play Germany tomorrow morning.'

'I am very aware of this!' Joachim said, nodding briskly. 'I will certainly be present. And perhaps you will be kind enough to allow me to take you to lunch afterwards? I know, of course, that an athlete in competition will be careful what she eats, so if you accept, I will inform myself of what will be appropriate to serve you.'

'Wow! Well, uh, thank you again!' Lori said, dazzled. 'We'd love to, wouldn't we, Sham—'

She turned to her teammate, but Shameeka had already headed back into the party a while ago, seeing that Joachim's interest was fixed on Lori, and wanting to give her a good shot.

'Um, I guess it's just me, then,' Lori said bashfully. 'Unless you meant—'

'I would be more than honoured by your company, Miss Makarwicz,' King Joachim said, taking her hand and kissing it once again, rendering her completely speechless.

It had been a lightning whirl ever since. A whirl of Olympic success, first of all: Lori and Shameeka had played their barely covered asses off and taken bronze, which, since they were the second-string US women's volleyball team, was pretty damn good going. Joachim had courted Lori all through the competition, but in such a gentlemanly way, absolutely taking for granted that her sporting obligations came first, that his presence had been hugely positive rather than a distraction.

And then, after their medal triumph, Lori and Shameeka had instantly been snapped up for a sponsorship endorsement by a Swiss watch company, which had been a big career step forward for both of them. The company had paid the girls to pose for a series of black-and-white ads, in which they were both jumping to spike a ball in unison, their lean, muscled bodies gleaming in chiaroscuro, their faces intent. The watch they were advertising was a chronograph with two dials, the tonneau split perfectly symmetrically, called the Duplex: under Lori and Shameeka's jumping bare feet ran the slogan: 'Twice the Power. Twice the Timing.'

Not exactly original, but what did they care? They had not only been paid lavishly for the ads, but had been contracted to embark on a month-long press tour around Europe in mid-September, as soon as the required American media appearances had been completed. The Duplex press tour was an infinitely higher level of travel than anything underpaid athletes in a not-really-famous sport ever got to experience: five-star hotels, unlimited expenses, first-class flights, and all they had to do was play some small exhibition matches and hold a series of press conferences with luxury goods journalists whose idea of a probing question was to compliment the girls' amazing bodies and ask if they'd met Prince Toby at the Olympics. Shameeka and Lori had been in sheer heaven.

Lori's burgeoning relationship with Joachim had grown exponentially as the press tour progressed. Europe was tiny, Lori had discovered. Really tiny. You could fly from country to country in, like, an *hour*. You could drive across three borders in one *day*. It was nothing for Joachim to charter a plane and fly to Madrid, or Rome, or Berlin, or St Petersburg, wherever she and Shameeka were staying, so that he could take her out to dinner. And he did exactly that with increasing frequency. Joaquim treated her like a queen: the dinners would always be at the Italian or Japanese restaurants she liked; he made sure they served her favourite cocktail, a Sea Breeze, since her regime meant she could only allow herself one alcoholic drink a day; she only had to mention casually how much she liked flowers, and the next time he took her out there would be a guided visit to a botanical garden planned before their dinner reservation.

And he was very pleasant company. He listened, he asked questions. He heard about her childhood in a small, dying town in upstate New York, which had flourished during the days of the Erie Canal, when heavy industry had sent all its goods by water. Its population was shrinking every year; kids left for college and never came back. But Lori's parents, loyal to a fault, wouldn't have dreamt of leaving Dorchester.

'I'm the only one who even went out of state to university,' she said, over dinner in Barcelona, after Joaquim had organized a private tour of Gaudi's Sagrada Família. They were sitting on the terrace of L'Orangerie, an exquisite restaurant in the Gran Hotel la Florida, their chairs turned so that they could see the city stretching out below them and watch the sun falling slowly in a hot red ball into the blue waters of the Mediterranean Sea. 'My brother and sister are still back home. Both of them went to the community college, they'll settle down ten minutes' drive from my mom and dad. Hometown kids all the way.'

'Family is very important to you, Lori, I can see,' Joachim had said appreciatively.

'Oh, *very*,' she said wholeheartedly. 'I don't see enough of them. I try to get back for Thanksgiving, but, you know, an athlete gets a pretty short window at her physical peak, and they totally get that I want to go for it while I can.'

'And what do you plan to do after you—' Joachim smiled, which was rare for him; his expression was usually so composed. His rather plump face creased up into pleasant lines as he did so, a little dimple popping out on each side of his full lips. 'I was about to say, after you retire, but you are so young and beautiful and full of life, it seems very wrong to say retire to a woman who looks like you do.'

'Oh! Thank you!'

Lori found the formality of King Joachim's compliments charming, and, frankly, refreshing, after the highly charged sexual atmosphere of the Olympic Village. Whenever an athletic event had finished, all the competitors were unleashed to party freely, and in the later stages it had been a Bacchanal, with drunken guys staggering between the Heineken and Budweiser Houses, pockets full of condoms – a hundred thousand had been handed out in the Village at the start of the Games – slurring 'Hey, hot stuff, wanna fuck?' at her and Shameeka.

Shameeka had; Lori hadn't. It was all too public for her. And halfway through, she had met Joachim, and his poise and sophistication, not to mention the fact that he was over a decade older than her, had made her contemporaries seem extremely young and callow.

'I guess I'll coach, back home,' she said. 'I'd love to work with young people.'

She took a careful sip of her Sea Breeze – she'd learned years ago to pace herself – and so missed the approving look Joachim was directing at her.

'You like children,' he commented, sounding very satisfied.

'Oh yes!' Lori said ingenuously. 'Of course!'

Setting down her glass, she missed, too, the smirk that said that Joachim had successfully crossed the last item off his list of essential qualities in a queen-to-be . . .

A short time later, the press tour wrapped up as the ad campaign raced into newspapers, magazines and billboards in order to capitalize on Lori and Shameeka's bronze medals. It was early October, and the girls were due to return to Miami, back to their routine and training schedule, when Joachim asked Lori to postpone going back home in favour of a visit to his homeland, Herzoslovakia. A small tax haven nestling between several other European countries, all much larger but not necessarily richer, Herzoslovakia had not been included in the press tour, as it had very few permanent residents. Its hordes of passport-holders were domiciled there instead, which allowed them to benefit from its very low tax rate while not having to live in a tiny little country year-round.

'He's really serious!' Shameeka had whooped on hearing about Lori's invitation. 'He wants his mom to check you out to see if you're marriage material! Which you totally are,' she added fondly. 'And you know, he's *ready*.'

Ever since it had been clear how interested Joachim was in Lori, Shameeka had been combing the European gossip magazines and blogs for information about him: he was thirty-seven, an only son, King of Herzoslovakia since his father had died over twenty years ago. And he had a doting mother, the Dowager Queen, who was apparently pushing him hard to marry and produce the next generation of heirs to Herzoslovakia.

'Whenever you say some guy's "ready",' Lori observed dubiously, 'you mean that they marry the next girl who comes along once they've decided to settle down. I don't think that's really romantic—'

'The next girl they *fall for*, dipshit!' Shameeka did a pretend-smack to Lori's head. 'Look, Joachim went to, like, every Olympic event there was going, and you're the one he asked out! I asked around the Village and no other chick got even taken on one date by him! So he liked *you* – it wasn't some weird multiple audition process! Just tell me I can come to the wedding and hook up with Prince Toby. I want a redheaded, freckled, corn-rowed royal baby . . .'

Lori had giggled, pretend-smacked Shameeka back, and made a huge effort to put her friend's words out of her mind. OK, so Joachim was reaching the age when guys who'd held out up till now found their thoughts turning to marriage and kids: but they'd only met a couple of months ago, and even to entertain the thought was way too soon for a normal person, let alone for a guy who wasn't just marrying a wife, but choosing a queen to help him govern his country.

No, she wasn't even going to think about where this court-ship might end up. She was going to visit Herzoslovakia, enjoy having Joachim show her around his home country, which sounded like the quaintest, prettiest, most charming little monarchy in the world, and then go home to Miami; the Duplex watch people had been very happy to change the date of her return ticket. She'd tell Shameeka all about the trip, soak up some much needed Florida sunshine, and, if things went well, she had no doubt that Joachim would come to visit her. Distance was clearly nothing to him – he'd even come to Russia overnight to visit her on the press tour. And if the Miami visits went well, and he invited her back ... well, then, *maybe* she would allow herself to start thinking about the *possibility* that he might want to make her his Queen ...

That was how Lori had envisaged the process – assuming, naturally, that they liked each other more and more with every visit, that the liking blossomed into something stronger. The oddest thing of all about the situation in which she, quite unexpectedly, found herself, was that she wasn't even sure that the blossoming, as it were, had actually happened. She couldn't actually *remember* Joachim telling her that he had fallen in love with her, that evening in the tower terrace of Schloss Schwanstein, the ugliest name in German for the prettiest one in English, Castle Swanstone. It was as lovely as its English name, not an adjective Lori had expected to use for a castle: she'd thought of them as being imposing, domi-nating, with castellations from which boiling oil could be poured on invaders, slits in towers for archers to rain down arrows on ditto, surrounded by a wide moat, barred by a huge clanking drawbridge.

But Herzoslovakia's castles weren't like that, not at all. They were beautiful, fairy-tale creations, perched on hills high over rivers with exquisite views over the countryside below, clustered with towers and turrets and balconies, designed in a Gothic Revival style but with nothing gloomy about their interiors at all; the rooms were charming, painted in light clear blues and creams and greens, furnished with delicate, priceless furniture, hung with gilt-framed watercol-ours and oil paintings of landscapes. Clanking suits of armour, displays of historic weapons and heavy dark portraits had been discreetly moved to attic storerooms by the Dowager Queen, whose taste was impeccable.

There was so much to admire in Herzoslovakia: the beauty of the tiny, mountainous country, the friendliness and affluence of its citizens; as a tax haven, Herzoslovakia's wealth meant that there was full employment and more than enough money to go round. Joachim had taken her on a tour of the castles, stopping for a couple of days in each one, barely an hour's drive between each – when, of course, they didn't travel by river, on his private motorboat.

Each castle was prettier than the last, each suite of rooms reserved for her use more enchantingly decorated, and by the time they reached Schloss Schwanstein, Lori was in an absolute daze. Dinner that night, in the tower terrace, hundreds of candles in crystal sconces and candelabras providing the only illumination, gas flames flickering outside on the stone balcony in huge wrought-iron torches, had been utterly perfect: blinis with caviar, delicate curls of smoked salmon on golden beetroot canapés, tiny steamed dumplings, each topped with a dot of sour cream, all served on priceless, gold-edged, royal-crested china, vintage champagne from the royal cellars poured into crystal coupe glasses . . .

For once, she had said hell to her eating plan and the one-drink-a-night rule. A soft Hungarian red wine had followed the champagne, served with seared beef with foie gras and miniature puffed soufflé potatoes; then elderflower and champagne sorbet with Italian rosé dessert wine, Rosa Regale by Castello Banfi, in smaller crystal glasses from the vast matching set. By the time coffee came, in paper-thin gold-rimmed china demi-tasse cups, Lori's head was swimming with enchantment. The string quartet at the far corner of the room, partially concealed behind a two-fold Chinese gilded screen to afford Joachim and Lori some privacy, were playing Borodin's ridiculously romantic String Quartet No. 2 in D major, written to evoke the memory of the composer's bliss-ful courtship of his beloved wife; Joachim held out his hand to Lori, asking her to step out onto the terrace and admire the night stars, timing it as the quartet reached the famously dreamy Nocturne.

The strains of the Borodin, the first violin and cello soaring together in an intense, silvery thread of melody, was the final touch. It had all been planned to perfection. Joachim took Lori in his arms and kissed her with the gentle, sweet, chivalrous kisses which had ended every evening of her stay in his country; the embraces had lasted longer every night, but had been confined to kisses on her lips and her hands, caresses of her hair and shoulders, and soft compliments to her beauty, charm and grace. Lori had fallen asleep enveloped in twin clouds of starched linen sheets, fresh each day, and the praise which Joachim had rained down on her, feeling already as beautiful as a queen.

When Joachim pulled back from the kiss, looking fractionally up at her – Lori was a little taller than him in heels, but he had assured her that he preferred tall women, and Lori had always liked short men – his round blue eyes were wide and sincere as he told her that she had swept him away as no woman ever had before, that her beauty, her bearing, her natural modesty, her manners, her fresh, unjaded American charm, had carried him away until he could think of nothing but her. That showing her his country over the last ten days had been the greatest pleasure of his life. That the time was drawing close for her to go home, and he couldn't bear to let her go. That he wanted her to stay for ever with him, by his side, learning about his country, becoming its Queen. Would she? Would she stay with him, here in Herzoslovakia, agree to make it her new home? She would make him the happiest man in the world if she would say yes. At this moment he was not a king, but a man, a man asking the woman upon whom he had set his heart to marry him.

From the pocket of his dinner jacket, he had produced a velvet box, easing it open with a flip of his thumb. Lori couldn't help gasping, even though she was worried about seeming vulgar. Inside was a ring with the biggest diamond she had ever seen in her life, set inside an oval of other, perfectly matched diamonds, each of which would have been quite satisfactory on its own. The entire effect, even in the velvet-dark night by the flames of the gas torches, was breathtaking; by daylight, the clarity and colour of the jewels would, literally, be dazzling.

Lori's mouth dropped open. Joachim, taking silence for consent, reclaimed her left hand and slid the enormous door knocker of a ring onto her third finger. It fitted as if it had been made for her.

'I took the liberty of having it sized to fit you,' he said, smiling at her reaction. 'A maid measured your rings for me and the jeweller estimated the correct size for this finger. It is exact? Good!' He kept hold of her hand, looking at it with great approval. 'A family heirloom. Only a woman like you, Lori, could carry off such a magnificent piece. As I looked through the family jewels, I knew that this was meant for you. It once belonged to Queen Elizabetta of Herzoslovakia, who was called the most beautiful woman in Europe. There is a portrait of her I will show you tomorrow – like you, she was tall, statuesque, beautiful. Regal. You will look superb in the crown jewels of Herzoslovakia. You will be the most beautiful queen in the whole of Europe – the whole of the world.'

Joachim enfolded her in another embrace, his kisses becoming more passionate. Lori, her head spinning from his proposal, the romance of the setting, the confidence with which Joachim was kissing her, the music in the background (the quartet were playing the Nocturne on repeat, as per instructions) and the unusual quantity of wine she had drunk, kissed him back with a passion that easily matched his. Joachim allowed his hands to slide down to her waist, pulling her even closer. She felt the warmth of his hands through her simple black cocktail dress and shivered in pleasure, wanting more; she twined her fingers through his thick short curls, pressed herself snugly against him, tasting the sweet wine and the elderflower sorbet on his tongue, losing herself completely.

Her eyes closed, and she felt her nipples stiffen against the light silk fabric of her bra. The sensation was delicious. It had been so long since Lori had let herself be carried away like this, to eat a three-course meal, drink wine with every course, to kiss a man and feel her whole body respond. She had been measured in her response to Joachim previously, echoing his decorous kisses, unsure of what proper etiquette was with a king when she wasn't even his official girlfriend, but knowing that she certainly didn't want to seem in any way too eager, a vulgar American girl who didn't know that European kings pursued their courtships with gentlemanly restraint.

But now, his hand was behind her head, holding her tightly against him, his other hand caressing the upper slopes of her bottom, and the relief was overwhelming. Joachim *was* capable of passion, as she had secretly begun to doubt. Now that they were engaged, he could allow himself to show her how much he wanted her as a woman. And Lori was more than ready. She'd spent the last two years training exceptionally hard, had broken up with her college boyfriend because he was resentful of her commitment to making the US Olympic team, and had barely got laid since. Being courted by Joachim had been a fairy tale, but she was a red-blooded girl who definitely enjoyed sex; if he had made a pass at her days ago, she would have been overjoyed. She certainly wasn't the kind of woman who would have made him propose before she agreed to go to bed with him.

And it's so important to make sure that you're sexually compatible before you get married, she thought seriously. *I couldn't marry anyone who I didn't enjoy having sex with!*

Joachim's penis was now pressing between her legs; their relatively equal heights meant that it fit, almost exactly, where she wanted it, and a soft moan issued from her lips as she felt it rub up against her. She couldn't quite feel how big it was, but it was hard and ready, and her thighs parted a little, her feet shifting apart, so that his leg could drive in between them, his cock butt closer into her. The black silk thong that matched her bra was damp; she longed to be alone with him, to unzip her dress and see the appreciation in his eyes for her body, hard and toned in sexy underwear she'd worn tonight in the hopes that he would see it, want to peel it off her, finally crack the perfect-king façade and – *kiss me like he's dying to get me in the sack, twist his fingers into my hair . . . yes, just like that . . .*

Eagerly, Lori pulled back, looking at Joachim's gleaming eyes, his pink cheeks. She drew her hand from round his neck, reaching up to stroke his face, saying: 'Shall we—'

But it was the hand with the ring on it, the gigantic, heavy rock of a diamond. Its facets scraped Joachim's cheek, and he let out a little squeal, flinching back.

'I'm so sorry!' she said, laughing. 'It's just so big! I'm not used to wearing anything so huge.'

'You will become used to wearing many large jewels before you realize it,' he said fondly, taking her hand and kissing the palm. 'My Lori. Tomorrow, after we have made the announcement, we will visit the vault and I will show you the tiaras.'

Her eyes widened.

'And now—' Joachim drew her arm through his and folded her hand against his chest, a charming, old-fashioned gesture with which Lori had become very familiar – 'now I will walk you to your rooms, my dear. It will be a big day tomorrow. We will return to Hafenhoffer—' this was the King of Herzoslovakia's official residence, overlooking Valtzers, the capital – 'and tell my mother. She will be delighted! Overjoyed! She has taken so much to you, she thinks you have all the qualities required to be a wonderful queen . . .'

As they re-entered the terrace room, the quartet shifted smoothly to the last movement of the Borodin, the Vivace. It provided a fittingly joyous note on which Joachim could lead his bride-to-be back inside; unbeknownst to Lori, the exit onto the terrace had been the staff's signal to clear the sorbet dishes and dessert wine glasses, and Lori and Joachim were greeted by a footman carrying a silver tray bearing two champagne coupes.

'Let us toast, my dear,' Joachim said, handing one to Lori.

'How did they *know*?' she whispered to him as she took it, taken aback by the fact that the staff were so aware of the situation.

He smiled, a genuinely amused smile, and stroked the hand that was resting on his sleeve.

'Ah, this is something you will have to become used to, Lori,' he said gently. 'You are no longer a private person. You belong now to us, to this little country. We will honour you, treasure you, look after you. Anticipate your needs, treat you like the queen you are.'

'I don't know what to say,' Lori blurted out as Joachim toasted her, clinking his glass against hers, the cut-glass crystal ringing pure and clear for a moment.

'You have said yes, and that's all I needed to hear,' he said, smiling fondly at her as he sipped his champagne. 'My very dear and sweet Lori.'

But I never actually said *yes*, Lori realized now as she stood on the dressmaker's stool. The women had finished pinning the hem, and were stepping back to coo at her in a stream of Herzoslovakian: Lori was studying the language, but couldn't have got close to making out what they were saying. Still, it was indubitably positive. Their hands were clasped at their breasts, their heads cocked to the side, their faces wreathed in sentimental smiles.

'Come!' the head seamstress said, holding out her hand to Lori and nodding imperatively. 'You come!'

Taking her hand, Lori stepped off the stool. Clicks of the tongue, hisses and gestures from the little women, indicated that she should walk slowly, as the dress was bristling with pins. This was the first time that she was wearing the actual wedding dress; previously, as per couture tradition, Lori had had fittings for the *toile*, a test-run dress of heavy unbleached cotton, made so that the design and fit could be perfected for the seamstresses to reproduce in satin and lace.

Lori glided across the marble floor of the Green Drawing Room to the enormous, gilt-framed cheval mirror which had been wheeled in for the purposes of the fitting. She watched herself approaching, a long, slim white figure in heavy duchesse satin, a notoriously demanding fabric that only a perfect figure and equally skilled tailoring could carry off. Her bob-length blonde hair had been pinned up on the crown of her head with kirby grips as best she could manage, showing off the length of her neck; her blue eyes were wide with disbelief as she came to a halt, taking in her transformation from all-American girl to Herzoslovakian Queen-to-be.

The seamstresses flocked around her, sighing with appreciation, clapping their hands, the smiles almost splitting their old lined faces as they saw how well the dress moved and how regally Lori carried it off. The design had been kept very simple, it had been explained to her, in order to set off the extraordinary Herzoslovakian crown jewels which she would be wearing; it was a sheath of bias-cut satin which followed the lines of her slim figure in a way that would have been overly sexual if Lori's body had not been so elegant, with its flat stomach, small breasts and narrow athletic hips. Priceless ivory antique lace was draped at the bodice in overlapping panels that formed a boat neck, skimming Lori's collarbones, falling into cap sleeves that covered her shoulders. At the neckline was pinned a wide strip of exquisitely soft, silky ermine: more ermine would trim the sleeves and the hem of the long, curving train, an abundance of rich fur considered suitable for a winter wedding.

'Too much!' the dressmaker said, smiling still, squeezing Lori's upper arms. 'Too much! Like man!'

The other women giggled, nodding in agreement, as Lori realized that they meant her shoulder muscles and her biceps.

'Don't worry,' she said, smiling back. 'I won't flex my arms on the big day.'

Teasingly, she raised one arm a little, turned the palm to face the ceiling, and contracted her muscles; her bicep and tricep popped up impressively. The women shrieked, the dressmaker grabbed Lori's arm and pushed it down again, shaking her head.

'No! Not like man!' she wailed, continuing in a stream of urgent Herzoslovakian, stabbing Lori's tricep with a pointing finger, gesturing at the lace that now sheathed Lori's magnificently square shoulders.

'We make sleeve longer,' the dressmaker said firmly to Lori. 'To here.' She stabbed halfway down Lori's arm. 'We not see arm like man.'

The main door of the Green Drawing Room suddenly swung open, a footman entering first and holding it for the

Dowager Queen, who swept in with her usual light, swift gait. The seamstresses instantly fell into curtseys – not quick bobs of the head and hips, but full, halfway-to-the-ground obeisances, heads ducked, gazes to the emerald malachite and marble inlaid floor that, along with the matching fireplace, gave the room its name.

'Oh, how magnificent!' the Dowager exclaimed, tapping the tips of her fingers together to avoid doing anything as vulgar as actually clapping. 'My dear, you look like you were born to be a queen!'

It had been a huge relief to Lori that her prospective mother-in-law was so enthusiastic about Joachim's lightning-swift courtship of his fiancée. As the King had assured Lori, the Dowager had been utterly delighted at the news of the engagement, kissing her daughter-in-law-to-be again and again, pouring her tea and handing her the cup with her own hands, rather than instructing the footman to do it – a sign of very high esteem – and launching into a stream of enthusiastic plans for the future. She was already occupying the Dowager's apartment at Schloss Hafenhoffer, so Lori mustn't think that there would be any awkwardness; on the marriage, Lori would join Joachim in the Imperial Suite. She wouldn't interfere in any way with any changes Lori wanted to make; it would be a positive *relief* to finally have a reigning queen, the Dowager was *much* too old now for all the state duties and had been nagging Joachim for a *decade* to get married and bring a bride to Herzoslovakia! But he had held out for the right girl, and now he'd found her. The Dowager *couldn't* be happier.

Despite her self-deprecating comments, the Dowager Queen had barely passed sixty, and, thanks to careful maintenance and judicious nips, tucks and tweaks, she looked much younger than that. In her elegant Yves Saint Laurent crepe suit, her classic Ferragamo court shoes, and a wonderful multi-stranded pearl necklace at her throat – she always wore pearls, she had told Lori, as they were extremely flattering to the complexion – she was intimidatingly elegant. At this moment, in her couture wedding dress, Lori felt for the first time that she was on a par with the Dowager, and certainly the open appreciation in the older woman's eyes spoke volumes about the success of the dress.

'Wonderful!' she exclaimed, nodding vigorously. 'Absolutely wonderful! My dear Lori, you have an excellent figure. A very hard design to wear – satin makes women look fat *so* easily – but you are perfect!'

Behind the Dowager, two more footmen entered the room, each carrying a large, elaborately carved wooden box; she pointed with one ring-laden hand to the huge malachite table, and the footmen scurried to set down the boxes as instructed.

'We must decide now on the tiara and parure you will wear,' the Dowager said, producing a small key from the pocket of her jacket and unlocking the boxes.

With a superbly theatrical gesture, she flung one after the other open, and stepped back, revealing the contents, a small smile playing on her face as Lori and the seamstresses gasped in unison. It was immediately obvious why the boxes were so big: inside each, on moulded beds of dark burgundy velvet, sat a lavish tiara, surrounded by matching sets of jewellery. Both tiaras were so heavily crusted with pearls and diamonds that they looked, Lori thought in a rare, disloyal moment, more like something a drag queen or a gypsy bride would wear than an actual royal queen.

But then the Dowager lifted one up, easing it gently out of its case, and carried it over to Lori, who bent to allow her future mother-in-law to set it on her head. It felt as if it weighed ten pounds, the metal sides spiking down through her hair, pressing tight as a clamp. She thought suddenly of that medieval torture device she'd seen in a film, an iron ring that fitted round the skull and could be tightened, slowly and agonizingly, by screws on each side. Gingerly, she straightened up again, to even louder gasps: one of the seamstresses burst into loud, gulping tears, and the Dowager produced a tiny, lace-trimmed handkerchief from somewhere and dabbed at the corners of her eyes with it.

Lori felt like crying herself, to be honest. The tiara was perfect, breathtakingly so: the Dowager's good taste was unerring. Lori didn't even want to imagine the value of what she was wearing on her head: it was more like a crown, imposing and regal. Diamonds the size of quails' eggs were fixed into the elaborate golden curlicues, pearls almost as large weaving around them in swirls that echoed the gold setting, rising to a central curve in which the largest diamond of all towered high above Lori's temples.

'Only you could wear this, Lori,' the Dowager said with great fondness. 'Your height, the lovely wide forehead ... magnificent! It would dwarf a smaller woman. I could never – how do you say, *carry this off*? This tiara has not been worn for over a hundred years. Oh yes.' She nodded in great satisfaction as she folded up the handkerchief and replaced it in her pocket. 'It waited for you a long time.'

Lori was speechless. She stood, staring at herself, as the Dowager bustled back to the jewellery box, and returned with a pearl and diamond collar, the jewels set in a gold framework that matched the design of the tiara.

'I instructed Dagmar to cut the neckline *so*,' she said, nodding vigorously as she looked at the lace that followed the line of Lori's collarbones. 'It is excellent, Dagmar.'

The seamstress went bright red and swallowed hard.

'Help me,' the Dowager commanded, as they lifted and eased the collar to lie around Lori's neck without damaging the delicate lace. It weighed almost as much as the tiara; Lori thought again, oddly, of torture devices. 'See!' the Dowager said happily. 'The diamonds *en tremblant*! Perfect!'

She touched the diamonds that were suspended all around the base of the collar on minutely fine gold wires.

'They move, a little, as you do,' she explained to Lori. 'They catch the light, like a fire around your neck. Beautiful! Dagmar, the earrings . . .'

The little seamstress was already holding out the matching earrings to the Dowager, who clipped them onto Lori's lobes. *I'm like their doll*, Lori thought with amusement, *their giant, larger-than-life doll that they get to dress up* . . .

'Such an Aryan beauty!' the Dowager observed happily. 'So blonde! And such lovely blue eyes, just like Joachim's! You will have very beautiful fair babies.'

The seamstresses nodded vigorously as Lori braced herself not to flinch at the ice-cold metal tightly fastened to her scalp, bare neck and earlobes: *wow, these boxes must have come from deep in the vault. They do feel as if no one wore them in a hundred years.* As promised, Joachim had taken her to see the family jewels on their return to Schloss Hafenhoffer, but there had been so very much to view that it was impossible to take it all in. Some preliminary selections had been made, jewellery which Lori would wear for official engagements and State dinners, but he had suggested that she spend some days there, going through the collection with the help of the Dowager, familiarizing herself with what was at her disposal and considering what she might want to have reset, as many of the pieces were old-fashioned and could do with a more modern setting. Which would have been lovely, if Lori had had the faintest idea about jewellery settings.

'Joachim was *very* blond when he was small, like his father,' the Dowager was saying comfortably, 'but then his hair became more dark. Mine, of course—' she smiled as she touched her ash-blonde locks – 'mine has a little help! But I have always been proud that my eyes are so light.'

Like a husky, Lori thought, looking at the Dowager. *That pale, pale blue, like water over swimming pool tiles . . .*

'Aryan?' she said hesitantly. 'Isn't that a bit—'

But the Dowager had already moved on to the subject of Lori's bouquet and the flower arrangements in the cathedral.

'White roses and *anemonen*,' she was saying with great satisfaction. 'Tied in lace sewn with pearls—'

She reached up to touch the heavy lace bodice of the dress. 'Like this. It will be sewn with many, many seed pearls,' she said to Lori. 'Dagmar and the women will be very busy. Much work for them, very tiny stitches! But we are very proud of our sewing skills in Herzoslovakia. We will take you to Paris, of course, Lori, for the collections. But your dress must be designed and made here, as is the tradition. I, too, had my wedding dress made in Herzoslovakia, by Dagmar's mother.'

Dagmar beamed and nodded vigorously.

'Now, Dagmar,' the Dowager continued, 'the Queen-to-be has been standing still for a long time, and she must be tired. She is used to running and jumping, not being still! Take this off her. The next fitting is in three days, correct? I want to see at least a third of the pearls on the bodice by then. And loosen it fractionally at the bosom. Oh, and I think the sleeves should be a little longer—'

'She's already said that,' Lori said, grinning. 'To hide my big man arms.'

The Dowager smiled back. 'You are very fit and healthy, my dear!' she said tactfully. 'That is a wonderful thing. But yes, a bride is not a . . .' She shook her head, not finding the word in English.

'Bodybuilder?' Lori suggested.

'Yes! Bodybuilder! What is good for the beach is not good for the church. Now, Dagmar will take this dress off you, very carefully, and you will meet me for tea in my rooms so that the florist can show us the sketches for the flowers. I want to make sure everything is *just* the way you want it . . . I will arrange everything, of course, but we must be sure that it is all how you would like . . .'

Really, I'd so much rather she just chose everything, Lori thought ruefully as a footman led her along panelled corridors to what the Dowager called her rooms, but was actually an entire wing of the castle. *We're doing this dance, her and me, like we're in one of those balls from a Jane Austen movie – I want her to pick what's best, she wants me to pick what I'd like, we're pirouetting round and round in ever-decreasing circles . . . the trouble is, everything she suggests is so pretty and perfect and suits me so well, but if I just say I love it she gets worried I'm being too polite and starts picking holes in it . . . and if I make a suggestion it takes half an hour for her to explain to me that it sounds lovely but unfortunately there's a very good reason why it won't be possible . . .*

Which was exactly what proceeded to happen with the florist. It took two hours of negotiation over lapsang souchong and almond madeleines to assure the Dowager that the roses and anemones, the ribbons trimmed with seed pearls, the large arrangements in the cathedral – rose bushes carefully bedded into huge eighteenth-century *famille rose* Chinese porcelain jars – all sounded exquisite just as the Dowager and the florist had conceived them. The florist left, and Lori, shattered in a way she had never been in all her years of hardcore physical training, set down her teacup and prepared to go back to her own apartment for a much needed nap.

'So I will send someone to collect you at two-thirty for the formal engagement announcement,' the Dowager said, setting down her own cup and consulting the ruby-studded dial of her wristwatch; though her style in dress was elegant, rather than ostentatious, Lori had never seen the Dowager wearing anything less than what must be an absolute fortune in jewellery. Pinned to the lapel of her jacket was a brooch as large as a saucer, shaped like a flower, the ruby centre vying to outshine the sapphires and diamonds which made up the petals.

'Thank you,' Lori said gratefully; she still got lost in the palace if left alone to find her way. There were just so many turret staircases, and they all looked exactly the same to the untrained eye.

'We are all so very happy,' the Dowager said, rising gracefully to her feet. 'You have brought a wonderful new energy to the family, Lori.'

Not feeling it right now, Lori thought ironically, trying valiantly not to yawn: the Dowager was quite right, sitting or standing still was much more tiring than working out.

'You aren't worried that it's all happened so fast?' she asked a little timidly, standing up too; she knew never, ever to remain seated if her future mother-in-law was on her feet. 'Sometimes *I* feel that maybe it's all been such a whirlwind, and—'

'So romantic!' the Dowager interrupted, clasping her hands together. 'So beautiful and romantic! Joachim tells me that he knew you were the girl for him as soon as he met you.' She tapped the clasped hands lightly against her heart, or rather the enormous, glittering brooch pinned over it. 'After all these years, it happens so fast! Wonderful! To me, this says that it is true love for him. And it must be the same for you, because you accept him when he proposes so beautifully.'

'Well, yes – that is – it's just—'

Lori didn't even know quite where she was going with this. She felt impelled to say it, however, to try to register some small – not *objection*, exactly – almost like a disclaimer, a clause you inserted into a sponsorship contract to say that you might need a cooling-off period. Not that you ever did that with a sponsorship contract, of course – not that she even wanted, really, to cool off . . . it was merely that, as she had tried to say, everything was happening so very *fast*, and it felt as if no one else remotely noticed or cared about the lightning speed of events, from meeting to engagement to marriage, and that she ought – *someone* ought – to at least register that speed, even just mention it in passing . . .

'Oh, my dear!'

The Dowager, seeing Lori's hesitation, hearing her voice tail off, stepped forward quickly to embrace her. The smaller woman's head rested against Lori's shoulder; Lori, hugging her back carefully, looked down at the Dowager's meticulously tinted and sculpted ash-blonde hair, every strand in place, sweeping round her scalp in a perfectly smooth swirl.

'You could not be more welcome here in Herzoslovakia,' the Dowager assured Lori, taking a small pace back, hands sliding down Lori's arms to grasp her just above the elbows. 'Joachim is settling down at last with such a lovely healthy girl!'

I wish she wouldn't keep mentioning me being healthy, Lori found herself thinking. *It always makes me feel like she's going to pull back my lips and check my teeth, like they do with horses.*

'I can't help feeling a bit out of my depth,' she admitted. 'You know, two months ago I was living in a little two-bed apartment in Miami with a view of the beach if you leaned off the edge of the balcony and sort of squinted round the corner of the apartment block next to us. And now . . .' She couldn't move her arms, as the Dowager was still gripping them, so she rolled her head to signify the grandeur of their surroundings. 'I mean,' she blurted out, 'don't you wish that Joachim was getting married to a queen, or at least a countess, or something? Someone from Herzoslovakia? Even someone from *Europe?*'

The Dowager nodded sympathetically.

'Frankly, Lori, that *was* my original hope,' the Dowager said, smiling up at her sweetly. 'I mustn't lie to you, must I? You are going to be my daughter, the only daughter I will ever have, and we must always be honest with each other. I must admit that I *did* hope Joachim would find a girl from maybe Austria, Hungary, Germany, where there are many aristocrats who would understand all of our ways. But the heart must have what the heart wants, and my son is a man of integrity who would not marry just to please his mother and his country, but also to make himself happy. And he has chosen a beautiful angel of a girl, with a lovely sunny personality! Happy, smiling—'

Please don't say healthy! Lori crossed her fingers.

' – blonde, like a true queen, a true Herzoslovakian, who will give him lovely healthy children, and me lovely healthy grandchildren . . .'

Gah, I knew she wouldn't be able to avoid saying it . . .

But the mention of children softened Lori instantly. She did want to have children, always had, the more the merrier, the sooner the better; she couldn't wait to get started with Joachim, fill the royal palaces with a whole brood of – yes, healthy little rug rats, tumbling down the staircases, sliding along the polished marble floors, bringing some life and noise and much needed chaos to the perfectly organized formal atmosphere that presently reigned in Schloss Hafenhoffer.

'I want to have *loads* of kids,' she said to the Dowager, who beamed approvingly.

'And you won't lose your lovely figure, even if you have many children,' she said reassuringly. 'You have a nice long waist – that is a *very* good shape for having babies! You must be careful not to put on too much weight, though, so you don't get the stretch marks . . .'

So after her nap, standing next to Joachim in the Throne Room, posing for photographs as journalists eagerly called out questions about when they were planning to start a family, Lori found herself remembering this comment from her future mother-in-law and smiling with such genuine amusement that the photographers cooed in pleasure at how beautiful she looked. *It's just the kind of thing that Mom and Grandma would say. They've got that same bluntness. If they think something about you, they'll just come out and say it. Grandma even worried that I'd turn into a lesbian if I played volleyball!*

Well, I've definitely proved her wrong there, she thought, smiling. *Not just engaged to a guy, but a king to boot! They couldn't believe it when I rang to tell them – oh, I can't wait till they come to visit next week—*

'Miss Makarwicz, please to raise your hand so we see better the ring?' one photographer asked, and Lori obediently placed her left hand on Joachim's uniformed chest, turning it from side to side slowly to give different angles, make the diamonds blaze in the flashes of the cameras.

Last month I was showing off the Duplex watch, this month it's my engagement ring, she found herself thinking ironically. *What is this selling, though? The happy monarchy of Herzoslovakia, safe as houses for all your tax haven needs?*

The cynicism was utterly unlike her; she had no idea where it had even come from. Shaking her head to dispel it, she leaned against Joachim and smiled happily at the ranked mass of media.

'Miss Makarwicz, are you going to compete playing volleyball in future?' a journalist called. 'Maybe competing for Herzoslovakia!'

Laughter greeted this, and Lori, smiling, waited for it to die down before she said: 'No – I couldn't do better than taking a medal at the Olympics! I hope to coach and work with children in my new country to promote the importance of health and sport, but I don't think it would be appropriate as a queen to be jumping around in the sand. Besides, I want to settle down in my new country, not be travelling around the world.'

'May I say, Miss Makarwicz, you would look very attractive in a volleyball costume in the Herzoslovakian colours!' called a brave man, who was immediately shushed by a volley of disapproving hushes from the other journalists.

'Ugh, a Communist!' Joachim hissed crossly in Lori's ear. 'I am very sorry.'

But Lori was looking in the direction of the 'Communist' and smiling even more beautifully, her perfect teeth on display as she said easily: 'You know, I was never happy competing in that small outfit. Joachim has handkerchiefs that are bigger than that!'

She let them laugh at this, and then added: 'But seriously, no, I won't be playing in any future tournaments. As your future queen, I will be putting my new country and my king first, I promise you that! My family are going to be visiting me soon from America, and I am very much looking forward to showing them my new home, of which I am very proud. *Erçeŝs Herzoslovakia!*' she finished. *Long live Herzoslovakia!*

The journalists broke into applause. Joachim's arm, around her waist, squeezed her tightly in approval at the perfect way she had handled the press conference.

'*Erçêss Kirá Lori!*' he said proudly. *Long live Queen Lori!*

She smiled at him, tilting her head slightly back at the angle which she knew, from her years of press conferences, sports channel interviews, photo shoots, sponsorship material, was the one best way to present her face: the line of her jaw was perfectly smooth like this, the slight bump on her nose blurring to straight. Her king, the man for whom she was changing her life, was looking his absolute best in the dark blue uniform of an honorary colonel in the Herzoslovakian army, its high collar, with its gold flashes, concealing the soft little bulge of flesh under his chin, the dark red sash and rows of medals adding to his authority, the custom-tailoring of the uniform narrowing his waist and lengthening his legs.

My king, she thought happily, seeing the pride in his eyes as he gazed at her. *He's chosen me, out of all of the women he could possibly have had – me, Lori Makarwicz from Dorchester, New York, from a blue-collar family about as aristocratic as a sack of potatoes. He's lavished me with jewels –* around her neck she was wearing a multi-strand turquoise and pearl necklace with a diamond and pearl clasp, and in her ears diamond and pearl stars – *welcomed me to his country, his home, his family, asked me to be his wife and the mother of his children . . . his mother's already treating me like the daughter she never had . . . I'm the luckiest girl in the world!*

Joachim's arm was warm around her, his breath fresh on her cheek. She turned into him and reached up to stroke his cheek lovingly, careful now not to scratch him with the enormous rock on her hand; it was a source of perpetual anxiety to her, that ring. She couldn't bathe or shower or sleep while wearing it, but she had to keep checking that it hadn't rolled off the shelf or the bedside table she'd put it on; she was still waking up several times in the night to touch it before falling asleep again.

All alone in the enormous four-poster bed, of course. Because King Joachim didn't think he should be sleeping with his fiancée before the marriage.

Lori couldn't get her head around that. OK, he hadn't thought it proper to have sex before they'd become engaged, she got that, but now that they *were* – well, didn't it seem like a really good idea? Even if he didn't want it known, they didn't have to flaunt it. There were a couple of months to go before the wedding . . . they had plenty of time to sneak off somewhere and get on with it . . .

I'm going to have to seduce him, she told herself determinedly, as he held up a hand, signifying the end of the press conference. *It's the only way. I'm sure he's holding back out of some scruple, because he thinks he should wait until the wedding night. Well, that may be how they do it in Europe, but everyone here keeps telling me how healthy I am, and they're right. I'm a healthy, red-blooded American girl, and I'm not going to marry a man I haven't had sex with! I'm going to pick my moment, get Joachim back to my rooms, and show him how we roll back home in the States.*

Lori smiled at her unsuspecting fiancé, who was beaming at her as fondly and protectively as if she were an angel come down to earth.

Well, he'll find out I'm not that much of an angel.

Belinda

Twenty years ago

The woman who had, until earlier that day, been Princess Belinda, stepped slowly out of the helicopter, steadying herself on the outstretched hand of the co-pilot, who had jumped down to help her out. Her legs were wobbly, and she was very grateful for the instinctive courtesy that kept him standing there, waiting politely as she gathered herself, found her balance. It wasn't the long ride in the helicopter that had made her so shaky; she was used to travelling by this mode of transport, and had been too dazed to even notice their route, the frequent stops for refuelling on the journey from Oukaïmeden.

They had crossed Morocco, landing briefly in Algiers, then buzzed over the Mediterranean to Cagliari, right at the base of Sardinia; from there it had been another jump over the bright blue Tyrrhenian Sea to their final destination. If Belinda had looked out of the small window of the military helicopter during the journey, she would have seen nothing below her at all; no islands, and barely any boats apart from the occasional ferry taking passengers from Naples to Corsica. In the summer, there would have been many more ferries, carrying tourists from one beautiful Italian island to another; but it was the beginning of March, far too early in the year for sunbathing or swimming, and the boats were on their winter schedule, the islands inhabited only by their year-long residents, a fraction of the people who would swarm to them in the summer.

Which made the tiny island on which the helicopter had landed an ideal location where one of the most famous women in the world could take refuge after having faked her own death.

It was the shock of what she had done that morning which was making Belinda's legs tremble. Everything had gone exactly as planned. So much so, in fact, that she had had nothing to do but follow the meticulous instructions which had been drummed into her for weeks beforehand, once the entire plot had been constructed.

She had rehearsed it again and again. Nothing had been left to chance; even the ski lift, after she had ridden it up to the summit of Jebel Attar, just after dawn had broken, had been temporarily disabled for twenty minutes by the operator, who had thought he was being bribed by a hireling of Belinda's to ensure that she wasn't followed by any photographers or nosy parkers. Of course, the real reason had been to make sure that no one could follow her too closely, or even, from the lift itself, spot a clue that the avalanche which entombed her might not have been quite the tragic accident that it had seemed . . .

Even before she had reached that stand of tightly packed Spanish firs, Belinda had started to execute a hockey stop, shifting almost all her weight onto her left ski, then letting the skis turn to parallel the instant the first tree blocked her from view, leaning hard up the slope, driving the edges of the skis hard into the packed snow, forcing her to a halt. The man waiting for her caught her arm, steadying her as she skidded to a stop, nodding in appreciation of her skill as the other man, poised at the far end of the line of trees, set the fake Belinda into motion.

The real Belinda watched in something close to horror, her breath coming in swift pants from the rapid exercise, as the dummy set off. Modelled bending over its skis, the poles tucked under her arms, it looked almost exactly like her, folded into the shape which Belinda had been careful to make in her swift descent. The model was dressed in an identical blue ski suit and the same hat and goggles that Belinda was wearing, a dark wig that matched Belinda's hair streaming out from under the hat.

It only took a few seconds. The second man deftly operated the dummy's radio controls, sending it down the slope underneath the hanging ridge; a moment later, he triggered the hidden explosives planted beneath the rocks along the ridge, sending them and their heavy covering of snow crashing down on the speeding figure below. No one else was anywhere nearby. The previous skiers had long gone, the jamming of the ski lift's cable had ensured that there would be no others who might be put in danger; as Nigel Slyme, tears pouring down his face, snapped away, capturing the ''death' of his idol, the real Belinda was quickly pulling on a bright red jacket over her blue suit, as the first man, on his knees, unfurled a pair of black ski trousers, specially made to snap on over her existing ones. She dragged off her hat and goggles, handing them to him to slip in his backpack; in return, he tossed her a new pair of goggles and a red hat with a blonde ponytail sewn to the back.

It had barely taken half a minute to completely transform Belinda's appearance. They had practised this drill again and again, getting it as fast as possible, in the days leading up to today. A weekday had been chosen so there would be fewer people on the slopes. It was a morning clear enough for any photographs to be unmistakably of Belinda. Finally, a discreet tip-off to Nigel Slyme to ensure his presence and the crucial documentary photos of Belinda's 'death' – in exchange for a backhander, of course, so that Nigel believed he had paid a bribe to catch the princess quite unawares in a rare early-morning moment of solitude.

Then, after the successful entombment of the remotely controlled dummy, the breathlessly fast cross-country ski in the opposite direction from Oukaïmeden, down the steep slopes of the Toubkal National Park, to where a Jeep was waiting to take them to an impromptu helipad. The scramble into the helicopter with Italian military markings, the two men left behind in the Jeep, Belinda alone with the two pilots as the machine lifted into the sky. And the hop, skip and jump flight across the sea to this little island, her final destination on the escape route.

Belinda looked down at herself. She was still in the double layers of skiwear; it had been cold in the military helicopter, which didn't have the insulation of the more luxurious models. The small heliport was on the highest point of the island, a peak that had been flattened and concreted over, and Belinda could see almost the entire landmass of the islet below, grassy slopes leading down to little white beaches, the roof of a pale stone villa on a terraced plateau: the only building, it seemed, on the whole island. The sea was a delicate emerald-blue, lapping softly at the shoreline. It was the perfect retreat from the world.

Belinda had not known where she was headed, hadn't wanted to know; planning her own death had been almost more than she could cope with. Even now, the magnitude of what she had just undergone had barely sunk in. She was still shaking, and not from cold. It was a bright spring day, the sunlight bouncing off the sea, and she was more than insulated in her double layers of skiwear. She had pulled off the goggles, and the hat, with its itchy attached ponytail, in the helicopter; she raised a hand to shade her eyes from the midday sun, but was still unable to let go of her grip on the co-pilot.

And then she saw the man she loved running up the path from the villa, and with a sobbing cry of relief she dropped the supporting hand and took off, positively sprinting into the arms of Prince Rahim Mohajeri bin Azhari. A Saudi prince with a Berber mother, Rahim was half international playboy, half humanitarian, and the only person in the world to whom she had been able to confide the shocking truth about the sham that had been her marriage.

She slammed into Rahim, crying fully now, crying for everything she had left behind and for the uncertainty of how she would live out the future. His arms closed tightly around her, and she buried her face in his neck, breathing in the warm, musky scent of his Acqua di Parma cologne and the delicious, infinitely reassuring smell of his skin. Behind them, the helicopter, its rotor blades spinning, took off again, so noisy that by the time the last echoes of its progress had died away, its dragonfly silhouette disappearing across the sea to the Italian mainland, Belinda's sobs were dying down into little gulps and sniffs. Rahim, into whom his Harrow education had instilled formal manners, produced a perfectly ironed handkerchief from the pocket of his blazer and dried her eyes with loving care and attention.

'Come, my darling,' he said, wrapping his arm around her shoulders and leading her down the stone steps set into the side of the hill. 'We will have some mint tea and something to eat, and you will settle into this lovely place.'

'Where is it?' Belinda asked, blowing her nose. 'You know I've never been any good at geography! We flew for absolutely ages . . .'

'We are in the Tuscan archipelago of little islands,' her lover informed her. 'Over there—' he pointed across the sea in an easterly direction, where a faint dark outline could just be made out – 'that is Elba, where Napoleon was imprisoned after he abdicated. And there—' he swung around – 'you will not see it, because it is too small, but below is the island of Pianosa, a nature reserve on which for many years there was a high-security prison. They kept Mafiosi there, in extreme isolation, so they could not communicate with their *capi* back in Sicily.'

'Goodness!' Belinda sniffed with wry amusement. 'You make it all sound so depressing! All these prison islands!'

Rahim laughed. 'I'm telling you this to show how secure it is here, my love. Elba is a pleasure resort now, but most of the little islands are nature reserves, like Pianosa. They can scarcely be visited at all, unless you have a special permit from the European Union, or if you are in the forestry department. You see, I've done all my research! And this island, Montecapra, is leased from the government by Massimo Benefatti—' this was an Italian billionaire well-known to both Belinda and Rahim on the international party circuit. 'Ostensibly, it is a wildlife sanctuary, but Massimo comes here also to enjoy the peace and tranquillity. The airspace and the waters are protected by the Italian airforce out of Pisa, to prevent fishermen and tourists visiting the nature reserves. So you see, it is impossible for a paparazzo to come anywhere near Montecapra.'

They had reached the villa by now, a beautifully restored eighteenth-century building, its high windows framed by traditional dark green shutters. Belinda paused, taking it in. During her marriage to Prince Oliver, she had stayed in most of the royal palaces in the world, hotels for which the designation five-star simply wasn't enough, private mansions of incredible luxury, even the White House. But right now, this simple, elegant villa, on an island in the middle of the serene Tyrrhenian Sea, was the most perfect refuge she could imagine.

Rahim took her into the villa, through a central hallway with Roman-style mosaic floors which led straight through the ground floor of the house to a long loggia at the back, its glassed-in high windows giving spectacular views over the sea below. Belinda divested herself of the jacket and snap-on ski trousers, but shook her head when Rahim suggested she go upstairs to change.

'Tea first,' she said, managing a watery smile. 'Tea and biscuits for shock. It's the English way.'

'The English way, but Moroccan tea,' Rahim said, smiling back. 'It is the perfect blend of you and me, darling.' His grin deepened. 'I know what you would say if you were more yourself – you would tease me and tell me to stop being such a flowery Arab. But I can't help it sometimes. I like to say poetic things, you know.'

A servant was holding the back of a delicate velvet armchair, waiting for Belinda to seat herself. He pushed in her chair as Rahim poured tea from a clear glass pot, fresh mint leaves steeped in hot, not boiling water, pale green aromatic steam rising from its surface. Rahim trickled a little thyme honey into each cup, stirred them well, and then handed one to his lover. The servant had retreated discreetly: Belinda, very gratefully, reached for the plate of fluted, sugar-topped lemon biscuits and started to work her way through it. She had never had to watch her weight, having always been very physically active; she had skied and ridden horses all through her teens, and had actually met Prince Oliver not, as the press had reported initially, working as a chalet girl in Verbier, but teaching beginners to ski on the nursery slopes.

Rahim watched her with great approval; he liked a woman with a healthy appetite.

'We will spend some weeks here,' he said to her. 'Or, if you wish, I will leave you to be alone, as long as you need.'

Belinda, her mouth full of biscuit, shook her head so vigorously that some sugar crumbs sprayed out onto her ski suit. Normally, she would have been mortified by this breach of good manners, but as she looked down at the crumbs, she realized that she didn't give a damn. She was no longer a princess. She wasn't even Lady Belinda Lindsey-Crofter any more. She had no idea, in fact, *who* she was.

So all she did was dust the crumbs onto the floor, swallow the rest of her bite, and say vehemently: 'I don't want you to go. Stay with me. I couldn't cope on my own, not at all.'

'Good.' He looked very grave. 'But Belinda, you must take this time to decide if this is really what you want. It is still not too late to go back. It will be a scandal, yes, but we can manage that. We will say that you were frightened for your life – which is no more than the truth – but that you could not bear to never see your children again.'

'I don't know if I *can* bear it,' Belinda said quietly. 'I honestly don't. But Oliver would have killed me if I'd stayed. I know he's tried once already. And if I admit to something as wild as staging my own death in an avalanche, that'll be *exactly* what he needs to make me look completely bonkers. It'd be even easier for him to try again. Slip me an overdose and say that I popped too many pills by accident.'

Rahim nodded slowly, taking in her words. Belinda had

desperately hoped that her divorce from her ex-husband, Prince Oliver, heir to the British throne, would protect her from his malice; but Oliver had been violently opposed to the divorce, had fought tooth and nail to convince her to stay married to him. If anything, his anger towards her had worsened after they were no longer man and wife; he had been terrified that she would spill his secrets, despite a condition of her divorce settlement being utter discretion about his private life. An aide of his had come to her, in absolute terror, to warn her that someone in her inner circle was in Oliver's pay, planning to doctor her food so that it looked as if she'd taken an accidental overdose.

And I believed every word. I know that Oliver was capable of doing it.

I may not be able to be with my children as they grow up and have children of their own. But at least I'll be alive to see them from a distance.

Wordlessly, she picked up the teacup and sipped the sweetened mint tea, staring out over the waves below.

Living with Oliver gave me two near-breakdowns, sent me onto antidepressants and to therapists I couldn't confide in properly, because I was absolutely forbidden from telling the truth about the future King of Britain.

But when I divorced him, I realized I was in more danger than ever.

She turned to look at Rahim, seeing the concern in his dark eyes as he gazed at her. He had always believed her, had loved her for years. Had intuited that the reason she was so nervous, so twitchy, wasn't that she was a neurotic prescription-pill addict, the rumour that Oliver's camp had so gleefully spread about her. Rahim was the only one who had ever loved her for herself. All the other men who had courted her had been attracted not just by her looks and her status, but by the reputation for instability that had grown around her.

Men love crazy women, she thought ironically. *Just like women love bad boys. I was guilty of that too. I thought Oliver was a bad boy, a wild prince, who was settling down finally, because he'd fallen in love for the first time. I bought into that whole idiotic, romance-novel, Mills and Boon story that Oliver was selling me. I thought I was The One. I had no idea at all that I could never have been what Oliver wanted, or needed . . .*

The slowly dawning realization that Oliver had married her for all the wrong reasons – while still expecting her to play the perfect wife and mother, not just in public but to his family – had sent Belinda into a terrible downward spiral. She *had* become reliant on antidepressants, but never as much as Oliver's spinners had elatedly whispered to the press. She *had* been close to breakdown, but she had never tipped over the edge, as they had said. And she had resisted the temptation to sleep with Rahim until she had been officially divorced. Bad enough that Oliver had not even been faithful to her for twenty-four hours; she had learned from the same aide who had warned her about the murder attempt that Oliver had cheated on her the night of their wedding. She wasn't going to sink to his level, even if she had every justification.

And Rahim had waited patiently for her. He was the man she had thought Oliver was when, as a naïve eighteen-year-old, she had walked down the aisle of Westminster Abbey to become Oliver's bride.

Well, first she had turned her back on the prospect of one day becoming Queen, and now she had rejected, too, the social status of being a princess. She had given up so much, but she was alive and safe, where Oliver's plotting couldn't reach.

'I would never have said a word about him,' she said, setting the cup back on the table, still gazing at Rahim. 'Not a *word*. For the sake of our children, if nothing else. But Oliver was too paranoid to believe me. If I go back, he'll have me killed.'

She swallowed hard.

'Then I won't try to persuade you to go back any more.' Rahim reached out and took her hand. His skin was soft; he moisturized with almond oil night and morning.

Belinda felt her throat close up. Now that she had lost the last sliver of opportunity to turn back, to be persuaded by Rahim to do so, it was the moment at which she truly absorbed how her life had changed for ever. She would never hold her children again, never see Hugo and Sophie grow into adults. Never see them smile up at her, run to her, wrap their arms around her legs and hold on for dear life, call her Mummy. There had been complications at Sophie's birth; Belinda would never have another child, something that hurt her deeply every time she remembered it. She might still have been young enough to try for a baby with Rahim if not for that.

But Oliver would have killed you if you'd stayed. This way, at least you can see Hugo and Sophie, the only two children you'll ever have, from a distance.

Her fingers tightened around Rahim's.

'This will be our honeymoon,' he said softly. 'A few weeks together, on this island. Out of time. It's a very odd honeymoon, I know, but to me, you're my wife, Belinda. And this is the start of our life together.'

Belinda was a survivor; she had fought her way through her appalling marriage without losing her mind or her life, and the decision to fake her own death in order to be free of Oliver had been all hers. She was determined not to cry any more. She didn't have everything she wanted, but she had her life, and the man she loved, and that was a very great deal.

So she picked up Rahim's smooth hand and kissed it as she said: 'Darling, you know something? You mustn't call me Belinda any more. Belinda's dead and gone.'

Rahim nodded.

'I thought that maybe,' he said, 'if you like it, from now on I would call you Hana. It means happiness in Arabic. No—' he thought quickly. 'More than happiness. Bliss. It means bliss.'

'I think that's *lovely*,' the woman who had been Her Royal Highness, Princess Belinda, and was now Hana, the official consort of Prince Rahim Mohajeri bin Azhari, said, smiling at her lover. 'I'm about bloody due some bliss.'

She stood up, and with one swift movement slid onto her lover's lap and wound her arms around his neck.

'You know what? Let's get started on some bliss right now. I've got *years* to make up for!' she said, and kissed him so hard he tipped back in the chair, and they nearly both went crashing down to the mosaic floor.

Chloe

Present day

'Bollocks! Bollocks bollocks fuckety-fuck!'

As Chloe emerged from the treatment room of the clinic, patting her chin rather gingerly after the vigorous salt microdermabrasion and UV light treatment she had just undergone, the loud voice of her new lady-in-waiting could be heard even through the glass entrance door; it sounded as if Lauren were standing on the staircase that led down to the ground floor.

'What is she *doing*?' Chloe muttered, as Lauren burst back through the door and stood, arms akimbo, in the hallway, shaking her head so furiously that even the several layers of hairspray she had applied that morning couldn't hold her extensions perfectly in place.

'Chlo, I'm sorry, babe, but the paps are outside!' Lauren announced. 'What a fucking disaster!'

'What? Oh *no*!' Both Chloe's hands rose to her face now in an instinctive effort to cover it.

'I didn't say a word to anyone!' Sujata, the owner of GiGi Medical Aesthetics, assured both girls, her expression horrified. 'I cleared the whole appointments book so that no one would come in while you're here, Chloe! I do all your treatments myself so I'm the only technician in the clinic—'

'I know, I know,' Chloe said swiftly to reassure Sujata. 'I don't think for a moment it was you.'

'Client confidentiality is *so* crucial!' Sujata wailed, going into her office, which had a window on the street, and angling herself to look down without showing her face at the glass. As soon as she did so, she screamed. 'Oh my God, there's a whole *crowd* of them!'

'It's all the foreign press too,' Lauren said grimly. 'Fucking hell, it's a sodding mess, isn't it? Let's have a look at you, Chlo. Shit.'

She winced at the sight of Chloe's face, which was not only pink and shiny all over, but dotted with small red marks where the tracer gun of the salt microdermabrasion had taken off the tops of several little bumps on Chloe's skin. Chloe didn't have a perfect complexion, and had been plastering on increasing quantities of foundation to protect herself from the scrutiny of the paparazzi over the years, clogging her pores more and more, which only compounded the problem. Facials had failed to help, so Chloe had resorted to more serious methods: the skin polish to smooth out her bumpiness, the light treatment to kill bacteria below the surface of the epidermis, and then a soothing papaya mask. She could already feel how much smoother her skin was, but Sujata had warned that she wouldn't want to go on somewhere directly afterwards, because of the possibility of temporary red rash marks, and she had been absolutely right.

'What am I going to *do*?' Chloe moaned, looking in the large mirror in the elegant reception room.

'We can cover up the dots,' Lauren said. 'I've got enough slap in me kit to make an orang-utan look nice and smooth. But—'

'I don't want to be papped coming out of here!' Chloe broke in. 'Oh, sorry, Sujata – no offence—'

'Oh, none taken! None at all!' Sujata interjected. 'I *quite* understand about your wanting to be discreet!'

'It just looks so *vain*!' Chloe sank into one of the leather chairs. 'I *can't* be seen here! They'll go on the website and start looking at all the treatments you do here, and start speculating about what I'm having, and the next thing you know they'll be printing that I'm having anti-cellulite treatments and photoshopping me to look all cellulitey—'

'You *are* having cellulite treatments, you dozy mare,' Lauren pointed out. 'That Indiba thingy-whatsit.'

'It's really helping!' Chloe said, perking up for a moment. 'And my tummy's definitely flatter, too.'

'The high radiofrequency treatments are really *very* effective,' Sujata said happily, forgetting about the paparazzi as she smiled at her client.

Lauren rolled her eyes. She never lost focus for a second on whatever goal she had fixed upon; it was a huge strength of hers, one of the main reasons Chloe had chosen her when the Palace had instructed her that she needed a lady-in-waiting. The job was, effectively, to be Chloe's personal assistant, organize her schedule and her calendar, and keep her life running smoothly as she embarked upon a series of official engagements. Chloe was determined to use her status as a way to publicize Rescue Children, the charity for which she had worked for years, and to expand her remit to a raft of not only other children's charities, but ones for trafficked women too, which was a new cause behind which she was determined to throw all the power and influence that she could muster.

So who better than Lauren, who had risen through the ranks at Rescue Children with Chloe, and was now head of fundraising at the impressively young age of twenty-eight, to work with Chloe on what Chloe saw, in great part, as a whole new charity venture? Chloe had been worried that Lauren would be hugely offended by effectively being asked to be Chloe's assistant, plus taking a salary cut into the bargain – the Palace considering, naturally, that ladies-in-waiting would already have their own family money, and be prepared to take on the role for a sum that would simply allow them a few extra holidays and some custom-made Philip Treacy hats for summer weddings.

But Lauren had jumped at the opportunity.

'Once in a lifetime, innit?' she'd said excitedly. 'I'll get all me expenses paid, too, won't I? Cars and food and that. Tell you what, I'll do it for a year, see you married, wedding done and dusted, then I'll train someone up for you, start me own charity and you can be the patron. Sorted!'

The Palace – incarnated in the person of Lady Margaret McArdle, ex-lady-in-waiting to Princess Belinda and now the unofficial doyenne of Royal etiquette – had raised its eyebrows almost to its hairline at the introduction of Lauren Plodger into its hallowed inner circle. But Chloe had held firm. Lauren was the best person, the *only* person for the job. No, she did not want someone of a more 'suitable' back-ground; Chloe had bitten her lip to avoid saying that Princess Sophie, the Hon Araminta and the rest of the poisonous females in their circle had left her completely unable to trust anyone remotely 'suitable'.

'It's a new generation,' Chloe had said firmly to Lady Margaret. 'Hugo's marrying a middle-class girl who works for a living. The Civil List has been cut down radically – the King's not supporting half the minor royals he was maintain-ing financially ten years ago. The royal family's moving forward, modernising—'

Lady Margaret flinched at this brutal word, but Chloe pressed on regardless –

' – and that's the right thing to do.' She smiled. 'Lauren's a twenty-first century lady-in-waiting. You'll see. She'll run things wonderfully efficiently. I really hope you'll help her in any way you can. She'll have so much to learn from you.'

Lady Margaret was experienced enough to yield to defeat graciously, while extorting any concession she could from the victor.

'She will *have* to agree to modify her language,' she said firmly. 'I will be *quite* unable to recommend a lady-in-waiting who swears like a stable boy.'

'I wouldn't know – I've never met a stable boy,' Chloe said dryly. 'But don't worry – Lauren hasn't worked for Rescue Children for years without being able to posh up her accent for rich donors and board meetings. She'll be fine in public, though she won't exactly sound like Sophie or Minty. And I'll tell her to watch the language with you, of course.'

Lady Margaret had winced again at the expression 'posh up', as Chloe had known she would. *But now I'm engaged to Hugo*, Chloe had thought, smugly looking down at the cabochon emerald ring on the third finger of her left hand, *I don't need to worry quite as much about that, do I?*

And then Chloe had realized that Lady Margaret, post-instinctive wince, was regarding her with a surprisingly sympathetic gaze.

'No one is suggesting that Sophie or Araminta are role models *anyone* should be emulating, my dear,' Lady Margaret had said. 'You are a nice, hard-working girl with good moral values. Hugo has made a choice of which I thoroughly approve.'

Chloe had stared at her, genuinely taken aback: prim and proper in her camel cashmere twinset over tweed trousers, pearl stud earrings contrasting with the weather-beaten skin of an outdoorsy woman who gardened, rode to hounds and hacked with the dogs out of hunt season, Lady Margaret, an Anglo-Irish duke's daughter, incarnated the British aristocracy. Chloe had never imagined eliciting this degree of approval from her.

'Thank you,' she managed to say. But Lady Margaret hadn't finished.

'Hugo remembers his mother a little,' she said. 'Sophie really doesn't – she was too young when darling Belinda died. I did my best for them, but Sophie has grown up without any maternal influence at all. And Oliver is . . .' She removed her gaze from Chloe and transferred it to the arrangement of salmon and yellow roses on the console table on the far wall of the Buckingham Palace sitting room in which they were meeting.

'Oliver,' she continued, 'was brought up in a children-should-be-seen-and-not-heard atmosphere which has obviously very much fallen out of fashion nowadays. Hugo and Sophie had very pleasant nannies, but that isn't really a substitute, is it?'

Chloe wasn't sure whether this required a response; she shook her head tentatively as Lady Margaret concluded:

'Sophie may take a little time to welcome you into the family. But I'm sure that you two will end up being the best of friends.'

Chloe had taken great amusement in relating this to Lauren, who had laughed like a drain and translated:

'Sophie's a fucking bitch who'll screw you over any way you can. Watch your back, girl. *Especially* if she starts pretending to be your mate.'

Well, Sophie might not be pretending to be my friend yet, but she's doing enough damage as my enemy, Chloe thought grimly now.

'Could they have followed you here?' Sujata was asking of the paparazzi outside.

'Doubt it,' Lauren said tersely. She exchanged glances with Chloe, mouthing 'that bitch Sophie' behind Sujata's back; Chloe nodded. Neither of them had any doubt that Sophie had set them up.

'What we need to concentrate on right now,' Lauren went on, 'is sorting out some way so Chlo isn't photographed anywhere sodding near this flipping clinic. There a back door?'

Sujata shook her head.

'Fuck,' Lauren said. 'It's a bugger that I can't pass for you, Chlo. Walk out with a scarf round me face, get them to follow me down the street, you nip out when they're all racing after me, then I take the scarf off and they all feel like wankers. But me arse'd give me away if I tried to get your coat on over it. Not to mention me tits.'

Lauren was a statuesque size sixteen, and proud of every curve.

She tapped her foot, shod in a ponyskin high heel whose leopard print echoed the lining of her belted raincoat.

'I *could* bell someone to come over and pretend to be you,' she meditated out loud, 'but who knows how long that'd take? I need to think about that for the future. And check out back exits. OK, Lauren, lesson bloody well and truly learned. But what are we going to do now?'

Sujata opened her mouth to say something; Chloe quickly raised her hand to hush her to silence. This was how Lauren operated, talking her thought process along until she reached a solution.

And Lauren *always* reached a solution.

'Ooh, something popped into me head. Something I saw coming in. Hold up. What's downstairs here again, Sujata love? On the ground floor?'

Addressed directly, Sujata could answer.

'A Pilates studio,' she said. 'They're—'

But Lauren had already turned on her heel.

'Chlo, go into me bag and cover up every spot on your face, OK?' she snapped over her shoulder. 'I don't want to see one mark on it, nothing. Then slap on lots of me Tarte blush, the gel one, but no eye makeup at all. Got it?'

Chloe dashed to obey as Lauren headed out of GiGi's offices and clumped downstairs as fast as her high heels and tight pencil skirt would permit. A mere five minutes later she was returning, followed by a pink-cheeked, excited Pilates teacher whose enviably lean-muscled body was on display in the regulation capri leggings and bra-top vest, her hair pulled back in the equally regulation Pilates ponytail.

'Hi!' the teacher said, her eyes widening on seeing Chloe's very familiar face, now even-toned (from a safe distance) and lightly flushed. 'Wow, you're even prettier in real life!'

'Thank you,' Chloe said gratefully.

'Yeah yeah, whatever!' Lauren snapped. 'Sorry, love, but we ain't got time for that. Here, put these on, Chlo. Tasmin here's lent you a set of exercise gear. You're going to come out of the studio, say goodbye to Tasmin – you were having private Pilates session to tone up for your wedding dress, no one'll blink at that. Tasmin gets the publicity so she's happy, and if she tries to tell the papers you were really up here she screws her business and looks like a twat, so she won't be tempted to do that, will you, Tasmin?'

'I – *no*!' Tasmin exclaimed, horrified.

'Good.' Lauren leaned forward to squint at Chloe's face. 'Nice one – that blush makes you look like you just got all sweaty.'

'*Great*,' Chloe said, rolling her eyes as she nipped into the treatment room to change.

A few minutes later, her sweater pulled on over the exercise clothes, the jeans she had been wearing rolled up in Lauren's bag, Chloe slipped downstairs and into the studio by the side door; luckily, it shared its toilets with the office at the back of the building, so had an internal door to the lobby. Tasmin, her face bright with excitement, had applied two extra coats of mascara and alternated plank position with Pilates press-ups while waiting for her celebrity 'client', so that her arms looked phenomenally lean and cut as she held the street door open for Chloe and posed there while the photographers sprang to life, clicking away madly.

'Had a nice workout, Chloe?'

'Struggling to get into the wedding dress, Chloe, love?'

'Take off the sweater, Chloe, eh? Let's have a look at your nice new shape!'

You never said a word, no matter what they shouted. You smiled, the polite smile that you had perfected over the years, and your security officers jumped out of the car when they saw you emerge and escorted you back to the vehicle so the waiting press couldn't get dangerously close to you. Lauren followed behind, enjoying the attention; she was well on her way to becoming famous in her own right, with her Fifties-style airbrushed makeup, her high-piled hair, her belted raincoat and the flashes of animal print that were her signature look. You waited until you were safely in the car, pulling away, and the paps were turning back to photograph the delighted Tasmin, to turn to Lauren and say bitterly:

'It *was* Sophie, wasn't it?'

'*Oh* yeah,' Lauren said grimly, pulling out an e-cigarette from her bag and toking on it hard. 'That fucking cunt. Know what, Chlo? I blame meself. She was only in my office earlier having a snoop around, wasn't she? Wandered in to ask what Hugo was up to, cos she couldn't get him on the phone and his secretary was off out somewhere.' She exhaled smoke, shaking her head in self-reproach. 'I should've known that was bollocks. That Tristram's always around when I need to check something with him.'

Since the engagement, Chloe had moved into Kensington Palace. She had refused to live with Hugo before he proposed, though he had asked her to repeatedly; she had had an awful superstition about it. It hadn't been so much that old line about men not buying cows if they could have the milk for free (though Lauren had trotted that one out a couple of times), but the awareness that if things didn't work out, it would be an even bigger comedown to have moved into Kensington Palace only to leave it again.

Because, after the initial euphoria of dating a really nice guy who not only seemed very keen on her, but was a prince into the bargain, had worn off, Chloe had had to do some very serious thinking. They had kept it quiet as long as they could, but eventually, of course, the press had got wind of Hugo's new love interest, and Chloe's comparatively humble background had not only sent them into overdrive, but demonstrated how much the girls Hugo had previously dated had been protected by their aristocratic connections.

Posh girls, it emerged, all came from families who knew people who owned newspapers, holidayed with them in Barbados, sat next to them on the benches of the House of Lords, lunched with them at the Garrick Club. If Hugo and Araminta had had a fling, for instance, it would barely have been mentioned in the press. No one would have stalked Minty outside the South Kensington apartment building where she lived, tried to get upskirt shots of her getting out of cabs, tracked down her exes and bribed them to spill the beans on when she'd lost her virginity. It simply didn't happen to the Mintys of this world: they were defended by their powerful male relatives.

But Chloe had no such protection. And the worst thing of all, the part that really grated on her last nerve, was that if *she* broke it off with Hugo, it would be assumed by almost every single person in the world that *he* had been the one to do it. If she moved out of Kensington Palace, having decided that Hugo wasn't The One, the only story the media would glee-fully embrace was that Hugo had chucked her out.

Thank goodness, she had made the right choices every step of the way. Taken her time to be quite sure of her feelings, moved into Kensington Palace only when she had that ring on her finger. Chosen Lauren as her lady-in-waiting, one of the best decisions she'd ever made, installing her in an office across the courtyard from Hugo's bachelor suite of rooms.

'Sophie must've had a squint at me diary,' Lauren confessed. 'She was smoking, and she perched on the desk and had a rummage around for something she could ash in. I bet she was really getting a gander at me big desk diary. Last time I fuck up like that. Sorry, Chloe. My bad. I just had GiGi in it, but, you know, she's posh but she ain't thick. She'll've gone off and Googled it and called the paps pronto.'

She sighed.

'And you know the flipping irony? I only went and got that desk diary cos I thought if I had an electronic one, it might get hacked by some bleeding journo! I don't care if they're all supposed to be behaving better after all that Leveson stuff, I bet they're all still bloody at it! I'll have to get a lock for it. Like a little girl's diary. Pretty sodding funny, I *don't* think.'

Chloe nodded.

'From now on,' she said firmly, 'close it the moment she or Araminta come in, okay? And tell her you can't help her, whatever she asks. You've got my authority to be as rude to her as you need to be.'

'Got it,' Lauren said. 'The bitch is fucking with us anyway, so we might as well take the gloves off and punch her in the face with a lot of rings on.' She thought for a moment. 'Big, cocktail ones that really leave a fucking mark.'

'I don't know what I'd do without you, Lauren,' Chloe said, reaching out and squeezing her friend's hand.

'Not get caught out having your sodding face sand-papered!' Lauren said gloomily. 'Does it hurt?'

'They shoot salt at you from a millimetre away,' Chloe said grimly. 'It's like lying still while you get tracer-fired by a machine gun. Lucky I've got a hair appointment tomorrow – I've got salt crusted in my roots now. But it's totally worth it. Feel how smooth my skin is.'

She tapped her cheeks. Lauren stroked one cautiously, not wanting to smear the makeup.

'Bloody hell, that *is* good,' she said. 'Couldn't do it meself. Low pain tolerance. But then, I don't have an official engagement photoshoot at Buckingham Palace tomorrow.' She snarfed a gust of laughter. 'Bloody hell, Chlo! Photoshoot at Buckingham Palace! You bricking it?'

This was one of the many reasons Chloe loved Lauren: it was so much easier to answer a question asked with brutal honesty than one cloaked in layers of politeness.

'Of course,' she said, feeling her stomach tense at the prospect. 'But I'm okay with being photographed now.'

'You take a lovely snap,' Lauren said. 'Just remember to stand on his left, okay? Your nose looks straighter from that side. And your dress is flipping *perfect*. Goes lovely with that big old rock.'

She leaned over and tapped the enormous emerald ring on Chloe's finger. Chloe looked down at it, turning her hand back and forth slowly: it was a family heirloom, which Hugo had picked because she loved green, and Lady Margaret had supervised having it re-set by Garrard's, the historic jewellers who had once cut the Koh-i-Noor diamond for the Royal Family. They had done a lovely job. The old-fashioned diamond-crusted filigree setting had been replaced by a modern platinum frame that held the huge, oval, cabochon emerald almost invisibly. On each side of the emerald sparkled a perfect one-carat diamond.

'*This*'d do some damage if I punched Sophie in the face with it!' Chloe said, giggling.

'I'd fucking *love* to see that!' Lauren said wistfully. 'Well, you're going to look bleeding perfect for the pics, babe.'

'Thanks to you,' Chloe said with complete sincerity.

Another reason Chloe valued Lauren was her excellent strategic brain: about a year before the engagement, Chloe had agreed to be Hugo's escort to official outings – again, Chloe had put this off as long as possible, not wanting to look as if she were eagerly pushing herself into this aspect of his life. But she had planned with Lauren how to present herself, how to work on her appearance. Lauren had told her to sort her teeth out, and Chloe had resigned herself to the necessity of Invisalign braces, which had sorted out her slightly crossed lower teeth by pulling them slowly, achingly apart, and then holding them straight until they learned, painfully, to do it on their own. Then she had submitted to regular teeth whitening sessions. And she had had to pay for it all herself, not even accepting the discounts which the dentist would have been delighted to give the girlfriend of Prince Hugo; it mustn't be reported that Chloe was in any way exploiting her unofficial status.

It had been Lauren, too, who worked out what Chloe should do about her clothes: buy them on the high street, but have them tailored to fit her perfectly. Thank goodness, Lauren knew a Cypriot tailor who did great work at rock-bottom prices; Chloe couldn't have afforded anything more. Chloe picked out dresses from Hobbs, J by Jasper Conran, LK Bennett, and Chris Spyrou sucked his teeth, complained about the difficulty, pointed out all the problems inherent in the alterations, and then executed them perfectly for practically nothing. Chloe was careful never to buy anything tight, and Chris's professional standards meant he was as aware of what a dress would look like when Chloe sat down as when she was standing up. As a result, Chloe never had to worry about a wardrobe malfunction. She not only looked ladylike, marriage material, but a champion of British high-street brands.

For the shoot, she and Lauren had picked out a white silk Hobbs dress with a big green flower print. It had three-quarter-length sleeves, and was nipped in at the waist, with a full enough skirt to flatter Chloe's English pear-shaped figure. Green patent Bertie stack heels – *not* peep-toe, they had decided. The future wife of the second in line to the British throne did not need bitchy fashion journalists commenting on her toenail polish. The dress was Fifties in style, so Chloe's hair and makeup had been done in a sleek, modern fashion, with loose, finger-curled waves around her face; she was at the height of her beauty, her eyes glowing with happiness, the picture of a young woman who couldn't wait to get married to the man she loved.

Lady Margaret, coming in to supervise an hour before Chloe and Hugo were due to meet the massed cameras of the press in the gardens of Buckingham Palace, nodded approvingly at the sight of the bride-to-be.

'I must say,' she commented, 'you girls *do* know what you're doing.'

'We picked out one with a nice high neckline so we can't see a flipping *hint* of her tits,' Lauren said. 'I don't even want 'em seeing her sodding *collarbone* till she gets married.'

'God, Chloe, your lady-in-waiting doesn't mince her words, does she?' came Sophie's high-pitched drawl as she strolled into the sitting room of the Belgian Suite. This set of rooms was where eminent foreign visitors were housed when they visited London – the Obamas had stayed there most recently – and since it was on the ground floor, in the garden wing, it had been the most convenient place for Chloe to get ready for the engagement photos. Its dark yellow walls hung with Gainsborough and Canaletto oil paintings, its priceless cut-glass chandeliers and petit-point upholstered Chippendale furniture might have been designed specifically to intimidate commoners into a state of whimpering inferiority; even Lauren had glanced at the portraits of King George the Third and his unfortunate Queen, Charlotte, and muttered:

'Blimey, Chlo. Hard to believe you're marrying into all this, babe.'

But Sophie wandered in and plopped her tiny little bottom onto the arm of one of the Chippendales without the slightest concern for their value or historical worth, quite indifferent to the creaking sound of the delicate wood.

'Quite a mouth on you, Laura,' she continued, staring up at Lauren, a cigarette dangling from between her fingers; Lady Margaret gestured swiftly at a footman, who dashed over with an ashtray a mere second before the trail of grey ash hit the hand-woven silk carpet. 'I must say, you'd fit right into any massed gathering of squaddies.'

'It's Lauren, not Laura,' Chloe snapped. 'And she doesn't swear any more than any of your lot do in private. It's her accent you're really talking about, not her effing and blinding.'

'I did say "squaddies",' Sophie pointed out lightly.

'Well, if we're talking about massed gatherings, that's your friend Minty, right? Pulled more trains than Thomas the Tank Engine, by all accounts,' Lauren said, hands on hips.

'Actually,' Chloe chipped in, 'it would really be Toby. He did the heavy goods pulling, didn't he?'

'Or Mavis,' Lauren said, really getting into it now. 'She was the diesel engine, right? Didn't she do lots of shunting?'

Chloe had been trying to keep a straight face, but Lauren pronounced 'shunting' with such relish that she snorted a little. Lauren was more than equal to continuing on her own, however.

'But I'll bow to Princess Sophie's experience of squaddies,' Lauren added. 'I heard you like a bit of rough, love,' she said directly to Sophie. 'Uniforms and all.'

The footman who had handed Sophie the ashtray and retreated to his post by the main door went as red as the satin waistcoat he wore under his black tailcoat. Lauren winked at him and flicked her mass of extensions over one shoulder.

'At least I'm not so ignorant that I bitched about being given an old ring, rather than my fiancé popping out to a *shop* and getting me a new one,' Sophie snapped.

'I *never* said that!' Chloe exclaimed, outraged: she knew much better than that now, was fully aware that one should not buy, but inherit, one's own furniture and jewellery and paintings.

'Oh dear, didn't you?' Sophie said, a smile curling her pretty lips. She tossed back her blonde locks. 'What a shame! Because I read something on the internet about that – you getting all ratty with Hugo because you didn't get a nice shiny new ring. How *terribly* unfair, if you didn't actually say anything like that! I wonder who could *possibly* have told people the story?'

'*Sophie*,' Lady Margaret said reproachfully. 'Chloe is going to be your sister. I really think it's time for you to—'

'She's *not* going to be my sister!' Sophie said furiously, jumping to her feet. 'She'll never be my sister! God, I *wish* Mummy were still around! Mummy would never have let things get this far! She'd have put a stop to things before Hugo got in too deep with Little Miss Dog Rose!'

'*Sophie!*'

Lady Margaret was furious now. Chloe couldn't help but be mortified that this scene was taking place in front of two footmen; it was yet another difference between born aristocrats like Lady Margaret and Sophie and commoners like Chloe and Lauren that the former took no notice whatsoever at the presence of staff members.

'I *knew* your mother very well,' Lady Margaret said to Sophie icily, 'and let me tell you, she was *not* a snob! Besides, you must be aware that your parents' marriage wasn't exactly the success of the century, you silly girl, and Belinda's blood was as blue as—'

'Ink,' Lauren filled in, as Lady Margaret flailed for a metaphor.

'Yes! Ink!' Lady Margaret flapped her hands impatiently. 'Belinda's blood was as blue as ink, and much good it did her and Oliver! If I were you, Sophie, I'd concentrate on the fact that your brother has found a nice girl who's very compatible with him, and be pleased that Chloe is so suitable in many respects!'

'Ow,' Lauren muttered to Chloe. 'Bet you want that on your tombstone, eh? "Suitable in many respects".'

Lady Margaret, towering over willowy, slight Sophie, continued:

'And Lauren, who is a *very* efficient young woman, and *extremely* gifted at all this public relationship thingywhatsit that we're all forced to engage in now—'

'She's actually nicer about me than she is about you,' Lauren noticed, very amused.

' – *does* have a point about your reputation, Sophie! I can't deny that I've heard the rumours myself! One of the house-keepers at Kensington Palace told me that when you get back home the worse for wear not a single footman is safe from your attentions!'

Lauren's heavily pencilled eyebrows shot up as she tried her best not to snigger. Both footmen standing with their backs to the walls of the Belgian Suite's sitting room were now avoiding each other's eyes.

'You and your friend Araminta are *notorious*!' Lady Margaret continued, and even Sophie flinched at this: clearly it was a very bad word in the posh lexicon. 'Both of you need to take a good hard look at yourselves before you end up in serious trouble. Honestly, Sophie, sometimes I think I should tell Oliver to make you join the army! You need serious discipline!'

'Don't know if that'd be the best idea, Lady M,' Lauren said irrepressibly. 'All those squaddies in their camos – you'd have to bury her in a Y-shaped coffin.'

One of the footmen nearly broke Palace protocol by bursting out laughing; only the strict discipline of his training allowed him to choke it back at the last minute.

'*Not* helpful!' Lady Margaret rounded furiously on Lauren, her weather-beaten face creased into a frown so deep that even Lauren muttered:

'Sorry. Too far,' in instant apology, shuffling her feet like a schoolgirl being hauled over the coals by the headmistress.

'I'm *so* sick of this!' Sophie exclaimed passionately, throwing her cigarette at the ashtray and managing, through some miracle, to hit the target. 'Everyone's always picking on me! Hugo's so bloody perfect, he does everything right, never gives anyone a moment's trouble, and *I'm* always the one people get cross with! It's *so* unfair! You *know* Daddy's livid that Hugo's marrying her, but he doesn't get it in the neck like I do! It's like everyone just *makes* me out to be the bad one! But at least I just *shag* my commoners, I don't *marry* them!'

Lauren's fists clenched; Chloe took a step forward, allowing herself, for a brief, glorious moment, the fantasy of doing what she and Lauren had talked about yesterday, planting a punch in the middle of Sophie's pretty face with her left hand, seeing that cabochon emerald smack into her cheekbone. Sophie's eyes met Chloe's, read the fury in them, and the colour drained from her face in fear; but the actual blow that landed was, quite unexpectedly, from Lady Margaret. The slap, from a hand calloused and strong from decades of trowelling earth and reining in horses, sent Sophie reeling.

'*Oww!*' she shrieked, just as the door opened, held by the footman outside, and Hugo, in a smart blue suit and Britannia Royal Naval College silk tie, his shoes polished, his hair brushed back as smoothly as his curls would allow, walked into the sitting room. Chloe blinked as she took in the tie, which had wide diagonal stripes of bright yellow, red, blue and burgundy and was pretty much the ugliest thing she had ever seen.

'What's going on?' he exclaimed, looking from his fiancée to his sobbing sister. 'Honestly, we're all supposed to be *happy* today!'

Letting out a long, bubbling sob, Sophie pushed past him and dashed for the door.

'She's upset that she wasn't invited to the wedding of King Joachim and that beach volleyball girl that you're off to in a couple of months,' Lauren said smoothly, adding insult to injury. 'She's feeling all left out, poor thing.'

Sophie turned by the door, shot Lauren a glance of utter hatred, and then made her exit, grabbing the door from the footman's hand and slamming it herself to demonstrate the level of her rage.

'Goodness,' Hugo said, staring, baffled, after his sister. 'I had no *idea* Soph liked weddings so much! Shall we see if we can bag her an invite to Herzoslovakia? It'll be dull as ditchwater, but if she's getting *that* upset . . . Isn't she going to be one of your bridesmaids, Chlo? That should cheer her up too, shouldn't it?'

'Not when she sees her dress,' Lauren muttered happily to Chloe. 'Peach is going to absolutely *fuck* with her colouring.'

Belinda

Present day

'Fatiha, your back's so much straighter!' Belinda said encouragingly, bending down in front of the Berber woman who, in loose linen clothes, was executing Downward Dog on a bright purple mat spread out on the marble floor. She considered Fatiha's alignment thoughtfully for a moment, then took up a position in front of Fatiha's wide-spread hands.

'Grab onto my ankles,' Belinda instructed. Fatiha lifted her head in surprise, saw her mistress nodding, and then, giggling a little, reached out and cautiously lifted one hand and then the other, holding onto Belinda's ankles.

'I'm just going to stretch you out a bit,' Belinda said, stepping back fractionally, increasing the pull on Fatiha's arms, making her spine straighten as she did so. 'Can you feel that?'

'Yes, *madame*,' Fatiha said obediently, and Belinda hoped she meant it; one of the troubles of teaching yoga and Pilates to the Berber women who staffed Rahim's estate in the High Atlas mountains was that they were so fiercely loyal to Rahim, the prince of their tribe, that they found it very difficult to tell Belinda, his consort, if something wasn't working.

'Can you see?' she said to the three other women in the class. 'Zahra, Souniya, Asmaa, stand up for a moment – she can't hold this for ever—'

The three others gratefully abandoned their own Dogs, walking their hands up to their feet and rolling up to stand. Belinda watched them with pride, aware of how supple their backs were now after years of her lessons.

'See how her shoulder blades are really sinking into her back now?' she said, leaning forward to lay her fingers lightly on either side of Fatiha's spine. 'Her back's getting so lovely and straight!'

'Yes, *madame*,' they all murmured in unison.

'Right, Fatiha, you can let go now and walk back into Child's Pose,' Belinda instructed, and felt the tight grip on her ankles release as Fatiha obeyed. 'All of you, take up Child's Pose now,' Belinda added. 'I'll come round and give you each an adjustment.'

She pressed down on each woman in turn as they folded forward onto their mats, their stomachs relaxing between the spread of their open knees. It had taken years, too, to stop them automatically giggling every time their mistress touched them; now, they positively sighed in release as Belinda's hands pushed their shoulders further down, her knees bracing back against their hips, lengthening out each of their backs in turn.

'Come up by rolling onto your right side and pushing yourself up gently, raising your head,' she said. 'And then lie down for Corpse Pose.'

As they stretched out, she walked around the room, laying a scented lavender cushion across their eye sockets to blot out the light completely, running through a gentle litany of how to relax, from the top of their head right down to their toes; the forehead melting into the hairline, the eyebrows separating gently, the cheekbones spreading out to the ears, the tongue resting on the roof of the mouth, the lips slightly parted . . . by this time, Asmaa, as always, had begun to snore lightly, and the other women were breathing regularly, the clearly audible breath that was called Ujjayi by yogis.

Belinda surveyed her little group with immense fondness as she sat down softly and folded her legs into full lotus, hands in prayer position at her breastbone. This had been one of the things that had kept her sane and focused in her exile with Rahim, first learning the discipline of Iyengar yoga, and then realizing that she wanted to teach it too. Her regular classes were hugely satisfying to her; she had seen the posture and strength of her pupils improve, and recently she had started a children's class too. She ran a mat Pilates class, too, which she had had to modify for her students – none of the Berber women had the slightest interest in flattening their stomachs.

'You can remove your eye mask and start to open your eyes now,' she said, pitching her voice loud enough to wake up Asmaa, who snorted, caught her breath and spluttered into consciousness. 'Then roll to your right sides and come up slowly to sit.'

The women sat up and swung their legs into excellent cross-legged positions; used, unlike Westerners, to sitting on the ground frequently, their hips were much looser than Belinda's had been when she first started practising yoga. Their hands rose to their breastbones in an echo of Belinda's pose, their heads bowed with hers: they all murmured 'Namaste' together and as they lowered the backs of their hands to rest on their knees, their heads rose again, wide smiles mirroring back hers.

'Thank you all,' Belinda said happily. 'Very good class, everyone.'

'Thank you, *madame*,' they all chorused cheerfully.

Calling her *madame* had been Rahim's idea; as they were not married, Belinda was not, technically, his princess, and besides, that title was the last one they wanted to associate with her in her new life. The Berbers all spoke fluent French, and *madame* had seemed a neat solution to the problem. Her new name, Hana, was barely spoken; lovers rarely need to use each other's names, and to everyone else at the Tarhouna Palace, Belinda was simply *madame*, their adored prince's beloved consort.

Belinda stood up and left the room so that her class could put away the mats, yoga bricks and bolsters they had used that session. The wooden door, carved with decorative chinks and curlicues, allowed light and air to filter through, but even so the bright Moroccan sun outside was always a shock, like walking on stage, a sudden blinding burst of white hitting her square in the face. The sky seemed already bleached of its blue by the force of the sun; Belinda skirted the edge of the shallow tiled pond in the centre of the courtyard, water trickling gently into it from a high fountain – a modern, sculptural shape that looked like loose slabs of Carrara marble stacked carelessly one on top of the other. There were pools and fountains scattered throughout the palace, oases of water in the dry heat of the sun, encircled by cloistered courtyards which provided shade, and whose elegant arches threw darker silhouettes across the tiled floors.

If I have to be shut away from the world, I couldn't have chosen a lovelier place, Belinda thought, her bare feet warmed by the stone. She often sat and watched the play of water from one of the many fountains, flicking through magazines or listening to music; the palace was fully wireless, Rahim loving anything to do with technology, and she could program her laptop or iPod to play through concealed speakers in all their sections of the palace. This wing was hers, and gradually she had turned it into a sanctuary. Across the courtyard was a fully equipped Pilates studio, into which Belinda had recently had a ballet barre installed: she went inside, switched on the mild air conditioning which she allowed herself when working out hard, pulled out one of her current favourite DVDs and slipped it into the player.

The familiar music started to play, the big white smile, bouncing ponytail and determined stare of Carrie Rezabek, Belinda's latest exercise guru, filling the fifty-two-inch screen. 'Welcome to Pure Barre!' Carrie said brightly, and Belinda grimly settled in for forty-five minutes of hardcore suffering. These, ironically, were the times when she felt most alone. She missed doing classes with other women, missed the grunts and groans of misery that made the workout so much less painful when shared with other sufferers. It was much harder to make herself wedge the special Pure Barre ball beneath one knee after another as she rested her hand on the barre and copied the exercises Carrie had specifically designed to lift her buttocks and give her the Pure Barre Ledge, her hamstrings and glutes screaming in pain; to drop to the ground and place the ball high up between her thighs, squeezing it firmly as she executed a series of torturous twisting sit-ups.

Carrie was American, and Americans were always in a hurry. There was barely any time for Belinda to recover between sequences, to stretch out and let her body assimilate what it had just managed to achieve. But afterwards, when the DVD was paused on Carrie's resolutely cheerful face, Belinda felt absolutely wonderful. She had achieved something. It would be so easy, here in paradise, to let herself go, to eat more and exercise less, to slip into a lazy, spoilt, indolent way of life. But she had known that, if she took that path, depression would set in very quickly. Exercise had been the only thing she could cling to as her marriage exploded, sending splintered shards of glass raining down on her, and exercise had saved her again when she had escaped.

Sweat practically dripped from Belinda as she stood up and surveyed herself briefly in the floor-to-ceiling mirrored walls. She was in better shape than she had been when she had fled to Montecapra twenty years ago, leaner, stronger, with more muscle definition. And of course, it wasn't just her body that had changed. Discreet plastic surgery on her face had altered it just enough for Belinda to be unrecognizable to anyone who might associate her with the woman she had once been; her nose was shorter, her chin rounder. Combined with her now-blonde hair and lightened brows, it was inconceivable that anyone who didn't already suspect her true identity would guess who she was.

And frankly, being blonde at forty-six is much more sensible than being brunette, she thought wryly. *It's so much easier to cover the grey!*

Leaving the studio, she came out once more into the courtyard, passing swiftly around it to the far side where a wide flight of steps led down the outer wall of the palace. On a promontory below was Rahim's supreme gift to her, a private swimming pool, partly recessed into the cliff-like side of the citadel, partly extended out into space, an infinity edge allowing the water to flow invisibly over the rim, a glass bottom providing spectacular views of the ancient rock below, overlapping spurs folding over and over each other like waves of a long-frozen golden sea. High above, birds which she had learnt, with great amusement, were called Atlas horned larks, circled in the sky, riding the currents of air, and a buzzard hovered far in the distance over the white-peaked mountains beyond.

Rahim was already in the pool, happily ensconced on his favourite lilo, a mauve blow-up armchair with wide arms on which his own rested; it looked as if he were sitting on a floating throne which moved graciously across the water, impelled by the random setting of the wave machine. He smiled on seeing Belinda run swiftly down the steps, his white teeth flashing under his black moustache as he raised a hand in greeting. Belinda stopped underneath the big built-in rainforest shower head by the side of the pool; it turned on automatically, cool water pouring down on her as she soaped off her body, peeling off her exercise clothes as she did so, rinsing them out at the same time, letting them fall in sopping wet heaps to the cut-stone floor of the shower – bra, thong, all dropping until she stood naked, rinsing out her hair one last time, and then, with a whoop, raced towards the silvery pool and dived in smoothly.

There was nothing like swimming naked. The water pressed between her legs, entering her as they opened and closed in a strong powerful breaststroke; it lifted her small breasts, which bobbed lightly, buoyed up, her nipples already hardened by the cool shower. The pool had been situated to be completely invisible from the rest of the palace. No windows overlooked it, no balconies or walkways provided even the tiniest glimpse over the expanse of water that stretched out miraculously over the rocky mountains below. Belinda and Rahim could swim and sun themselves here in total privacy, the rarest of privileges when you were usually completely surrounded by servants. So Belinda, seeing clearly underwater, could swim up on Rahim, see his dark cock rising up between his legs from the sight of her stripping under the shower water, watch it bob gently in the waves of her approach, and duck her head to close her mouth around it, sucking hard for a long delicious moment, before the need to breathe forced her up to the surface.

Rahim's hands grasped her arms, pulling her higher, helping her slither onto his lap, their limbs slick against each other's. She straddled him, bracing against the inflatable chair, finding their familiar angle, gasping as his cock nudged between her legs, finding its entry place, sliding up inside her, forcing a rush of cool water inside her and then its own heat, filling her as she let her weight sink onto his lap.

'God!' she sighed in happiness, his arms wrapping round her waist, her legs around the inflated back of the chair, his calves kicking gently beneath their floating bodies, balancing them, leaning back a little to keep them suspended upright in the swimming pool. This was why Rahim so loved this particular chair; the back was a separate piece, allowing Belinda's long legs to extend behind him, close around him, keep her pressed down hard on his cock as they let the lapping waves of the pool move them around in slow circles. The root of Rahim's cock rocked between Belinda's parted legs in a rhythm they had long perfected, building slowly, agonizingly slowly, stoking a fire inside her which grew and grew.

Sun beat down on her shoulders, larks called to each other as they spun high above the citadel, the jets of the wave machine beneath them kept the lilo constantly circulating; Rahim began to tilt his pelvis back and forth, his cock pushing even more insistently inside Belinda, against her. She was biting down on his shoulder now, the smooth wet skin pressed into her mouth, moaning and gasping, trying to hold on as long as she could, not to rush what she knew was coming, to make this build-up last as long as possible; but she heard herself cry out, louder and louder, a plaintive, desperate wail that echoed the cries of the larks above them. She couldn't bear it any more. With a fierce push of her legs, she rammed herself against Rahim, pulled back for a split-second, letting cool water pass between them, rammed herself in again, the friction intense, three or four rubs of her spread legs against him all she needed to send herself spilling over the edge like the water that was lapping over the rim of the pool.

Rahim rocked harder, rearing back, the heel of one hand jammed into the small of her back, the other rising up to tangle in her hair, pull her head back, drive his tongue into her mouth. His cock was driving up faster and faster inside her, and Belinda came again, kissing him back as frantically as he was kissing her, the rough rub of his moustache against her upper lip an extra stimulant, rough hair and smooth skin against her face, her body, his hard cock inside her and his wet pubic hair grating against her mound, the network of nerve endings that radiated between her legs on fire now, almost too stimulated, burning up under the cool water.

Rahim's thighs under her were pumping faster and faster, bouncing her body up and down. It was harder and harder to hold onto his slick wet skin, to keep herself steady. He grabbed out behind her for an edge of the pool, caught the stone, wrapped his hand around it and, still kissing Belinda, holding their bodies up, grunting now with the muscular effort, let himself go, yelling as his cock exploded inside her, vibrating between her legs so strongly with the relief of release that Belinda was hit by another orgasm she hadn't expected, rippling through her so powerfully that she lost her balance and her grip on Rahim. She fell against him, onto the arm that was holding them locked to the edge of the pool, knocking it loose; the inflatable chair flipped sideways and tumbled them both into the water, Belinda's legs still wound around Rahim's waist.

The cool water was a shock on their scalps after the heat of the sun. They thrashed for a second or two, untwisting themselves, legs floating down to find the bottom of the pool, pushing up to the surface, grabbing for the side; they hung there like two beached mer-people, their torsos resting on the warm stone, gasping in the aftermath of their orgasms, their chests rising and falling fast. Gradually their panting gasps turned into laughter; with great love, Belinda watched Rahim's moustache quivering, his dark eyes dancing with amusement.

'One day,' he said, 'we won't fall off.'

'We always fall off sooner or later,' she said.

'That was much better,' he said firmly. 'And really, it was your fault. I had a terribly good grip. We would have been fine if you hadn't fallen on top of me.'

'I had a bonus orgasm,' she said. 'When you came. It took me by surprise.'

'A bonus orgasm! I must be *really* good,' he said complacently.

'It was a bonus,' she said. 'I don't think, technically, you had anything to do with it.'

'Excuse me, of course I did! My penis was inside you at the time!'

His smile was wide, his teeth dazzling against lips the colour of pale mocha, shading into rich pink where they were parted; his moustache was rich dark coffee, but Belinda was beginning to see a few silvery hairs in it now, the same silver that gleamed in his short sideburns.

'I love you so much,' she said.

His hand closed over hers.

'It was worth it?' he asked, a question he tried not to put to her more than every other day. And she gave him the answer she always did, with a smile that echoed his:

'It was. It was worth it.'

They lay there for a little while longer, still beached, cast up on the shore, their legs dangling in the water.

'I have to move,' she said eventually, regretfully. 'I'm going to get burned. I haven't put on sunblock since this morning.'

'Your nose is going red,' he agreed, reaching out to touch it.

'You should have told me!' Belinda started to pull herself out. 'God, my arms are like jelly . . .'

'It's so cute when it goes red,' Rahim said, dropping back to stand in the pool, gripping her thighs and hoisting her up and out. 'I like it. You look like a bunny rabbit.'

'*Men*,' Belinda said witheringly. 'The things you think are cute.'

She wriggled to her feet and walked around to the palace wall, where a wooden chest held fresh towels. Wrapping one around herself, she sat down on a lounger in the shade provided by the white overhanging canopy. Rahim followed, winding a towel at his waist, sarong-style; then he picked up an iPad from a mosaic-tiled table, clicked it into life, and ran his thumb over the screen.

'Are you *sure* that it was worth it?' he asked, sitting down next to her, drops of water standing out in relief on his rich brown skin, tanned dark even in the winter sun.

'Darling—' Belinda snaked an arm around his waist, rested her head on his damp shoulder. 'You *promised* you wouldn't keep asking and asking—'

'There's something you need to watch,' he said, his voice serious now. 'I was wondering how to tell you, but I think I will just show it to you instead.'

He tilted the iPad towards her as he thumbed the Play button below the BBC News 24 window that was open on the screen. Belinda's heart pounded against her ribcage as she saw the face of her son, that blend of her and Oliver all grown up. She was extremely familiar with how Hugo looked as an adult, of course she was, having eagerly followed his and Sophie's transition from toddlers to skinny-limbed children to preternaturally sophisticated adolescents to fully formed, beautiful descendants of the House of Sandringham, royal heirs in waiting. She asked Rahim not to keep questioning her about whether it had been worth it precisely because she asked herself the same question on a daily basis; she had tried not to Google new pictures of her children more than once a week as they grew, and she had always failed.

Without them, she would have walked away from Oliver much sooner and never looked back. They had been the umbilical cord that kept her tethered there for years, and the wound that she had caused to herself, severing it, ached with as much pain now as it had the day that she had left, a scar that would never heal.

But once they had turned twenty-one, Belinda had forced herself to stop. The pain was not abating; it actually, perversely, grew stronger when she watched them as adults, realized that they had entire lives of which she knew nothing. She had had the willpower to leave, to face the truth, that she had to make a new life for herself rather than stay and face being murdered by her ex-husband. Now she needed a second, equally strong burst of willpower to say goodbye, once and for all, to the children she had left behind.

She hadn't seen Hugo for eight years. Greedily, she feasted on the sight of him. He was fully a man now, with Oliver's blond hair, his long aristocratic nose and strong jawline. *Thank goodness he's so clearly Oliver's son*, she always thought, looking at him. *With all the dirt that Oliver tried to throw at me in the divorce, that piece of mud he could never have flung.*

Not that he would, of course. It wouldn't exactly have been in his interest to imply that he wasn't capable of fathering children.

But her son had her eyes and brows, and, above all, he had her smile. She had always secretly hated her smile; it was too wide. One of her nannies had even called her 'Gummy'. The media, the world, had fallen in love with that smile of Belinda's, so open and unforced, and during her engagement, even the first few months of marriage, she had smiled constantly, dazzled with happiness, by her fairy tale come true, by her ridiculously handsome prince, who could have had anyone in the world and who had chosen her.

She reached a hand up to the screen, tears forming in her eyes. Hugo was smiling just as she had done, twenty-five years ago, a positive grin that creased his whole face as he looked down at the young woman beside him. His arm was wrapped protectively around her, sheltering her in his embrace.

Belinda flashed back for a moment to her own engagement photographs; Oliver had held her hand, raising it so that the gathered press could see her ring, smiling at the cameras, not at her: *look, I've finally done it! All those years with my name linked to every eligible princess in Europe, one after the other, a whole bevy of aristocratic girls, with a few models and actresses thrown in there for spice – and now, at thirty-seven, I've settled down with a young, pretty, more-than-eligible duke's daughter who stares up at me as if I were Prince Charming come to life.*

Are you happy now? Oliver's almost defiant eyes asked. *Father, Mother, are you happy now?*

By contrast, Hugo was smiling down at his fiancée; his love for her was abundantly clear. His cheeks were pink with excitement, his gaze, as he looked down at her, positively melting. And what made Belinda's tears fill her eyes and start to trickle down her cheeks was that this – she read the name as it scrolled beneath them in a news trail – this Chloe Rose was staring up at Hugo just as blissfully. Their hands were clasped as they talked about how happy they were, about when the wedding was to be held; the photographers had to call to them to turn Chloe's hand so that the ring could be seen, and Chloe giggled, the sweetest little laugh, said: 'Oops!' and rotated her left hand, saying reprovingly to her fiancé, 'Darling, you're distracting me!'

'She's so pretty!' Belinda breathed. 'Oh, she's a *darling*!'

Not a model, not an actress. As if Hugo would ever have married one – of course that would have been impossible. But a normal style of beauty, a nicely curved figure in that charming silk dress, not a clotheshorse or a skinny minnie.

'He looks very handsome too,' Rahim said. 'But what *is* that tie? It's truly awful.'

'It'll be something naval,' Belinda said abstractedly. 'They're mostly ghastly. She'll have to pick his ties better at public events.'

Rahim, a dandy who had his suits tailor-made in Jermyn Street, his shoes by Lobb's of St James, and his silk ties personally chosen for him by Giorgio Armani, nodded vehemently in agreement.

'She's *exactly* the kind of girl you hope your son brings home,' Belinda said softly to Rahim, her eyes still on Chloe. '*Exactly* the girl you hope he ends up with.'

Chloe's future mother-in-law feasted her eyes on her daughter-to-be, taking in every choice that Chloe had made with the eye of one who'd already been through the royal bride mill. Belinda approved each in turn. The dress, so perfect, which fitted Chloe nicely and looked current without being over-fashionable, was from Hobbs, the shoes from

Bertie, as Chloe was now revealing in answer to the questions thrown at her.

Oh, good girl! Belinda thought. *Good girl – not only British designers, but traditional high-street ones too! She couldn't have done better.* Chloe's cheeks were as pink as Hugo's, her pretty heart-shaped face attractively framed in her waves of light-brown hair, her eyelashes fluttering as they talked about how they had met – *in a coffee shop?* Belinda thought incredulously. *Goodness, things have changed. Oliver would never have dreamt of going into a coffee shop – he'd have sent someone in for him!* – her plans for charity work for the future, how Hugo, now that he was engaged, would not be going out on active service with the Navy but seconded to naval intelligence at Northwood, HMS Warrior Permanent Joint Headquarters.

'Though in my case,' Hugo interpolated with a self-deprecating smile, 'I'm afraid that "naval intelligence" is a bit of a contradiction in terms.'

It was an old joke, but everyone laughed as if they were hearing it for the first time, and Chloe rounded on him prettily, telling him not to put himself down.

'It'll be so wonderful to have him home!' Chloe was saying, beaming. 'I do feel so lucky,' she added seriously. 'To have Hugo home and safe. I know what it's like to have the one you love serving his country overseas, how frightening and lonely that is for the family and friends left behind. And I know how lucky I am, too, that Hugo's coming home now. But that doesn't mean I've forgotten all those months waiting for him, worrying about him. I want to become involved in working with military spouses and families now that I'm becoming one. It's going to be one of the causes I really want to focus on.'

'Isn't she wonderful?' Hugo said, beaming idiotically down at her.

Thousands of miles away, his missing mother burst into hysterical tears.

'Oh *no*!' Rahim switched off the iPad. 'I debated this so much with myself – should I tell you or not – but in the end I thought, I must! It is such an important thing, your son getting married – we never discussed how we would handle this, the big milestones—'

But his words tailed off as he saw Belinda wrapping her arms around herself, her head hanging forward as she sobbed in a paroxysm of misery, the darker roots of her hair showing as the dyed blonde locks fell over her face.

'Darling,' he said hopelessly, 'my sweet darling . . .'

Belinda raised her head eventually. Her eyes were red, the skin around them puffy, but they were narrowed in an expression of determination that sent chills down Rahim's spine.

'Don't say it!' he blurted out, panicking. 'Don't say it! You *promised* you would *never*—'

'I have to go back,' she said, and he let out a wail so loud that the Atlas horned larks scattered in a cloud of panic; even the distant buzzard removed itself even further.

'I *have* to!' she insisted. 'I have to meet them, just once . . .'

'Bel – *Hana*, you promised!' he wailed even louder.

'Rahim, I swear, I'm going back to England to see them even if I have to wear a burkha from head to toe so no one recognizes me,' she said with absolute resolve.

Rahim jumped up from the table, standing over her. His dark eyebrows drew together, his lips tightened, his moustache bristled, his arms folded over his chest: legs planted wide and dominating, he was the picture of a commanding, despotic Arab sheik of legend, dominating his woman, laying down the law to her once and for all.

'Under no circumstances!' he barked. 'I utterly and completely forbid it! It's much too dangerous! You are staying here, where I can keep you safe!' His index finger shot out, pointing down at the ground. 'Right here! And that's an end of it! I don't want to hear another word on the subject!'

But Belinda was on her feet too, wrapping the towel firmly around her.

'I need to go and plan this out,' she said, paying no attention to her lover's magnificently imposing stance. 'Take my time, work out how I can possibly manage to pull it off . . .'

She headed up the steps back to the palace. Rahim stamped his foot so hard in frustration that he bruised a toe on the stone and jumped around, cursing furiously.

'We might as *well* be bloody married!' he shouted after her, shaking his fist at her retreating back. 'You don't listen to a damn word I say!'

Lori

'Mom! Dad! Randy! Hailey!' Lori called in joy as her family emerged from a limousine in the magnificent courtyard of Schloss Hafenhoffer, looking around them in amazement and disbelief at the encircling wings of the castle, barely noticing the January chill. It was much milder in Europe than their home town close to the Canadian border, and the Makarwiczes were cocooned in the warm padded coats vital for the upstate New York winter.

Lori dashed down the balustraded stone staircase, her athletic legs taking the steps three at a time; if it had been the superb cantilevered double-balconied staircase in the main hall, she would have jumped on the polished banister and slid all the way down, such was her haste to welcome her family to her new home.

'How was the journey?' she demanded, even though Randy and Hailey had been keeping her, and the rest of their friends, up to date with every stage of the process through Twitter and Facebook and Foursquare, all the way, from their flight from Buffalo, New York, to JFK, to Munich and then to Graz in Austria; then the helicopter transfer across the border to Valtzers, and thence into a limo which brought them up the mountain to Schloss Hafenhoffer. The entire process, capped by the dramatic approach to the castle which towered over the capital city, was so imposing that the entire Makarwicz family were literally struck dumb.

'It's way cosier than it looks!' Lori assured them, throwing herself at her mother and hugging her so tightly that she almost squeezed the breath from Sandy Makarwicz's body. 'The Dowager's decorated everything beautifully, you'll be blown away by how modern and smart it all is. Wait till you see the rooms we've picked out for you! You have amazing views over Valtzers and the river – we thought we'd let you settle in for the rest of the day, and then tomorrow we'll go on a river cruise with a lunch at Schwanstein, where Joachim proposed to me – it's too cold for a picnic, even with heaters, but the view will still be stunning—'

Joachim, who had been waiting by his fiancée's side at the top of the steps, as befitted a reigning king, had deigned to follow her down at a much more measured pace, and now approached as Lori turned to gesture him forward.

'Joachim, my mom and dad, my sister and brother,' she said unnecessarily, her eyes shining with happiness. 'Everyone, this is King Joachim, my fiancé!'

Joachim's appearance, in the full dress uniform he had considered suitable for meeting his future in-laws, did not help the Makarwiczes manage to get a word out of their gaping mouths. Nor did his brisk, formal nod of greeting, combined with the click of his polished heels. It was one thing to hear that your daughter was marrying into one of Europe's oldest ruling families, to Google pictures of Herzoslovakia, its castles, its history, its King, and shake your heads in disbelief: it was quite another, for people who had never left the United States before, to apply for passports (fast-tracked at the request of the Herzoslovakian ambassador to Washington), fly across the Atlantic, and then be transferred on a scenic helicopter ride through mountain passes to a country which looked like a fairy tale come to life and whose ruler was dressed like the hero of a musical.

'This is like a cross between *The Sound of Music* and *The Slipper and the Rose*,' Sandy finally said to her daughter in a tone as hushed as if she were whispering in church. 'Oh! And *The Prisoner of Zenda*.'

'Uh, pleased to meet you, Your Majesty,' said Bob Makarwicz, stepping up to the plate manfully, holding out his hand to Joachim, who pumped it up and down. Mr Makarwicz towered over Joachim; Lori had inherited her height from both sides of her family, and the Makarwiczes, their tall genes enhanced by plentiful American protein, were giants in Herzoslovakia. Joachim, however, didn't bat an eye at being dwarfed by his future father-in-law, which Lori was happy to see.

'Joachim, please,' he said. 'I am to be your son.'

'Well! Yeah!' Bob Makarwicz blinked at the sunlight glinting off Joachim's medals, the gold braid on his epaulettes. 'I guess you are, uh, Joachim! This is my wife, Sandy.'

Joachim raised Sandy's hand to his lips, causing her to emit a surprisingly girlish giggle.

'Welcome to the family!' Hailey, even taller than Lori, plunged forward with great enthusiasm, hovered on the tips of her toes as she leaned forward to hug Joachim, then, at the last moment, found herself defeated by the rigidity of his posture, and held out her hand instead. 'Ooh!' she exclaimed as he kissed it. 'Wow! I get what Lori sees in you! Do you have a brother?'

Joachim cracked a smile at this.

'I am afraid not, Miss Hailey,' he said regretfully.

'She had two Cokes in the limo,' Sandy Makarwicz hissed to Lori. 'Sorry, hon. I tried to stop her. You know how buzzed she gets on sugar.'

'It's okay, Mom,' Lori reassured her mother. 'They like energy here. They think it's American and modern.'

'Huh.' Her mother absorbed this. 'Gee, it really *is* a shame Joachim doesn't have a brother. Maybe a cousin?'

Joachim greeted Randy and turned to lead the little party up the steps to the Schloss, and inside to the Throne Room, where the Dowager was waiting to receive them. Lori had suggested somewhere less formal – *anywhere*, frankly, in the entire castle, would have been less formal than the Throne Room – but no. The Dowager had maintained, very sweetly, that it was the only place suitable to meet Lori's family, considering Lori's own importance to the country. As a result, the *entente cordiale* that was blossoming between Joachim and the Makarwiczes ground to a screeching halt the moment he ushered them into the red and gold interior. They stood, overwhelmed, looking around them at its vaulted, ribbed stone ceiling, its magnificent tapestries, its elaborately carved dais on which stood the central throne, flanked by two other smaller ones, the scarlet silk velvet of their upholstery gleaming dully by the light of the many chandeliers.

The Dowager Queen was not actually sitting on a throne, but she could scarcely have been more impressive if she had chosen to make the Makarwiczes walk up the burgundy silk carpet into which the insignia of the Herzoslovakian royal family was woven, and kneel before her. Standing in the centre of the room, hands folded at her waist, a footman in full formal regalia flanking her on each side, she was wearing a brocade, ankle-length dress, with a satin sash over her chest on which were pinned a great deal of jewelled stars and brooches, more diamonds flashing at her earlobes and on her fingers. The Dowager might be tiny, compared to the hulking Makarwiczes, but she utterly dominated their first meeting with her, and, Lori suspected, would do so at every single encounter from then on.

'It is such a pleasure to meet the family of the future bride of Herzoslovakia and mother of its heirs,' she said, with a gracious nod of her head in welcome that had Bob and Randy ducking into bows and poor Sandy and Hailey trying their best to curtsey, despite the fact that Sandy was wearing mom jeans and Hailey velour tracksuit bottoms from Victoria's Secret that she had put on to be comfortable for travelling. When their heads came up again, Lori saw with great distress that her entire family were mortified, red with embarrassment.

'I think my mom and dad would like to change, see their rooms—' she began, but the Dowager raised a small, plump, ringed hand.

'We will have tea in the Pink Salon, to greet our very important visitors,' she announced imperiously. 'I wish to show them how important their daughter is to us, how Herzoslovakia has taken her to its heart.' She smiled regally at Mr and Mrs Makarwicz. 'Here is where Lori will be crowned Queen, after her marriage to my son in Valtzers Cathedral. Joachim has chosen his bride, who will bear children to inherit his throne, and we are all delighted with his choice.'

'Uh, thank you,' Bob Makarwicz managed, looking dazed. 'We're all very proud of our Lori too . . .'

But the Dowager had already turned on the heels of her court shoes and was gliding across the carpet, away from them, past the throne dais; the Makarwiczes had no choice but to follow her, gawking at the huge carved and gilded chairs of office as they went, imagining their daughter sitting in one of the lesser thrones, a crown on her head, a distant, regal expression on her face. More footmen threw open a long series of doors as they went through drawing rooms and salons to their eventual destination at the far end of the Schloss, with a magnificent terrace outside which offered commanding views over the red-roofed town of Valtzers clinging to the hillside below, and the river that followed the curve of the mountain, a blue-grey ribbon glittering in the sunshine.

'Here we are!' the Dowager said, sinking onto a pink silk sofa and gesturing for Lori, Joachim and the Makarwiczes to take their places on the formal arrangement of sofas and armchairs around a low table on which a silver tray held a priceless bone china tea set.

'Oh, how pretty!' Sandy Makarwicz commented spontaneously. Lori winced; she had learned already that you didn't compliment possessions here in Europe. It was a sure way to spot a *nouveau riche*. To fail to take for granted the sheer lavish opulence with which you were surrounded was to proclaim that you hadn't grown up in such luxury. You could, of course, lean forward and comment knowledgeably on the differences between Meissen and Sèvres china, perhaps, if you knew that your hostess was also interested in such fine distinctions; but if she wasn't, you ran the risk of looking like a show-off, which was almost as bad as looking vulgar, so you needed to proceed with caution.

'It is Limoges,' the Dowager said politely to Sandy. 'Made for the Herzoslovakian royal family in the nineteenth century, in France, with our crest on every piece. The set is still perfect – we only bring it out on the most important of occasions. Like today.'

A footman came forward, but she waved him away. 'I shall pour myself,' she said, 'for our honoured guests. It is China tea,' she added to the Makarwiczes. 'I prefer China, but perhaps you would like Indian?'

Four horrified faces stared back at her. She might almost as well have been speaking in Mandarin or Hindi for all they knew how to answer her. Lori cringed; the only tea the Makarwiczes ever drank was from a can or a plastic bottle, sweetened and flavoured with peach or strawberry, served at Denny's or Arby's on the rare occasions they went out to dinner.

'They'll be fine with China tea,' she said quickly to the Dowager, from her privileged seat next to her future mother-in-law. 'We're really more coffee drinkers in the States.'

'I can certainly send for some coffee—' the Dowager began, but Lori shook her head vehemently. She would have it sent to their rooms, later. With Coke, if there was any in the Schloss. *Oh boy, Mom and Dad aren't going to be able to drink coffee or sodas with meals*, she realized. *Just wine or water. Dad's going to hate that.*

None of the worry showed on her face; years of competitive sports had taught her to keep her expression neutral under pressure, and that training was coming in very useful now. In her excitement to have her family visit, she hadn't considered how very different their social customs were from that of Europeans, let alone European *royalty*, for goodness' sake.

I'm going to have to sit down with them all as soon as I get them alone and explain a whole bunch of stuff to them – God, where do I even start?

'Milk? Sugar?' the Dowager was asking Sandy, who looked to Lori for help. That was another minefield, Lori was pretty sure; you didn't have milk in China tea, she thought. Or at least the Dowager never did.

'They'll all have it with two sugars,' she said quickly.

'Ah, the American sweet tooth,' the Dowager smiled. 'Here in Herzoslovakia we are famous for our baking skills. Pastries, little biscuits – what I think you call "cookies". Please.' She indicated a little plate of pale yellow-tinted macaroons. 'These are one of our specialities, filled with jam made with a berry from the hillsides. *Hangönştelïn*, they are called.'

Randy reached for one, the yellow *hangönştelïn* tiny in his huge hand. He wolfed it down in a single bite, wincing as he did so; Lori knew it was because the berry jam was actually quite sour. It was considered a delicacy here, but she tried to avoid it as much as possible. She looked round at her family, now all holding miniature china teacups and saucers, looking like adults at a children's tea party, sipping their tea in disbelief at its odd, aromatic taste, trying to fight through their jet lag to look polite and enthusiastic, visibly uncomfortable on the stiff, buttoned and tasselled chairs, their jeans and sneakers and sweatshirts looking ridiculously inappropriate next to the Dowager and Joachim's extremely formal wear and Lori's own Jil Sander navy silk dress and topaz earrings.

The dress, like most of Lori's current wardrobe, was a recent acquisition. The clothes which Lori had brought to Herzoslovakia on what she had thought was to be a short visit had by now been considerably extended in the boutiques of Valtzers at the royal family's expense: Lori had barely objected, since, if she were staying on in Herzoslovakia, she clearly needed many more clothes than one suitcase would carry, and only a few of her outfits were at all suitable for a queen-to-be. And Valtzers was a shopping paradise for her specific needs: its main streets, like other hideaways for the truly rich – Geneva or Montenegro, for instance – were lined with extremely expensive and chic boutiques, which sold taste as well as quality. No flashy leopard print Versace or

Cavalli for the ladies who shopped in Valtzers: they were wives, not mistresses. Lori had swiftly assembled an entire dressing-room full of Helmut Lang, Balmain, Temperley London, Reed Krakoff, Proenza Schouler: elegant, restrained, fashionably cut garments in superb quality wool, crepe and silk. They felt a little like costumes to her still, and it was hard to take in that a silk blouse could easily cost a thousand dollars, a day dress three times that. It was a fortune to pay for clothes, but she could, at least, see what the money was buying. When she got dressed every morning, she immediately felt more confident, more assured, knowing that she looked exactly right for the role of fiancée to a king.

While my family looks like they came to do manual work in the Palace! Why didn't I get them up to their rooms straight away to change and settle in? she thought in frustration. *I should have planned this all so much better!* But the Dowager – who had suggested that Lori call her *Mušsi*, or 'Mama' in Herzoslovakian, a cosy name which Lori did not yet feel comfortable enough to use – and Joachim had wanted so much to greet the Makarwiczes as soon as they arrived, and in the most impressive, regal way possible.

Lori had been so flattered by this, so happy at the lack of snobbishness the Herzoslovakian royal family were showing to her blue-collar relatives, that she hadn't paused to realize that visiting royalty arrived already dressed in a style appropriate for this kind of reception. Randy was in a Syracuse University sweatshirt, for goodness' sake; the pockets of Hailey's pink velour jogging pants had diamanté trim around them. There was probably some slogan on her ass – 'Pink' or 'Juicy'. And the exquisite manners that Joachim and the Dowager were demonstrating, the way they were behaving as if their guests were Prince Hugo and Princess Sophie from the British royal family, for example, just made it worse.

By the time they come back for the wedding, she told herself grimly, *I'll have this all under control. Mom, Dad, Randy, Hailey, they'll all know what to expect and how to dress. I'll make sure they look great for the official photos – I'll take them out and buy them a whole set of new clothes.*

She glanced sideways at the Dowager as she replaced her cup and saucer on the table. To her surprise, she realised that the Dowager was looking at her too, and as their eyes met, her future mother-in-law gave Lori a little nod, like a sign of agreement, as if she had read Lori's mind; *which*, Lori thought, *she probably has.* By the time of the wedding, the Makarwiczes would be dolled out from head to toe in outfits suitable to their status as the family of the bride, whatever Lori and the Dowager needed to do to achieve that.

Lori had thought there might be some issue convincing her family that they would need to accept what they might perceive as charity from her fiancé and his mother; the trip, of course, had been entirely paid for by the Herzoslovakian royal purse. Instead, the problem turned out to be convincing the Makarwiczes not to turn round and go home almost immediately after they had arrived.

'We just don't fit in!' Sandy wailed as soon as she and the rest of the family were alone with Lori, in the suite of rooms set aside for Sandy and Bob's use. Plopped down on the chaise-longue at the foot of the four-poster bed, she stared around her with as much distress as if she were in a sunless maximum security prison cell, rather than a huge, brocade-walled bedroom with a balcony overlooking the river below, another huge bedroom leading off this one for Bob's use – the Herzoslovakians had very old-fashioned ideas about spousal sleeping arrangements, as Lori had already learnt with Joachim. Priceless hangings draped the carved mahogany frame of the bed, yellow roses were arranged in equally priceless vases on the marble mantelpiece.

'We don't belong here!' Sandy continued.

She gestured down at herself, her 'comfort-cut' jeans, her lime Gap sweater with attached white collar, cuffs and hem, her white sneakers, the bobble at the back of her ankle socks just visible. And then at her husband, in his stay-pressed chinos and checked shirt. To Lori, they were exactly what a mother and father should look like, exactly what all the other moms and dads back home in Dorchester looked like. People shopped at the Gap and Macy's and Bon Ton, maybe went for the day to the Carousel Mall in Syracuse for Ann Taylor Loft and Lord and Taylor if they were rich and fancy. No one wanted to stand out: that would embarrass themselves, their children and their community. One of the oddities that Lori had always noticed about Dorchester was that you never saw anyone wearing the sexier, tighter clothes that were available in shops like Bebe in the Carousel Mall. She had no idea who bought the stretch satin minidresses there or where they wore them: if you ate out at one of the chain restaurants in the mall, Uno Chicago Grill or Ruby Tuesday's, say, in anything but a T-shirt and jeans or denim skirt – with a turtleneck over the tee in colder weather – you'd get the kind of stares that implied you were a hooker plying for trade.

Lori took a deep breath.

'*I* belong here now,' she said: there was no point reassuring her folks that they fitted in here, because it was obvious that they did so about as well as the Dowager would queuing for a table at TGI Friday's. 'So we need to figure out a way that you guys can too, anytime you come visit. And at the wedding, of course.'

'Oh Lori, honey, I don't think I can do it!' Sandy was on the verge of tears. 'It's too much for me and your dad! I don't understand half of what Joachim's mom says, though I'm sure she couldn't be kinder and nicer! And the way they look just puts us all to shame.'

'We're small-town folks, and proud of it,' Bob Makarwicz chimed in. 'Maybe that's where we should stay.'

Randy, leaning against the fireplace, nodded in vigorous agreement, nudged a porcelain vase with his shoulder by accident, turned to catch it before it fell, an agonized expression on his face, hit the fire-irons below with his feet and sent them crashing down to the marble floor as he stood, gripping the vase, afraid to move. Hailey, who had been smoking on the balcony, dashed in, relieved him of his burden and shooed him towards an armchair, where he sat nervously, his large body filling it so completely that he had to remove the silk pillow from behind his back to fit into the chair properly.

'See?' Sandy said. 'Your brother's going to break something every time he turns round!'

'I feel like a bull in a china shop,' Bob confessed. 'Everything here's so dainty and delicate. Scares the hell out of me.'

Lori looked over to Hailey for help, but her sister was fully occupied setting the vase back on the mantelpiece, trying to arrange the roses exactly the way they had been before Randy disturbed them, her back turned to the room. The slogan on Hailey's pink velour ass turned out to be 'Princess': Lori tried not to wince.

'We *have* to make this work!' she insisted. 'You're my family, Joachim's my fiancé, he and his mother are trying so hard to make you feel welcome – I know it was totally overwhelming, but that's my fault. I didn't think it through. I should have planned it all better. Look, get some rest, have a shower, unpack, I'll get you sent up some coffee and sodas . . .'

'They unpacked for us already!' her mother wailed. 'They went through all of my clothes! Lori, I couldn't be more mortified!'

Bob pulled open one of the huge carved doors of the armoire to show his daughter. Sandy's meagre wardrobe was exposed, a few dresses hanging lonely in the giant cupboard, her sneakers and a sensible pair of two-inch-heeled court shoes below them, her jeans and T-shirts folded neatly in a small stack on the high open shelves lined with scented paper.

'My *underthings*!' Sandy was moaning. 'They folded all my *smalls* up individually!'

'Hey, I hope they had fun with my Vicky's Secret push-up bras,' Hailey said bravely from the fireplace, where she was down on her knees picking up the fire irons.

But it wasn't the image of her mother's sensible underpants, double-folded into the little lingerie drawers in the marble-topped chest of drawers, that made Lori's heart sink. It was the sight of Sandy's suitcase, stacked away on the top shelf of the armoire, bought new for this trip at the mall, because her parents rarely travelled and obviously wanted to arrive with a nicer set of luggage than their battered old cases; they'd gone to Target and picked up a matching set on sale, Sandy had told her in an email. Dark green, trimmed with a silver metal, it was familiar to Lori because of all the travelling she did; she'd seen that same, supermarket-brand suitcase circulating round a thousand luggage carousels all over the world. By the time her parents got home, the canvas would already be stained, the metal scuffed, the cheap materials betraying all too obviously their chain-store origins. She thought of Joachim's matched, monogrammed set of Vuitton luggage, and cringed inwardly – not at her parents, but at the sheer scale of the gulf that now existed between their two worlds.

For a moment she was dumb, unable to think of anything to say.

'*You* fit in here, honey,' Sandy said, taking Lori's hand and patting it. 'Don't you worry about that. We can see how much they love you. You've been all round the world, you're sophisticated now. You're not a Dorchester girl any more.'

'You've always been my princess,' Bob added. 'Well, you're going to be a queen now, and I couldn't be prouder of you. Joe's getting the best girl in the world.'

'Hey,' Hailey muttered. 'Other daughter alert.'

'But your mom and I probably should back out of the limelight before we make fools of ourselves,' Bob continued. 'Or Randy knocks over some fancy heirloom that costs a million dollars.'

'We should pack up and go back now before we mess things up for you,' Sandy said in heartfelt tones. 'Your new family seems just lovely, hon.'

'They *are*!' Lori exclaimed, really worried now. 'And you have to stay to get to know them a bit better! If you turn round and leave now, I don't know what I'll do! You can't just go like that—'

'No, she's right – we can't!' Hailey said, and Lori felt herself exhale in relief at having an ally. 'Mom, Dad, you're being totally ridiculous, okay? We said we'd come for a week, we all took time off work – which turns out to be, like, incredibly easy when you say you're going to Europe to meet a king that your sister's marrying, FYI,' she added to Lori. 'My supervisor was like, bring me one back and you can go for a month on full pay! *Any*way, we all scrambled to come over, the whole of Dorchester knows where we are, and we'd look like total failures if we went home as soon as we got here . . .'

This aspect of the situation had not occurred to the other Makarwiczes. They stared at Hailey, Bob and Randy's large Adam's apples bobbing as they swallowed hard, her words sinking in.

'We have to stick it out,' she insisted. 'We can't go home with our tails between our legs. Besides, Mom, Dad—' she looked at each of them in turn, very pointedly – 'you were both worrying about Lori getting engaged so fast! Jeez, you've been going on and on about it nonstop ever since she told us. I've been, like, *switch the channel!* for the last few weeks. And now you've got here, you want to go back home before you've even had a chance to figure out if Joachim's a good guy or not, and Lori's happy?'

She grinned at her sister. '*I* think it's insanely romantic,' she assured Lori. 'So no worries here. And Randy doesn't give a shit, apart from getting a free holiday so soon after coming over for the Olympics. But Mom and Dad have been freaking out.'

'So you *can't* go home yet,' Lori said firmly, very grateful for Hailey's excellent handling of the situation. 'I totally get that you'd be worried, that's only normal. You have to stay and see how great it is here. They all treat me – well, like a queen. Honestly.'

'They don't look down on you because you're American?' her mother asked timidly.

'Of course they don't!' Lori was genuinely surprised by this idea. 'They didn't look down on Grace Kelly when she married the Prince of Monaco, either! Of course, she was a movie star—'

'And you're an Olympic athlete, honey,' her father said with great pride. 'You deserve to be a princess. You sure as hell look like one right now. All elegant and classy.'

I'll have to tell them not to say 'classy' any more, Lori thought, making a mental note. *It turns out that if you truly are, you'd never dream of using that word.*

'You do look just beautiful,' Sandy agreed, looking at her daughter in the sleek Jil Sander navy crepe dress with its flashes of white, the topaz earrings that glowed almost as golden as Lori's hair.

Even Randy gave Lori the thumbs-up.

'It's just a different style here,' Lori said tactfully. 'Tomorrow, I'll take you shopping for some European clothes.'

'Nothing will fit your father and Randy here!' her mother said worriedly, but her eyes did light up at the prospect of shopping.

'The tailors will take their measurements today and get something made in a couple of days,' Lori promised. 'You should see how fast they make alterations on my wedding dress and my trousseau. I'm sure they can fix a suit each for Dad and Randy. And of course they'll sort out your wedding outfits.'

'What's a trousseau?' Hailey asked eagerly, but was overridden by Randy whining:

'I already got a suit! I don't need another one!'

'Oh honey,' his mother said. 'Somehow, after seeing Joachim's get-up today, I don't really think your Men's Wearhouse Big and Tall that you got in the Black Friday sale's going to cut it, do you?'

'Plus, I can't drink any more tea from those tiny little cups,' Bob said decisively, as if that were the line in the sand he was drawing to remain sane. 'I just can't. I could barely get my finger through the handle. I was crapping myself the whole time—'

'*Bob!*' his wife said crossly.

'Sorry, honey. But when Joachim's mom said they were hundreds of years old, and a perfect set, I was, like, kill me now before I fuck this up,' Bob said, to vigorous nods from his son.

'Yeah! It was like something in my head told me just to drop the damn thing and get it over with,' Randy chimed in.

'You too? Man, I was *this* close!' his father said, holding up his thumb and index finger, pressed tightly together. Father and son sniggered together.

'Okay,' Lori said firmly. 'No more tea. We can deal.'

'When can we go shopping?' Hailey asked excitedly.

But just then there was a knock on the door; all five heads turned as Lori called: 'Come!' as she had learned to do. Philippe, Joachim's private secretary, entered, his dark grey suit discreet but so exquisitely tailored to his slim figure that Lori grimaced for a split-second, vividly imagining the contrast between Philippe and Randy with the latter dressed in his Men's Wearhouse Big and Tall finest.

'Hello, Philippe,' she said.

'*Bonjour, mam'selle,*' Philippe replied. Behind his wire-rimmed Maison Martin Margiela glasses, his eyes flashed with considerable interest to Randy for just a moment, clearly focusing on the Big and Tall aspects of Lori's strapping brother rather than the deficiencies of Randy's sartorial taste. His gaze returned to Lori, once more a hundred per cent professional, as he said:

'As you know, I have planned the itinerary for the visit of your family – *bienvenue en Herzoslovakie, mesdames, messieurs* – and His Majesty has just informed me that perhaps the gentlemen would enjoy to participate in some sporting activities during their stay? During his pleasant conversation with the *messieurs*, His Majesty learnt that they delight in the hunting and the shooting in America, and he considers that maybe they would like to join him on a wild boar hunt. Also, possibly, the shooting of the pheasants? It is not the season for the pheasants, of course, but for this special occasion His Majesty is happy to have me arrange it for the gentlemen.'

Lori was familiar by now with Philippe's habit of using several words where one would do, spoken in a heavy Parisian accent. The other Makarwiczes, however, goggled at this slender, elegant apparition, as dumbstruck as if Philippe had just teleported into the room wearing a Star Trek uniform and holding up his fingers in the Vulcan peace greeting.

'Wild boar hunt, pheasant shoot, Dad and Randy,' she translated for their benefit. 'Wanna go while you're here?'

'*Hell* yes!' the two men chorused in unison, their eyes lighting up.

'It is perfectly safe, *madame, je vous assure*,' Philippe said smoothly to Sandy, whose eyes had widened nervously at the words 'wild boar'. 'The gentlemen will be in no danger at all.' He allowed himself a small smile. 'It is not like in the ancient times. We do not hunt here on the horses with the spears.'

'Oh, good,' Sandy said feebly. 'Because they don't know how to ride. Also, you wouldn't have horses big enough.'

'The gentlemen are certainly most magnificently proportioned,' Philippe commented. 'It is to be envied. If it is permitted, Her Majesty *la reine douairière* informs me that she will send to your rooms our seamstresses for some initial measurements, as a gesture of hospitality from herself. Perhaps in a few hours, after you have all had time to repose yourselves?'

'That would be lovely, Philippe,' Lori said, grateful that the Dowager was forging ahead with this.

'The ladies will wish to see *Mademoiselle*'s wedding dress, *bien sûr*,' Philippe said. 'Some shopping in Valtzers, also, I will arrange. The cousins of His Majesty, *mademoiselles les comtesses* Katya and Kristin, will be very happy to take the ladies on a little tour of our most charming capital.'

'Shopping sounds great!' Hailey said enthusiastically to Philippe. 'And I *love* your accent.'

'*Mademoiselle* is very kind,' Philippe said smoothly.

'Is it, like, French? 'Cause it *sounds* French,' Hailey went on. 'But we're not anywhere near France, are we?' She looked at her sister.

'*Mademoiselle* is correct,' Philippe agreed. 'We are not near my country, which is indeed *la France*. But, *me voici*! Here I am, all the same.'

'Countries in Europe are a lot closer,' Lori muttered to Hailey. 'It's like he's from New York State, working in, uh, Louisiana.'

Philippe smiled politely at the extreme unlikeliness of this comparison.

'Anyway, he was talking about Katya and Kristin,' Lori said quickly to her mother and sister, under her breath; Bob and Randy were now pestering Philippe with questions about the boar hunt. 'They're Joachim's cousins – really nice and fun and friendly, you'll love them. They said they were really keen to spend some girl time with us while you're here.'

'Oh, that would be nice,' her mother said, cheering up at the thought of female company that would be less intimidating than the Dowager Queen's.

'Mom, you *have* to stay,' Lori said in an undertone. 'I was counting the days till you came. I'd be in pieces if you just turned round and left now.'

'It's all so soon,' her mother said, looking at Lori with worry now for her daughter rather than her own social inadequacies. 'But, you know, it's so *romantic* that he's swept you off your feet – you're okay, aren't you?'

'I am! It *is* romantic,' Lori assured her. 'He's such a gentleman. And they're taking really good care of me. He said he didn't mean to propose so fast either, but he just couldn't help himself.'

'Oh, that's lovely,' Sandy said, her eyes brightening.

'But I need you guys here too,' Lori said seriously. 'I *was* feeling a bit . . . not lonely, exactly, but waking up every morning in a strange country, it's a shock.'

'I guess it's a good thing for you to be staying here,' her mother said. 'That way you know what you're getting into.'

Lori cracked a smile.

'Exactly,' she said. 'And I like it here. I really do.'

'You can stand living in Europe?' Sandy asked. 'It's all so different!'

Lori's smile widened. 'I can,' she said. 'Really, I can. I kinda like it. It's an adventure. And this country is so beautiful.'

'It sure is,' her mother said, nodding vehemently. 'It sure is. And it seems real safe, too.'

'Hey, fella,' Bob was saying to Philippe, which made Lori wince but didn't ruffle Philippe's immaculate surface at all, 'this boar hunt? I have another question.'

'*Oui, monsieur?*' Philippe clasped his hands across his chest and tilted his head a little to one side, expectantly.

'The guys here – they don't drink tea on a hunt, do they?' Bob asked, winking.

Philippe let out what was almost a titter.

'Oh, *monsieur, non, je vous assure! Absolument pas!* But not at all. There is the brandy, usually. The whisky also. But if *monsieur* would prefer the beer, we have truly excellent Herzoslovakian and also German ales—'

'No need to worry about that now,' Bob said with a wide smile. 'Just checking.'

'Hey, I'd like to try some of that Herzoslovakian beer!' Randy said enthusiastically.

Philippe's eyes flashed behind the lenses of his glasses.

'I will myself, personally, bring a selection to *monsieur's* room *tout de suite,*' he assured Randy. 'I will be *most* happy to oblige *monsieur* with any request he may have, no matter *what* it may be.' He smiled at Randy. '*Monsieur* has only to ask.'

From that moment on, there was, at least, no more talk of the Makarwiczes leaving Herzoslovakia precipitately. Cautiously, tentatively, they settled into what Bob was now calling their orientation week. The castle visits were a huge hit, as they had been with Lori; no one from the New World could fail to be entranced by the history, the charm, the breathtaking perfection of the centuries-old turreted stone castles clinging so prettily to the sides of the steep slopes, the sunshine glinting off the light sprinkling of snow on the velvety green grass lawns that flowed down to the river, the trips down the Danube on Joachim's powerboat, and the lunches on a moored, heated barge floating peacefully beneath the castle walls, a string quartet playing Mozart as they ate. Lori, taking a hand in the menus, had made sure that there were always cheese, ham and smoked sausages for her family: cold cuts were easily understandable food for the Makarwiczes, washed down with beer for Randy and Bob and Riesling for Sandy and Hailey, who were used to sweet wine. Back home, raspberry merlot was one of the most popular alcoholic drinks.

And the weather cooperated, to Lori and Joachim's great relief: it barely snowed, the sun stayed out, it was a clear crisp day for the boar hunt. This idea turned out to have been a masterstroke of Joachim's. Bob and Randy looked forward to it for days, went off before sunrise, equipped with monogrammed hip flasks and Barbours presented to them by Joachim, and returned, mud-stained and blissed out, babbling about how well the hunting dogs were trained, how expertly the drivers handled their Land Rovers, how fast the boar scampered through the brush. Joachim was tactful enough to give Bob the credit for the one they killed: roped onto the roof of one of the Land Rovers, it was taken back to the Schloss, butchered and marinated in red wine and vinegar for forty-eight hours to tenderize it before it would be served at the Makarwiczes' farewell dinner.

Meanwhile, Sandy and Hailey were shopping, lunching and attending another fitting for Lori's wedding dress. The lace was being carefully pieced over the bodice, the embroidery pattern of the seed pearls was taking shape, the ermine trim had been shaped by the furriers to perfection. Sandy burst into hysterical sobs on seeing her daughter in the exquisite creation even before the Dowager, smiling, showed Sandy and Hailey the jewellery that Lori would be wearing.

The tiara and choker sent Sandy completely over the edge; she collapsed onto a love seat, sobbing her heart out in the Dowager's arms, as the Dowager patted her head and told her how much they all loved Lori in Herzoslovakia and what good care they would take of her daughter, while swiftly dabbing Sandy's slightly snotty tears away before they stained the shantung-silk lapels of her immaculate suit. Katya and Kristin, Joachim's cousins, who were almost always around now, having bonded with Hailey, ordered more champagne from a footman and strolled out on the terrace, gossiping and smoking with Hailey as Lori, standing on the dressmakers' plinth, felt tears pricking at her own eyes at the sight of her mother crying with sheer joy.

By that evening, the Dowager and Sandy had bonded sufficiently for them to decide to have a quiet dinner in the Dowager's rooms, followed by a viewing, in the private cinema, of *The Sound of Music*. It had transpired that this was one of both women's favourite films: parts of it had actually been shot in Herzoslovakia, and the Dowager was going to point them all out to Sandy. Bob and Randy were out with Joachim at a beer hall, which left the four young women free to hit the chicest nightlife that Valtzers had to offer. Katya had actually suggested that they fly to Paris for the evening, which had rendered Hailey speechless in wonder for a good five minutes, but Lori had nixed the idea, pointing out that as Joachim's fiancée she couldn't possibly be seen to prefer anywhere to Valtzers.

They had dinner in a very smart Italian restaurant – though Katya and Kristin, who were glossy, full-on Eurotrash, mostly smoked, drank white wine and pushed their food around their plates, Hailey emulating them eagerly. The conversation was mostly about boyfriends, past, present and future; Hailey was wide-eyed at the list of pop stars, film actors and European royalty that Katya and Kristin reeled off; particularly fascinating was the revelation that Prince Toby even had freckles on his cock. In return, responding to their teasing questions, she described every single man that Lori had ever dated, to Lori's great mortification: 'always blond and built,' Hailey spilled, giggling. 'Lori's high school boyfriend was just like a short Liam Hemsworth – you know, Thor? She goes for the jocks.'

'Jocks?' Katya asked, unfamiliar with the American word.

'Sporty guys – you know!'

'Oh yes, I like those very much!' Kristin agreed, promptly reciting a list of tennis players and Formula One drivers with whom she had been sexually intimate. It mercifully turned the conversation away from Lori, and they were still on the subject of sporty guys when they left the restaurant, climbed into the limo waiting outside, drove three blocks to Coco Bongo, Valtzers' most expensive nightclub, and got out again. Coco Bongo was very dark and very plush, catering to tax-avoiding million- and billionaires visiting their legal place of residence on advice from their accountants. At its bar clustered the kinds of very expensive young women who gathered in the exclusive bars and clubs frequented by tax-avoiding million- and billionaires. Katya and Kristin swept past them regally, up the steps to the VIP area, where the manager was already jumping to unhook the velvet rope for them personally.

It was the best night out for Hailey that Lori could have imagined, and she was hugely grateful to Joachim's lively young cousins for organizing it. Lori was much more sedate than her sister, which, of course, made her perfect queen material; but they were completely safe inside Coco Bongo, pictures being absolutely banned, and the Herzoslovakian countesses and Hailey, having had very little to eat, swiftly got absolutely hammered on vodka shots and tumbled around the dance floor on high heels to Rihanna and Pitbull. Lori sat in the VIP area in a booth that overlooked the dance floor, sipped a glass of white wine and watched her sister with satisfaction; every single visiting member of the Makarwicz family had found some activity they genuinely enjoyed in Herzoslovakia. Their visit had been much more successful than she had ever dreamt it would be, the royal family bending over backwards to welcome their new in-laws.

'Darling!' She looked up to see her fiancé sliding into the booth beside her. 'You are having a good time?' he asked.

Putting his arm around her, Joachim kissed her with enthusiasm. She tasted beer on his breath, a dark, rich ale, so much nicer than the generic chemical flavour she was used to from previous boyfriends who had been hitting the Buds or the Millers all night.

Everything in Europe is so much more sophisticated. She smiled at him and settled herself against his solid body, his arm resting on her shoulders.

'Where are Dad and Randy?' she asked, seeing that Joachim was alone.

He grinned.

'They enjoyed Herzoslovakian beer *very* much,' he informed her. 'It was very nice to see how much they enjoyed it. But then we came outside the beer hall and the cool air makes them feel suddenly very tired, so the driver takes them home and I think I will walk here to see how you are getting on.'

'Oh no, they'll have awful hangovers tomorrow!' Lori said, wincing.

Joachim shrugged. 'They can sleep for a long time,' he said easily. 'It is not a problem.'

His body was warm against hers, and it was lovely to feel his arm around her, smell his now-familiar scent. She snuggled in even closer, draping a leg daringly over his. They still hadn't had sex yet; Lori had made an attempt at seducing Joachim after a romantic dinner, just as she had planned. But Joachim, taking her hands, kissing each of her fingertips in turn, his eyes wide and blue, had expressed how glad he was that she loved him and wanted to be with him in that way, but that, since she was being housed under his roof, it would not be proper for them to 'live as man and wife' before the ceremony.

Lori had doubtfully said that she understood what he was saying, but she still felt weird about it. Joachim had replied that things were different in Europe when a man really loved a woman, and they were especially different when a king respected a woman enough to want to make her his queen. Perhaps he was too serious, too old-fashioned – could she wait a little, could she forgive him for his scruples? But he wanted to be with her for ever, to marry her for life, just like her father was with her mother. He remembered that Lori had told him before how much that meant to her, that her father and mother had such a strong marriage: that was what he wanted for them.

These words, of course, had made her melt. It was what she wanted too: a marriage that would last for life. And though it definitely felt increasingly strange and frustrating to kiss her fiancé goodnight every evening, go to separate sets of rooms, and climb into a huge bed every night alone, often pulling out her Rabbit vibrator from the drawer of the bedside table (thank goodness *that* had not only been in her suitcase, but she'd gone straight to her room on arrival and unpacked the case herself!), she could also see that qualities like seriousness and an old-fashioned perspective were excellent ones to have in a husband.

And worth waiting for, she thought now, cuddling up against him. *We've got the rest of our lives together – I can wait a couple of months if I have to.* She felt undeniably horny, pressed against her fiancé like this in a dark nightclub, with a few drinks in her and sexy music playing. But then she remembered the free-for-all at the Olympic Village, the near-orgies that had ensued after each medal ceremony, the drunk, lecherous guys perpetually coming on to her, not caring who she was, just that she was attractive female flesh, and she took a deep breath.

That's not what I want. I've never had casual sex; I've always dated the guys. Nothing wrong with Shameeka having fun – and God knows she did in the Village! – but that's just not me. I've found a guy who wants me for life, and I guess the price is that he comes with principles even more old-fashioned than mine.

She couldn't help smiling at this thought: she'd never met a guy who'd turn down sex if you offered it to him on a plate. It just went to show how committed Joachim was, how important this marriage was to him. Like her, he wanted to do it once and do it right, as her mom always said.

Her heart full with happiness at the choice she'd made, the king who wanted to treat his queen so respectfully, Lori picked up Joachim's hand and kissed the back of it. His arms tightened around her in response.

'The girls are having fun, yes?' he said, spotting Katya, Kristin and Hailey, who were surrounded by men egging them on to dance as sexily as possible, tossing their hair, wiggling their hips, arching their backs much more provocatively than the girls who were there in a more professional capacity. 'Good, I see that my cousins take care of your sister.'

'I'm not sure if I'd call it taking care,' Lori said dryly, as an admirer summoned a waiter over with a tray of shots: the girls whooped, grabbed one each and clinked glasses before downing their contents.

'Oh, they are young, they like to dance and have fun, it's normal,' Joachim said easily.

'Wow,' Lori said, twisting to look at his face. 'I thought you'd be a bit more disapproving. They're getting kinda smashed.'

He shrugged. 'Katya and Kristin are only minor royalty,' he said. 'Like Prince Toby in Britain. They will not inherit, they are more free to dance and drink and enjoy the parties. I must be more careful, because I am the ruling king. And I am a very clever king, because I have picked a bride who is careful too. Serious. A lady. Who does not have more than two glasses of wine when she goes out in public, who sits politely instead of—'

'Shaking her ass,' Lori suggested, seeing that Joachim's vocabulary did not quite stretch to describing his cousins' and her sister's antics.

He laughed and stroked Lori's arm appreciatively. 'Yes! You know, it is funny – I see you first jumping around in the sand, shaking your ass, as you say, wearing very few clothes. And yet there is something that tells me I want to meet you, and as soon as I do, I know you are the one for me. And for Herzoslovakia.'

Joachim was always saying wonderful things like that, things that made Lori's heart melt with happiness. She was as careful with his and his country's reputation as he said, and he was right: it came naturally to her. She had never been a big drinker or a big partier, being too serious about her sport, and not liking to lose control and make an idiot of herself. At last she had found somewhere that those qualities were prized, appreciated, rewarded. As the Queen of Herzoslovakia, her modest nature would finally be an asset, not a liability. She had been teased for it at high school and even more so when she went to college in Miami, a huge party town.

But here, I'm normal, she thought with great relief. *Here I fit in. Here they actually like that I don't want to go to tequila bars and do body shots off other girls to turn the guys on.*

All I want is to get married, fall into bed with my husband and start making babies.

She pulled Joachim's head to hers and kissed him with such passion that he was laughing when he gently eased her away from him again.

'You have had *three* glasses of wine, I think!' he said teasingly.

'I'm just so ready to get married,' she said, feeling suffused with happiness. The pounding bassline was building inside her, heating her blood, making her libido surge; they were a bare month away from their wedding date, and right now, it felt much too long to wait. 'To get married,' she said, sliding her hand along his leg, towards his crotch, 'and start making lots of little heirs to the throne . . .'

Firmly, Joachim picked up her hand before it could reach its destination.

'This is not the time or the place,' he said, kissing her hand, holding it to make sure it didn't venture downwards again. 'But I too want many little heirs.'

Lori shifted on the velvet seat of the booth; now she had allowed her excitement to grow, it was hard to turn it off. She was getting even more horny by the moment. Despite her previous resolve, she couldn't help feeling that seducing her fiancé this evening might be just the right way to finish the night.

'We could practise tonight,' she suggested, leaning into him, running her tongue seductively around the curve of his ear. 'We could use protection, so I don't get knocked up before the wedding. Maybe I should sneak into your rooms when we get back to the Schloss . . .'

'It would not be fitting, I am afraid,' Joachim said, shaking his head sadly. 'You know how I feel, Lori. Much as I would like it, it would not be fitting. But very soon, we will be married. And I have something to tell you, something I know you will like. Lori, as a wedding present, I have decided to pay off the mortgages on your parents' house and to offer Randy and Hailey interest-free loans for them too. I have come to very much enjoy my new family that you have brought me from America, and I want to make their lives a little more easy.'

Lori stared at him, open-mouthed.

'Oh my God,' she stammered. 'I don't know what to say.'

'Then say nothing,' he said, smiling, and kissing her forehead. 'You make me so happy, so proud. I want to make you happy too, and your family as well.'

'Oh my God,' Lori repeated, her head spinning. 'You don't need to do this, honey, you really don't . . . that's like, above and beyond anything I could possibly have expected . . .'

'I *want* to do this,' he said simply. 'Please, indulge me. We will say no more about it. Your family will know when they return to America – the Herzoslovakian Embassy will inform them. It will be easiest that way. They will not be embarrassed by learning it here.'

Still reeling from this news, Lori was even more overcome when, on the Makarwiczes' departure, Joachim presented Sandy and Hailey with diamond earrings and Bob and Randy with Cartier watches. They protested, of course, that they couldn't possibly accept such expensive gifts, after all Joachim and the Dowager had done for them already, but Joachim deftly distracted them by showing them a stunning pink, blue and white diamond parure which he had had made specifically for Lori. The parure was so extraordinary that the earrings and watches seemed modest by comparison, making it easier for the Makarwiczes to yield. Joachim was clearly a skilled diplomat.

'Look,' he said proudly, fastening the necklace around his fiancée's neck and stepping back to appreciate the effect. The matching earrings were already glistening in her ears, the bracelet on her wrist; Hailey and Sandy were gasping at the brilliance of the colours reflected in the crisp-cut facets of the diamonds.

'It is a *demi-parure*, technically,' the Dowager said. 'The *grandes parures* have also a ring and a brooch. But they are out of fashion now, the young people do not wear a whole set. The clothes are not formal enough to balance the effect.' She smiled at Lori. 'You were born to wear this jewellery, my dear,' she said with great satisfaction. 'Your height, your bearing, your complexion – truly queen-like.'

Sandy flushed with pride and squeezed her husband's arm as they looked at their tall, fair, beautiful daughter bedecked in diamonds.

'Katya says you need to be tall to wear a tiara,' Hailey commented: most of her sentences these days started with 'Katya says' or 'Kristin says'.

'Ah yes, Katya – I have another another little surprise,' Joachim said. 'Katya and Kristin will fly back with you. We thought you could all stop in New York for a night at the Carlyle, as my guests of course, and do some more shopping for the wedding. They will guide you round the best places, where we have charge accounts.'

'Oh, how lovely!' Lori exclaimed. 'Hey, why don't I come too? Just for a couple of days? We could have a really lovely time – I'm really going to miss you so much—'

But the Dowager was shaking her head regretfully.

'There is the school opening tomorrow afternoon,' she said smoothly, 'and then the Parliament visit. Philippe has scheduled a great deal of appointments for when your family leaves. It is back to business, as you say in America.'

Joachim was nodding too.

'You see, it is not all diamonds, being a queen!' he chimed in jovially to the Makarwiczes. 'Lori works hard at her new job. She is a very busy girl here. Everyone wants to see her, to meet her, to have her come to support their charity.'

'We can do a trip after you're married,' Katya said comfortingly to Lori, whose face had fallen. She knew that the Dowager and Joachim were right: she couldn't possibly skip official appointments, even ones of which she had not been aware. But she was suddenly conscious of how much she longed to be with her family for just a day or two longer, back home in the States . . .

'Yes!' Kristin added. 'It will be lovely, we will all go together! We will plan it very soon.'

Lori smiled at her and Katya gratefully.

'You have your Herzoslovakian lessons, too,' Joachim said. 'You have skipped a whole week, and you told me you wanted to be fluent by the wedding. It is only six weeks away! So much to do!'

'And they'll all be back so soon,' the Dowager said quickly. 'Time will fly by.'

'It does make sense, honey,' Sandy said, hugging her daughter. 'I'm sorry you can't come, but we'll be back real soon. We'll see you before you know it.'

It was true. They would be back in less than six weeks. And yet as the tall Makarwiczes climbed into the limousine that would take them to the heliport, Lori sobbed her heart out as she watched them go.

'I'm sorry!' she said to Joachim, whose arm was wrapped around her waist supportively as they waved goodbye. 'I'm so sorry! I'm happy here, I really am – it's just, it was so lovely being with them, and I'm going to miss them so much . . .'

'Of course,' he said gently. 'You are a good daughter, you value your family. I love this about you. It is natural that you are sad when they go away.'

He turned, guiding her so she moved with him; the limousine, negotiating the steep curves down the hill, disappeared from sight, her back to it now, the castle looming up before them. And emerging from the main doors were two young men dressed in black, both muscly and well-built, but very different physical types. Lori's eyes went immediately to the blond god, a total jock, though his brushed-back hair and clean-shaven jaw were much more in the European than the American style. Bright blue eyes sparkled at her as brightly as the diamonds in her parure. He ran lightly down the steps, his body moving with the fluid lightness of an athlete, his pecs clearly defined under the black turtleneck sweater, his waist very narrow. She felt guilty for staring, but it was impossible not to, on first view of him, at least: he was as handsome as the film star he resembled, with his sculpted features and full pink lips.

The sturdier, stockier young man bringing up the rear, taking each step of the stone staircase much more heavily, was like the ugly duckling behind the beautiful swan, darker, wider, his muscles tightly packed, a weightlifter following a gymnast. His features were as solid as his physique, blunt and functional, his black hair growing low on his forehead in tight curls.

'Lori, these are Mihaly and Attila,' Joachim said. 'I have personally chosen them to be your bodyguards.'

Lori's eyes widened in surprise.

'Now that the wedding is coming closer, you will be beginning to attend some official engagements, at which I will not always be present,' he continued. 'I am very concerned for your safety at all times. Last night, in fact, was when I had this thought, meeting you at the nightclub where men could have bothered you and Hailey, for instance. And I was there to make sure you all returned safely. But in future, when I cannot be with you, there will be these two very efficient young men to take care of everything.'

'I really feel very safe already,' Lori said. She smiled at Mihaly, the blond, and Attila, the swarthier one. 'I don't mean to be rude, but Herzoslovakia is so incredibly quiet – there's barely any crime here at all.'

That was, of course, due to its tax-haven status that meant everyone was so comparatively wealthy; certainly there was no crime which sprang from social deprivation.

'Last night no one bothered us,' she went on. 'Or at least, in a way Hailey didn't like! Honestly, Joachim, it's really kind of you, but I don't think it's necessary.'

And also, I don't like the idea of these two following me round the whole time, asking me where I'm going, what I'm doing. I'm not used to living in a palace with staff around me every moment, checking to see if I want anything; I know that they're aware of everywhere I go, everything I do, how long I spend in the gym, when I'm due for my next Herzoslovakian lesson, exactly how I like my coffee – it's lovely, I shouldn't complain, but sometimes I want so badly to be alone, and having full-time bodyguards is going to make that so much less likely . . .

'They will be very discreet,' Joachim assured her. 'You will not find them waiting next to the bed when you wake up in the morning!'

It was a joke, and everyone laughed, but Lori had a quick flash of Mihaly doing exactly that, wearing not very much at all, and she hoped to God that her instant physical reaction to that image didn't show on her face. Sexual frustration was definitely nagging at her: somehow the enforced abstinence mandated by Joachim was prompting her to think about it more and more, about their wedding night, when they would finally release all this built-up tension. She was masturbating almost every day now, had had to buy new batteries for her Rabbit once already, and it was slowing down, which meant that she was due another set. But even that was only a temporary release . . .

And maybe I need a new Rabbit too, she thought. *It's bound to break down sooner or later, the way I'm going. I should definitely have a backup. Oh my God, how am I going to get a new one? Order it online? But I can't get deliveries from a sex shop!*

Maybe I could order one from Amazon. Does Amazon sell vibrators? No one would bat an eye at a package coming in from them. But what if they open my mail? What if my new bodyguards insist on opening all my packages for security reasons! What if Mihaly sees my Rabbit and thinks . . . makes a joke about it . . . Oh God, I'd be beyond embarrassed—

Jeez, this is crazy! I need to get a grip, I really do.

Lori glanced back at Mihaly, who was smiling at her, his hands, clasped below his waist, drawing her eyes perilously close to his crotch, and she was sure she went red. She was shocked by how quickly her thoughts had turned sexual about him with her fiancé standing right next to her, and though she felt guilty, of course, she couldn't be *too* ashamed. She was a healthy young woman, her fiancé's old-fashioned scruples meant that he was barely laying a finger on her (*let alone in me!* she thought naughtily), and she had just been presented with a bodyguard who was exactly her type; no wonder sex was at the forefront of her mind.

After the wedding, she thought with huge relief, *this will all sort itself out. Joachim and I will be at it all the time, making babies, honeymooning blissfully in Mexico. I can't wait. And though I'm frustrated now, it's great to know that he has strong principles. He'll make such a good father.*

She looked up at her fiancé lovingly, and realized with a shock that he had been speaking for a while; she'd been so absorbed in her thoughts that she'd missed quite a bit of what he'd said.

'. . . jewellery, too,' he was saying. 'That alone is a good reason for bodyguards. As the Queen, people will expect to see you wearing the jewels suitable to your station, and Mihaly and Attila will make sure that you can be safe wearing your new parure, for instance.'

Reluctantly, Lori had to admit that this did make sense. She nodded.

'I *would* be a bit freaked going out wearing that without someone keeping an eye on me,' she said.

'There you go! It is settled,' Joachim said cheerfully. 'And now I will leave you with them. I must go to do some work. Philippe is waiting for me. I will see you for dinner, my love.'

He kissed her, turned on his heel and went swiftly up the long stone staircase, back into the Schloss.

'What are your plans for the day, Your Highness?' Mihaly asked, clicking his heels. His voice was a light tenor, as charming as the rest of him.

'Oh,' Lori said, 'I'm not actually royal yet – you don't need to call me that—'

'To us you are already,' Attila said seriously in a deep bass-baritone. 'We guard you like you are royalty.'

'And besides, you will be Queen of Herzoslovakia very soon,' Mihaly pointed out, his smile revealing that he had a very cute little dimple dug adorably into each cheek. 'We would just have to change what we call you then. We might as well start now.'

'Okay,' she said, yielding to their insistence. 'As long as it's not against protocol or anything.'

'Philippe tells us to call you Your Royal Highness,' Attila said, which instantly dispersed all Lori's concerns: Philippe was the absolute arbiter of Royal protocol for her.

'Highness it is!' she said, smiling back at both of them, but guiltily aware that her eyes were warmer for the ridiculously handsome Mihaly. 'Okay, well, I guess I'll go for a run. It would be cool to do it outside, actually. You guys up for that? You could show me a good route – I've been using the gym, but we could get in some nice hill work out here. And then I'd like to go down to Valtzers. I need to get some batteries for my, um—'

What do people even use batteries for nowadays?

'Portable radio,' she said at random. 'Okay?'

'Whatever you say, Your Highness!' Mihaly said again, smiling at her, and Lori made a resolution, then and there, to avoid looking at her gorgeous blond bodyguard too much. Because those dimples were pretty much the cutest thing she'd ever seen in her life.

Chloe

'Now, I want you just to keep breathing and relax as much as you can,' the therapist said in a lovely soft reassuring voice which was completely at odds with the fact that she had just inserted a tube into Chloe's rectum. 'I know that's easier said than done! But just try to hold on as long as you can.'

'Um, when you say "hold on"—' Chloe mumbled, beyond grateful that she was lying on her side on the treatment table, facing away. 'It sort of feels like—'

'Keep letting the water come up inside you until you feel that you need to fart so badly you can't hold on any longer,' Sarika, the colonic hydrotherapist, said with reassuring matter-of-factness. 'Let me know when you're at that point, and I'll let some of the gas out. It'll happen a few times. Nothing to worry about!'

There was nothing to say in return to this but 'Okay'. Lying there, trying to keep breathing, relax, and not think about what was happening in her bottom area, Chloe stared at the white-painted wall and prayed to goodness that Lauren was right and that this colonic detox course would, as promised, help to flatten her tummy bulge for next month, when she would be on show at the wedding of Joachim of Herzoslovakia to Lori Whatsherface. Thank goodness, at least, the wedding was in February, which meant she wouldn't be wearing a light, clinging dress; she and Lauren had selected a Mark Fast knit with a Preen coat over it, a Philip Treacy hat and LK Bennett heels, in keeping with their policy of only choosing British designers. Lauren and the stylist had taken plenty of photos of Chloe in the outfit from all angles, and it looked lovely: bright colours, but not too clashing, nothing that looked as if she were trying to compete with the bride.

As if I could! I'm going to have to stand next to her at some stage, she thought ruefully. *Nothing like knowing the entire world media is going to compare you to a tall, stunning, Olympic-athlete, naturally slim blonde to make you feel paranoid about your weight! Oh, why did she have to get married in the same year as me?*

Herzoslovakia might be a minnow in Europe, its ruling family barely on the radar compared to the endlessly scruti-nized British royals, but as soon as Prince Joachim had proposed to Lori, who was already a minor celebrity due to her bronze Olympic medal and the watch ads with her team-mate, the upcoming marriage had been catapulted into the headlines. Pictures of Lori and Joachim were everywhere; the Herzoslovakian royal family certainly seemed to be enjoying its sudden fame. Chloe had seen Lori on the cover of *Hello!* three weeks running, posed against the stunning Herzoslovakian backgrounds of castles and mountain ranges, dressed in the couture that her enviable figure could wear so effortlessly.

She must work out every day, Chloe thought gloomily. *I just can't do that. I really hate exercise. But the thing is now, being slim isn't enough any more; you're supposed to look all muscly and super-toned as well.*

Ironically, it was Hugo's mother, Belinda, who had incarnated that ideal: Belinda, not only beautiful, but athletic too, with her lean body honed from skiing in the winter and swimming in the summer. Belinda, who had even died practising the sport she loved, in a freak accident which had left her son and daughter motherless. Belinda, whose shoes, in a way, Chloe was expected to fill, to whom, in the press, Chloe was endlessly compared . . .

And as if it wasn't bad enough knowing that, for the rest of my life, they're going to run pictures of me next to Hugo's drop-dead gorgeous mum, now they'll be doing the same with me and Lori of Herzoslovakia, who's five inches taller than me, twenty pounds lighter and could make a bin liner look like an evening dress.

No wonder a colonic detox seemed like a really good idea.

Lauren had done her research before suggesting the idea to Chloe; she'd asked around for experts, talked to several, and chosen Clarity Colonics partly because Sarika had been so enthusiastic and evangelical about the treatment. She'd raved to Lauren that colonics had helped take her down from a size 16 to the enviably slim, flat-stomached 8-10 she was now, even after having had two children.

But it's not bloody Lauren taking her clothes off and lying on a table in a paper robe and a paper thong with someone pumping litres of water up her bum, is it? Chloe thought savagely. She wasn't a particularly adventurous girl; she had been terrified about this appointment for days. It was only Sarika's smiling, cheerful demeanour that had enabled Chloe to go through with it, frankly, and as her bowels filled up with liquid, she was feeling weirder and weirder about the whole thing . . .

'I really think I need to—' she said feebly, but the able Sarika was already adjusting some kind of valve on the device up her bum, releasing the intense pressure that Chloe had started to feel. The terror, of course, was that she was going to lose control of herself and poo all over Sarika, and though Chloe knew that that was incredibly unlikely, that Sarika obviously knew exactly what she was doing, Chloe couldn't get that image out of her head . . .

'Right!' Sarika said brightly. 'I'm going to stop the flow and ask you to turn on your back now, so I can massage your tummy. Don't worry,' she added as Chloe's heart leapt in fear, 'the tube won't come out. I'm going to hold it as you turn over, okay?'

Feeling horribly clumsy, Chloe managed to manoeuvre herself onto her back, the tube still firmly in place, the soles of her feet on the paper covering the table.

'All those hard stools up there in your colon should be softening now, with all this water inside you,' Sarika said comfortably as she leaned over Chloe and started to push down firmly on her stomach through the thin robe.

God, the embarrassment of having anyone else touch her tummy! She didn't even like Hugo near it! *Though at least the fact that it's all swollen up with water is a good excuse for it sticking out*, Chloe thought ruefully. Sarika's pretty face wasn't showing any shock or revulsion at the size of Chloe's abdomen as she massaged away, though she commented:

'Yes, you definitely have some bloating issues! This is really going to help with that.'

'I eat a probiotic yoghurt every morning,' Chloe said quickly. 'And I really watch my diet. But my stomach's always stuck out a bit . . .'

'Yes, it's just a tendency to bloating,' Sarika said reassuringly. 'The probiotics are great, and I recommend one after the treatment. Lots of liquids—'

Chloe couldn't help shuddering at the mention of liquids, considering the litres her colon was currently struggling to hold in.

'– home-made soups, and no raw vegetables for three days. Fruit is fine, just chew it well. But honestly, after you've finished your detox package, you're really going to see a difference in your wellbeing.'

'I think I need—' This was all very exciting, but right now Chloe had two pressing things on her mind: first, she really, really needed to go to the toilet, and second, she had to make sure her wig didn't get dislodged as she did so.

'Yes, of course!' Sarika was already easing the tube out of Chloe's rectum; she seemed to know the current state of Chloe's bowels even better than Chloe herself. 'Just slip yourself down from the table and go into the loo. Take your time in there. I'll be waiting outside in the reception area, so no need to worry about me.'

One hand in Sarika's, the other carefully cradling her scalp to make sure her wig was in place, Chloe clambered down from the table and barely made it to the en-suite toilet before the world fell out of her bottom. Thank God there were two closed doors between her and Sarika; the noises she was making were definitely not for anyone else's ears.

Honestly, she thought ironically, *I could just have eaten a rotten mussel and had the same experience . . .*

But she had to admit that, despite the similarities to a bad case of food poisoning, her current experience was, actually, strangely satisfying. By the time she was sure that she had managed to evacuate everything that wanted to come out, flushed the loo a couple of times, washed very thoroughly with mercifully scented soap, and emerged, she was feeling surprisingly good about what she had just undergone.

Not only that, the bobbed wig, pinned very carefully over her own hair, which was secured in a wig cap, hadn't moved a fraction. Lauren, capable as always, had picked it out and affixed it to Chloe's scalp: it was a medium-brown, darker than Chloe's natural colour, and a style so different from Chloe's that it transformed her face. Lauren had done her makeup differently, heavier than usual, lots of eyeliner: 'Very North London,' she had said, wielding her Barry M pencil with a vengeance. 'They're all fucking Goths up there. You'll fit right in.'

Kensal Rise, it turned out, was more yummy mummy, Notting Hill spillover territory than Goth Central, but no one had given Chloe more than a glance as she got out of the cab and walked into the café below which Clarity Colonics had its treatment room. After the near-debacle of Chloe's microdermabrasion treatments, Lauren really had thought of everything. Even if someone recognized Chloe as she went into the café, it would just look as if she were going for an organic chai soy latte, or whatever the latest yummy mummy drink of choice was nowadays.

'All done! Brilliant!' Sarika said, summoned back in. 'So if you lie down again, Cathy, we can get started on your enema.'

'My *what*?' Chloe babbled frantically.

Sarika's pretty face scrunched up in confusion.

'Your friend booked you the full detox,' she said. 'That's a colonic plus enema for your first session to really get everything cleaned out. Do you think you're not going to be able to manage it? I've mixed you up a very effective one! You breezed through the colonic . . .'

'Did I? Really?' Chloe had always been susceptible to compliments.

'You absolutely did!' Sarika assured her.

Chloe looked over at the bottle Sarika was affixing to the wall, filled with an ominously coloured pale reddish liquid.

'It's a great mix of herbs,' Sarika said enthusiastically.

Oh well, in for a penny, in for a pound, Chloe thought. *But I'm bloody well making Lauren come in for this too, I swear to God.*

She climbed back on the table, trying not to look too grim; she didn't want to make lovely Sarika feel bad.

'It's two litres,' Sarika said, 'but we'll stop at one and a half if you feel you can't take any more. Right, I'm going to pop this back in . . .'

How did I get here? Chloe thought, as her first ever enema started flooding slowly into her bottom. *If you'd told me a year ago that I'd be getting my face sanded down with salt and my bum cleansed out with herbs, I'd have burst out laughing. I really thought I was doing all right with all the pressure and the paps and everything.*

But then I started having fittings for my wedding dress and no matter how lovely Stella McCartney is, white puts pounds on you, and so do TV and photographs, and I'm not going to do any crazy diets, so when Lauren suggested this and said that everyone in Hollywood has colonics to get their tummies flatter, it seemed like a really good idea . . .

She wasn't going to breathe a word of this to Hugo. She hadn't told him about the salt microdermabrasion, or the laser treatments to remove her leg hair, or the incredibly expensive LA eyelash-growing serum developed by a leading plastic surgeon she had had shipped over. He'd be totally against all of it, thinking it weird and unnecessary. Hugo was blessedly supportive of her in every way; he thought she was beautiful just the way she was, was hugely proud of her charity job and her plans, after the wedding, to establish her own charity foundation with Lauren. It was one of the reasons she loved him so much: his mother had been famously beautiful, his sister was gorgeous outside, if not inside, while Chloe was merely a nicely pretty girl, nothing more.

But Hugo looks at me as if I'm a film star and a supermodel rolled into one. He always has, right from the first time we met.

And he treats me like a princess. Even though I'm not one yet.

It was a tribute to how much Chloe loved Hugo that the thought of him made her smile sweetly even while a herbal enema was being pumped into her bottom.

Belinda

Twenty-five years ago

Belinda was restless. The baby was moving almost constantly now, or that was how it felt; maybe he wasn't, maybe it was just that she was so excited to feel him, so hyper-alert to every little kick and push and turn as he rolled slowly over in her womb. She pictured him turning in the amniotic fluid like a little dolphin, doing lazy, slow somersaults, the placenta tumbling equally slowly in his wake, tethered by the umbilical cord. Warm soft red walls surrounding him, wrapping him in love, this baby that she wanted so badly to hold and cuddle and feed from the body that was carrying him with such care. She couldn't wait, was counting down the days to her due date: only two weeks, but everyone was telling her that the first baby took longer.

'First one needs more time to cook. Like a batch of biscuits,' the Duchess of Wexford, the mother of Belinda's best friend, Lady Margaret, had told her briskly. 'Not that I've ever baked biscuits, of course, but that's what Cook always says. First tray takes a bit more time.'

The Duchess was the closest thing that Belinda had ever had to a mother; her own had died when she was three years old in a riding accident, and Belinda had been brought up by a long series of nannies, her father having been more interested in hiring young, pretty girls than picking a nice, sensible, experienced woman to take care of his only child. Unfortunately, the inevitable consequence of picking young pretty ones was that every time he would drop back in from his tax exile on Mustique, he would seduce the nanny and then sack her when she got too clingy. Poor Belinda had to watch the process repeat over and over again as the girls passed from euphoria to misery. Every time they packed their bags, sobbing, Belinda sobbed too. And in the background, her father's secretary resignedly got on the phone to yet another agency to hire yet another impressionable girl who would, yet again, be dazzled beyond belief when the Duke deigned to notice her on his next trip back to Worcestershire . . .

It was the Duchess of Wexford who had brokered the marriage between Belinda and Prince Oliver. Oliver, at thirty-seven, was being pressured by his father, the famously overbearing King Stephen, to marry and produce heirs to the throne; Belinda, at twenty-one, was a beautiful, healthy, sporty girl from one of Britain's oldest aristocratic families. Her inexperience meant that she was easily swept off her feet by the charming, dashing and extremely handsome Oliver. Having been recommended to meet Belinda by the Duchess, Oliver had flown to Verbier, where Belinda was working the winter season teaching skiing: 'Lady W', as Belinda called the Duchess, had been careful not to say a word to Belinda about her plan, to avoid making the latter a bundle of nerves.

Oliver had wasted no time. Lady Margaret, who knew him a little better, had been instructed by her mother to bring him and Belinda together. Within two months, in what the press enthusiastically described as a whirlwind courtship – off-piste runs by day, and by night, fondues, hot buttered rum and dancing till dawn to Europop at the Farm Club, punctuated by its legendary ice cube fights – Oliver had proposed, and Belinda had more than eagerly accepted.

So far, marriage to Oliver hadn't been quite the fairy tale that Belinda had imagined during those dizzy, glorious days of her engagement. She had been buoyed up on a cloud of sheer exhilaration then, the world at her feet, adored by the media; Belinda didn't have a bad angle to her face, was naturally, dazzlingly photogenic, and her lonely, unloved childhood meant that she was pathetically grateful to Oliver for his proposal and to the Royal Family for their instant acceptance of her. King Stephen could not have been kinder, belying his formidable reputation; Queen Alexandra was restrained and poised, as always, but welcoming. The wedding was spectacular, the nationwide street parties joyous; over a billion people watched on television or listened on the radio as a radiant Belinda blushingly said 'I do' to Oliver.

And then . . . well . . . a wife is different from a fiancée, isn't she? I can't expect Oliver to treat me as if we're still on honeymoon.

Not that the honeymoon was quite as wonderful as I thought it would be, either. But Oliver's a lot older than me, he's so sophisticated. He's had lots of girlfriends. I must seem really young and silly to him a lot of the time – no wonder he doesn't want to spend every waking hour with me. We had skiing in common when we met; that's why we were together so much, we could spend all day out on the slopes. And sports were the best parts of our honeymoon in Hawaii – waterskiing, wakeboarding, kayaking, learning to paddle-board—

She smiled at the memories. Oliver had the physique and the energy of a man ten years younger; he was incredibly fit, strikingly handsome, effortlessly physically competent. Belinda had watched his lean tanned body riding the waves, balancing skilfully, with awe and admiration and disbelief that he was hers now, that out of all the women in the world he could have had, he had chosen her, a twenty-one-year-old who had none of his sophistication or worldliness.

She wasn't in a complete haze of delusion: she knew that Oliver and everyone in his circle was happy that she was younger than him because she'd fit into his life better, adapting to his wishes, and her youthful body could conceive and bear babies more easily. But that was fine with her. He was her tall, handsome prince, who'd chosen her, and she could ask for nothing more than to fit into his life and have his children.

She'd just thought that the actual process of making them would be a bit more . . . fun. Would last a bit longer. Would involve Oliver kissing her, holding her. Looking her in the face. Letting her lie on her back, instead of her front, every so often . . .

She pushed the thoughts away as quickly as they had come. There was no point in going over this again. Oliver only had sex with her one way, and that was just how he liked to do it. He was very resistant to any discussion of sex, but in the early stages – when she'd tried to turn over – he'd explained that he had a bend in his penis that made it uncomfortable for him to have sex at any other angle. It didn't seem like *that* much of a curve to Belinda, but she didn't exactly have much experience in that area – she wasn't a virgin, but a few fumbling encounters with boys of her own age at ski resorts or hunt balls, boys who finished almost as soon as they'd started, hadn't given her much time to familiarize herself with the male anatomy in an erect state before it was inside her, whipping through its business in a matter of minutes.

Not that Oliver takes much longer, she thought disloyally. *But I'm sure with time it'll get better. And he's been so careful about the baby. I did show him all that research saying it was okay to have sex when pregnant, but he said that my body was a temple to him now, and he just couldn't think of me that way until I've given birth . . . gosh, it's been frustrating! He's so busy so much of the time with all his projects, and we had such regular sex when we were trying to get pregnant . . . I do miss being close to him like that . . .*

She sighed, her hands wrapped around her large, curving stomach, a lovely round ball which she found hugely satisfactory. Belinda loved being pregnant, had loved every minute of it – apart from not having sex with her husband. Even though their sex life might not be quite as amazing as she had hoped it would be, she was hugely attracted to Oliver, and every time he slid inside her, it made her feel beautiful, desired, attractive.

And she loved, too, the approval she got from everyone from the moment the news had got out: her husband, the Royal Family, the Duchess, the country – honestly, the entire world. Images of a radiant, glowing, pregnant Belinda, more beautiful than ever, had circulated round the planet, been plastered on the covers of glossy magazines in every language. From the perfect fiancée, she had become the perfect bride and then the perfect mother-to-be. The ideal woman.

It's just a bit lonely up on a pedestal sometimes . . .

Nine o'clock in Balmoral Castle, and it was as silent as the grave. The tartan carpeting, the heavy oil paintings hung in serried rows from the dado rail above the papered walls, all cushioned any noises. Belinda had not really had a chance to form any taste of her own when she married Oliver, having never lived anywhere but her own ancestral home, where the décor was as old-fashioned as the interior style preferred by the Royal Family. If she had been asked, she would have said that she found Balmoral much too busy. The Balmoral and the Red Stewart tartans especially created for Queen Victoria were everywhere, on carpets, curtains, and upholstery, while the rest of the chairs and sofas were covered in floral prints. The walls were all papered in equally busy prints and hung with endless still-lifes of dead animals – stags, pheasants, boar, deer. To someone unused to the British aristocracy's eccentric style in stately home decoration, it might have seemed both morbid and overdone.

Belinda was secretly relieved that tonight was the last she would spend in a set of rooms almost entirely hung with pictures of bloodstained corpses. She and Oliver were due to leave the castle the next day, heading back by private train carriage from Edinburgh to Kensington Palace to be close to the Chelsea Hospital, the breathtakingly expensive private clinic which was British celebrity mothers' first choice to deliver their babies.

I hope it's soon! Belinda thought eagerly. *I know I'm not supposed to want the baby to come early, but I just can't wait to hold him . . .*

Knowing that she was carrying a boy was very much the icing on the cake, as far as everyone who surrounded Belinda was concerned. If the firstborn was a male, it meant that any awkward feminist issues could be safely shelved for a whole royal generation; no worries about having to reform the rule of primogeniture, no consequent awkward legal messes as the tail of the legislation whipped back and forth to cause endless confusion as the entire British aristocracy – and the Church of England – struggled to follow suit. Belinda had done her duty by the country perfectly so far. A boy in the womb, another child hopefully to follow: the minimum requirement was an heir and a spare.

But as far as Belinda was concerned, she had no desire to stop at two. She wanted to keep going, pop out as many babies as she could, turn the cold, detached atmosphere of the royal family into a warm, loving, caring one which would gradually soften her husband into becoming the man she had thought she was marrying.

Oliver had gone to his suite of rooms after dinner, saying that he had a headache and wanted an early night; *but it's only nine*, Belinda thought, unable to settle, to nod off in front of the TV in her living room. *Olly won't be asleep yet. I could just pop in and say I wanted to double-check when we're leaving tomorrow – pregnancy is making me very dozy, I forget everything unless people tell me over and over again . . .*

The truth was, she wanted a goodnight hug and kiss from her husband before she settled into bed. Pregnancy had made her not only absent-minded but more vulnerable, in need of even more physical contact than usual.

I do wish we could at least share a bed, if we can't have sex, she thought wistfully. *But Olly says he's much too selfish a sleeper – he starfishes across the bed and he's never been able to share with anyone. I do wish . . . oh well, no point dwelling, as Lady W would say . . .*

In her silky slippers and her belted cashmere maternity dressing gown, Belinda drifted down the short corridor between her and Oliver's rooms, her young, lithe body so used now to the weight of the baby that she moved with surprising ease. Staircases were harder, but even so, everyone was very impressed with how effortlessly she was carrying her child.

Posh people never knocked on doors: that was for servants. Turning the doorknob, she thought for a moment that the main door to Oliver's suite was locked, but it was just stiff. She had hardly ever opened the door to her husband's rooms, as he normally visited her.

Oliver wasn't in his sitting room: he was probably reading in bed. Belinda thought, her heart leaping, that she might even dare to lever herself up onto the high four-poster with him. Sit there for a few moments, put her head on his shoulder, kiss his neck. She knew that his parents had been detached, undemonstrative to the point of neglect; she was trying to bring Oliver along in easy stages to be more affectionate, but she never knew how her advances would be received.

The door to the bedroom was open. Belinda's slippers, her light tread, made no sound at all on the blue and red tartan carpet as she approached. And her gasp as she saw what Oliver was actually doing on the four-poster bed, her stumble and grasp at the lintel of the door, were barely audible either over the noise being made by Oliver and his companion.

They were both naked, their bodies glistening with sweat and what looked, to Belinda, like a light application of oil. Oliver hadn't lied about preferring to be on top, and having his partner on their stomach. But it was only now that Belinda let herself realize that the story about the curve in his penis had nothing to do with the angle of her pelvic bone, the interior walls of her vagina, even an attempt to find her G-spot, which Oliver had once suggested. It was absolutely nothing to do with a vagina at all.

Because underneath Oliver, sweating, oiled, groaning and grunting, was Simon, one of the under-footmen, his uniform in a crumpled pile by the bed. Two pillows were propped under his hips, and his outstretched hands were clutching around one of the poles of the four-poster so that he could buck back against Oliver as the Prince of Wales fucked Simon's plump, raised arse in a regular, rhythmic motion that was horribly familiar to the Prince's watching wife.

Only Oliver never says a word, barely makes a sound, when he does it to me, she thought dumbly. *But with Simon—*

'I'm fucking your dirty little common arse!' Oliver was saying, his eyes bright and delirious with lust. He had never looked as handsome as he did at that moment. 'Your dirty little footman's arse!'

'Yeah, fuck me,' Simon moaned. 'Your Royal Highness! Fuck me harder!'

'Filthy little oik!' Oliver said, grabbing Simon's hips, his hands digging into the young man's pink bum cheeks. 'You've been asking for this all day, strutting around in your tight little trousers—'

'Yeah, give it to me!' Simon reared back even harder. 'Fuck, I wanted you to do it to me all day – I couldn't wait for tonight—'

'You were fucking gagging for it, you common little slut!'

'I fucking was!'

Oliver slapped Simon's arse so hard that the whole handprint showed up, deep red: Simon yelped.

'*What* do you call me?' Oliver demanded.

'Your Royal Highness!' Simon moaned. 'Your Royal fucking Highness!'

Belinda couldn't move. Inside her, the baby stirred, stretched its limbs, began to react to its mother's extreme emotional distress. But every muscle of Belinda's body was locked in place as she watched her husband's hips jerk even more wildly, his hand reach out for something beside him – something he was lifting, throwing around his neck in a loop.

Is that a tie? How weird— Oliver's just put a tie round his neck, and he's grabbing it with his hand, pulling it tight – oh God, it's like he's strangling himself!

With a jolt, Belinda suddenly flashed back to the only sounds she had ever heard from Oliver during sex: a series of stifled little grunts, almost as if he were choking, which started up when – she had learned through experience – he was on the verge of coming. She had been shocked at first, sensing that those noises were wrong in some way; but they either had sex at night, in the dark, or somewhere there was no chance of her ever being able to see his reflection behind her. The one time she had lifted her head, asked if he was okay, he had quickly pushed her nape down again, indicating that he wanted her to lie prone. And he hadn't been choking, clearly, because he had come, and then collapsed on her afterwards for a few brief lovely moments, so she had learnt to ignore those occasional sounds, not wanting to put him off.

But that's what he was doing, behind me. When he was making those noises. He was putting a tie round his neck, strangling himself, pulling it with one hand, making his eyes pop out a bit, his face go red – oh my God, my God, what's wrong *with him, why is he* doing *this—*

'Oh fuck yeah! I'm fucking coming, Your *fucking* Royal Highness!'

Simon's own bum heaved, and a long-drawn-out wail of pleasure indicated that he had spunked all over the silk coverlet; he lay there, his body spasming, as Oliver, above him, heaved a loud grunt that was horribly familiar to Belinda, tugged even harder on the tie, spluttered for air, and shot his own load inside his footman lover.

Belinda's entire body was as hot as fire – apart from her skull, which felt as if the bones were an icy clamp digging into its delicate contents. A terrible shooting pain exploded inside her womb; her entire lower body was burning up in agony. Water gushed from her, splatting over her pretty slippers, over the tartan carpet, water that felt as if it were sizzling as it flooded down her legs. She screamed, the hand clutching the door lintel weakening, losing its grip as she collapsed over herself, crumpling to the carpet. That alerted Simon, who was more conscious than his self-asphyxiated master.

'Sir! *Sir!*' he yelled frantically, his eyes bulging as much as the Prince's, writhing out from under Oliver. The latter's cock slid out from Simon's arse, still red and swollen. 'Sir, it's the Princess!'

'What?' Oliver blinked hard, put a hand up to massage his throat, took a long, painful breath and then another, turned slowly to look where Simon was pointing as he simultaneously raced to struggle back into his uniform.

'Oh, *fuck!*' he said. 'What the hell is she doing in here? What the *fuck* was the silly bitch *thinking?*'

Those words were not quite the last thing Belinda remembered of that awful night. That was Oliver bending over her, a dressing gown dragged on over his naked body, a wild, savage look in his eyes as he hissed warningly:

'You just came in here and tripped on the carpet, okay? Nothing happened! You didn't see anything! Nothing fucking happened! You keep your mouth shut and don't say a word! Understand?'

And then a stream of people poured into the room, summoned by a screaming Simon; they were bending over Belinda, trying to lift her, as someone cried:

'The baby's coming! The baby's coming early!' and a pain so intense hit her between the legs that she mercifully blacked out as the first, vicious contraction clamped around her uterus.

Lori

'It's so beautiful!' Lori exclaimed, looking around the suite of the spa hotel in amazement. She still hadn't got used to living like a princess, she realized ruefully: she was always gasping at luxuries that everyone around her took entirely for granted. And Kristin's reaction instantly emphasized that point.

'If you like Sixties architecture, I suppose,' Kristin drawled, pulling her cigarettes out of her Damien Hirst-designed backpack, made for The Row, black shiny leather with coloured capsules made to look like prescription pills stuck all over it. 'I prefer things a bit more modern. But the view's stunning, isn't it?'

Winding her arm through Lori's, she strolled with her towards the balcony, Attila jumping ahead to slide the floor-to-ceiling glass doors open before the two young women reached them. It was true that the spa hotel had been built at the end of the Sixties, and its style had been revamped to echo that decade, but Lori loved the open brick fireplace, the sheepskin rugs, the transparent tables and the modular beige furniture: somehow the décor managed to be both fun and sexy. Each of the three young woman had a large suite on the penthouse floor with adjoining glass .balconies which gave sweeping views over the terraces below, the pool – now closed in the winter season – and the skating rink beyond.

'I wish Joachim could have come,' Lori said wistfully, imagining how lovely it would be to share this beautiful space with her fiancé. 'They're making him work so hard, it's such a shame . . .'

'What, bring your fiancé on a girls' getaway?' Katya came up behind them, reaching for one of Kristin's cigarettes. 'No way! It's girls-only for the entire week! We're just going to pretend these two don't exist,' she added, winking at Mihaly and Attila. 'They're *certainly* not coming in with us when we get our massages!'

Lori turned to look over the view, the cold clear winter breeze, high up in the Alps, whipping her skin, providing the perfect excuse for any pinkening to her cheeks. In the fortnight she had spent with Mihaly and Attila almost permanently by her side, her attraction to the former had deepened perilously. Joachim was practically never around, while Mihaly – younger, sexier, flirtier – was a constant presence. Mihaly was a million miles away from being anything like good marriage material, and that was what Lori wanted, to settle down: but it was like announcing you were going on a diet only to have someone cover every available surface with Charbonnel et Walker pink champagne truffles.

When we get back to Valtzers on Tuesday, I'm definitely going to tell Joachim I feel really weird about this, she decided firmly. *Not about Mihaly, obviously. But I barely see anything of my fiancé, we're not having sex yet, it's a month to the wedding and I feel really . . . disoriented. I know that Joachim and I share the*

*same goals, we want the same things: a strong family life, lots of
kids, a commitment to build a future together.*

Lori had come to realize that it was Joachim's deep sense
of responsibility to his country that had drawn her to him
more than anything else: she found him very attractive, of
course, had done so ever since she met him in London, looking so sweetly formal and poised and mature in the middle of
the wild Olympic riot of free love. *That's it*, she thought now,
*that's why I fell for him. He was so grown-up. And that's what I
want.*

The world of professional athletics – in which Lori had
been living since she was seventeen – was not one that was
filled with stable, faithful relationships. People stayed with
their coaches and trainers much longer than they did with
their partners; all the travelling, plus the intense physicality
of sport, made the atmosphere highly sexualized, full of
temptation. She had seen pretty much everyone she knew
make promises they couldn't keep, had found out that both
her boyfriends had cheated on her while she or they were
away competing, had become, she realized now, utterly
disillusioned with the idea that she would ever find a man
who was willing to commit fully, the way her dad was with
her mom. Joachim was not only solid, secure, but a king to
boot, which made him almost too good to be true.

*And the downside is that, right now, he's putting his country
ahead of me*, she realized. It had been explained to her that all
the new tax legislation, the pressure the G-20 group of
finance ministers and central bank governors were feeling
obliged to put onto tax avoidance schemes, were pushing tax
shelters all over the world onto the defensive. Jersey,
Luxembourg, the Cayman Islands, Swiss banks, were all
re-examining the strategies and techniques they had used up
till now to protect the companies and individuals who were

domiciled in their territories from paying anything like a fair
rate of tax in their true home countries. Herzoslovakia was
by no means immune to the cold wind that was blowing
worldwide. Joachim was apparently in intensive meetings
with his economic team to decide what, if any, concessions,
Herzoslovakia should offer the G-20 group: this was a critical point for his country, he had told her.

To be honest, Lori barely understood much of this. When
you were at an American college on a sports scholarship, it
was taken for granted by all parties concerned that you
were only expected to do the absolute minimum of studying, and Lori was pretty humble about her lack of intellec-
tual abilities. She was perfectly aware that, like Randy and
Hailey, she'd have attended the local community college if
her sporting abilities hadn't catapulted her to the University
of Miami, and she had been horrified, since becoming
engaged to Joachim, at her absolute ignorance of practically
anything to do with the world outside America. Europe's
geography, history, culture, languages were all a closed book
to her; going from one sporting event to another, the travel
arrangements were all made for you, and everyone spoke
English, so you never needed to learn more than 'please'
and 'thank you'. In her regular lessons on Herzoslovakian
culture, she was mortified to realize how minimal her
knowledge was of so much stuff that Europeans took for
granted.

*But what I can't help thinking is that, with all this economic
crisis going on, maybe this would be a good time to focus on
moving Herzoslovakia from a tax haven to a tourist destination,*
Lori had thought. *It's so pretty! There's so much to see! And
honestly, it's so quiet – it would be nice to have some tourists
coming through, visiting the sights.* So far, she had been sensible
enough not to make this point to Joachim, but she was

hoping that gently, in time, she could; had dared to imagine that she could actually make a difference to her adopted country . . .

I won't talk about this with him now. It's the last thing he needs to hear, with all these strategy meetings. I'm going to focus on spending more time with him – I want him to see me as the first person he can turn to, talk things over with. Then, gradually, I can start making suggestions, become his partner.

She nodded to herself. One great thing about being a professional athlete was that you were very good at setting yourself achievable goals.

'So this afternoon,' Kristin was saying, blowing out smoke, 'we will have the vinotherapy treatment. A grapeseed peel, and then we soak in the wine bath, in a *barrique*.'

'That is a wooden wine cask,' Katya said, giggling. 'So much fun! Wait till you see! We all climb inside, we have one each, and then you look and see all our heads which stick out of the top of the wine. It is so funny! The last time we did that, Kristin and I laughed and laughed. And then they massage us in Sauvignon till we are all lovely and smooth.'

'And then we go to dinner and drink a lot of wine,' Kristin finished. 'Of course!'

'I had no idea what you meant when you said "wine hotel",' Lori admitted to them, leaning on the glass balcony, looking down at the snowy slopes below. 'I thought it was just— you know, wine tasting.'

'We do not taste,' Katya said, winking. 'We drink! But yes, this is a lot of fun. I like the grapeseed peel very much.'

'Does it actually make a difference?' Lori asked naïvely.

Katya made a dismissive 'fft' sound with her lips.

'Of course not,' she said. 'For that, you need a doctor, someone to give you an injection or a proper treatment. This is just to laugh and have a good time. With wine!'

A waiter, who had been uncorking a welcome bottle in the suite, appeared on the balcony with a tray containing three glasses of red wine: Kristin and Katya, whooping, descended on him, handing a glass to Lori, clinking theirs against hers.

'We are going to have the best week!' Katya said enthusiastically. 'And then we will be home on Friday, and Joachim will have all his boring work done, and he will be so happy to see you back!'

'Sometimes you need to go away so they will miss you more,' Kristin said wisely, smiling at Lori. 'Joachim has been so busy, so serious, all his life. He is always working. Now he has a lovely fiancée, but you are living in the Schloss with him, so maybe he is taking you for granted, like men do. He needs to miss you so that when you go back he will appreciate you.'

Lori was nodding: this all made perfect sense. And certainly, Joachim did seem to be missing her during her stay up in the mountains. He rang her every day, even from Berlin, where he had to fly for a couple of days midweek; he chatted about what he was doing, showed a lot of interest in her anecdotes of cross-country skiing, learning to skate, and the tremendous fun it was to sit in a wine barrel and soak in red wine, something she had never even known you could do. It was a return to the days of their courtship, where they had talked and talked, and Joachim had listened to her more than any man had ever done – *and looked at my face while he did it, too, not my boobs or my legs.*

But it was a weird disconnect, all the same. Talking to Joachim, but not being with him. Having new experiences, but not with him. Enjoying what could have been a very romantic time, but not with him. Mihaly, handsome as a blond god, smiling at her with those adorable dimples every time she turned around. And this evening, Katya and Kristin, on whom, frankly, she had been leaning heavily for company, had both announced that they had period pain – 'we're always synched up,' Kristin had said airily, 'it's being sisters, I suppose' – and retired to bed with cramps before dinnertime.

'So sorry to leave you alone, Lori!' Katya had said, wincing and clutching her abdomen. 'You could always have dinner in the dining room without us – they'll look after you really well—'

But Lori wasn't comfortable with that, as Katya had probably sensed she wouldn't be. She ordered dinner served in the suite, curled up in front of the fire with a bottle of red wine, and sat there, watching the flames burning, the curtains pulled back to give a view of the snowy landscape by night, feeling, suddenly, very lonely. Lori wasn't used to being on her own. She had shared her apartment in Miami with Shameeka, trained with her every day, been part of a larger volleyball team and entourage – coaches, physios, nutritionists. It meant that she had had very little practice in entertaining herself. And Joachim was out to dinner in Berlin with German bank contacts; she could scarcely ring him and whine about feeling lonely when she was living in the lap of luxury at his expense.

So when there came a knock at the door, Lori jumped up in huge relief. The waiter had said to ring room service when she was ready to have the dinner plates cleared; it couldn't be him.

It must be Kristin or Katya, feeling better, come to see how I'm doing, to have a nightcap with me—

She pulled the door open eagerly, and then stood there, surprised, because it was Mihaly there, by himself, Attila nowhere to be seen. This was very unusual; the two young men were almost always together.

'Your Highness,' Mihaly said easily, 'how is everything? You are happy?'

Lori didn't know how to answer that question honestly. She hesitated as Mihaly continued:

'I may come in for a moment? Perhaps I can check the fire for you.'

'Oh, sure!' She held the door wide. 'That would be great, actually. I've never had one of these open fires before – we don't really have much use for them in Miami! It's really gorgeous, but I wasn't sure if it was okay to put another log on – I was freaked about knocking the whole thing over—'

Goodness, I drank more wine than I realized! I'm babbling! She shut up as Mihaly strode over to the low, square brick platform on which the fire was burning, a wide copper flue suspended over it to carry away the smoke. Beneath the fireplace, neatly chopped logs were stacked tidily. Mihaly extracted a couple, cocked his head to the side, considering his strategy for a moment, and then, expertly, placed first one and then the other log into the slow blaze, angling them into a tripod shape to burn most effectively.

'Perfect,' he said contentedly, turning to smile at Lori, who blinked at the sheer wattage of his bright blue eyes and sparkling teeth. She stumbled a little, her foot catching on a tuft of the sheepskin rug beneath her, and Mihaly was swift to jump to her side, catching her elbow.

'Sit down, Your Highness,' he suggested, easing her to the rug. 'Watch the fire! But not too close – there may be sparks. Here.'

He refilled Lori's glass and handed it to her.

'Thank you!' she said. She hadn't meant to have any more, but it was delicious, and the glass was so enormous that even filled to the correct level it looked as if there wasn't that much wine in it.

'It's good, I hope?' Mihaly enquired. 'I can tell them they must send you a different wine if you do not like this.'

'Oh, it's great!' She giggled. 'I've had quite a bit already!'

And then she felt rude, talking about the wine being great and not offering him any.

'Would you like to try some?' she asked. She meant that he could get a glass; there were a few on the console table. But Mihaly must have misunderstood.

'Thank you!' he said, with an even more dazzling smile, and, with the fluidity of a ballet dancer, sank to the rug beside her, hitching up his slim-fitting black trousers at the knees as he did so in one smooth movement. He reached out his hand just a little, a perfectly judged gesture which didn't invade her space in any way. In fact, when Lori realized that he thought she had offered him some of her own wine, she had to lean towards him to give him the glass, putting her slightly off-balance for a moment.

'You are very kind,' he said softly. As he drank, a lock of his silky fair hair fell forward, into his eyes; he pushed it back, but it wouldn't quite stay. It softened his entire appearance. Suddenly Mihaly was no longer the sleeked-back bodyguard, arms folded across his chest, hair severely brushed out of his face, but considerably less professional. More approachable.

'Mmn,' he said, raising his head again. His pink lips were stained a darker red from the rich Sangiovese blend, and as Lori watched, mesmerized, the tip of his tongue slid out to lick them clean. 'It is delicious. Very tasty. Oh no!'

'What?'

Lori was really beginning to feel that she had drunk too much now; her head was spinning, and she felt a good few steps behind everything Mihaly was saying. Or maybe it was the heat of the fire? Now that she was on the rug with her back propped against the sofa, she was closer to the fire than before, and the extra logs had caught flame, popping and flaring away. He was moving, leaning over to the table, refilling the glass: she made a small protest, but he was shaking his head, smiling again.

'I drink too much of your wine,' he said apologetically. 'I give you more. This music is very nice, Your Highness.'

'Oh, thank you!' Lori said. 'It's just a mix on my iPod. Uh, lounge music.'

'Very relaxing,' Mihaly murmured.

He handed her the glass, and this time he was the one leaning towards her. She could smell his Versace aftershave, warm and spicy, and see the smooth line of his cheek, silhouetted against the leaping flames of the fire. She took the glass, and his fingers stroked hers for a second as he released it; the contact made her head spin.

'You are happy?' he asked again, moving back a little, and she realized she missed him being so close; *oh no. This shouldn't be happening.* She looked down at the glass in her hand, found herself taking another long sip of the wine, more and more confused; when she was drinking, she had an excuse to look down, avoid Mihaly's blue gaze.

She drew that out as long as she could; but when, finally, she raised her head, lowered the glass to her lap, she knew that her lips were a little wet with wine, as his had been. Lori watched helplessly as Mihaly put one finger to his lips, touched it to the point of his tongue, and then – slowly, giving her plenty of time to pull back – reached towards her, and, very lightly, smoothed the tip of his finger over her mouth.

'You have just a little drop of wine there,' he said, so softly she found she was tilting towards him to hear what he was saying. 'Just a very little drop ... let me wipe it away for you ...'

His other hand slid towards her lap, and she tensed in anticipation, so confused she honestly didn't know what she thought was going to happen. Or what she wanted to happen. Mihaly took the glass from her unresisting grip, placing it back on the table, which meant he needed to come in closer, cross her body with his arm. And then he was shifting on the rug, turning to face her fully, his back to the fire, his arm sliding back to stroke her shoulder.

'I—' Lori began, in the most feeble voice she had ever heard coming out of her mouth.

She was perfectly aware of what was about to happen, but she didn't have enough willpower to stop it. The wine, the fire, the music, the sudden solitude after being so happily in company with the girls, and Mihaly's ridiculous, film-star handsomeness; it was a perfect storm of temptation. If Mihaly had paused, waited to hear what she was about to say, she would have managed to go on, to say that she didn't think this was a good idea, *knew* this wasn't a good idea; but of course, Mihaly ignored her faint attempt at protest – which, if she were honest with herself, she wanted him to do. She was young, she was by herself in a strange country, her fiancé two – or was it three – countries away? She was in an incredibly romantic setting, extremely horny from Joachim's sex ban. She'd had wine at lunch, a spa treatment followed by another glass of wine, which they'd topped up, and now most of a bottle over dinner . . . *goodness*, she thought, *I've really had way more wine than I'm used to* . . .

Mihaly's lips touched hers, soft as satin, tasting of the Sangiovese, his tongue, sliding into her mouth, even more perfumed with the wine. It was intoxicating, delicious, a fantasy made real; a stunningly handsome man, easing her towards him, his muscled thigh pressing against hers, his fingers now stroking her neck in slow caressing circles, making her arch her head back in sheer pleasure.

'You are so beautiful,' Mihaly crooned against her mouth. His hands slid down her back, pulling her even closer, and Lori came more than willingly, her eyes closed in ecstasy, reaching up to wind her fingers through his cornsilk blond hair. 'So perfect.'

You're so perfect, Lori thought, her entire body burning up now with the need to get as close to him as she could. *So handsome, such an amazing kisser, such smooth skin, such silky hair, such a great body* . . .

Her brain was desperately searching for any tiny little scrap of conscience that would kick in, make her push Mihaly away, stop his hands from sliding even further down her spine, finding the hem of her light silk cardigan, easing his fingers underneath, onto her bare skin, making her gasp in delight and arch even further into him. But it couldn't, much as she tried. This felt so wonderful, so exactly what she had been craving for months; sex with a man who wanted to make love to her as much as she did to him.

She was too far gone even to bargain with herself. There was no attempt at justification running through her mind, no 'just this once', or 'Joachim's been neglecting me so I deserve it', or 'I'm pretty drunk and I don't know what I'm doing, so it's not my fault'. Her body, frustrated for so long, had taken over completely, as her brain, sodden with fine wine, lay back, too exhausted from its months of hard work learning the Herzoslovakian language, palace etiquette, and adapting to a whole new culture, to put up any moral resistance.

'Such lovely skin,' Mihaly breathed as he ran his fingers over the back of her bra, established that it was front-fastening, and laid her carefully down onto the sheepskin rug in one perfectly choreographed move. 'So fair and soft.'

He was lying next to her, unbuttoning her cardigan, baring her chest, unhooking her bra; his head bent over her small breasts, licking them in tiny, practised flicks as she gasped and wound her fingers through his hair again and pulled his head up so she could kiss him. He had removed his sweater at some stage, and his chest, bare against hers, was as smooth as her own skin. Now that his torso was bare, the scent of his Versace aftershave was even richer than before. His hair, falling forward into their faces, was freshly washed with citrus shampoo.

He shifted slightly, still kissing her, adjusting his weight, tipping her so they lay on their sides, facing each other on the rug, their legs entwined, his cock pressing against her thigh, but discreetly; everything Mihaly did was slow, steady, seamless, undressing her and himself as easily as if he had done it a thousand times, caressing her breasts and her stomach, licking his finger and running it around her belly-button till she thought she would scream with the need to feel him inside her. He smiled as he felt her buck towards him, whispering:

'So soft, so strong . . . you are so beautiful, so perfect . . .'

This is unreal, a voice inside Lori's head said suddenly, even as her hips pressed against his, as she reached down to grip his buttocks and rub herself against him, moaning with anticipation. *This is like something from a romance novel. When does a guy ever actually say these amazing things to you? When does a guy keep telling you how beautiful and perfect you are? Or undress you both so smoothly, as if your clothes were just pouring off your bodies like water, without a single fumble or awkward moment?*

'Your waist is so tiny,' Mihaly complimented her as he ran his thumb along the waistband of her jeans, hooking the button open with one deft, practised backwards flick. 'So slim, I could put both my hands around it . . .'

Totally unreal, the voice said, louder now. *It's like he's not thinking about himself at all, only you. When does that ever happen? This is too good to be true.*

Huh. Wow. It really is.

Lori pushed back, sitting up, gathering the cardigan around her shoulders, pulling it over her breasts to cover herself a little.

'I'm not sure about this,' she said, and heard her voice now sounding surprisingly grounded and sensible. 'I mean, this shouldn't be happening,' she corrected herself. 'This *really* shouldn't be happening.'

'Lori—' Mihaly, undeterred, took her hand, stroking it, tracing his thumb around her palm seductively. It was the first time he had used her first name, and hearing it from his lips made her tremble with excitement all over again.

Everything he does is sexy, Lori thought, feeling herself respond to his touch, grow even wetter between her legs. *He's like a . . . trained sex robot.*

'Let me make you happy,' he continued. 'This is you and me, together, being happy. That's all that matters. You know I can make you feel wonderful, Lori.'

He raised her hand to his mouth, nipping, licking at her fingertips, making her shudder with desire.

'I want to kiss you all over,' he whispered. 'Lick you, taste you. Make your pussy wet and ready for me.'

Huh, the voice said. *He's upping the sexy talk to get you back in the mood. But it doesn't feel real . . . he sounds more like an actor in a soft-porn film than a real man . . . what is this, some kind of weird fidelity test set up by Joachim?*

Lori realized she was shaking her head. That thought was crazy, of course: but the fact that it had even popped into her mind showed that things were very wrong here.

'We can't do this,' she said, easing her hand away from his. 'We *can't*.'

'But you want to!' he said, his tone remaining as seductive as ever. 'I know you want to. I feel your body responding to me.'

Whoah, the voice observed. *He's hot, yeah, but I just got a major cheesiness alert.*

He reached for her glass of wine, handing it to her.

'Here in Europe, things are different from America,' he continued, smiling at her conspiratorially. 'We are not so strict with ourselves. We let ourselves enjoy pleasure, quietly, discreetly. We make ourselves happy in our own way. Together. Let me make you happy, Lori. Believe me, no one will mind. Everyone loves you, everyone wants you to be happy.'

Lori stared at him dumbly, hardly able to take in his words. She glanced down at the glass in her hand, tempted for a moment, and then placed it on the table; the last thing she needed right now was any more wine.

'The King is away, he's busy, he has many important things he needs to focus on right now,' Mihaly said sweetly. 'Let me focus on you. Let me make you happy. I promise you, it will not be a problem for anyone. Relax, let yourself go . . .'

His blue eyes were fixed on her, his voice caressing and sweet, the entire effect hypnotic: he reached out, stroked her arm, sending a delicate tingle up and down her spine. Despite herself, Lori tilted towards him, and he was quick to lean in, his lips softly, kissing her again, the tip of his tongue meeting hers, wet and seductive. Lori heard herself groan deep in her throat with the sheer need she felt to get laid, to feel Mihaly's cock inside her.

But even as Mihaly eagerly pushed his tongue deeper into her mouth, wrapped his arms around her, his words were ricocheting around Lori's brain. Her hands came up, clasped his shoulders, and then, taking hold, pushed him back, away from her.

'I really can't do this!' she exclaimed, and now her voice was rising, sounding distressed. Mihaly, deft as always to read the signs, was already nodding as she continued:

'I can't, okay, I just can't! This whole "things are different in Europe" thing – okay, I'm American, but I can't believe it's always like that here! I mean, I have a fiancé! You work for him! You work for my fiancé, and I just – that isn't okay, it just *isn't . . .*'

She was getting hysterical. Mihaly said swiftly:

'Your Highness, please, don't distress yourself!' He reached for his sweater, pulled it back on, smoothed down his hair; in a few seconds, he was the perfect bodyguard again. The fireside lover had vanished. 'You must feel comfortable, be happy. That is all I care about.'

And there it is again. What about what he *wants? What about* his *wanting to fuck* me? *His cock must be really sore by now, but he's acting as if that doesn't even matter.*

Which is . . . weird.

With fumbling fingers, she managed to fasten her bra and button up her cardigan, though not half as deftly as Mihaly would have done it.

'What you were saying,' she blurted out, 'it's really confused me. I don't know what to think. This whole Europe/America thing! It's like you're saying everyone's okay with this? Like, everyone would be okay if they knew? Or they *already* know? But how's that even possible? I feel really, really weird now! Like, freaked out!'

Mihaly was rising to his feet; like a gymnast, he could stand from sitting cross-legged without using his hands. He leaned down, took her arm, and guided her up to stand too.

'I think I will take you to see Countess Kristin,' he said, walking across the living room with her in tow, picking up her key card from the console table, handing it to her as he opened the door, walked down the hall, tapped lightly on the door of Kristin's adjoining suite. Lori took the card dumbly, again taken aback by the sheer skill and efficiency of Mihaly's movements.

He does it so quickly, but there isn't any spontaneity, the voice observed. *It's like he plans everything out in advance.*

The door to the suite swung open, Kristin standing there in a dressing gown, Katya visible behind her, sitting on the sofa; there was champagne in an ice bucket, a film on the TV screen, glasses in both their hands, a bright sparkle to their eyes that indicated that whatever period pain they had been suffering earlier had long since dissipated.

'Mihaly!' Kristin exclaimed delightedly for a split-second before she noticed a shell-shocked Lori standing beside him. 'Lori!' she added, smoothly adjusting to what she saw on Lori's face. 'What's wrong? Come in, come in – thank you, Mihaly, we won't need you any more ...'

Shutting the door on Mihaly, she ushered Lori into the room, brought her to the sofa, settled her in beside Katya.

'Do you want champagne? A liqueur?' Katya asked, taking in Lori's state of distress.

'Just some water ...' Lori mumbled, as Kristin went swiftly to fill up a glass for her.

'Darling, what's happened? You look so ...' She shot a quick glance over at Kristin. 'Do tell us!'

Katya put an arm around Lori as the story came out. If Lori hadn't been so drunk, she would never have dreamt of telling her fiancé's cousins that one of her bodyguards had just tried to seduce her, and that she'd been very tempted; but she was not only far from sober, but in a strange country, disoriented by what had just happened, and by Mihaly's very confusing words to her.

And certainly, there was not a shred of disapproval on either of the girls' pretty faces as the story came out. Katya kept her arms around Lori, Kristin held her hand. Once Lori had stammered to a halt, the first thing that Kristin said, frowning in confusion, was:

'So you don't like Mihaly? I am very surprised!'

'We thought you would,' Katya chimed in. 'We thought he was your type, exactly.'

'From what Hailey said about your boyfriends before Joachim!' Kristin added. 'She said you liked them sporty, blond, handsome . . .'

'Who doesn't?' Katya giggled.

'Did he do something wrong?' Kristin asked, frowning. '*That* is very strange.'

Lori could barely catch her breath, she was so shaken by the direction the conversation was taking.

'No!' she said, even more bewildered now. 'He didn't do anything wrong! I mean – no, it's not that he isn't really hot . . . but I didn't even – I wasn't – I don't – I'm *engaged*,' she managed to say with great relief, having found it very difficult to get to the actual point she was trying to make, since it was so strangely absent from Kristin and Katya's response. 'I'm *engaged*! I shouldn't be making out with anyone but Joachim!'

'Oh, darling, it's different here,' Kristin said sympathetically, squeezing her hand. 'Mihaly tried to tell you, yes? We are not bourgeois. You can relax, really.'

'Yes, very much not bourgeois!' Katya agreed, smiling in confirmation. 'We know your culture in America is different—'

'Yes, we understand that,' Kristin said. 'Many marriages, many divorces. Sometimes five or six times! Crazy! Here in Europe we try to have only one marriage, if possible, but we are more . . . *flexible*.'

'It's so much more easy!' Katya laughed.

'Much more easy! Fidelity is not demanded,' Kristin said, shaking her head. 'Thank goodness! But we must be discreet, that's very important. Look, Joachim is a lovely man, a great cousin, but he is very reserved—'

'Very repressed,' Katya added.

'A fantastic man, very responsible. He will make a great husband. A good father. But a husband isn't a lover, is he?' Kristin said, looking very wise.

'No! Not at all! At least, not with his own wife!' Katya said, which provoked a burst of laughter from Kristin. 'So with a lover, you are discreet, and you use protection so you don't get pregnant,' Katya advised. 'Mihaly will very much know that. He will take care of you.'

'You should get a diaphragm,' Kristin advised, looking serious now. 'You can't be on the Pill, because you need to have heirs for Herzoslovakia who are of royal blood. And you should use condoms with your lover, just to be sure as well, I would say. But hey, you can have fun! You are so lucky – a queen-to-be, with a rich husband and as many discreet lovers as you want!'

Katya nodded enthusiastically. 'That is my dream!' she said. 'When I am ready to marry, that is what I want!'

'Me too,' Kristin agreed. 'That is perfect, isn't it? The best of both worlds.'

They finally came to a halt, looking at Lori, identical smiles of encouragement on both of their beautiful, regular-featured faces framed in manes of thick, glossy hair, their skin flawless and moisturized. Lori looked from one to the other, so dazed by this totally unexpected flow of information and encouragement that she couldn't get a word out.

'You are very tired,' Kristin cooed, stroking Lori's hair. 'I'm sorry, it's our fault. It's late, we talk too much—'

'She needs to sleep,' Katya said, nodding. 'Look, her eyes are closing. Do you have an Ambien?'

'Of course!' Kristin said, raising her eyebrows in surprise that Katya even needed to ask that. Kristin went to the bathroom as Katya noticed that the water glass was swaying dangerously in Lori's grasp and took it from her. They were right. Lori was utterly exhausted by the events of the evening, overwhelmed by the degree to which the rug had been pulled out from under her feet; there is a limit to how much unexpected information the human brain can process, and Lori was beyond hers. Add to that the wine she had drunk and the physical confusion from her makeout session with Mihaly, and by the time Kristin returned with the Ambien, Lori's eyes were already closing.

'Let's get you back to your room,' Kristin said, helping her up, Katya on her other side; they made quick work of taking Lori back to her suite, pulling off her clothes, settling her into bed.

'Should she even take this?' Kristin wondered, holding the Ambien, but Katya nodded efficiently.

'This way she won't wake up in the middle of the night,' she pointed out. 'She's drunk a lot – that could happen.'

'Oh no, we don't want that! She will have awful thoughts if she wakes up in the middle of the night! I hate that! Here, Lori, take this little pill . . .'

Joachim's cousins were very thorough in the care they took of his fiancée. They made sure she washed the pill down with a full glass of water, propped her up on pillows, tucked her in, and turned off the lights and the iPod as they slipped quietly out of the suite. The Ambien did its job, knocking Lori out very effectively; she was quite unused to any sleep medication, so one pill was plenty. She slept heavily and dreamlessly, and when she awoke the next morning at seven, to the clear light of morning sunshine reflecting off the snowy slopes outside – because no one had thought to draw the curtains – she had a few blissful moments of clear-headed, well-rested tranquillity before not only the events of the night before, but the consequent hangover, kicked in with a jolt.

Her head jerked up from the pile of pillows on which it had been resting, her eyes snapping fully open. A further stab of pain shot through her skull at the full impact of the white morning light, and she winced; but Lori hadn't achieved a bronze medal at the Olympics without a high pain tolerance, plus the ability to make swift decisions. Throwing the covers back, she jumped out of bed, ran for the wardrobe area, dressed swiftly, and grabbed her coat and bag. Necking two Advil and grabbing a bottle of water as she went, she headed down to the hotel reception, thanking the heavens that Herzoslovakian hotels, like many European ones, required all guests – even its Queen-to-be – to submit an identity document when checking in.

The concierge on duty was too well-trained to show surprise at Lori's requesting her passport from the safe at a quarter past seven in the morning, nor at her asking him to call her a taxi. Ten minutes later, a cab pulled up outside, and Lori, nervous that Mihaly or Attila might be up and see her exit, was already waiting for it on the steps, her coat pulled tight around her.

The doorman had barely got the taxi door open before Lori was bending to climb in, shoving a tip into his hand.

'To the heliport,' she said to the cab driver. 'As fast as you can make it.'

Belinda

'Squashy!'

'Lumps!'

Lady Margaret McArdle, slightly shorter than Belinda, buried her face in her friend's shoulder and gulped heavily a few times, the most emotion this extremely well-bred aristocrat would allow herself to display – even under the highly unusual circumstances of being reunited, after twenty years, with her dearest, oldest girlfriend, risen from the grave. Belinda had flown in from Morocco by private charter that morning, travelling on a passport Rahim had procured for her in her adopted name of Hana.

'You are *awful*, Lumps,' Lady Margaret said into Belinda's sweater. 'You really are. We were all in absolute pieces at your memorial service! And all those flowers everyone brought! They made the Palace gates absolutely *reek* for ages. Nothing like rotting flowers for a really foul pong. I felt so sorry for all those poor rubbish men who had to take them away. They were leaking all over the pavement.'

She pulled back, having found a non-sentimental tack that would allow her to swallow back any lingering tears.

'You could at least have told *me*, Lumps,' she said reproach-fully. 'I would have kept absolutely mum.'

'I know you would, Squashy,' Belinda said, hugging her again. 'But it had to be all or nothing. You do see that, don't you?'

Lady Margaret blew a raspberry against Belinda's shoulder.

'I suppose so,' she said crossly. 'I'm still bloody cross with you, though.'

'Oh, Squashy! Pull your socks up and pour me a drinkie-poo!' Belinda said, knowing that this was exactly the tack to take with her friend.

Listen to me, Belinda thought with great amusement, as Lady Margaret gulped, nodded, and went over to the drinks table. *A couple of minutes back with Squashy and I'm talking like a major Sloane again!* Rahim, having been educated at Harrow and Oxford, had a posh accent too, but the centuries of privilege, the absolute knowledge of being a descendant of several of the most ancient titled families in Great Britain, echoed behind Lady Margaret's every word. You were born to that very specific accent, or you weren't; Belinda had never heard an actor who wasn't posh, playing a character who was, managing to pull it off perfectly. Like the nick-names, it was another way the upper classes put up barriers to social-climbing interlopers.

Lady Margaret was mixing two gin and tonics so stiff that a spoon could almost have stood up in the tumblers. Belinda stood, watching her friend with huge affection, and taking in the beautifully proportioned living room which ran from one side of the classical late-Georgian house to the other. They were in the back section, overlooking the private garden, with the central doors closed. No one strolling down Eaton Square, one of the most prized addresses in Belgravia, could have looked in and seen the two women – and more to the point, no paparazzo could have taken shots of them.

'I don't think this room has changed at all in twenty years,' Belinda said happily.

'Mummy had the sofas re-covered,' Lady Margaret said. 'Even she could see they were getting a bit manky. But that was yonks ago.'

'It's so ... *English*,' Belinda said with great satisfaction, sitting down in one of the overstuffed, inevitably chintz-covered armchairs, looking around her at the clutter which had accumulated over the years: Lady Margaret's mother, the Duchess of Wexford, had never subscribed to the less-is-more philosophy. The décor would have given a minimalist an instant attack of hives. Vases, bowls of pot-pourri which had probably last been changed when the sofas were re-covered, tissue boxes, and endless bric-a-brac that came under the heading of '*objets d'art*' in auctioneers' catalogues littered every available surface, and there were a plethora of surfaces. Issues of *Country Life*, *The Lady*, seed catalogues and *Tatler* were piled high on side tables and magazine racks, the only reading material available; like her mother before her, Lady Margaret had never seen much point in books apart from *Debretts*.

'Well, what else would it be?' Lady Margaret said briskly, handing Belinda her gin and tonic.

'It needs some smelly dogs,' Belinda said rather wistfully. 'I suppose Pongo—'

'Oh God, he died years ago, darling,' Lady Margaret said. 'It was a merciful release for all of us. He stank like a toilet by the end. Mummy should never have let him on the sofas. That's why they needed to be re-done, you know. And he got awfully bitey, too. Bloody spaniels never age well.'

'And Lady W?' Belinda asked. 'How's she doing?'

'Oh, pretty much like Pongo,' her daughter said brutally. 'Bit smelly round the edges and liable to bite your hand off. Campaspe's welcome to her, frankly. Cheers.'

Campaspe was the long-suffering wife of Lady Margaret's brother, the current Duke of Wexford, who lived at their country pile in Rutland – the Irish estates were long gone – running the guided tours, the gift shop, and the jam-making workshops, while simultaneously dealing with her increasingly unbearable mother-in-law. Appropriately, the Dowager Duchess lived in the dower house on the estate, but she was so used to being in charge that she tried to spend every waking minute poking her ivory-handled cane into every aspect of estate business.

Lady Margaret plopped herself down in the armchair kitty-corner to Belinda's and clinked her glass with her friend's.

'Here's to not seeing Mummy any more,' she said cheerfully. 'Ever since she had an awful rumpus with Queen Alex and she sacked Mummy as Woman of the Bedchamber, Mummy's too bitter and twisted about her lack of access to Buck House to come to London any more. Lucky me, I get the house to myself! Poor old Campaspe, though. She's definitely got the fuzzy end of the lollipop, having to deal with Mummy on a daily basis.'

'Squashy!' Belinda said, shocked. 'That's your *mother* you're talking about!'

She took a sip of the cocktail and nearly choked.

'Bloody hell, did you put any tonic in this at all?' she muttered.

'Lumps, it was Mummy who got you into all the mess in the first place,' Lady Margaret pointed out bluntly. 'She knew you'd barely had any boyfriends – she knew you'd fall for Olly like a ton of bricks. You always had mad pashes on everyone's dads, because your own was barely ever around and busy shagging the nannies when he was. You were like a sitting duck for a gorgeous older chap who was a prince to boot. She shoved you at Olly when she knew perfectly well what was really up with him.'

Belinda stared at her friend as these words sank in. Without even realizing it, she raised the glass to her mouth and this time took a long pull at the nearly neat gin.

'I feel awful about it, too,' Lady Margaret said frankly. 'I had no idea Olly was a shirt-lifter till you told me. I'd never have told you to go for it. We all thought he was the catch of the century. Well, all of us girls did.' She shrugged. 'Water biscuit?'

She reached for a Minton plate that would have been priceless if it weren't a little chipped; it was piled high with Carr's water biscuits. She offered it to Belinda.

'No thanks,' Belinda said, still dazed at this revisionist version of history. 'I never really saw things like that.' She drank more gin. 'I thought Lady W was on my side. You know, almost like I was her second daughter.'

Lady Margaret barked out another laugh just as she had inserted a whole water biscuit into her mouth. Crumbs spattered over her twinset-covered chest as she said:

'Oh, being her daughter wouldn't have helped, Lumps. She'd have thrown me at Olly too if she'd thought I was the marrying type.'

Belinda, who knew exactly what this euphemism meant, nodded to acknowledge it; it had been obvious since their school days that Lady Margaret's sexual inclinations were entirely Sapphic.

'All Mummy ever cared about was getting further and further up the bums of the Buck House contingent,' Lady Margaret continued. 'Being Woman of the Bedchamber and made a Dame – she was potty about all that sort of thing. If she'd been the right age, she'd have married Olly herself and knocked out an heir and a spare without a murmur about what he got up to with the footmen in the evenings. Shame she *wasn't* the right age, actually,' Lady Margaret added, eating another cracker. 'She'd've been exactly the right wife for him. Run his household perfectly, made sure there were always some tight-arsed little oikey boys for him to bum. Sort of like Madame de Pompadour bringing in mistresses for Louis Quatorze. Mummy would have absolutely *loved* being Queen.'

'Which I didn't really care about at all,' Belinda said sadly. 'I just wanted Oliver to be in love with me.'

'You were a soppy little idiot,' Lady Margaret said, spewing more crumbs. 'Mind you, you weren't the only one. We all had a bit of a sob when we saw you in that wedding frock. You looked absolutely bloody gorgeous, and you were so happy!'

Belinda took a long pull at the gin to avoid crying at this.

'Oh well, no point dwelling, as Mummy would say,' Lady Margaret observed matter-of-factly.

'I say that to myself all the time!' Belinda exclaimed. The two women smiled at each other, the weight of their shared memories settling over them like a warm, familiar quilt.

'Lumps,' Lady Margaret said, 'honestly, it's like I just saw you last week.'

'I know, Squashy,' Belinda said with infinite fondness.

'I couldn't believe it when you rang me. After all these years! My God! How could you *do* it? Pretend you'd died, just disappear like that? Hugo and Sophie were in absolute pieces!'

'Don't, Squashy! *Please* don't!' Belinda was beginning to realize why Lady Margaret had made the cocktails so strong.

She finished the rest of hers, the gin burning a heat trail down her throat. 'I would *never* have done it if I hadn't been absolutely sure that Olly was going to have me killed!'

Lady Margaret looked around her in an automatic security check, even though she had made sure the house was empty before Belinda's scheduled arrival; the housekeeper had the week off, the secretary too.

'Oh my God, Lumps, tell me *everything*!' she said in horror.

The drinks needed to be completely refilled well before Belinda had told her best and oldest friend the full story about Oliver's plot to kill her after the divorce by faking an accidental overdose.

'You were such a mess by then, we'd all have believed it,' Lady Margaret acknowledged. 'Not that you'd done anything deliberately, of course. But popping a few too many sleeping pills when you were having one of your wobblies – yes, we'd all have thought that was pretty much par for the course.'

Belinda shivered.

'That's why we can't tell anyone about me coming back to life,' she said. 'You're the only person I trust, Squashy.'

She hesitated, looking at her friend, a grown woman now. Margaret was as slim as she had always been, due to her years of hacking horses, gardening, and long walks; when in London, she never let a day go by without a brisk circuit of Hyde Park. Her face had altered as much as Belinda's, though in a very different way; Margaret would not have dreamt of resorting to plastic surgery. The only moisturizer she ever used was Astral Cream. Her sensible, pleasant face was already weather-beaten, scored with lines across her forehead and at the corners of her eyes, faint traceries of red veins on her cheeks, sun damage beginning to dapple her with small brown sunspots. Her once-blonde hair was streaked with grey, cut into manageable layers that were brushed back from her face, her only concession to femininity her navy-blue mascara. Margaret looked every year of her age, and utterly content in her skin.

Squashy's got older, but she hasn't changed a bit, Belinda thought. *She's always known who she is, where she belongs. Just looking at her makes me feel incredibly secure. As if I've come home.*

Lady Margaret shook her head slowly, digesting this information.

'Good Lord, Lumps,' she said. 'This is a shocker.'

It was such a classic British upper-class understatement of the kind Belinda never heard in Morocco that she couldn't help smiling for a moment, despite the gravity of the subject under discussion.

'I *do* know how much you loved those children,' Lady Margaret observed. 'Even when you were at your utter loopiest, they always came first with you.'

'I wasn't actually *that* loopy,' Belinda pointed out. 'I honestly felt like Oliver was trying to drive me crazy. I was on a ton of pills, of course I was! But you try divorcing your gay husband when you're not allowed to say one word about him and the footmen, the drivers, the waiters – one of them on our honeymoon night, apparently, I found out later – he sneaked out to shag him when I'd gone to sleep ...' She drew a long breath. 'It killed me to leave Hugo and Sophie. It really did. Poor Rahim's had to listen to me babbling on about them ever since. There hasn't been a day I haven't thought about them.'

'But it didn't kill you literally,' Lady Margaret said grimly, swilling down the last of her gin and tonic. 'Which is better than the other thing.'

She set her glass down.

'You can't tell the children, you know,' she said to Belinda firmly. 'What's done is done. You can't expect them to keep such an enormous secret. And you can't explain why you did it without pulling their father into the story too.'

'I know,' Belinda assured her. 'I just want to see them – and her. I want to meet the girl Hugo's marrying. I want to know the chain's been broken ... that they're marrying for love, that they're not making the mistakes I made ...'

Her voice broke; she scrabbled in the pocket of her jeans for a tissue.

'I just want them to be happy!' she wailed. 'I can't be there for them, but I just want them to be happy!'

Lady Margaret, true to her aristocratic roots, was not someone who found it natural to hug a friend as she sobbed about the loss of her children. Normally, her response would have been to pour Belinda another stiff gin, but her friend had clearly had more than enough of that already. So instead, she sat there, letting Belinda have her cry out, shoving a box of tissues across the table at her when she had exhausted her own meagre supply. And when Belinda's sobs had slowed down to the occasional bubbling breath as she blew her nose, Lady Margaret picked up the plate of crackers and handed them forcefully back to Belinda.

'For fuck's sake, Lumps, eat something!' she instructed. 'I know you're watching your weight, you always were, but you're drinking nearly neat gin and you need to eat. I've got some cheese somewhere, too. And I ordered absolutely loads of nibbly stuff from Ocado. Still can't cook, but one doesn't need to nowadays.'

'Ocado?' Belinda asked, confused.

'It's online. You point and click and a nice man comes round with it in a van.'

'What happened to Harrods Food Hall?'

'Oh darling, you *have* been away for yonks!' Lady Margaret was very happy to have distracted her friend away from the painful subject of her lost children. 'No one goes there any more, it's only for tourists! *Beyond* vulgar – you can't get quails' eggs in aspic any more, it's gone *totally* downhill.'

Night was falling: Lady Margaret clicked on some lights, staring at her friend's face.

'You know, because your voice is just the same, it's like you haven't changed at all for me,' she observed. 'But the surgery's jolly clever. Just enough so it doesn't look like you any more, though they actually didn't change much, did they?'

Belinda shook her head. 'I've got these glasses, too,' she said. 'Clear lenses – Rahim and I both had Lasik – but they make me look really different as well.'

'The hair colour, the eyebrows—' Lady Margaret squinted at Belinda. 'Very good work! It's like another version of you. Similar but different, as Hugo used to say when he was little.'

Oops, Margaret thought. *Made a boo-boo there. Mentioned Hugo. Unavoidable, really. Hope she doesn't turn on the water-works again.*

Belinda had accumulated a pile of tissues on the cluttered coffee table. She looked at her oldest friend, pleading with her eyes.

'What's she like, Squashy? Tell me honestly.'

'She's lovely,' Lady Margaret said with unusual gentleness. 'Absolutely the right girl for him. Worked for a charity before she met him. Wants to set up her own foundations. Sensible, down to earth, loves him. All the good stuff. Don't worry about them, Squashy.'

Belinda's ears pricked.

'Who *should* I worry about?' she asked nervously.

Lady Margaret drank some more gin and got up.

'Time to draw the curtains, I think,' she said bluffly. 'Light's going.' She walked over to the wide bow windows that over-looked the garden and started to haul on the tasselled draw-cord. 'Sophie's running a bit wild at the moment,' she tossed off over her shoulder. 'Nothing really to be done, I don't think. She'll settle down in her own time.'

'Can I see her?' Belinda asked, hope lighting up her eyes.

'Don't think that'll work, actually,' Lady Margaret said lightly. 'She's all over the place. Off in Ibiza at the mo, I think, with Toby and some of their gang. Mainly goes to parties, as far as I can see. *But*,' she continued, 'we're off to meet Hugo and Chloe tomorrow! Got an appointment with 'em about the wedding plans. You're my temporary secretary. Gave Emma the week off. Keep your mouth shut, put your glasses on, pretend to be doing lots of clever stuff with the iPad whatsit she uses, we'll be fine.'

'I can't *wait*,' Belinda breathed.

'Come on!' Lady Margaret stood up. 'We should get some food down us. I've got all these TV dinner thingies, practically live off 'em now. I'll put about six in the microwave. You need a lot of 'em, I find. Just one barely touches the sides.'

One thing Belinda really hadn't anticipated was how much Britain would have changed; she'd watched the TV shows, the news, in her Moroccan exile, followed the politics much more than she had when she'd actually lived there and, in a way, been part of it. But the day-to-day details, the Ocado vans, Harrods being vulgar now – there would be a lot that was surprising to her in the coming days, and she'd have to be careful, out in public, not to walk around wide-eyed, commenting on how different everything was.

She followed Margaret downstairs to the kitchen and pulled up a bar stool at the counter while Margaret extracted brightly packaged containers from the fridge.

'Oh, the latest *Tatler*!' Belinda said, seeing a glossy magazine strewn among piles of post. 'I never recognize anyone in it nowadays – funny, it used to be like our diary, didn't it? With someone else taking pictures to save us the bother!' She glanced at the cover. 'God, she's stunning! She looks like she ought to be on a fitness magazine! Can't quite say the same for him . . .'

It was a photograph of a beautiful young blonde woman in a pale blue ballgown, glowing with health, skin tanned, her perfect white teeth on display as she smiled widely in that open, familiar American style. She was leaning against an older, more stolid man who, while not unhandsome, was certainly not her physical equal. His smile for the camera was considerably more reserved, the expression in his eyes more watchful.

'*Amazing* jewellery,' Belinda commented, looking at the white, pink and blue diamond parure the woman was wearing. 'God, that's perfect for her colouring! She looks rather familiar, actually . . .'

'That's the beach volleyball player who's marrying Joachim of Herzoslovakia,' Margaret said, putting a bottle of red wine and two balloon glasses on the counter. 'Took bronze at the Olympics. Fantastic bodies, all those girls. Absolute poetry in motion.'

'Joachim? That perv?' Belinda looked at the picture again, recognizing him now. 'Eww, isn't he the weirdo who likes the really fat black prostitutes who wee on him? Do you remember that story? He'd lie down in this big shower he had – way before those things were fashionable – and they'd squat over him – two of them, I think it was – and let loose.'

'Gives a whole new meaning to "wet room"!' Margaret said, sliding containers out of their packets and piercing them with a fork. 'Lucky tarts, I always think. I mean, when you get paid to do something like that. They're just doing what comes naturally, they don't even have to shag him, and then they get paid a fortune to keep their mouth shut. Jolly nice job, really.'

She frowned thoughtfully as she poured half the bottle of red wine into each huge balloon glass.

'Like being a dominatrix,' she added. 'Always thought that must be a fantastic job. You get to tell men they're disgusting, flog 'em as much as you want, and then they have to clean up their own mess. I should try it if I'm ever short a bob or two. Did you read about that chap who wanted to pretend he was in a Nazi dungeon? I bet I could pull off a jolly decent German accent.'

Belinda giggled. 'I can just see you doing that, Squashy,' she said. 'Riding crop and all. This Joachim chap had a place in Berlin, didn't he?' she remembered, wrinkling her nose as the memory came back. 'That was the story – he'd pop over there every so often. That's where the shower set-up was. He had it built specially, I think.'

'Makes sense. He couldn't do it closer to home,' Margaret said dryly. 'The kind of woman he likes would stand out like a sore thumb in Herzoslovakia. They're *very* white there, and they want to keep it that way. I mean, look at the fiancée! Hitler would burst into tears of happiness if he clapped eyes on her!'

'She's called Lori Makarwicz from some small town in upstate New York,' Belinda said, now reading the article. 'The back of beyond. Some nice, pretty, American athlete girl. Gosh, she hasn't the faintest idea of what she's getting into. There's simply no way she knows that old Joachim likes to be wee'd on by two big black women at a time.'

'No,' Margaret said, even more dryly. 'I think we can safely say she has NBI.'

This had been their slang for No Bloody Idea for so long that Belinda recognized it automatically.

'Just like me,' Belinda said quietly, looking at the beautiful, happy, carefree face of Lori Makarwicz. 'I had NBI either.'

She thinks she's marrying Prince Charming. She thinks the fairy tale has come true. I remember just how that felt . . .

'Not like you at all!' Margaret exclaimed hastily, swivelling round to look at Belinda. Behind her, the microwave pinged, but she ignored it, concerned now that Belinda was going down a dangerous road. 'Look, Lumps, this girl's much more experienced than you were. She's an athlete, she's travelled the world, met all sorts, probably had tons of boyfriends. She *must* know what she's getting into.'

'But we just agreed that she *didn't*, Squashy,' Belinda said intently. 'She *doesn't* know what she's getting into. I mean, she's American. A nice, clean-cut American girl. She's *not* going to be fine knowing that her hubby sneaks off to Berlin to get wee'd on in a specially built shower.'

'Wet room,' Margaret couldn't help muttering as she reached into the fridge and pulled out a pre-packaged cheese selection tray.

'They're using her as a breeding mare,' Belinda said darkly. 'Like they used me. And once you have kids, they have you locked in for life. You have to stay if you want to see them.' She drew a deep breath. 'I know that better than anyone.'

Margaret picked her glass up and took a long swig from it.

'Lumps—' she began.

'And look at this one's background!' Belinda went on. 'She comes from nothing! Even with my family, and having my own money, I couldn't stand up against Oliver!'

'You managed to get a divorce and custody of the children,' Margaret interrupted. 'You didn't do so badly. I'm sure this one will be able to—'

'She's got nothing! They have all the power!' Belinda rode over her. 'They picked some little girl from nowhere who'd be dazzled by Herzoslovakia, all those pretty castles—'

'They *are* lovely,' Margaret said, feeling increasingly as if she were trying to stop a runaway train with her bare hands. 'Look, you should eat some cheese—'

'I'm sure he's done a huge charm offensive on her!' Belinda was drunk by now, and oblivious to Margaret's attempts to wave a large piece of Stilton under her nose. 'But she's going to wake up and realize that she's stuck there, thinking her prince married her for love, when actually he didn't at all! And honestly, Squashy, that's the absolutely worst feeling! The worst thing of all! Even *worse* than finding out he's trying to kill you!'

'Can't argue with you on any of that,' Margaret said frankly. 'I doubt anyone could, really, apart from maybe some of Henry the Eighth's wives. You've had a bit of an unusual experience all round, Squashy. But, that being said—'

'Someone has to warn her!' Belinda, her kidneys swimming in gin and red wine, pounded a fist on the countertop, nearly knocking over her wine glass. 'Someone *has* to let the poor cow know exactly what she's getting into! I can't just stand back and watch this happen all over again to someone else!'

Lady Margaret sank her head into her hands in despair, completely forgetting that she was still holding the Stilton until she got some in her eye.

Chloe

'I'm very worried about the whole street party thing,' Chloe's mother Eileen said, easing a crocheted tea cosy over the pot of tea she had just made. 'I honestly don't know how it's all going to work. What are we going to do about the raffle?'

Chloe frowned, looking at her mother through the serving hatch that divided the kitchen and the lounge.

'Why is there a problem with the raffle, Mum?' she asked. 'I don't understand.'

'Here,' Eileen Rose said. 'Take the biscuits, will you, Geoff? I made you the special walnut ones again, Hugo,' she added to her prospective son-in-law with a motherly smile. 'Your favourites.'

'Oh, lovely! Thanks, Mrs R,' Hugo said, perking up eagerly. 'I love those! Did you put the white chocolate chips in too?'

'Of course!' Eileen said, tipping her head back and nearly dropping the plate of biscuits.

'Love, you know you can just roll your eyes,' her husband Geoff said, grabbing the plate from her. 'You don't need to tilt your whole head.'

'I've tried, Geoff!' Eileen said impatiently. 'I even tried in front of the mirror after you went on about it! It just doesn't work for me.'

'I worry about you doing it when you're driving,' Geoff mumbled, passing the biscuit plate through the hatch to Chloe.

'We worked that out! I said I wouldn't listen to Radio 4 in the car! Honestly, Geoff, you do go on,' Eileen said. 'You're embarrassing me in front of Hugo.'

'Scout's honour, nothing to worry about here, Mrs R,' Hugo said, waiting politely until the plate was put on a doily on the coffee table in front of him, and then diving in.

'Have you got the serviettes for crumbs?' Eileen asked anxiously. 'I've just had a new carpet put in. Hugo, did you notice the new carpet?'

'Of course the boy didn't notice the new carpet, Eileen!' her husband said.

'I did, Mrs R,' Hugo said, winking at Geoff. 'Or rather, I thought how nice and bright it looked when I came in.'

Chloe was still wincing at her mother's use of the word 'serviette'. Her relationship with Hugo had caught her in a nasty clash of cultures. The vagaries of the British class system meant that, with her Durham University education and publicity job in London, she already spoke with a posher accent than the rest of her family. Chloe tended to fit in with whatever group she spent the most of her time with, adapt to the way they spoke and acted. It made her very suitable as a bride for Hugo – Lauren, for instance, would never have altered her accent, remaining a proud Essex girl wherever she went.

Lauren would totally take the piss out of anyone who looked down on her for saying 'serviette', Chloe thought ruefully. *But she doesn't have to socialize with Sophie and Minty on a regular basis. Not to mention the King and Queen.* She shivered at the thought of her new in-laws: Stephen was simply terrifying, dominating every room he entered, a cold, detached presence who showed no affection to his quiet, composed wife, let alone to his only son. Hugo's father, Oliver, wasn't much better, though at least Chloe had to admit, with great relief, that she didn't detect any snobbishness in Oliver's attitude towards her.

In a way, it's even worse than that, she thought gloomily. *Sometimes I think that Oliver doesn't actually care at all about who Hugo's marrying, just that I'm female and of the right age. Box ticked, that's it. Which is less trouble for me, but means that his father doesn't actually care about him as a person . . . just an heir . . .*

'Right! Geoff, take the tea tray through, will you?' Eileen said. 'But *do* be careful of the—'

'New carpet!' her husband, daughter and future son-in-law all chorused happily.

'You three,' Eileen said, clicking her tongue. 'Honestly!'

Chloe smiled at Hugo, who was beaming at Eileen and Geoff as they came through into the lounge. Geoff put down the tray, whose base was covered with more doilies, and politely waited for his wife to plop down on the suede John Lewis sofa, which matched the one on which Hugo and Chloe were ensconced.

'No need to worry about the sofas, though, with the tea,' Eileen said happily. 'I Scotchgarded them myself. It's very interesting, Scotchgarding. You have to do a fabric test before to make sure the fabric's safe to do it on, did you know that? I made Geoff tip one of the sofas over so I could find a bit of fabric sticking out and spray that. Then you have to wait for forty-eight hours to see if there's a reaction.' She frowned.

'Or is that hair dye? I just did my roots, so I might be confused about that one.'

'What's Scotchgarding, Mrs R?' Hugo asked, leaning forward to take the cup of tea that she had poured, just the way he liked it: one sugar, a dash of milk.

'Oh! It's my new thing! I did all the doilies, too!'

Eileen launched into a description of how the stain-proofing spray worked, Hugo listening with genuine interest. Chloe and her father exchanged amused glances. She had long stopped worrying about Hugo with her parents. After the initial shock and awkwardness of having the second-in-line to the British throne brought round for tea, the Roses had adjusted surprisingly quickly to Prince Hugo sitting on their sofa on a regular basis. It helped, of course, that the family were royalists to the core and completely unpretentious; Lauren might have a take-me-as-I-am-attitude, but Geoff and Eileen Rose had no attitude at all, just a refreshing inability to pretend to be anything they were not.

And then it turned out that Hugo really loves all the silly little details of family life – especially Mum and her endless redecorating. The stuff that drives me and Dad crazy is what he eats up with a spoon. At first I thought Hugo was just being polite, but then I realized he's been so starved of that growing up, he can't get enough of it now . . .

It hadn't taken Chloe long to realize that not only did she not have to be embarrassed of her parents around Hugo, in fact, they were one of her greatest assets as far as he was concerned. Her warm, cosy, loving family was a haven for Hugo, a safe place to curl up and simply be himself, free from all the pressures of his own heritage. He really enjoyed seeing how Eileen had revamped the house every time he visited; she was constantly altering the rooms, moving Geoff into what had been her craft room, shifting her sewing machine and crochet table to the back bedroom and taking the front one for herself instead. They were very happy in their house, a generous semi in a cul-de-sac in Waltham Forest, would never have dreamt of moving away from their neighbours and thriving community. Someone else might have moved every few years, but redecorating the house was Eileen's hobby instead.

That reminded Chloe: Eileen had been worried about the street party the cul-de-sac was planning for their August wedding.

'Mum?' she said, interrupting Eileen's detailed description of exactly how far you had to stand from whatever you were spraying with Scotchgard, paired with sweeping arm gestures that demonstrated the correct figure-of-eight action required to cover the fabric completely without going over the same spots again and again. 'Sorry, I know that this is rivetingly important info you're giving Hugo—'

Geoff snorted, and Eileen elbowed him crossly. They were a very nice-looking couple, Geoff enviably fit still, as busy with DIY projects as Eileen was with her sewing machine, and Eileen adorably fluffy and pretty in the layered tops she usually wore over trousers, accessorized with jewellery made by equally craft-conscious friends.

'It's just you mentioned there was a problem with the street party for our wedding?' Chloe went on.

'I'd *love* to go to a street party,' Hugo said wistfully. 'They look like so much fun on TV.'

'Ooh, they *are*!' Eileen's eyes shone with excitement. 'We have so much going on, Hugo, you wouldn't believe! Me and Jo and Sue – not Sue next door, Sue on the opposite side, four doors down. Or is it five? Geoff, is it five? Anyway, *nice* Sue, and me and Jo, we're like a highly trained fighting unit now.'

'Honestly, Eileen, the boy's in the Navy!' Geoff said. 'You shouldn't muck around saying things like that when he's fighting for our country!'

'I really do just drive the boat,' Hugo said self-deprecatingly. 'Honestly. I don't do any of the death or glory stuff.'

'Oh, Hugo knows just what I mean,' Eileen said comfortably. 'Have you had enough biscuits? There's more in the kitchen. Finish those ones, won't you? Not you, Chloe, love, you're excused till after you're married.'

'Thanks, Mum,' Chloe said gratefully.

'Don't diet too hard, though,' her mother said firmly. 'You've got a lovely figure. No one wants to see you wasting away to nothing.'

'I couldn't agree more, Mrs R,' Hugo said, smiling at his fiancée.

'Aww,' Eileen cooed happily. 'I do like to see you two getting on so well. Birds in their little nests agree, eh, Geoff?'

'If they have separate nests because one of them snores the house down,' her husband said. 'Naming no names.'

'I have a condition!' Eileen snapped. 'You *know* I have a condition!'

'What happens exactly at street parties?' Hugo asked, deftly diverting Eileen from her perpetual grievance at her husband bringing up her snoring issues. 'It always looks so jolly in the photos, with all the bunting and everything.'

'Well—' Eileen, as easily distracted as a kitten chasing competing balls of wool, launched happily into a description. 'We have the raffle, of course, but also the competition to dress up someone in toilet paper, one to see who can eat a doughnut fastest without licking your lips, the fancy dress race, the guess the weight of the giant teddy bear, the quiz – this year we're going to do one on the names of chocolate bars, that'll be very popular – the Pass the Parcel for the kiddies, the sack race, the three-legged race, the egg and spoon race . . . ooh, loads!'

'Excellent,' Hugo said enthusiastically. 'I bet I'd do really well at the doughnut-eating competition.'

'You should come!' Eileen said. 'Anyone can enter!'

'Mum, we'll be getting *married* that day!' Chloe pointed out. 'It's the street party for our wedding!'

'Oh dear! I keep forgetting!' Eileen said, distressed. 'Well, you see, that's exactly my problem! Geoff, pour me more tea, will you? I'm so confused. I think there's another cup in the pot.'

She looked earnestly at Chloe and Hugo.

'You see, this is the first street party I've ever not been able to go to,' she said wistfully. 'And I'm very worried about how Jo and Sue are going to cope without me. We *have* asked Sheila onto the committee as well, but between you and me, she's a bit of a broken reed. Honestly, you should see her in Zumba class.'

'What on earth does Zumba have to do with it?' her husband asked, handing her a freshly filled cup.

'She can't keep up,' Eileen said, shaking her head. 'No coordination. Just stands at the back and flaps her arms like a goose trying to fly. I mean, how can someone like that be expected to organize a raffle?'

'Would you rather be here, Mum?' Chloe asked, grimacing at Hugo, who shrugged hopelessly back.

She looked at her mother's distressed face.

'I mean, Mum, of course we want you at the wedding, but I don't want it to make you unhappy, either! If you'd rather be here—'

'Well, I can't say I haven't thought about it,' Eileen admitted.

'*Eileen!*' Geoff said.

'I'm being honest, Geoff! I'm being honest with the children! I *did* think that it would be very sad if we had the worst street party ever because our daughter's marrying the future King of England! I mean, I do get words wrong sometimes, but even *I* know that would be ironic!'

Eileen was panting a little with the vehemence of her words. A lock of her hair fell down into her eyes, and she pushed it back as crossly as if it were trying to grope her.

'We can't miss the wedding,' Geoff said. 'I'm going to put my foot down on this one, Eileen. I'm not watching my daughter's wedding on the telly just because you think Sheila isn't going to weigh the teddy bear properly.'

'Oh God, Geoff, she *won't*.' Eileen turned to him and clutched his hand. 'She *won't*. You have to take it to the butcher's and make sure he cleans his scales first – either she won't bother, or she won't be careful that he's wiped them down – she's *not* very hygiene-conscious! Oh my God, everyone's going to catch salmonella off the teddy bear!'

'I could take it to the Palace and weigh it there,' Hugo said swiftly. 'We're bound to have big scales there. Huge amount of catering for State dinners and so on.'

'Would you, Hugo? Oh, that would be so kind of you!' Eileen said, swivelling to look at him, hugely relieved. 'Bless you for being so thoughtful!'

Geoff, behind her head, shook his own and mimed his throat being cut to indicate that this drastic action would not be necessary.

'So you're coming, Mum?' Chloe raised her hands, the dazzling sparkle of her engagement ring still taking her by surprise every time she noticed it, and pressed them briefly to the sides of her scalp. 'My head's just beginning to feel a bit tight – there's so much to organize—'

'We're coming. No more to be said about it,' her father said firmly, patting his wife's hand. 'We wouldn't miss it for the world.'

'Oh *good*!' Hugo said with flattering enthusiasm. 'It just wouldn't be the same without you.'

'No problem, son,' Geoff said bluffly, and Hugo, who had never been called 'son' in his life before by his own father, smiled at Geoff so happily that Chloe's incipient headache dissolved immediately.

I'm not posh, my mum says serviette, can't keep a coherent thought in her head and once ironed her stomach by accident trying to steam out some wrinkles on her top, but I'm better for Hugo than any girl of his own class could be, she thought confidently. *I've barely seen a single happy aristocratic family in all the years I've been with Hugo. Practically all the parents are divorced, and the ones who aren't hate each other's guts and live in separate houses.*

That's what I can give him. Happiness.

She leaned over and kissed her fiancé's cheek with a spontaneity totally normal to the Roses, but completely alien to the royal family: sweet, affectionate Hugo went pink with pleasure.

'Aww,' Eileen said happily, 'isn't that— oh! Foxy! Here, foxy foxy!'

Her always wandering attention had been caught by something in the garden at the back of the house, visible through the patio doors behind the sofa on which Chloe and Hugo were sitting. She stood up eagerly, clapping her hands in excitement.

'He's back, Geoff! He's back! Ooh, look, he's found the food!' She clapped again. 'Clever, clever foxy! You see, he's eating the Sheba! I *said* he'd eat it! Told you so!'

She looked at Chloe, shaking her head, as her daughter and Hugo both swivelled round to look. Sure enough, on

Geoff's immaculately maintained lawn was a large, ruddy fox, its head bent over a bowl placed between the ornamental fountain and a large, imposing greenhouse.

'Your dad said foxes were dogs, not cats!' Eileen continued triumphantly. 'And that I shouldn't give him that leftover Sheba we had from taking care of Jo's cat! But look, he's eating it! He loves it! Clever foxy!'

'What I *actually* said was that you shouldn't feed the bloody thing at all,' Geoff muttered. 'Bloody hell, look at it gobbling up that food, eh?'

Hugo goggled at the sight of the fox snarfing up cat food, its long muzzle shoved as deep into the bowl as it could get.

'I've never actually seen someone – um, *feeding* a fox before,' he observed.

Chloe winced; Hugo's father rode to hounds, as his father had done before him; the whole royal family considered themselves fully fledged country dwellers, despising townies who sentimentalized animals in general and foxes in particular. She knew Hugo wouldn't breathe a word of this to his family, thank God: if Sophie ever got wind of it, however, she would use it to mortify Chloe forever more.

'Mum, *please* don't tell any of Hugo's family about this,' she said. 'They wouldn't understand at *all*.'

'Yes,' Hugo agreed, casting a speaking glance at her. 'It'll be our little secret. I say, he's quite a jolly chap, isn't he?'

The fox, having finished the cat food, was now approaching the patio doors, sniffing around and nosing up to them, trying to see if it could find a crack through which it could try to wedge itself.

'You'll have him hanging out in here in no time if you leave those doors open,' Hugo added.

'Sleeping in bed with us,' Geoff said dryly. 'Taking baths with Eileen.'

'He could definitely do with a bath,' Hugo said. 'Probably crawling in fleas.'

'Oh, Hugo!' Eileen said reproachfully, as Geoff sniggered. 'Don't talk about Foxy like that! I'm sure the poor thing can't help it, having to sleep outside like he does.'

'*Having* to sleep outside! It's a wild animal!' Geoff said.

'I do hope none of your neighbours has chickens,' Hugo said. 'I hear it's quite fashionable nowadays to keep them.'

'Or kittens,' Chloe added. 'Foxes go after kittens too.'

'Foxy would never do anything like that!' Eileen said, genuinely outraged. 'Honestly, you two can go too far sometimes. You can just tell by his lovely sweet face. Ooh, maybe he will come in! I wonder if I'll ever get to tickle his tummy.'

'I think it's a bitch, actually,' Hugo said, squinting at the fox. 'Her teats look engorged. I wonder if she's dropped a litter recently.'

'*Hugo!*' Eileen exclaimed, horrified at this casual use of country-folk language. 'Honestly!'

'What?' Hugo swung round, shocked. 'What did I say?'

Eileen could not bring herself to repeat the word 'engorged': she hesitated, trying to find a way to paraphrase it, and in that moment Geoff and Chloe swung into action.

'We should get going,' Chloe said, jumping up and pulling a baffled Hugo with her. 'We have that meeting with Lady Margaret and Lauren about the allocation of charity and veterans' places to the guest list ...'

'Sounds riveting!' Geoff said, exchanging a sympathetic glance with Hugo. 'And I thought organizing *our* wedding was a nightmare! Good luck, my son.'

He clapped Hugo on the shoulder and went to get their coats.

'Mum, are there any biscuits for Hugo to take with us?' Chloe asked a still-vibrating Eileen. 'You know how much he loves them!'

It was the perfect distraction: Eileen forgot about Hugo's inappropriate language entirely as she bustled off to box up biscuits for him.

'I've got some lovely new containers from the Lakeland catalogue,' she called from the kitchen. 'They have a *really* tight seal. Wait till you see them, Chloe!'

'Ooh! I don't know if I *can* wait, Mum,' Chloe said, earning herself an elbow in the ribs from her fiancé.

The biscuits were produced, Hugo and Chloe complimented the 'Lock & Lock' plastic box as Geoff rolled his eyes, coats were donned and more goodbye hugs and kisses were given than Hugo had exchanged with his entire family in the whole of his life. As soon as they were back in the car taking them to Buckingham Palace for the meeting, Hugo unsnapped the container.

'Goodness, your mother was absolutely right,' he said appreciatively. 'This seal really is very tight indeed. Impressive.'

Chloe giggled.

'I love how she can talk about tight seals, but you can't say "bitch" or "engorged teats",' she commented, looking wistfully at the biscuits.

'What'fff wrong wiff tha'?' Hugo said, mouth full.

'It's rude,' Chloe informed him. 'Body parts. "Engorged"! You said "engorged" to my mum! And "bitch"!'

'Iff wha' you *call* a female foffss! Or dog!'

'Well, *don't*. Not in front of Mum. I must say, it's a good thing that my family and yours have no interest in socializing, *ever*.' Chloe said with huge relief. 'I mean, they have nothing in common.'

'Your mother and my great-aunt Lavinia would probably get on,' Hugo said, having washed the crumbs down with some of the water that was always provided in the car. 'They're both very sweet. I think, to be honest, Great-Aunt Lavinia would have loved to have a life like Mrs R's. Much more quiet and domestic. She really doesn't enjoy the pomp and ceremony that much. That's why we never trot her out in public unless we absolutely have to.'

He looked a little wistfully at Chloe.

'You'll be fine with all of it,' he said. 'I know you don't love it, but you'll be fine with it.'

'Someone had to take you on,' she said, cuddling up to him.

'I'm bloody grateful that you did.' He wrapped his arm around her. 'I'm so lucky to have found you, Chlo. *I'm* the lucky one. It's not an easy thing to ask a girl to do, sign up for everything that comes with marrying a king.'

He hesitated, then forged on:

'I know you probably think that I left it a bit late to propose,' he said bravely.

Chloe was curled up in the crook of his arm, her back pressed against the side of his body, her shoes kicked off so she could stretch her legs along the seat; luckily, this meant that Hugo couldn't see her expression. She relieved her feelings by pulling a gruesome face, but her voice stayed even and cheerful as she lied:

'Oh no, it was fine! You needed to feel ready . . .'

'I think it was more that I was scared about what happened to my mother,' Hugo said quietly. 'She was so unhappy, you know. Went off the rails in a very big way. It's odd, because as far as I can work out, she and Pater really did have an awful lot in common. Both massively sporty – they met skiing, you know. And she did like the pomp and ceremony, by all accounts. She looked so lovely and smiling whenever she was out and about. Everyone who met her on official occasions said she was so happy to be there.'

Chloe could hear there was a lump in his throat, but she knew better than to comment on it.

'So that was why I probably waited too long,' he continued. 'Because Mater and Pater seemed like a very good match, and they didn't manage to stay together. I was worried that it might be the same for us, you know? I mean, if it was all the pressure of the paps and the foreign magazines and everything that weighed on her so much, how would we know it wouldn't be the same for you? I can see that it's a lot harder for women.'

It was the first time he had ever said this, and Chloe relaxed against him with the pleasure of hearing the acknowledgement that parts of her job were infinitely more strenuous than his.

'It *is*,' she said in heartfelt tones. 'It *so* is. You can just wear the same suit again and again and again – though actually, Lauren thinks you should be getting some made from Ozwald Boateng and Richard James – support a range of British designers, like I'm trying to do. Oh, and Paul Smith. But you know, even if you didn't, no one would remotely criticize you for it. With me, if I wear something too much, they go on about it, and if I wear something just once, they go on about that too! I feel I just can't win! And they're just *clothes*, you know? I have important charity stuff to set up, my whole foundation with Lauren – I honestly don't care about what I wear half as much as they do! Only I *wish* they wouldn't bang on at me about my shoes. I'd like to see them stand around and smile in high heels in the rain all day long!'

She caught herself, realizing that her rant had taken her away from the subject under discussion, Hugo's dead mother

Belinda; Hugo barely even mentioned her, and Chloe was on high alert now, wanting to tease out anything she could about Belinda from him. So much about Belinda's life and death was a mystery to Chloe: why Belinda had become so discontented with her handsome, seemingly devoted husband, when it had been so clear to everyone how much she adored Oliver on their wedding day; why the divorce proceedings had been so strangely curtailed, with wild rumours about non-disclosure agreements and gagging clauses; how, so soon after the divorce, Belinda had died in such bizarre circumstances, in an avalanche in an area not known for them, with a paparazzo photographer coincidentally taking photographs . . .

'Do you remember your mother much?' she asked Hugo, thinking that it was ideal that she wasn't facing him; men found it so much easier to talk openly about their feelings if you couldn't see their expression.

She felt him shake his head.

'I don't think so,' he admitted. 'I do have memories, but I don't know how real they are. People tell you things, and then you sort of trick yourself into thinking that you actually remember them. And because there are so many photographs and videos of her – I used to look at them so much when I was little – I think I've made up memories from those too, you know?'

He hesitated, then went on:

'The thing I'm sure I remember is all the crying and shouting. She was so angry with Pater. I do remember all of that. She used to cry and hold me and tell me she'd never leave me.' His voice got very small. 'And then she did.'

Chloe bent to kiss the arm that was wrapped around her waist.

'Not deliberately,' she said. 'She fought for custody of you and Sophie. The avalanche was just a horrible accident.'

'Sometimes I wonder . . .' He took a long breath. 'Never mind. Anyway. Poor Sophie, she doesn't have any memories at all of Mater. And being a girl, it was rougher on her, I suppose. I know Mater wanted to bring us up herself, it was in the divorce settlement. She wasn't keen on the way Grandpa and Granny did it with our father – you know, nannies and governesses and having to make an appointment every time they wanted to see their own parents.'

Chloe, who knew this already, still had to bite her tongue to avoid making a comment on how Oliver had been brought up.

'But that's sort of what happened, all over again,' he said sadly. 'Though Lady M was a real trouper. Did her best to be a sort of super-aunt. Visited all the time, talked about Mater and how much she loved us, all that sort of thing. Really pulled us both through.'

So what's Sophie's excuse for being a complete bitch? Chloe thought cynically. Still, having just left the cosy home in which she'd grown up, loved and cosseted, she couldn't help contrasting it with Hugo and Sophie's upbringing in the nursery wings of various royal palaces, motherless, making appointments to see a father who showed no interest in them even when they were in front of him. It was amazing that Hugo had turned out as well as he had.

But then, he was the firstborn, the heir. He was probably cooed over by everyone, with Sophie feeling that she was trailing in his wake. That can't have been easy for her.

Wait, did I actually think something sympathetic about Sophie? Wow. I must be getting really confident if I can afford to do that!

Chloe realized that she was smiling. She turned round, easing the seat belt around her as she did so, and reached up to kiss Hugo square on the mouth.

'I hate that you had to grow up without a mum,' she said. He kissed her back, hard.

'I love you, Chlo,' he said. 'I love you so much. Look, how long is this meeting going to last?'

'Oh, an hour at most,' Chloe said, reading his mind. 'And then we can nip back to ours.'

'We can pick up fish and chips on the way back!' Hugo said, looking blissful. 'Fish and chips, *The Walking Dead* and Gü key lime pie for afters! Can't *wait*. Honestly, Chlo, you have no idea how much I look forward to just crashing on the sofa with you, eating takeaway. Best evenings ever. Two nights in a row! How lucky are we!'

'If I have to watch *The Walking Dead*, I get two episodes of *Friends* afterwards,' Chloe bargained.

Hugo groaned.

'Oh come *on*, you know you love it really,' she said, poking him.

'It is bloody funny,' he admitted. 'I absolutely wet myself when Joey had all that jam on his face.'

'And then, I want a lovely long bath, and some *major* banana action,' Chloe whispered. 'I mean *major*. I want to do everything two people can do with a banana.'

'Sod it, let's do that first!' Hugo said eagerly. 'I'm *totally* fine with the fish and chips getting cold.'

'We can heat it up in the microwave afterwards,' Chloe pointed out.

'We are *so* married already,' Hugo said, kissing her. 'Apart from the having sex bit. Talking of which, when you say *everything* two people can do with a banana – you know that thing we were talking about the other night – I was sort of hoping—'

'Yes! I was thinking that too! Let's try it as soon as we get home!'

'God, Chlo, I must be the luckiest guy in the world,' he said. 'Now you've *got* to get off my lap. I've got huge stiffie action going on and it needs to go down before we get to the Palace, okay?'

Lori

Over the hills and far away. It was a line from a song she'd heard somewhere, ages ago, on a TV series maybe, and hard as she tried she couldn't remember any more of it. She could have Googled it, of course, but she wasn't turning any of her devices on. Not her phone, not her tablet. She was flying under the radar, avoiding the risk that Katya or Kristin might ring her and try to talk her into abandoning her precipitate flight from Herzoslovakia.

Over the hills and far away. It was in her mind because of the swift hop in the helicopter over the hills into Austria, looking down at the mountain peaks that were perpetually snow-covered, winter or summer, densely crowded together, the reason that Herzoslovakia didn't have its own airport. There were always helicopters for charter at the heliport; it had been a very fast process taking one. The only speed bump had been when the manager initially refused to take her credit card, assuming that he would simply send the bill to Schloss Hafenhoffer. But Lori had insisted. You couldn't run away from your fiancé and get him to pay for the flight. Not that she had said that to the manager.

And not that I'm even running away from Joachim! she
thought as she queued up at the passport control line at Graz
airport. Check-in had been as fast as the ticket purchase;
with no hold luggage to hand over, she had raced through the
process at one of the machines, printing out a boarding pass
and heading straight for Departures. *I'm running away from
the feeling that everything yesterday was set up – my God,
before yesterday! It sounded as if Katya and Kristin picked out
Mihaly for me weeks ago, when we went out with Hailey and
they asked her about my type . . .*

She realized that she'd started to shake: she felt weak
whenever she thought about the fact that Joachim's cousins
had set her up with a lover.

*Those girls! This whole 'we're different in Europe' thing! Every
time I remember what happened last night, I feel like I'm going
crazy! I don't know what to think . . . I tried to tell myself it was
all some kind of practical joke, but it didn't feel like a practical
joke . . .*

*Stop thinking about it, Lori. Just stop. Listen to your relaxing
iPod playlist. Over the hills and far away.*

She'd bought a ticket to New York without even a second
thought about her destination; she was going back to her
folks, not to Shameeka and the Miami apartment. She was
crawling back into the bosom of her family, with no idea
about what was going to happen next. Just that she needed
to get away from this messed-up situation, away from a
country that wasn't her own, which seemed, based on yesterday evening, to have an entirely different moral compass
from everything she believed in . . .

There was only one person ahead of her in the security
line. She opened her passport to the photograph page and
placed the boarding pass on top of it, an experienced traveller used to moving through airports as fast as possible; the

flight was on time so far, and hopefully she'd make her connection at Frankfurt smoothly too. Then JFK, and the next flight available to Buffalo. She didn't even know if she'd call her folks from the city, or just turn up on their doorstep—

The official was beckoning to her. She stepped up to the counter, handing her documents over, expecting a quick glance at her photo, her face, a confirmatory look down again and the swift return of her passport and boarding card. But almost as soon as the security officer looked at her photograph, matters took a very different turn. He frowned deeply, staring up at Lori, whose hair was hidden under a wool beanie hat, and who, makeup-less and pale, was not an instant match for the deeply tanned, smiling girl in the photo.

'Wait, please,' he said in accented English, holding up the palm of his hand to her.

Is there a problem with my visa? Lori thought, suddenly panicking. Everything had been organized for her post-Olympics when she and Shameeka were doing the watch campaign; she was sure that all her passport stamps were in order. Besides, she didn't quite understand the whole Schengen border thing, but was pretty sure that it meant that once you were inside whatever Schengen was – and that surely included Austria? – you could move around freely and didn't need your passport stamped every time.

Plus, I'm going home. Back to the USA. There shouldn't be any problems with a US citizen going back home!

The officer was looking over her shoulder, and she turned to see why: two more uniformed officials were walking briskly towards them, a man and a woman.

'You will come with us, please, Miss Makarwicz,' said the woman, smiling at her. 'We need to make some checks.'

Lori felt horribly like a criminal.

'What's wrong?' she said. 'I thought I had my visa situation all sorted out.'

'It is just a matter of a few checks,' the woman said, still smiling.

'If it's because I don't have an entry stamp – I flew in just now on a helicopter charter, you can check – they never stamp your passport at the heliports—'

Oh God, my voice is going up – I do sound like a criminal now, a really bad, panicky one – I'm telling the truth, so why is it coming out as if I'm lying?

'We will just ask you to come with us now,' the man said, and all she could do was follow them. They had her passport and boarding pass; what other option did she have? They took her through an unmarked grey metal door into a short corridor with what looked like interview rooms leading off it; they indicated that she should go into one of the rooms and take a seat in front of a metal table. Everything was grey, extremely clean, and completely neutral.

'Would you like a glass of water, Miss Makarwicz?' the woman asked. 'We will ask you to wait for a supervisor.'

'No! I don't want water! I just want to get on my flight!' Lori said, trying to tamp down the rising hysteria that was threatening to overwhelm her. 'I really need to make that flight! I have to change planes in Frankfurt – please, how long is this going to take? What's the problem? I can explain – if it's just because I don't have an Austrian entry stamp—'

She still didn't want to say 'Herzoslovakia'. It was such a small country; as soon as she named it, people would instantly make the connection between herself and Joachim, would wonder why the fiancée of its king was heading off to the States with no luggage apart from her handbag. The last thing she wanted was any scandal at all. Joachim had done nothing wrong. He didn't deserve that. She just needed a break, a place to calm down and try to figure out how she felt about him, about everything; she would freak if she were plastered all over the tabloids as a runaway bride.

But do they know already? she thought suddenly, her heart racing. *They called me Miss Makarwicz before they'd even had a chance to look at my passport! And the guy at the counter didn't say a word to them, he must have just pressed a button or something. So how did they know my name?*

Oh my God, what's going on? What the hell is happening?

'Maybe some coffee?' the man asked, ignoring her outburst of questions. 'It is the morning still, perhaps some coffee would be welcome?'

Lori shook her head, her brain now tearing along a very unwelcome track of speculation.

No way they're this nice to everyone they pull in for a passport issue. No way does the average person get offered water and coffee.

And they knew my name!

She took a deep breath. *Don't get paranoid, Lori. It's probably just some sort of glitch.*

The officials were leaving the room, smiling at her as they backed out.

Backed out! Like you'd do to royalty!

She bit her lip, hard. *Or maybe like you do to a suspect, when you don't want to turn your back on them. Though goodness knows what they suspect me of . . .*

There was a hubbub in the corridor now, further down; doors slamming, feet tapping quickly along the linoleum floor, voices talking swiftly in German. Lori didn't speak the language, had no idea what was being said, but was sure that she heard her name at least a couple of times; she couldn't stay sitting there in this mess of uncertainty and nervous

confusion. She jumped to her feet, staring at the open doorway of the interview room; the two security officials hadn't
closed it behind them, which surely indicated that they
couldn't seriously be thinking of her as a suspect.

Which means . . .

'Lori! Darling Lori! Oh my dear, my dear! Where is she –
in there? Lori! What is *happening?*'

The Dowager Queen of Herzoslovakia swept through the
door, holding her small, gloved hands out to her son's fiancée.
She was wearing a floor-length fur coat, which, on her short
stocky figure, made her look like a small furry animal standing on its hind legs, her black-gloved hands the outstretched
paws. An otter, perhaps. Or a beaver.

'Lori! Here you are, in this horrible room! Oh my darling,
what is happening? I don't understand!'

Without a moment of hesitation, she glided right up to
Lori, who towered over her. The Dowager's outstretched
arms wrapped, as much as they could, around Lori's torso,
pulling her into an embrace, her tightly coiffed ash-blonde
curls resting on Lori's breast. The Dowager hardly ever
hugged Lori, or anyone. She preferred to limit herself to
kisses on the cheek, arm pats, hand-holding. This display of
physical expression made the older woman seem suddenly
human. Lori looked down at her scalp, noticing the thinning
hair carefully disguised by the elaborate coiffure, the pink,
vulnerable skin under the teased, roller-set hairstyle, and she
felt a lump in her throat. She hugged Joachim's mother back,
the fur coat oily and sleek beneath her hands.

The Dowager tilted her head back, her eyes bright and
beady as she took in Lori's pinched, tense face.

'Darling! Tell me what has happened. Sit down. Look, I
will shut the door . . .'

She bustled over to the door of the interview room,

closing it firmly, coming back to sit down in one of the metal chairs; she patted the seat of the one beside her.

'Sit!' she repeated. 'Please, Lori, you must tell me everything. I am so worried for you and Joachim.'

'How did you know I was here?' Lori sat down; she couldn't stand, towering, over the tiny, seated Dowager.

'A problem with the stamps on your passport,' the Dowager said smoothly. 'You have entry for Herzoslovakia, but no exit. They were confused, so they want to talk to the Herzoslovakian passport control, and of course, that office called me immediately to find out where you were because it was all so strange for you to be in Graz, leaving for America. Leaving for America!' she repeated, shaking her head. 'How is this possible? I call Joachim, of course, in Berlin, to see if you have had a fight, and he is horrified, he says nothing has happened, nothing at all! And I ring the hotel – by now, I am already about to take the helicopter, my dear – and they say you have left.'

She raised one hand and placed it over her heart.

'I think I will have a heart attack!' she said, breathlessly. 'I know it is true, you are in Graz! I am just so lucky that I get here before you leave!'

Really? Because it feels like they were holding me here until you arrived . . .

'You must do exactly what you want, what you choose,' the Dowager said, reading Lori's mind with unnerving accuracy. 'If you want to go, to leave us, then you must go. Any time you want. You must be free. But please, Lori, make me understand *why*. We love you so much, we have taken you into our hearts. My son loves you, he brought you to our country and it has made us all so happy to meet you and to love you too. You *must* tell me why we are here, in this horrible room, like prisoners!'

She cast a glance around the grey metal room and shuddered.

Lori took a deep breath. Hearing that she was free to go was a huge weight off her mind; her whole body relaxed. Of course she knew that no one was going to hold her by force in Austria, or drag her onto a helicopter back to Valtzers, but knowing something and hearing the Dowager say it so clearly were two different things. She felt her back sag into the metal back of the chair, felt, too, tears pricking at her eyes.

'I'm embarrassed,' she heard herself blurt out. 'I'm embarrassed to tell you.'

'This horrible room!' the Dowager said, grimacing. 'It's like I am the interrogator! I would so like to be in my cosy study, with you, drinking tea, and so nice and comfortable that you feel you can say anything. But we must stay here. You must not come back till you feel ready.'

Lori nodded slowly, feeling even better. And better seemed to be synonymous with exhausted; the weight of last night's events, and her precipitate flight, had been a huge burden, and now that she was being reassured rather than coerced, she felt a wave of exhaustion sweeping over her.

'Do you hate us, Lori?' The Dowager reached out one small, gloved hand and tentatively took Lori's. 'Is it Herzoslovakia that you hate? Our life, our country, maybe is very small to you after America. You cannot stay where the place does not make you happy.'

'Oh no!' Lori's fingers closed around the Dowager's in instant reassurance. 'No, I love Herzoslovakia! You know that! It's the most beautiful place I've ever been. I've been doing outdoor runs and every new trail in the woods, there are the most gorgeous views – it's like paradise. And the people are so lovely too—'

'You have learnt the language very well,' the Dowager said encouragingly. 'I hear you speak Herzoslovakian now in shops! Everyone is very impressed with you, so excited for the wedding, so happy to have you as the new Queen—'

She caught herself, her voice breaking. Her head ducked; she scrabbled, with uncustomary inelegance, in the pocket of her coat, which was so voluminous that it took her some time to find the opening in its folds. Eventually, she produced a linen, lace-trimmed handkerchief with which she dabbed her eyes.

'I'm so sorry,' she whispered. 'I just need a little moment. I don't want to put on pressure. But my heart is breaking a little, for you and Joachim. All I want is for you both to be happy . . .'

Lori thought her heart might be breaking a little too. *What was I thinking, just running away like this? I owe everyone much more than that, after the wonderful way they've taken me into their country, made me feel so welcome from the very first moment! You hear all sorts of terrible mother-in-law stories, but the Dowager has been nothing but lovely to me.*

She deserves better than this.

'I'm so sorry,' she said, both her hands now wrapped around the older woman's tiny one. 'I'm *so* sorry. Look, I can't promise anything – I feel so confused and messed up – but you're right, this room is nasty. Can we – if I say I might want to leave afterwards – but can we go back to the Schloss, and sit down in your room, like you said, with some tea – and I'll try to tell you what happened . . .'

The Dowager was already rising to her feet with impressive sprightliness, especially considering that the coat must weigh at least a stone.

'I have a helicopter waiting,' she said happily. 'We will be home very soon, and then you must tell me *everything.*'

*   *   *

This, however, was easier said than done. Once ensconced in the Dowager's pretty little silk-walled study in one of the turrets of Schloss Hafenhoffer, it took a long time for Joachim's mother to coax the full story from a halting, morti-fied Lori. But it *was* the full story: Lori was determined not to lie or shade the truth. Yes, it was awkward and embarrass-ing to tell your fiancé's mother that you had been tempted into making out with your bodyguard, but matters were at such a crisis that Lori couldn't avoid that part of the story. If the Dowager were appalled, disgusted by her behaviour, then Lori deserved every ounce of condemnation that could be poured on her head. Lori wasn't making any excuse for herself, not at all, but she *did* want the Dowager to under-stand how lonely she had felt with Joachim so absent, to realize that this wasn't Lori's idea of a marriage, and that the lack of physical contact, too, had made her so very vulnerable . . .

She stumbled and stammered through the tale, with plenty of pauses for tears, sips of tea, and bites of lemon tuile biscuits; mostly, she looked down at her lap and out of the turret window beside her, at the view of Valtzers and the river below, sparkling in the winter sun. She was too ashamed to meet the Dowager's eye.

But the Dowager was nothing but sweet, encouraging, and, crucially, unshockable. Lori found herself relaxing, surprisingly, and feeling a definite echo of her relationship with her beloved grandmother, who also possessed a surpris-ing knowledge of how the world worked behind her fluffy, cardiganed exterior. The Dowager said very little, giving Lori all the time and space she needed, but every word she did speak was to the point. Lori mentioned Joachim's busy work schedule, and the Dowager agreed that it was too much for a bridegroom-to-be. Lori alluded, as tactfully as she could, to needing more intimacy, and the Dowager said that the physical aspects of marriage were crucial. Lori reached the point where she and Mihaly were on the sheepskin rug, and the Dowager murmured that everyone was human and to forgive was divine.

In fact, the Dowager's wrath was entirely reserved for Katya and Kristin. She was deeply, profoundly shocked at their conduct and their total lack of morals. She could assure Lori that the girls' glib comparisons of Europe versus America were merely that, glib and shallow and utterly unprincipled.

'I am afraid that they are not fit company for you, Lori my dear,' she said, shaking her head. 'I knew they were young and frivolous, but I did not realize that they were so . . . I do not know the word in English, but it is like "loose". I did not know that they were so *loose*.' The disdain the Dowager managed to invest in this word was impressive. 'Their parents are not together,' she added. 'Not divorced. Our family does not allow divorce. But it was not a good marriage. Both of them have many affairs, are very wild. What the girls have done is very wrong, but they have not learned the right way from their mother and their father. Not like you.'

She nodded in approval of Lori's family.

'Your mother and your father, such nice people. A very strong marriage. Good morals, you can see that. And from good morals, a strong family, comes a good girl like you.'

'I don't *feel* very good right now!' Lori sobbed. 'I feel like the worst person in the world! And so *confused*!'

'Lori, my darling,' the Dowager said gently, 'you are a very sweet and lovely girl, and you know whose fault I think this problem is? Mine. First of all, mine.'

'*Yours?*' Lori stared at Joachim's mother in shock, the tear-soaked handkerchief dropping to her lap.

'I brought Joachim up on my own,' the Dowager said, setting down her tea cup, fixing Lori with a steady gaze. 'It was a difficult time with his father dying so young. I was the regent of the country till Joachim came of age. And he had to be a man very young. It is good for Herzoslovakia. Joachim is strong, firm, a good king. But for the modern young woman, it is different. You want what I think they call a partner – that's correct?'

Lori nodded, blowing her nose.

'Joachim maybe does not know how to be that,' the Dowager said. 'Always I tell him he must be strong, he has to stand on his own. Not to cry for his father, but to become the king to rule his country. And he has no brothers or sisters to help to carry the weight, to play with and have fun. So now, it is hard for him to show his feelings, to ask for help. He feels he has all the weight and responsibility of Herzoslovakia on his shoulders.'

'I don't know if I could help with that,' Lori said feebly. 'I mean, I'm an athlete, not an International Relations graduate—'

The Dowager swept that objection away with a flick of her hand.

'You have brains,' she said. 'You are learning our language, you know just what to say at press conferences. You are a very good partner for Joachim. But he must let you join, explain things to you. Do you know why he is working so hard? Yes, to make your honeymoon without problems, so you can relax together without stress, as you should. But do you understand the details?'

'I know it's about Herzoslovakia's status as a tax haven,' Lori said.

'We have no industry,' the Dowager said sadly. 'We are such a small country. You know, we are very proud of our independence, our own language. But when Joachim's ancestors fought for Herzoslovakia, for its borders, they were . . .' She searched for the word. 'Like pirates. Wild. They thought of their castles, of defending them. They did not think that they needed land big enough for factories, for an airport. And our country is very beautiful, but for tourism, for film companies, it is hard for many people to come without an airport! So—' she spread her hands – 'we become a tax haven. It is very pretty here, and rich people can come with helicopters, they do not mind that there is no airport. And now there are big scandals with the tax avoidance, the European Union is making changes. And we are very worried! Monaco has the seaside, its yachts, the Grand Prix car race. Jersey is an island, they have tourism, they have farms. But us – even our mountains are too steep for skiing! What can we do? We want to help, to talk to the EU, to make things fairer for people. But we are frightened to lose our living as well.'

Lori was nodding earnestly by now.

'I really wish Joachim had talked to me like this,' she said. 'I mean, I knew bits and pieces, but it does help when you say it all clearly like that.'

The Dowager smiled at her. 'I said it was my fault, but it is my son's fault too,' she said gently. 'He is a very good man, a very good King, but he has been a bad fiancé. He needs to learn how to be a good one.'

'*I've* been a bad fiancée!' Lori was crying again. 'You're being too nice to me – I made out with someone else, and I'm engaged to your son – you ought to be so much crosser with me.'

'Why would I want to make you feel bad, when you are so busy doing it for yourself?' the Dowager said, raising her eyebrows sympathetically. 'My dear, Joachim neglected you. For the best of reasons, to try to make all the work and business disappear for your honeymoon, but still, he should have been with you much more. You cannot just propose to a young woman and then put her—' she searched for a metaphor – 'put her in the refrigerator until you marry her! I should have seen this too, realized that he is not spending enough time with you.'

Put in the refrigerator summed up so perfectly how Lori felt that she heaved a gasping sob of relief; it wasn't just that the Dowager was forgiving her, it was that she *understood*.

'You are in a strange country, far from your family,' the Dowager was continuing. 'And you were so upset when you kissed Mihaly that you tried to run away because you felt guilty. This is not how a bad girl behaves. Please. Forgive us for not taking care of you as we promised your parents, for making you feel so lonely here with us.'

The phone on the Dowager's desk shrilled a ring; she picked it up, said a few words in Herzoslovakian, and then, turning to Lori, asked tenderly:

'Lori, my son is here. He has flown straight back from Berlin. May I tell him that you will agree to see him, to talk to him? Believe me, he will understand everything, feel that it is we who are to blame ...'

Lori's cheeks were flaming red.

'I'm so embarrassed!' she muttered, hiding her face in her hands. 'He's been working really hard, and I've just been doing nothing but get into a mess ...'

The Dowager spoke a couple more words into the phone, and hung up.

'You will start again, both of you,' she said. 'And now it will be better.'

'Lori!'

The door burst open. Joachim, panting, stood there, in jeans and a sweater, his hair rumpled, looking as if he had run all the way from the heliport; exercise and more informal clothing suited him, brought a flattering colour to his face, brought out the blue of his eyes. He looked from his mother to his fiancée; Lori hung her head, feeling mortified by what she had to tell him.

'I will leave you two alone,' the Dowager said, rising to her feet. 'Joachim, you have much to apologize to Lori for.'

'No!' Lori blurted out, as the Dowager made her exit, closing the door tactfully behind her, but not before she had given her son a look that said more clearly than mere words could do: *Don't fuck this up*. 'No, it's my fault! Oh, Joachim—'

She stood up, feeling that she ought to look her fiancé in the eye.

'I made out with Mihaly last night!' she confessed. 'Oh God, I feel so awful! I've never cheated on anyone in my life! Joachim—'

He crossed the room to her in a couple of fast strides.

'You are so beautiful!' he said, taking her in his arms. 'So lovely, so sweet. And I left you by yourself, I neglected you. My beautiful, lovely fiancée. I am a stupid idiot! You are a young woman, you have needs, and I left you alone because of a stupid idea about waiting for marriage – I am an idiot!'

He kissed her more passionately than he had ever done. It was not the most experienced kiss – Mihaly's had been infinitely more seductive. But that comparison only made Lori even more relieved to be in Joachim's arms. It was real, honest; his embrace, a little clumsy, squashing her a bit, so she had to push back a fraction, tilting her head to get a better angle, was so much the opposite of Mihaly's careful choreography that she could have cried with sheer relief. And he was kissing her, even knowing that she had done the same with Mihaly yesterday! He forgave her! She grabbed onto his sweater, her fingers sinking into the wool, pulling her whole body as close to his as she could, as if she were trying to climb into him, mash them together.

'Joachim—' she managed to say against his mouth. 'I really need—'

'Yes! Me too!'

He grabbed her hand and practically ran with her to the door. Down a winding flight of turret stairs, along a hallway, no staff anywhere to be seen, which was very unusual for that time of day, late morning; the Dowager had clearly instructed everyone to stay away from that wing of the Schloss. Joachim and Lori tumbled into the Imperial Suite, into the bedroom, kissing as they went; Joachim pulled away briefly to go to the windows and pull all the curtains closed, shutting out all the bright winter daylight. It wouldn't have been Lori's choice, but she was just so relieved that Joachim didn't hold her slip with Mihaly against her, that he understood why it had happened and how sorry she was, that she had been honest with him and the Dowager and they had listened to her, had forgiven her, that this truly was the right man for her, the right family to be marrying into—

She pulled off her clothes, kicked off her trainers, was stripped down to her underwear when he came back to the bed. It was dark in the room now, and she couldn't see his expression, but he was just as fast at undressing himself. Now they had decided to do it, they were throwing themselves into having sex at full speed; the antique bed creaked as they collapsed onto it. Joachim's body was very smooth against hers, and she gasped happily in the shock of going from nought to a hundred, at suddenly being naked with her naked fiancé, his cock pressing into her leg, knowing that he wanted her.

Everything had been so wrong, so off-kilter, and now it was coming right. She and Joachim had lost their way, got their priorities confused, but they were back on track now. This was how things were supposed to be. She and her fiancé were making love, they were sexually compatible, this crucial part of the equation had been resolved . . .

There was no question of using contraception. It wasn't her fertile time of the month, but even if she did get pregnant, the wedding was a mere four weeks away and it wouldn't matter remotely if she had a baby eight months afterwards. A baby! They were doing it, they were actually having sex, sex that could get her pregnant, make the first of the many children that she longed for . . .

Eagerly, she pulled Joachim on top of her, opened her legs. They were kissing madly, his hands running up and down her body, and they both moaned as the head of his cock butted against her. He reached down, stroking her, making sure she was ready, clumsy in his haste; his fingers grazed her clitoris and she squealed in sheer relief.

That was her overriding emotion as her body responded, so grateful to have someone else's hand between her legs, rather than her own or a vibrator that she came almost at once. Relief. Relief from the months of tension and frustration. She hadn't realized how great her doubts were about Joachim, how much she had been worrying about their future sex life, until his cock slid into her, finding her more than wet and ready for him, and she heard him grunt above her as he started to fuck her hard. Relief, even more than release; Joachim *did* want her, *could* fuck her, would be a real husband to her. She was crying a little in sheer – God, she couldn't think of any other words but *relief*. His weight on her, his heavy pelvis weighing her down, his smooth, almost completely hairless body pressing into hers, his cock inside her. Finally, finally things were right: this was how it should be. She and her fiancé, not even making love, but fucking;

honestly, at that moment it was exactly what she wanted, a good hard fuck.

He yelled something in Herzoslovakian, grunted, jerked and came in a series of final, shuddering thrusts against her. It hadn't lasted long, but it was their first time; that was okay. Normal. Again, the opposite to Mihaly and his inhuman ability to control his physical urges. Joachim, now collapsed on top of her, stroking her hair, was a normal fiancé, not a sex robot. She had finally had normal sex with the man she was going to marry. Her doubts were resolved. Everything was going to be fine.

And hopefully, next time they could do it in daylight, and Joachim would last just a little bit longer . . .

Chloe

Goodness. Chloe couldn't help gawking for a moment as Lady Margaret's tall, blonde, elegant secretary entered the room behind her boss. *She has an amazing figure.* Chloe sat up straighter, sucked in her stomach, made a mental note to get Lauren to schedule another colonic for her as soon as possible; it did seem to be helping. And when a woman at least twenty years older than you had a body this good, it made you want to work even harder on flattening your tummy.

Still, never in my life will I be able to wear a tailored shirt tucked into a pair of fitted trousers like this Henrietta. She must have been a model, back in the day; she certainly walks like one. Though a model wouldn't be as shy; she had barely managed to whisper a 'How do you do?' on being introduced to Chloe, Hugo and Lauren. And her head was perpetually ducked, as if she were not confident enough to look anyone in the eye. Surprising, really, considering that she was so striking, with her perfect bone structure and smooth, tanned skin.

Hugo and Chloe were meeting Lady Margaret in the Belgian Suite of Buckingham Palace, which had become the unofficial headquarters for the wedding planning committee, at least for any matters that required them to be at the Palace. Lauren had had an earlier meeting there, consulting on the best location for the wedding after-party reception with the major-domo, Martin Frensham. She and Martin were by no means natural allies; Martin had started as a footman decades ago and risen through the ranks, leaving behind his Essex accent very swiftly. The fact that Lauren was entirely unabashed about her own Estuary vowels and occasional dropped 'h' made him both defensive and snobbish.

Lauren, sensibly, had dealt with it by simply ignoring Martin's attempts to patronize her, and they had reached an uneasy accord based entirely on the fact that they were both top-class organizers. Lauren regularly relieved her feelings after meeting Martin by doing a lively imitation of him looking down his nose at her while saying: '*Not* exactly the way things are usually done here, Miss Plodger.' Chloe could tell as soon as she laid eyes on Lauren that a raft of Martin impressions were due after Lauren's afternoon spent going round the State Apartments with him.

'Can I offer anyone a drink?' Martin asked now, looking around the room as if he were the host. 'Lady Margaret, I know you won't say no to a G&T at this time of day.'

'I most certainly won't!' Lady Margaret said briskly. 'Three p.m. – sun's over the yardarm somewhere! Nothing for Henrietta, though,' she added swiftly, glancing at her secretary. 'She's got to keep her wits about her.'

The secretary nodded silently, looking down at the tablet computer she was holding.

'I'll have a voddy and tonic, please,' Lauren said. 'Slimline tonic.'

'Slimline. Of *course*,' Martin said. He placed just enough emphasis on the first syllable of 'slimline' to allow it to carry a raft of unflattering connotations as far as Lauren was concerned.

'Oh, go on then, me too,' Chloe said.

'Gin for me,' Hugo said easily, sitting down so that everyone else could too. He was by no means a stickler for protocol, and wouldn't have cared less if anyone sat before him, but he knew that others – especially in a royal palace – would be insistent on following correct form. Chloe had pointed out to him, too, that if he relaxed too much, he would lead people like Lauren, who hadn't been brought up in royal circles, into error and cause them to make a terrible faux pas in front of his father or his grandfather – a fate which would be almost worse than death.

'Is gin a posh thing?' Lauren wondered aloud. 'Probably is, isn't it? We never had it at home.'

'It certainly wasn't posh in the nineteenth century,' Lady Margaret informed her as they all settled around the low coffee table, Lauren and the secretary, Henrietta, placing their tablets in front of them and tilting the screens up on their stand cases. 'Gin was cheap as chips then. Poor people's drink. They called it Mother's Ruin.'

Oddly, the secretary flinched at this, her heavy tortoiseshell glasses slipping a little down her nose. She pushed them up with a manicured finger, saw Chloe looking at her curiously and ducked her head to avoid making eye contact.

It's a shame she wears the glasses, Chloe thought. *Her eyes are so stunning. You can tell she lightens her hair, but that's probably just to cover some grey.*

Goodness! I have to stop staring at her! Why am I gawking at her like this?

She glanced at Lauren and Hugo, but neither of them seemed to have the same interest in this Henrietta as Chloe did. They were both looking at Martin, who was personally

bringing over the tray of drinks, having waved away the footman; he liked to minister to Hugo himself whenever
possible.

'I've stiffened yours for you, just the way you like it, Lady
Margaret,' he said sycophantically to her.

'Good, good,' Lady Margaret said rather absently. Her
attention was elsewhere, though on what, precisely, Chloe
couldn't be sure.

The silver tray was so huge that it covered a large part of
the coffee table's surface; Martin distributed the drinks. As
he handed them out, Henrietta, the secretary, ducked so far
down, looking at her tablet, that only the crown of her head
could be seen. It went beyond shyness, Chloe noticed; she
was positively awkward. *Not* a good trait in a social secretary,
even a temporary one.

'Bottoms up!' Lauren said cheerfully, hoisting her glass
and clinking it with Hugo's.

'Bottoms very much up!' he responded, grinning at her.
'How's everything going on the after-party front?'

'No bloody bagpipes, that's for sure!' Lauren said, patting
her elaborately arranged and sprayed hair, which was pulled
back into a modern version of a beehive. 'Old Marty here's
mad keen for bagpipes, but I put the kibosh on that fast. No
way are you celebrating the happiest day of yer lives to the
sounds of cats being strangled.'

Lady Margaret barked out a laugh. Her secretary
goggled at Lauren, clearly unable to believe the latter's
frankness. And Martin, about to close the door, shot
Lauren a look of absolute loathing, which Lauren answered
with a complacent curve of her bright pink lipsticked
mouth.

'*Old Marty!*' Hugo chortled once the door had shut.
'Lauren, you really do know how to get his goat.' He tilted

his head at her. 'Do you think you might be a little bit too hard on him sometimes?'

'Sorry,' Lauren said contritely; she would never have apologized if Hugo had reprimanded her, but this polite concern worked wonders. Chloe felt warm with pleasure at how well her fiancé handled her temperamental, if brilliant, best friend. 'He's just – *you* know, he's been here for donkey's years, and he really likes to rub it in that I don't know anything about anything.'

'Catch more flies with honey than vinegar,' Lady Margaret said in a way that was so clearly meant to be kind that Lauren mumbled a 'Sorry' again.

'Staff here *do* tend to be very possessive about the Family,' Lady Margaret added. 'You'll get the hang of dealing with them. Takes time, though.'

Henrietta nodded in agreement with her employer; strange, Chloe thought, since Lady Margaret had made a point of mentioning before that it was Henrietta's first visit to Buckingham Palace.

'Right, well, shall we get down to business before we all get too sloshed to focus?' Lauren said rather gruffly. 'Thanks. I'll try harder with Martin.' She picked up her tablet. 'I've pinged you over a guest list from the two sectors we discussed previously, Lady M – veterans and charity volunteers. Did you get a chance to look at it? I think we could expand the parameters of—'

The sitting-room door burst open with such force that it banged against the wall behind it and set the pendants in the chandelier overhead tinkling like ice crystals. Everyone jumped: Lady Margaret, Henrietta and Lauren, who, having lesser status than a prince of the realm and his fiancée, were seated with their backs to the door, swivelled round to see who on earth could be barging into their meeting like this.

Hugo and Chloe, with a clear view, were already rising swiftly to their feet.

'Hugo! Your *bloody* sister!' yelled Prince Oliver, storming into the room with such fury that Chloe was extremely grateful there were people and furniture between her and him. She preferred to spend as little time as possible with her future father-in-law; not only was he patronizing and dismissive, she had the sense that he didn't care for women at all. Nothing she had ever said to him had been greeted with anything more positive than a grunt or a sneer, so she had pretty much given up talking to him at all, which he clearly preferred.

She had to admit, however, that he was one of the most handsome men that she had ever seen. Even more handsome than his son; Hugo was good-looking, but his father was like a film star. Tall, brooding, his hair barely silvered with age, he was Heathcliff or Mr Rochester or Mr Darcy grown older: *which*, Chloe thought, looking at the frown on Oliver's forehead, the snarl of his perfectly sculpted lips, *just goes to show that you shouldn't pick the romantic hero who spends the entire book stamping around on moorland or being rude to the heroine. Because can you imagine what miseries they'd be to live with?*

Her idea of a romantic hero was Henry Tilney in Jane Austen's *Northanger Abbey*: funny, sweet, always nice to the heroine and her family. Someone who'd always be in a good mood at breakfast. Someone supportive, someone you could grow old with, knowing he wouldn't turn into a grumpy old curmudgeon.

Well, Oliver was a curmudgeon already. *No wonder he never remarried after Belinda died. No one could face living with that.*

'Sir! What *is* it?' Hugo stammered, looking terrified. Oliver in a rage was nothing new to him, but he had never got used to it.

'Your *bloody* sister!' Oliver shouted again. 'She's been behaving like a tart for years, and it's caught up with her finally! Not only that – sodding Toby's messed up in it as well! Her cousin! Christ, it's disgusting! I *knew* she took after her idiot mother!'

'Pater, *please*!'

Hugo was vibrating with distress. Chloe didn't know if she should touch him or not; tentatively, she put her hand on his, and knew she had done the right thing when he pulled her tightly to him, winding his arm around her. He was shaking from head to toe. A tide of resentment rose in her against his father: she hated Hugo being upset like this. And she was shocked, too, at the way Oliver had just spoken of his daughter and ex-wife. His language in private was always salty, but this was far beyond anything she had heard from him before.

She had mainly seen Oliver cold, dismissive, snubbing her when she tried to say something. Hugo had mentioned his parents' fights, his fear of Oliver's rages, but she hadn't realized how truly bad it had been. Chloe, brought up in a happy, loving household where cross words were rarely exchanged, had no experience of anything like this. She realized that she was trembling too. Oliver looked as if he were demonically possessed, his eyes almost entirely black with anger.

Not only that, his face was suffused with blood; he was turning his head from side to side like a wounded bull. Striding over to the mantelpiece, he grabbed a silver candelabra from the marble shelf, swivelled and threw it to the floor with such force that the candles burst out and rolled across the carpet. Everyone gasped; Henrietta let out a shriek, and then clapped her hand over her mouth as Martin, who had appeared in the doorway, glanced curiously at her.

Oliver kicked viciously at the candles that were rolling towards him, punting one into the delicate leg of a Chippendale table. The consequent smash seemed to relieve him a little; he looked towards Martin, who was closing the door discreetly, and barked:

'Get me a fucking *drink*!'

'Sir, what's happened?' Hugo managed to ask, his arm still clamped around Chloe. 'Did you say Sophie and *Toby*—'

Sophie, Minty, Toby and a large part of their crowd were in Ibiza, celebrating a friend's birthday. The friend was called Pasty: Chloe thought his real name was Rory, but practically none of them used their real names. The three other young men in Toby's inner circle were Shirley, Tex and Chewie, for Chewbacca; Toby himself was called Silver, which was short for Silver Spoon.

'They went to some club, picked up some cheap tarts, brought 'em back to where they were staying and were stupid enough not to take their phones off 'em,' Oliver barked, taking the glass of whisky that Martin scurried over to hand him, downing its contents in one, and shoving it back at the major-domo with a curt: 'Again.'

'But their security officers—' Hugo blurted out.

'*Exactly*,' Oliver said grimly. 'Apparently they got drunk and joined in. Sounds like they had a bloody orgy. And a couple of the trollops documented it all. Photos and film. The press office just rang because the pictures got offered to the *Herald* half an hour ago.'

Lauren and Chloe exchanged a glance; years of having to cope with the tabloids meant that the young women knew very well what a mistake this was. No British paper would print compromising photographs of Sophie and Toby: the sellers should have gone abroad, to Italy or France – whose gossip magazines were legendarily unscrupulous – or to America's downmarket weeklies.

'We'll buy them up,' Hugo said bravely, but his voice wobbled.

'Of course we'll bloody buy them up! But there'll still be *talk*!' his father yelled at him. 'This is a bloody PR disaster! They fucked each other all over the place, drunk off their heads, and took drugs too! What were the stupid little cunts *thinking*, letting commoners in to film them at it!'

'We should go over there straight away,' Chloe heard herself say in a very small voice.

'*What?* Speak up!' Oliver took a couple of strides towards her; it was all she could do not to cower. She and Hugo were clinging onto each other for dear life.

'We should go over there,' she said, trying, and not really succeeding, to raise her voice. 'Hugo and I. See if we can help put a lid on this.'

'That,' Lady Margaret said crisply, 'is a *damn* good idea.' She looked at Lauren, who nodded vigorously. 'Take Lauren too,' she added. 'She's a bright spark. Done wonders for Chloe and Hugo.'

Lauren was clearly bubbling with ideas, but didn't dare to speak up in front of Oliver. Chloe hoped fervently that Lauren would agree with her as she said:

'We could say we were there . . .'

Instantly, Lauren started to nod fervently. Emboldened, Chloe went on:

'Hugo and I stayed in last night – we didn't have any official engagements or anything, and today we went to see my mum and dad.'

Oops. Oliver winced pointedly at the common usage, never too distracted, even by a sex and drugs scandal featuring his daughter, to look down at someone who wasn't well brought up enough to refer to her 'father and mother'.

'So we could say that we went over to join Sophie and Toby last night, on a whim,' Chloe forged on over her etiquette slip, 'and that we were with them. No one's going to believe they got up to anything shocking with the two of us there.'

'That's true, sir,' Hugo said eagerly. 'We're famously boring, me and Chloe. Never had so much as a whiff of anything untoward.'

Hugo was so petrified of his father that he always ended up talking like a pompous parody of himself around Oliver; he would never have used the word 'untoward' in normal conversation. It had used to irritate Chloe until she first saw Oliver in a bad mood, and then she understood the desperate need to try anything that might avoid increasing Oliver's wrath.

'We'd need to take a private plane,' Lauren said, as Oliver gulped down half of the second glassful of single malt; she had calculated that the edge had been taken off Oliver's anger – enough, at least, for him to be able to hear a working-class accent without instantly bridling. 'Shall I go and organize that now? No time to waste. And I'll get KP to pack some cases for you?'

Oliver ignored her, but Lady Margaret gave her a brisk nod, and that was all the approval Lauren needed. As fast as her high heels and tight houndstooth print suit would allow her, Lauren bustled from the room, pulling her phone out of her bag, about to arrange for a plane and to ring Kensington Palace; the staff there would pack suitcases for Hugo and Chloe according to Lauren's efficient instructions.

'That little slut Sophie,' Oliver said, finishing his second whisky; Martin was hovering ready to take the glass from him before he decided to throw that across the room too. 'Takes after that stupid fool of her mother. Best thing *that*

one ever did was kill herself skiing before she could drag the
whole family down with her—'

'Sir! *Please*!' Hugo was still holding onto his fiancée tightly,
but he had got control of himself now, enough to strengthen
his tone so that he could cut his father off before he said
anything worse. 'I don't want to hear you talk about my
mother like that! And I don't want Chloe to hear it either.'

'Yes, and nor do I, Oliver,' Lady Margaret snapped. 'Keep
your tongue between your teeth on that subject.'

Chloe had been staring fixedly at the Prince's handsome,
contorted face, afraid to look away, much like someone
confronting a snarling dog; you didn't dare to avert your gaze
unless he attacked. But now she glanced over at Lady
Margaret, whose jaw was set, her eyes narrowed, looking
very much like an angry dog herself as she glared at the
ex-husband of her dead best friend. Beside her, the poor
temporary secretary was white as a sheet under her golden
tan, one hand raised to half-cover her face as if for protection; she must have had the shock of a lifetime, seeing Prince
Oliver burst in and make such a terrifying scene.

'Can one make sure the pictures won't run?' Lady
Margaret asked, her question mainly directed at Hugo and
Chloe. 'I mean, even if you buy them up, what with the inter-
net nowadays . . .'

'The press office will make them sign a cast-iron confidentiality agreement in return for a big payout,' Chloe said. 'It'll
go through the *Herald* people as a backstop. Then if anything
shows up on the net, all the money would have to go back,
and they won't want that. The trouble would be that if there
were lots of people there, some of them could have just taken
a few photos and not gone to the press, and they're bound to
show those around . . . those could leak out. That's why if
Hugo and I shoot off there, and we can have a go at denying

the whole thing, we can at least try to pretend that any others are fakes.'

Lady Margaret raised an eyebrow approvingly.

'You *do* know what you're doing,' she said, and it was almost as if she were speaking for someone else's benefit. Oliver's? But Oliver was glaring viciously at his son, paying not a whit of attention to what the women were chattering about. And Hugo was staring back at him. The two men looked suddenly very alike, their eyes locked, as if they were wrestling silently.

Chloe pulled on her fiancé's arm, but she couldn't move him, not even a fraction. From being dangerously vulnerable, trembling, Hugo's body was entirely tense now, and that felt even more dangerous to her. She shot a look of sheer panic at Lady Margaret, feeling that the situation could spiral out of control any moment. If Oliver said one more rude word about Hugo's sister or mother, Hugo would lunge for him, she was sure. And Oliver's narrowed eyes, his head jutting forward, indicated all too clearly that he knew that Hugo was throwing down a silent challenge.

Oliver's lips parted. Chloe, desperate to avoid a physical conflict at all costs, started to say something, anything: what actually came to mind was to ask if anyone knew what the weather was like in Ibiza this early in the season. So she was hugely grateful for a totally unexpected interruption from Henrietta, the practically mute secretary, who, quite abruptly, burst out into a hysterical wail, so loud and shrill that it broke the Mexican standoff between father and son. Both of them swivelled to stare in shock at the blonde woman.

'Jesus Christ!' Oliver snapped. 'What the *fuck*, Margaret? Who *is* this?'

You might have asked that before you started abusing your daughter and your ex-wife! Chloe thought, as savagely as her nice nature would permit. *You might have bothered to check whether there was a stranger in the room!*

'My secretary,' Lady Margaret said, swiftly putting her arms around the woman, pushing her down to sit on the sofa, ignoring formal etiquette. 'She's rather sensitive to bullish men storming around yelling in foul language about their nearest and dearest. I can't for the *life* of me think why! Do take a breath, Henrietta,' she added to the woman sotto voce.

'Well, get her under control!' Oliver ordered. 'Bloody hell, this is a madhouse!'

'We should go off to find Lauren,' Chloe said to Hugo, tugging on his arm. To her great relief, it yielded, no longer seemingly carved from stone.

'I'm going to the gym,' Oliver announced, turning on his heel, casting a glance of utter disgust at the now softly sobbing Henrietta, a crumpled heap in Lady Margaret's lap. 'If there's one thing I can't abide, it's a crying woman. Makes me want to upchuck.'

Chloe dug her fingers so deeply into Hugo's arm that she made creases in his shirt that only an iron would remove. It was partly to stop him from answering back, but partly also to relieve her own rage at his father; she only unclasped her grip when Oliver had stamped out of the room. Hugo muttered:

'*Ouch.*'

'Sorry!'

He massaged his arm, looking over at the two women on the sofa.

'Lady Margaret,' he began. 'I must apologize – that was really intolerable language in front of ladies—'

She was already holding up a hand to stop him.

'Please,' she said scathingly. 'Oliver's always been an abso-lute bastard. He's very good at putting on the charm as long as he needs to, but when it doesn't matter, he's a total shit. Among other things,' she added a little cryptically, patting her secretary's arm. 'Henrietta, get a grip!' she said to the latter. 'He's gone.'

'Martin, I think, um, Henrietta could do with a cup of tea,' Hugo said. 'Or something stronger.'

'She'll be fine,' Lady Margaret said quickly. 'I'll take her back to Eaton Square. She's a little sensitive, that's all.'

Understatement of the year! Chloe thought. *Honestly, that scene was awful for all of us, and she isn't even related to Oliver! This woman's much too sensitive to be able to work for Lady Margaret . . .*

But just then Lauren's heels clicked down the corridor and paused in the doorway to assess the situation inside.

'He went off in a huff,' Chloe told her.

'Right.' Lauren grimaced in a very speaking way. 'Well, we're ready to go. I've got a car sorted for Heathrow, and we'll stop at KP on the way to get the luggage.'

'Lauren, you're amazing,' Hugo said with great gratitude.

'Well, don't hang around! Get going!' Lady Margaret said briskly, knowing that otherwise Hugo would feel obliged to go through the polite farewell ritual.

Hugo and Chloe walked quickly to the door, following Lauren; they did not look back to see Lady Margaret and Henrietta gather themselves and start to leave. Which meant, also, that neither of them noticed that Martin, who had been standing with his back to the wall during the lurid scene, was easing forward, fixing Henrietta with a very acute stare, doing his best to get a look at her face.

'What were you *thinking*? Soph, *honestly*!'

It was evening in Ibiza, a comparatively balmy night compared to drizzly, grey London; they had found Sophie sitting on one of the many terraces of the Villa Clarita, a stunning, super-modern construction that looked like a series of white boxes with glass walls stacked randomly on top of each other. In the huge outdoor pool, which had a net stretched across the middle and water-polo goals on each side, were floating various inflatable animals and what looked like two Swiss balance balls.

The tables by the pool were covered with empty bottles, beer cans and glasses, and overflowing ashtrays. More empty cans and cigarette butts littered the cream marble patio surround. Clearly the villa had been on lockdown since the party last night, and the usual team of cleaners had not been allowed in as there was no way this kind of mess would normally not have been whisked away before the privileged young people who had so carelessly strewn it around woke from their slumbers.

'This is an absolute tip,' Hugo added, looking around him as Chloe pointedly cleared some of the empty bottles off the low white wall behind which the cliffs dropped away to the Cala Jondal beach and the Balearic Sea below.

'I don't want anyone knocking these over the edge,' she said.

'No, totally,' her fiancé agreed responsibly.

He looked back at his sister, who was huddled up in a ball in one of the modular charcoal rattan chairs that surrounded the matching glass-topped table; she looked less like a princess than a guttersnipe, her greasy hair pulled back in a tight knot at the back of her head, dark circles under her eyes, her skin sallow, mascara smudged into the roots of her eyelashes. She was wearing a cream silk pyjama set with boy-short bottoms – *of course Sophie has to show off her legs*, Chloe thought sarcastically, *even when she's in a huge amount of trouble and there's no one around who fancies her.* Her upper body was swathed in an oversized double-sided cashmere Brora wrap, pale pink and pale blue, which, Chloe noticed with great disapproval, was speckled with little burns from cigarette ash.

That wrap must have cost at least £500, and she's treating it like a Slanket.

Chloe might have an extensive clothes budget since her engagement, but she didn't think she would ever get used to the careless way Sophie and Minty trashed their possessions. Clothes, jewellery, shoes; sets of bed linen that cost over a thousand pounds; if you ever dropped in on Sophie wherever she was staying you would find piles of violently expensive things bought on a whim, scattered all over every surface together with wine glasses with only dregs at their base, overspilling ashtrays, half-eaten packets of dusty almonds and edamame, and scented candles whose wax had dripped onto the priceless furniture.

'Soph, this is a pigsty,' her older brother said reprovingly. 'You knew we were coming. You could have tidied up a bit.'

It's not like you had anything else to do! Chloe bit her lip. It wouldn't exactly improve her already problematic relationship with her fiancé's sister to weigh in on this.

Sophie picked up her packet of Silk Cut and lit a second cigarette from the butt of the one she was finishing.

'Don't go on, Huge,' she muttered. 'I've got the most stinking hangover ever.'

'It's not just a hangover, from what I hear!' her brother snapped. 'It's a coke and E comedown!'

Sophie shrugged crossly, the wrap sliding off one thin shoulder; she hoicked it back up again, pouting.

'Come on, Huge,' she mumbled. 'It's a birthday weekend, we're in Ibiza, of course we're going to be having a party. I honestly think everyone's making *much* too much of a big deal about this. No one's going to see the photos, it's all been dealt with – can't we just calm down a bit? God, I need a drink.'

The Ibiza night was soft and beautiful, a dark velvety-blue pricked with clear white stars. The outside illumination which suffused the lavish grounds of the villa had come on automatically as the daylight faded, built-in spots outlining the pool and the elaborate topiary that surrounded it; pale green uplighters picked up the decorative cacti planted in raised gravel borders. And the villa itself brimmed with light, its giant glass boxes softly lit, not a single visible lamp or overhead fixture. Everything was diffused, spilling smoothly out onto the terrace on which the three of them were sitting.

It should have been an idyllic evening atmosphere. So when Hugo stood up and banged his fist on the rattan table, making its contents jump and shudder dangerously, it was even more of a shock. Ash dropped off the tip of Sophie's cigarette, smearing onto her wrap. And Chloe looked up at her fiancé with tremendous admiration. Earlier, he had stood up to his father; now he was telling off his sister. If there had been anything she had wanted to change about Hugo, it was that he was too deferential with his family, too eager to please. It had made that aspect of Chloe's relationship with him difficult; she didn't actually need to say outright that Oliver was a terrifying bully and Sophie was a spoilt bitch, but Hugo had always been averse to any hint of criticism towards either of them.

Well, that's changed! Chloe thought with almost gleeful satisfaction, as Hugo positively bellowed:

'Sophie, you *have* to take this seriously! Are you fucking *joking*? There's video and photos of you and Toby and about twenty people having a fucking *orgy*! Where the hell *is* Toby?

Toby!' he yelled towards the villa. 'Get the *fuck* out here! I'm
not going through this twice!'

It was hard to read Sophie's expression in the dusk, which
was doubtless why she was sitting out here. Chloe and Hugo
hadn't even entered Villa Clarita yet; Sophie had been waiting on the front porch as the car bringing them, Lauren and
their security officers from the airport had pulled up outside.
Sophie had led them round the side of the villa while Lauren
went inside to roust out Toby. As Hugo's sister, Sophie had
clearly been chosen as the person to get the brunt of his
wrath: everyone else was hiding out in their rooms. Normally,
they would be down in Es Cubells, the pretty little village
nearby, but both Es Cubells and Cala Jondal were swarming
with journalists hot on the scent of a huge story, and the
villa's occupants were effectively under house arrest.

Hugo and Chloe, plus their entourage, had been picked up
directly from their plane in a Range Rover with blacked-out
windows, so that the hordes staking out the entrance gates
would not be able to see who was arriving at the villa.
Fortunately, Pasty's father, who owned Villa Clarita, was very
keen on his privacy, as he threw his own parties here as well,
ones to which neither his wife nor the press were invited.
Surrounding the villa were high walls, discreetly concealed
behind thick stands of pine trees and topped with barbed-
wire curls to deter photographers with long-range lenses.

Toby emerged through the glass doors of the recessed
sitting room and ambled around the under-lit pond, passing
a curling topiary shrub set in a matt black planter. He was
wearing a T-shirt that read 'Squirrels Protect Their Nuts', and
pyjama bottoms which hung low on his hips, low enough
that at least an inch of bare skin showed above their tie waist;
Chloe averted her eyes from the red curling hair twisting
around the cord.

'Sit down, Toby,' Hugo said in such a cold tone that Toby flinched and promptly obeyed, sinking to the closest available seat, an oversized black resin pebble with a flat top that rocked a little back and forth on the marble.

'We have a *responsibility*,' Hugo said, looking from Sophie to Toby and back again. 'Do you two not see that at *all*? We're paid an absolute fortune to represent our country, and you two just pissed on that from a great height! Not only that, you've caused a ton of work for people who have *much* better things to be doing – like organizing our wedding, which is actually going to be a *positive* thing for Great Britain, you know?'

He glanced at Chloe, who nodded; Hugo clearly didn't need any more help than the occasional sign of agreement. She was realizing that, long term, this crisis might actually turn out to be the best thing that had happened to her and Hugo. Chloe had been dying for some help from him on the Sophie front, but had felt that he coddled his younger sister too much for her to be able to tell him anything approaching the truth about how awful Sophie and her cohorts were to her; now she settled back in the modular chair, crossed her legs comfortably and enjoyed the spectacle of her fiancé finally stepping up and reading the riot act to his sister.

'Palace officials have scrambled and paid bribes and called in favours all over London because you two couldn't even take the most basic precautions to be discreet!' Hugo fumed. 'You were too drunk and messed up to make sure that everyone left their mobiles at the door with a security guy! Oh, hang on, it was worse than that – I understand that Soph actually *fucked* a security guy!'

Up until then, the villa had been so silent that you could have heard a pin drop onto its black tiled floors, the kind of silence that isn't empty, but full, its remaining inhabitants listening very intently to what was being said outside. But with this, a dull thud could be heard. Somewhere in the depths of one of the white-and-glass boxes, someone had reacted to this.

Probably the protection officer who Sophie shagged, Chloe thought. She knew that the security detail which had flown over with them was tasked with hauling the team in Ibiza over the coals: the Commissioner of the Metropolitan Police was livid at the total breakdown of professional standards for their conduct. Drinking, doing coke, and having sex with the royals you were supposed to be protecting was bad enough. Letting it be recorded for posterity was infinitely worse.

'They're supposed to be taking care of us,' Sophie whined. 'They're supposed to stay sober and make sure we don't get into trouble. It's their fault if they can't control themselves, isn't it? Not ours.'

Toby shifted awkwardly, the pebble rocking again.

'Soph—' he began, but Hugo was already coming down on his sister like a ton of bricks.

'What do you do, exactly, Sophie?' he asked in a frighteningly controlled voice. 'Can you please tell me exactly what you do?'

Sophie stubbed out her cigarette.

'I don't know what you mean,' she mumbled.

'In return for the money you get from the Civil List!' her brother said. 'What the *fuck* do you do to justify that?'

'I'm a trade ambassador for Britain!' Sophie said crossly. 'You know that! I promote British fashion and design . . .'

Her head was ducked, however, so that the words came out blurred.

'Christ, Sophie, you can't even look me in the eye and say that rubbish!' Hugo said furiously. '*Trade ambassador?* You go to parties and get free clothes! You know who really promotes British fashion and design? *Chloe!*'

He pointed at his fiancée, who was beginning to feel that this might actually turn out to be her best day ever. After the distress of seeing Oliver in such a tearing rage, the scramble for the airport, and the two and a half hour flight to Ibiza with Hugo vibrating like a tuning fork, torn between anger at Sophie and Toby's irresponsibility and distress at his father's foul language, Chloe hadn't thought for a moment that today could possibly end on a high. It was hard, of course, to say that any day could finish even more satisfyingly than the one on which Hugo had proposed to her, but that had been such an amalgam of emotional extremes: she had been too exhausted by the time she had fallen into bed an engaged woman to fully relish her triumph.

This time, she could. She could relish every single moment. All she had to do was keep her face relatively serious, avoiding anything that might be interpreted as a smirk, while she sat back and heard Hugo say pretty much everything that she and Lauren had always fantasized about telling Sophie.

'When Chloe wears something, it sells out the next day!' Hugo said. 'Chloe makes sure she only picks British designers! And she pays for them – she doesn't get anything for free!'

Wow, Hugo knows all of that? I didn't realize. Chloe couldn't help a satisfied smile raising her lips as she gazed up at her fiancé happily.

'Are you really telling me that you tarting around in leather hot pants made by some pervy Italian does anything positive for British fashion?' Hugo demanded of his slumped sister. 'The only message I can see *that* sending is that the Royal Family can't afford enough clothes to wear!'

Toby snorted at this. Sophie wrenched herself round to stare at him crossly.

'What?' he said, spreading his hands. 'Sometimes it does look like you've gone out in your knickers.'

'You are a disgrace to the family,' Hugo said deliberately to his sister. 'You have to work out a way to justify your keep from now on. Toby gets much less from the Civil List than you, and he's in the army, so at least he's got a bloody job. We're under an awful lot of pressure, you know. The public wants to see value for money from us in a serious recession, and I can't blame them one bit. I couldn't make a case for giving you a penny, the way you behave. People who have to live on less in a year than you squander in a week look up to us to set an example. Can you give me one positive example that you set, Soph? *Can* you?'

Sophie gulped.

'What does *Father* do that's positive?' she whimpered, trying a deflection strategy now. 'Apart from yell and shout and bully us and wait for Grandpa to kick the bucket?'

Toby nearly fell off the giant resin pebble.

'*Soph!*' he exclaimed. 'Steady on!'

'It's true!' Sophie said defiantly, but her brother was already cutting through her protest.

'So it's all up to me, is it?' he said, and his icy tone almost sounded like their father. 'Because that's what you're saying – it's all left up to me, right? Father's pretty useless, you're *completely* useless, Toby's a party animal at the best of times, besides getting himself mixed up in the worst scandal ever to hit this family, and *I'm* the only one that's supposed to maintain our reputation? Carry the monarchy forward in the twenty-first century? Because that's what I'm doing, Soph! It's all on my shoulders! If we all behaved like you and Father, the monarchy would be in pieces! Is that what you want?'

'Of course it isn't!' Sophie wailed.

'Thank God I have Chloe!' Hugo's voice was rising again. 'I tell you, she's the best thing that's ever happened to me! And believe me, I *know* how badly you've treated her! She's been an absolute rock, and I wouldn't have blamed her at all if she'd decided that the shit she's got from you and Minty just wasn't worth it! She's done more for us already than you have in your entire life, Sophie!'

I really never have been so happy, Chloe acknowledged to herself, allowing herself a smile as Hugo strode behind her chair and put his hands on her shoulders.

'Chloe and I are a team,' he said. 'A really good team. And from now on, I don't want to hear one rude word about her from you – or from any of your friends,' he added. 'Got it? You've forfeited any right you ever had to say anything about my wife-to-be that isn't a hundred per cent positive.'

Sophie was huddled into a tight little ball, her forehead resting on her knees.

'And Toby—' Hugo rounded on his cousin.

'Hey, I've never been anything but nice to Chloe!' Toby said defensively, as Chloe nodded vigorously in agreement.

'I know. But you have to help us,' Hugo said soberly. 'You can't pull this shit any more. Keep it behind closed doors, Tobes! Is that too much to ask?'

Toby shook his head. Chloe judged that it was time for her to change the subject somewhat. Hugo had definitely made his point, and she knew that it wasn't just his erring sister and cousin to whom he had made it. The villa was full of listening ears; Hugo's impassioned speech had reached plenty of the party-going culprits as well.

'Toby, what actually happened last night?' she asked quietly.

'Well, we all went down to the Blue Marlin mid-afternoon,' Toby said, naming one of the island's trendiest beach lounges. 'They were having this private opening party – you know, before they properly open for the season. It was really cool,' he added, brightening up. 'Not too crowded, and loads of gorgeous people. They had this DJ we knew from Boujis, plus this flamenco guitarist called Paco with his band. Fucking awesome. So we had a brilliant time, dancing and drinking and all that sort of thing, but the thing is, it was Sunday yesterday and the Marlin closes at midnight, and we were *so* not ready to, you know, wind down . . .'

He cleared his throat, looking at his cousin, looming behind Chloe's chair.

'Um, so we all thought we'd pile back here. And lots of people from the Marlin came too. Y'know, we're mostly unattached males here, and it's Pasty's birthday weekend, and we were all celebrating, and there were a *lot* of hot chicks at the bar – Dutch girls, all sort of big and meaty and lovely – *sorry, sorry* – shit, Chloe, *sorry*—'

'Get on with it,' Hugo snapped.

'—so *anyway*,' Toby said in embarrassment, 'we all piled back here and, you know, it's Ibiza. Lots of coke and E and champers. I mean, *obviously*. But I think some of the girls were hookers. Off duty, you know, letting their hair down. I mean, no one *paid*. But they were *very* professional. And some of them put on a bit of a show and that was, um, *really* distracting. I mean, none of us could think about anything else. I know Billo and Petey were supposed to be keeping a lid on things,' he added, referring to the two protection officers, 'but honestly, Huge, you really can't blame them that much. These girls were *super*-bendy. And then the other girls sort of got competitive – well, you know Minty – and started doing stuff of their own. I mean, it was a total free-for-all. Someone put a candle up my bum. I think it was a candle. God! I *hope* it was a candle!'

He reached round to the back of the pebble, putting a protective hand over his buttocks. *Closing the stable door after the horse has fled,* Chloe thought, trying really hard not to laugh: she would have rocking back and forth in the chair in silent spasms if she hadn't been anchored by Hugo's hands on her shoulders.

'All right, everyone?'

Lauren emerged from the living room, following the same route around the pool that Toby had done. Ever the gentleman, he stood up, indicating the giant pebble next to his with a courtly gesture, but Lauren looked down at it, huffed a dismissive laugh and remained standing.

'We've got a bit of a sitch,' she said, and Chloe sat up straighter at the tone of Lauren's voice, which she recognized as very smug: something had clearly just happened which had given Lauren huge satisfaction. 'Did anyone know there's CCTV in all the public rooms 'ere? Not the bedrooms and bathrooms, obv, but all the lounges.'

Sophie got it right away, her head snapping up from her knees.

'Delete it!' Sophie squeaked. 'We need to delete all of it right now!'

Toby was a few moments behind.

'Oh, *fuck,*' he said, and fell off the pebble.

'It was recording?' Chloe asked, trying to sound calm, though her heart was soaring in her chest with utter pleasure at the sight of Sophie's agonized expression.

'*Oh* yeah,' Lauren said, as flatly as she could manage; Chloe, who knew her best, could tell that she was struggling to control her unholy amusement. 'Got the whole thing, by the sounds of it. I had a quick gander with the Met guys who came over with us.' She cleared her throat. 'I think someone should watch it. You know, one of us. So we know what we're dealing with. Like, if someone else tries to sell photos or whatever, we know if they've got the genuine article, or they've just Photoshopped something.'

'That's a really good point,' Chloe agreed. Her eyes met Lauren's, and the two young women shared a moment of triumph. 'Lauren, would you be okay with that?'

Lauren nodded sombrely.

'Yeah, I think I should,' she said.

'You shouldn't have to do it by yourself, though,' Chloe said. It was as if the two young women had planned this in advance, their dialogue all scripted: they were in such accord that they didn't even need to think about how to respond to each other. The words tripped off their tongues as fluently as if they were actresses in a play they had performed hundreds of times already.

'I dunno,' Lauren shook her head. 'Can't really ask the Met guys to sit through it, you know? I mean, some of the stuff this lot got up to—' She drew in her breath pointedly, glancing briefly at Sophie, who was practically trying to smoke two cigarettes at once, and Toby, who was slumped on the patio now, his head in his hands – 'well, not a good idea for the coppers to see it, eh? I mean, you can't expect 'em not to gossip a bit. They're only human.'

It was time. Chloe had had a long day, she would normally have been ready for her bed by now, but the prospect of taking this most elegant of revenges on Sophie was invigorating her as if she had just drunk four double espressos. She rose to her feet, Hugo supportively at her side as she said, attempting to achieve a brave, stoic tone:

'I'll watch it with you, Lauren. It's not fair to ask you to do it alone.'

'*Would* you?' Lauren said, clasping her hands at her breast. 'Wow, Chlo, that's well nice of you.'

Chloe shook her head swiftly: Lauren was overdoing it there. Lauren, always quick on the uptake, dropped her hands as Chloe said nobly:

'Hugo, darling, *you* mustn't see the footage, of course. But poor Lauren – she needs someone else with her—'

Hugo nodded vigorously at both parts of this.

'Right! Hugo, we've got a room for you and Chloe all sorted out,' Lauren said, moving into a brisk change of pace now that her main aim had been achieved. 'Your cases're already up there. Nice en-suite, all the works – fuck, this place is stunning. Got a couple of the lads to bunk up together to make space. Sophie, Minty's moving in with you and I'm taking her bedroom.'

'*What?*' Sophie was outraged. 'I'm not bloody sharing with Minty!'

Hugo started to speak, but Lauren got in there first: it was very obvious, to Chloe at least, that she had set Sophie up with expert skill.

'Really?' she said, her tone of light surprise perfectly judged. 'Because we only, like, did a quick fast-forward through the footage, but when you and Minty were on the coffee table it looked like you were sharing *really* nicely!'

Grabbing her cigarettes, swearing horribly under her breath, Sophie jumped up and dashed for the house, only narrowly avoiding tripping and falling into the pond.

'Hugo, love,' Lauren continued, 'why don't you go and settle in and unpack for you and Chlo? We might be a while. There's sarnies in the kitchen if you're peckish.'

'Lauren,' Hugo said gratefully, 'I honestly can't thank you enough.'

'Yeah you can,' Lauren said cheerfully. 'You can give me a raise.'

'Consider it done,' Hugo said sincerely.

'Lauren?' Toby mumbled as the three of them passed him on their way into the house.

'Yeah?' She stopped and looked down at him.

'If it wasn't a candle?' Toby asked, in a small, pathetic voice. '*Please* don't ever tell me.'

Lauren didn't trust herself to answer without laughing; she managed a swift nod and kept going. Waiting in the sprawling living room, looking very incongruous sitting side by side on the long white leather sofa, were the two Met officers who had accompanied Hugo and Chloe; at least their black head-to-toe outfits toned with the black silk cushions and the ceramic waist-high vases filled with pussy willow branches. They jumped up on seeing Hugo following the two women into the villa.

'Kev, would you show the Prince where he and Chloe're bunking down?' Lauren said. 'Dave, love, have you made the sarnies yet?'

Dave, a short, wide, Irish-freckled young man, grinned up at the statuesque Lauren.

'Your wish is my command, milady,' he said. 'Ham and cheese *and* tomato. I put a plate for you in the office. And a bottle of wine.' He winked. 'I thought you might need it.'

'Thanks, love,' Lauren said, sweeping past him majestically. Chloe noticed with amusement that despite Lauren's cool tone, her hips were switching back and forth, an extra wiggle in her step for Dave's benefit. He was a brand-new recruit to the team, as naturally Toby and Sophie's disgraced protection officers had needed to be replaced in a hurry. He and Lauren had only met a few hours ago but the mutual attraction had been instantaneous; Chloe had noticed them flirting discreetly but continuously on the plane ride over. Now that Hugo was heading to his room, they didn't need to be quite so formal in front of the Prince, and Chloe saw

Lauren's cheeks pinkening with pleasure at Dave's thoughtfulness.

Still, when Lauren was working, business always came before pleasure. She had barely been in Villa Clarita for an hour, but already she had familiarized herself with the complicated layout; she led Chloe round a Japanese bonsai garden wrapped behind glass walls and into a small, sleek office at the back of the property, as dark as the rest of the villa was white. Black painted walls, black carpet, a wide wenge wood desk with a wall of built-in monitors behind it, images paused on the four screens that made Chloe gulp as she took them in. Unlike almost everything else in the room, they were in colour, which made them even more vividly explicit.

'Brace yourself,' Lauren said gleefully, pulling up a luxurious black leather desk chair. 'This is going to be un-fucking-believable.'

Dave had considerately uncorked the wine, and Chloe filled the two glasses he had left for them almost to the brim: they had just settled down in the chairs, sandwich plate in front of them, Lauren rewinding the footage to its start, when a tap came on the door.

'Um, Lauren?' Dave eased it open and put his head around it. 'I made you some popcorn. Found one of those bags you put in the microwave. You know, cos you're watching a film.'

Lauren swivelled her chair around and took the bowl.

'You usually eat popcorn when you watch an X-rated film, Dave?' she asked, her heavily pencilled eyebrows raised.

Dave was more than up to the challenge.

'Not at all, milady,' he said, quick as a flash. 'I prefer to eat something else entirely.'

Lauren raised one eyebrow.

'Good to know,' she said, maintaining her composure as a grinning Dave made his exit.

'Wow, Lauren, you two are at Flirt Level Red,' Chloe observed, noticing the complacent smile and bright eyes of her friend as the latter swivelled back to face the screens, kicked off her heels and put her feet up on the desk.

'I like cheeky ginger short-arses,' Lauren said, taking a handful of popcorn and handing the bowl to Chloe. 'And I *particularly* like cheeky ginger short-arses who talk to me face, not me tits. Right! We ready to see what went up Toby's bum?'

Chloe spat red wine over her own, much less substantial bosom.

'Damn, this top's dry-clean only,' she said, wiping herself down. 'I might not be able to watch all of this. You're scaring me.'

'Oh, sod that for a lark! You're watching every bit of it!' Lauren said merrily. 'I'll get Dave to bring us some more booze if we need it.'

She looked at Chloe.

'And forget dry-clean only,' she said, grinning even more than Dave had done. 'By the time you've seen this, you'll need a fucking bib.'

At first the lack of sound made the experience very odd: then Lauren had the idea of putting some music on, plugging her iPod into her travel speakers, and her R&B mix was perfect for the developing action on the screens. Toby, it turned out, had given a pretty accurate description of how the party had degenerated into a full-blown sex romp. Almost immediately after coming into the living room, a small group of girls dressed in tiny, stretchy dresses and high strappy sandals had climbed onto a white moulded plastic coffee table, dancing to unheard music, or rather, wriggling against each other, writhing so close that when the first boob popped out of the top of a dress being peeled down by one of the wearer's dance partners, it took a while for anyone else to realize.

But when they did, word got round the gathering as fast as wildfire. For a few seconds, Chloe thought that Lauren had fast-forwarded the sequence where about fifteen young men suddenly shot into view, clustering around the table, their faces upturned. But no, she hadn't. Men just moved at the speed of light when they heard that women were taking their clothes off.

They were cheering and clapping the girls on: more bandage dresses were unrolled, more breasts, miraculously able to point upwards without support, unveiled. A tall blonde girl bent down, took hold of one of her ankles and stood up again, the ankle coming with her, wrapping behind her head: it was particularly impressive considering that she was wearing five-inch heels.

'Ex-gymnast from Eastern Europe,' Lauren commented, eating a sandwich. 'Lots of 'em on poles nowadays. Pretty hard to compete with.'

Chloe's eyebrows were higher than they had ever been. She couldn't help being grateful that Hugo wasn't here, watching with them. These girls had absolutely amazing bodies, long and lean with bolted-on breasts the size of grapefruit halves and just as firm. The ex-gymnast's stomach was almost completely flat, even with one leg a hundred and eighty degrees in the air.

'The worst thing about porn is that the girls have such mental figures,' Chloe commented gloomily. 'You just feel you'll never be able to compete.'

'Not a prob for me,' Lauren said complacently. 'Lads who fancy me want all the bulges – they're watching Big And Beautiful DVDs.'

One of the other girls knelt down on the table, pulled aside the gymnast's G-string thong, and started to lick her in long strokes that were more for show than for effect; she was darting her eyes from side to side, making sure that the men crowding in were getting as good a view as possible.

'They know how to keep an audience happy, eh?' Lauren said. 'Won't go on for long, though. That table'll be murder on her knees.'

'Oh!' Chloe exclaimed. 'Look!'

She pointed to another monitor, where Sophie, always competitive with other women, had clearly decided that she needed to put on a rival show. Aided by Minty, who was holding her hand, she had climbed onto the dining-room table, and was hoicking her already short skirt up to her waist.

'Is she even *wearing* underwear?' Chloe asked, squinting her eyes.

'Bloody well hope so,' Lauren said, as Sophie began to sink into the splits, a rival group of male viewers gathering around her viewing platform. 'Cos we're going to be eating off that table tomorrow.'

'Eew!' Chloe put a hand, briefly, over her eyes as Sophie settled into the splits, throwing her arms wide, mouthing: 'Ta-dah!' The young men surrounding her applauded, and Minty, who couldn't bear Sophie getting more attention than her, climbed onto the table, standing behind her friend, and started grinding her white jean-clad crotch into the back of Sophie's head.

'What *is* she doing?' Chloe marvelled.

'Trying to go a bit lesbo to turn the boys on,' Lauren said. 'Remember what I said?'

Sophie, swinging her front leg around, turned to face Minty, pulling her down to the table; the two young women writhed on top of each other rather inexpertly.

'Two bags of bones going at it,' Lauren said. 'Lovely. Bet they're both bruised to pieces today, all those knees and elbows digging into each other . . .'

Chloe huffed out a laugh as Pasty, the birthday boy, sat down on the table, which rocked a little under his weight; his nickname hadn't been bestowed on him ironically. He pushed between Sophie and Minty, pulling them onto his lap, which had plenty of room for both of them; by now, their upper bodies were both stripped down to their bras. Chloe had to give Minty reluctant points for being slim enough to sit on one of Pasty's meaty thighs, wearing only white jeans and a skimpy silk chiffon bra, and not have a single roll of fat, not even a minimal one, show on her skinny torso. Minty and Sophie were now straddling Pasty's enormously spreading thighs, one on each side, their hands behind their heads, rocking their hips back and forth as if they were riding mechanical bulls in synchronized motion.

'Look back there,' Lauren said, pointing to the first monitor. The boob-job dancers were completely naked now, and Toby was snogging one with great enthusiasm, his hands wrapped over her round breasts as if he were a chef at a market stall feeling melons for ripeness. All around the table, the young men were dropping their trousers, pulling down their boxers, their cocks springing out. Chewie, another of the house party, ran into view, holding a bowl; he threw its contents high into the air, and both Lauren and Chloe flinched back instinctively, expecting the group to be soaked in liquid.

But what rained down on the orgy in the making looked, quite unexpectedly, like very large pieces of confetti. Some people, hit by it, jumped back, rubbing whichever part of their body had been struck, mouthing what were clearly curses at Chewie: most of the group, however, fell eagerly on the scattered shiny squares. And as they began to rip off the corners, both Lauren and Chloe let out '*Aaah*'s' of understanding in unison. The confetti was actually a bowlful of condoms.

'Thank God for Chewie,' Chloe said.

'Why's he called – oh God. Oh, Jesus Mary and Joseph. Fucking bloody hell. Don't bother, I can tell.'

Chewie had followed his condom-throwing act with a striptease; he was standing on the table, legs splayed wide, unbuttoning his shirt and wiggling his hips, cheered on by the naked girls. As the sheer extent of his hairiness was gradually exposed, some of the girls actually clapped their hands over their eyes: Chewie whirled his shirt around his head, let it go flying across the room, and started unbuckling the belt of his jeans.

'Fuckin' '*ell*,' Lauren said respectfully, reaching for the popcorn again. 'He's like a walking ad for loft insulation. D'you think his willy's got hairs on it as well?'

Chloe gagged, and promptly drank some wine to get rid of the acid taste.

'I can't stop looking!' she said, dribbling some wine down her chin and wiping it off with the back of her hand. 'I'm going to need more wine – pass me the bottle. God, it's like a freak show!'

She had seen Chewie on holiday, but Chewie in Vilebrequin board shorts was a very different proposition to him naked. The skin of his upper thighs was entirely invisible; it looked as if he were wearing a pair of black mohair shorts.

'Fuck, it ain't a bush, it's a fucking shrubbery!' Lauren said, riveted. 'How the fuck's his willy going to make its way out of all those pubes – oh look, one of 'em's going for it, brave girl – that's right, love, get your hand in there and have a good rummage around – yay! There it is!'

One of the strippers had extracted Chewie's cock from the heavy mat of pubic hair that blanketed his crotch and was rolling a condom onto it.

'No *way* is she going down on him,' Lauren said, shaking her head and shoving another mouthful of popcorn in without ever taking her eyes off the screen. 'No *way*. You'd never get some of them hairs out from between your teeth. And your face'd be all torn up. Like going down on a Brillo pad, only less soap.'

The girl had obviously come to the same decision. Pushing Chewie back onto the table, she was climbing on top of him, throwing one leg over his body and swivelling round, settling down into the reverse cowgirl to give as much of the room as possible a view of her jiggling breasts and her hands running up and down her body.

'Good choice,' Lauren commented, agog. 'All that hair must be a really nice comfy cushion. Bounces you up and down, does half the work for you.'

'We're *definitely* going to need a second bottle,' Chloe muttered, emptying the rest of the wine into their glasses.

The girl started to play with herself in a very porn-film style, parting her lips theatrically and inserting a finger, tipped with a curving acrylic nail, inside herself.

'Ugh, I can't watch that,' Chloe said, getting tipsy now. 'Whenever they put those long nails down there, I always think they're going to scratch their fannies up.'

'I know, right!' Lauren agreed. 'Especially bouncing around like that! You get one of them nails caught inside you, you could rip your twat right out.'

'Ahh! Lauren, *please*!'

But Lauren was already distracted, reaching for her mobile phone and dialling a number.

''Ello?' she said. 'Yeah, all right? Oh mate, you have no idea. They're doing all sorts. We're definitely going to need more vino . . . What? Fuck me, did you just say – that is *outrageous*. It's like, *blackmail* . . . Hah! Fuck me? Fuck *you*! Oh, all right then. I'm gagging for it . . . for the *vino*, you plonker! . . . Yeah, all right then. You got me over a barrel . . . No! Oh, you dirty bird . . . Yeah. All right then. One thing they do in the vid. But you'd better get that vino in here pronto . . . yeah, I *do* blimmin' well speak Italian . . .'

There was a knock at the door, and a second later Dave entered, mobile phone to his ear, a huge smile on his face and a bottle of red wine in his hand.

'Give it here and fuck off and eat some greens,' Lauren said, snapping her fingers at him. 'You're going to need your strength later, young man, I can tell you. I'm getting well worked up here.'

Dave duly disappeared again, and Lauren refilled her and Chloe's glasses with a huge smile of her own.

'Well, that's me sorted,' she said. 'Thought I was going to have a lonely wank after this. Nice to have a face to sit on instead. What!' She winked at Chloe. 'I told 'im I'd do one thing with 'im I saw in the vid. I didn't say what.'

'Well, you can't do the splits,' Chloe said. 'You'd snap in two. Oh, Lauren, look – it looks like they're having a competition—'

'God, those two show-offs! They've just got to be on top of something, don't they. Got to be on display,' Lauren observed. 'Like it'd kill them just to get fucked on the carpet like the rest of us commoners.'

Sophie and Minty were both flat on their backs on the dining table now, legs spread, young men in socks and shirts enthusiastically pumping between their legs, their heads tilted back to take another pair of cocks into their mouths.

The cocks, shockingly, belonged to Billo and Pete, the two protection officers.

'No *wonder* they didn't check everyone handed in their mobiles,' Chloe said, shaking her head in disbelief. 'They were too busy getting sucked off. They must be in *so* much trouble.'

'Ooh, look at Minty deep-throating!' Lauren said. 'She could give lessons.'

'I wish they'd all taken their socks off,' Chloe said, slurring a bit on 'socks'. 'It's just *so* amateur-porn.'

'Don't look at Toby, then!' Lauren said, chortling and pointing at another screen, where Toby was now kneeling on one of the leather sofas, naked apart from a pair of white socks, passionately kissing one of the Dutch girls he had mentioned before. She was exactly as Toby had described, tall and blonde, clearly sporty, with one of those athletic, Low Country figures that had wide shoulders, a well-upholstered frame, and small breasts: big and solid, rather than fat. Arching back, she pushed Toby's head down firmly to her nipples and then further south. Toby crouched over her, his head down as he worked away between her legs, the girl writhing and moaning, his bottom up in the air.

'Ooh, he's got a nice arse,' Lauren observed appreciatively.

'Nice *body*,' Chloe said: she would never have admitted that to anyone but Lauren. 'He's *really* in shape.'

They had a good view of Toby's back and one side of his body; his muscular shoulders, narrowing to a slim waist, were smooth and freckled, and his plump buttocks, sticking up as he eagerly ate out the Dutch girl, made the palms of Chloe's hands damp; she had always fancied Toby. Not that she would ever have done anything about it, of course. She was completely loyal to Hugo.

But still, it's fun to look . . .

Toby's long, lean thigh muscle, folded underneath his body, the equally muscular calf, were almost as smooth as the rest of him. There was a very light sprinkling of copper hair just visible at his buttock cleft, and Chloe realized she was focusing on that, trying to see more, leaning forward . . .

'Hope we get to see his cock!' Lauren said, leaning forward excitedly too. 'Ooh, do you think—'

But just then another girl who looked very like the one Toby was eating out appeared in front of the sofa. Chloe and Lauren groaned, as she was blocking their view, but she kept walking till she reached the head of Toby's sex partner; in her hand was a white candle, which she dipped into the girl's open mouth. The girl sucked at it enthusiastically. Toby looked up and said something; the girl he was eating out pushed his head right back down between her large, muscled thighs, however. The candle came out of the girl's mouth and was carried back again, behind the sofa, round to Toby's arse.

'Here we go!' Lauren chortled. 'Well, he was right, it was a candle – oh my *God in heaven*— '

Because the girl holding the candle wasn't preparing to insert it into Toby. Instead, she was standing back, giggling, her hand over her mouth, the candle discarded, as a man beside her, who was also completely naked, stepped forward. He too looked Dutch, as smooth-skinned and blond as Chewie was hairy and dark, and so tall he loomed over the sofa. His cock was in one hand, and in the other was a bottle of what looked like lube; he was squeezing the latter over the former, working it in. He said something to the girl, who put out her hand to receive an extra squirt of lube into her palm. She bent over Harry, rubbing the lube between his arse cheeks, rubbing her breasts and upper body against him, too, letting him feel her; then she moved aside, and the man took her place.

Chloe reached out to Lauren, grabbing for her hand; they clung together as they watched the Dutch man working his cock into Toby's arse. He did it slowly, with practised skill; it was long, but comparatively slender, so slipped in without much resistance.

'Nice,' Lauren said. 'Pretty much the same shape as a candle, eh? Bet Tobes won't realize what's really going on . . .'

And the man was careful not to do anything that would give the game away. He didn't hold Toby's hips, or thrust his cock so far in that Toby would feel the unambiguous male anatomy connected to its base; he limited himself to thrusting lightly back and forth, just as if it were a candle being pushed in and out. Toby was jerking in response to the penetration, arching his back; his head came up from between the girl's legs, his mouth opening: clearly, he was panting in pleasure. His hands were braced on the sofa, letting him push back more, take more of the cock inside him: he started to turn his head and instantly the girl sat up, took his face between her hands, kissed him passionately, distracting him from seeing what was happening behind him.

'They're all in on it!' Chloe realized in shock. 'They totally set him up!'

'I don't want to sound like some awful rapey rapist,' Lauren said, 'but he's fucking *loving* it . . .'

The girl kissing Toby was reaching down, between his legs; Lauren and Chloe, now having lost almost all inhibitions, groaned loudly in unison as her hand closed around Toby's cock at the precise moment when they could have seen it. She was twisting and pulling with an expert action that had Toby, unmistakably, yelling:

'Fuck! Fuck! *Fuck!*' as his hips pounded faster and faster, his head tossing, his red curls bouncing.

'It's like watching My Little Pony getting bum-fucked,' Lauren commented, as Chloe spat more wine over herself in perfect synchronicity with Toby's cock, which shot simultaneously over the girl's breasts and stomach; feeling him coming, she had directed its action with perfect aim.

Behind him, the Dutchman, his face pink and contorted with imminent release, his lips dragged into a grimace with the effort of holding on, pulled out of Toby and promptly shot his load triumphantly, an impressive jet of white spunk curving through the air as he waved his cock from side to side.

'*All* the rugs are going to have to be dry-cleaned,' Chloe said grimly.

'Toby really needs to find a gel who'll peg him on a regular basis,' Lauren observed, looking at Toby's ecstatic orgasm face.

'Peg?' Chloe asked.

'Strap one on and give it to him up the bum,' Lauren said, thrusting her hips explicitly up in the air. 'You know, hit that sweet spot they've got up there.'

Chloe was about to blurt out something about her and Hugo's odyssey through 101 Ways To Use A Banana In Bed, but she thought better of it. There were some things she couldn't tell anyone, not even Lauren, although she trusted her completely.

One of the reasons Hugo proposed to me is that I've been a hundred per cent discreet the whole time we've been together. Even from the moment he asked me out, I never breathed a word to anyone until we agreed we were okay to talk about it.

It would have been lovely to share a confidence with Lauren, to have a giggle about it, but Chloe just couldn't risk it. Hugo was so sensitive about any aspect of their private life being in the public domain. He had been too young to realize, when his mother was alive, how badly she had been treated by the media, how much the incessant gossip had affected her; but he had learned about it since then, and it had left him very alert to any possible slip in the wall of privacy he wanted to feel encircled him and Chloe.

What if the three of us are out one night, and Lauren gets drunk and makes a banana joke? I mean, it's not as if men like people knowing about their sex life at the best of times ... and though I really don't think Lauren would say anything, I have to be much more careful than a girl who isn't engaged to the second in line to the throne ...

So she bit her tongue, skipped the anecdote about how much Hugo had turned out to love an unripe banana up his own bottom, and finished her glass of wine. On the screens, Toby was lying on the sofa in the arms of the Dutch girl, the man who had shagged him was now bracing himself against the back of the sofa while the woman with the candle inserted it into his own bottom, and Sophie and Minty were in a large group around one of the black modular tables, on which a man was pouring what was clearly cocaine from a clear plastic bag: he had snipped the corner from the bag and was piping the cocaine out – 'Looks like Mary Berry icing a cake!' Chloe said – in a long spiral, starting from the centre of the table and circling outward, growing with each loop.

'Nice steady hand – he's done that before,' Lauren said. 'Probably his party piece, bring a kilo bag of coke and show off his cake-decorating skills. Ooh look, there go Soph and Minty, ruining his nice little moment. Never been any good at delayed gratification, those two.'

The two girls, cut plastic straws in hand, were already ducking their heads over the table, to the obvious annoyance of the man, who was yelling at them. Chloe rolled her eyes.

'I think I might go up and see Hugo,' she said. 'Do you mind? I don't think I can manage to watch it all – it's been a long day—'

'Nah, I'll come up too,' Lauren said, pushing back her chair and standing up. 'All that stuff about having to see it all was complete bollocks. I just wanted to mess with Sophie. From now on, if she gives me or you any grief, we can just ask if she's sucked any security officer cock today. That'll shut her up.'

'Bit rich, though,' Chloe giggled, 'considering you're off to do exactly that . . .'

She stood up, bent down to pick up her shoes, and tipped sideways, grabbing the desk to steady her; she wasn't as used as Lauren to drinking a bottle of wine at a sitting, and she was definitely the worse for wear.

'Only if he begs me,' Lauren said happily. Switching off the screens, she slipped on her own heels and wound her arm through Chloe's, taking some of her weight, walking with her to the door. 'Here, I've got you. Blimey, you've dropped a few pounds, ain't you?'

'I've got that wedding in a few weeks!' Chloe said, trying not to slur. 'In Herzoslovakia – you know, that volleyball supermodel—'

'Ugh, her!' Lauren said as they went down the corridor. 'Yeah, you don't want to stand next to that one in photos if you can avoid it. Lucky bitch, she's got it all, eh? Bloody gorgeous Olympic medallist, marrying the king of a nice little country where the press don't buzz round you like they do with us lot . . .'

'Ladies? You all done in there?'

It was Dave, emerging from the kitchen, his expression hopeful.

'Yeah, thanks, love,' Lauren said, breaking into a big smile at the sight of him. 'Seen more than enough. Billo and Petey

– look, they've had their fun. But let's just say they can't do this job any more. I don't give a toss what they do off the clock, but they were supposed to be working, and they totally lost the plot.'

Dave nodded briskly.

'They're already back in London, pretty much directing traffic,' he said. 'And talking of being on the clock—' he cleared his throat – 'I've actually been off-duty for the last couple of hours. I was staying up to make sure you have everything you, um, need.'

'I'm going to need a thorough check of my room,' Lauren said, nodding seriously. 'I have a thing about making sure there's no one hiding under the bed.'

'Lucky for you we're specially trained at the Met in under-bed checking,' Dave said, standing back to let them pass and start up the staircase. It was one of those floating-step, rail-free designs, which gave Chloe vertigo at the best of times: with her internal organs floating on a red wine lake, she clutched Lauren's arm tighter and squeezed her eyes nearly shut. Lauren walked her to the door of the suite she was sharing with Hugo, gave her a quick kiss goodnight and swiftly turned away; as she pushed open the door, Chloe could already hear giggles and squeals further down the corridor as Dave, following hard on Lauren's heels, presumably started to claim his reward for bringing the wine.

Chloe had stayed in some lovely hotels and private houses in her time with Hugo, but she wasn't too spoilt to be impressed by the beauty of the master suite of Villa Clarita. It occupied the entire space of one of the big glass boxes, stacked so that it jutted out at an angle over the bay below, entirely free from being overlooked, despite its two front walls each being a huge, single sheet of glass. The view by daylight, of the cliffs falling away to the sea, would be breathtaking: by night, the moonlight rippling gently over the dark waves was scarcely less stunning. The enormous bed, in the centre of the room, was white padded leather, made up with crisp white, grey-bordered sheets and a grey silk coverlet, illuminated only by two built-in crystal reading lights on either side. Two doors beyond led to a bathroom and what looked like a huge walk-in closet.

Hugo had put everything away, or at least away from view. The room was perfect, as it was meant to be seen, ready for a photoshoot for *Condé Nast Traveller*. And Hugo, lying in bed watching something on his iPad, his fair hair ruffled against the piled-up pillows, looking flushed, sleepy and handsome, was ready, in his fiancée's eyes, for something much too intimate to be photographed by anyone.

'All done?' he said, raising his head. 'Oh, you look—'

'I'm drunk,' Chloe informed him, dropping her shoes to the floor and starting to unbutton her shirt. 'I'm drunk, and I'm really horny.'

'Was it very—' Hugo put down his iPad.

'*Very*. They fucked everywhere! So much fucking! We couldn't even *watch* all the fucking! And now—' she unzipped her skirt – '*I* want to fuck.'

'Good,' Hugo said happily. 'I must admit, I *was* rather hoping—'

'Oh, I'm going to fuck your brains out!' Chloe assured him. She pulled down her knickers and tights, balled them up and threw them on the floor, and reached behind her to unhook her bra as she walked towards him. Hugo stared at her naked body for a long moment, swallowing hard, then threw back the coverlet and started urgently dragging down his boxers. His cock sprang up, as eager for her as always.

'You look incredibly sexy all bossy like this,' he commented, licking his lips, an unconscious gesture he always made when turned on. It always threw a switch deep inside Chloe. She was wet already, but she felt an extra surge of excitement as she watched his tongue slide over his full pink lips; by the time she reached the bed, climbed up his legs, settled herself on top of him, she was practically dripping. She raised herself, angled his cock as precisely as you can only do when you have sex with someone so often that you know the exact geometry that works for both of you, and bore down on him, driving him right up inside her. Hugo gasped, grabbed her hips, and moaned:

'Fuck! You're so wet! Fuck, I could come right now—'

'Don't you *dare*!'

All the images that Chloe had seen were flooding through her head. Everyone fucking everyone else. Cocks in pussies, in mouths, in arses: she giggled at the memory of Toby being fucked, and the involuntary spasm tipped her just to the verge of coming. She reached down, flicked herself a couple of times, and with huge relief, had her first orgasm of the night, grinding down even deeper on the base of Hugo's cock. He could take it; they often went at it pretty hard, and all he did as she ground him into her was to grip her hips even tighter, throw his head back even more against the padded leather headboard, jerk his own pelvis up to meet hers.

'I want to come,' he moaned, 'I want to spunk inside you—'

'You can't! We're not using a condom! I am *not* getting pregnant before the wedding!'

Chloe bent over, grabbed his hair in both her fists, dragged him up to look at her.

'You can't – fucking – come,' she said, pounding down on him with every syllable. 'You can't – fucking – come—'

She was pulling his hair, hurting him a bit; it had to hurt. Hugo's eyes were bright, loving this new game.

'You're so wet, you're so tight!' he said, pushing back, managing to sit up, driving himself into her even more; she screamed as he pulled her head towards him, his hands in her hair too, dragging her mouth to his, kissing her so hard their teeth clashed. He let go of her hair with one hand, leaving the other clamped on the back of her head, reaching down between her legs to make her come again and again, his cock wedged inside her; she screamed in bliss, but finally it was too much and she had to wrench his hand away, panting, unable to get a word out.

She shoved him back down, her hands on his chest now with weight behind them, riding him for a few last blissful strokes. She couldn't let him come inside her, *couldn't*. As soon as she announced a pregnancy, everyone would be counting back the days to work out when she had conceived; no way were they going to conclude that she'd got knocked up before the ceremony. Plus, she didn't need one extra pound on her as she walked down the aisle with the entire world watching.

But Hugo's cock was shuddering inside her with that tell-tale rhythm, and she could feel that he was bare seconds away. It was like an action film where the heroine has to wait till the last possible moment to make her escape, hold out, hold off the villains so that the rest of her team can get away; as she dragged herself up and off him a bare second before his cock swelled and shot, she felt that she was throwing herself to the ground, rolling under an overhead door that was slamming down, making it through just in time. She was panting as if she'd just sprinted a hard-fought race, panting and laughing.

And Hugo was too. She fell to his side, onto the huge, insanely comfortable mattress, as his cock pumped out a final few plops of milky semen onto his flat stomach, heaving with his gasps and his laughter.

'Fuck, you left that till the last minute,' he mumbled.

'The last *second*,' she corrected him, kissing his shoulder.

'That was *amazing*.' He turned his head to kiss her lips. '*You* were amazing. I'll have to get you boozed-up more often.'

Chloe's head was swimming; the combination of the wine and the orgasms was tipping her happily towards the shores of sleep.

'I'm really pissed,' she said, kissing him back and then flopping back on the pillows. 'I'm going to pass out any moment.'

'Shall I get you some soluble Solpadeine?' he asked thoughtfully.

'Ugh, I think I'd vom if I drank that now,' she said. 'But I'll probably need it tomorrow morning.'

There was a momentary pause.

'Chlo?' Hugo asked, sounding unexpectedly insecure for a man who had just had such excellent sex with his fiancée.

'Mmn?' she managed.

'It was the booze, wasn't it? And, obviously, watching people shagging – I mean, that'd make anyone horny . . .'

Something was wrong. With a truly heroic effort, Chloe heaved herself over onto her side and dragged up her heavy, slumping eyelids. If she could have held them open with her thumbs, she would have.

'What is it?' she mumbled.

Hugo was looking up at the huge, hyper-modern glass slab lighting fixture on the ceiling, but his voice was as muffled as if he had his face buried in a pillow as he continued:

'It wasn't – um, well, I'm sure you saw Toby, obviously. And he's quite a – well, people think he's very handsome, you know – and I'm not quite as – everyone always says—' He cleared his throat. 'I'm sure he's put it about a lot more than I have, Toby's always been – he probably knows lots of stuff to do, sex-wise, really cool stuff ... I've always been grateful that I met you when Tobes wasn't around, you know, Chlo. I sort of thought that girls fancied Tobes more, but went after me because of who I was ...'

Chloe was shattered with exhaustion, but this obviously had to be tackled immediately.

'I love you,' she said, kissing his shoulder. 'I love you, and no one else, and I don't want to have sex with Toby. I don't want to have sex with anyone else for the rest of my life.'

'*Really?*' Hugo turned to face her, his eyes big and vulnerable. 'Really, honestly?'

'Of course!' Chloe lied without a twinge of conscience. She wasn't going to physically cheat on Hugo, ever; what did it hurt to tell him she wasn't going to do it mentally?

'You're the only man I'm going to have sex with for the rest of my life,' she said firmly. 'I love you. We just fucked each other's brains out. You're the only man for me.'

Hugo's worried expression softened with relief.

'Seriously, Hugo,' she added, bringing out the big guns. 'I came, like, twenty times – *and* I'm sore now, your cock's so big.'

There were no more reassuring words than these for a man; Hugo was positively beaming now. She kissed his shoulder again.

'And now,' she said, 'would you wipe yourself off, turn the lights off and work out how to draw whatever curtains there are so I don't get woken up at dawn with a stinking hangover? Oh, and get me a glass of water from the bathroom? Thank you, darling. I love you *sooo* much ...'

She was asleep, and snoring, by the time Hugo brought back the glass full of water. Gently, he turned her onto her side, stroked her hair back from her face as she snuffled something in her sleep, and slipped into bed beside her, spooning her. Down the corridor, in their own glass box, Lauren and Dave were still hard at it, Dave's ginger head buried happily between Lauren's capacious thighs; but they were on their first time, and wouldn't get much sleep before dawn.

Lori

Lori was very calm. Blissfully, transcendently calm. It was rather unusual for a young woman on the verge of matrimony, when severe attacks of nerves, mood swings, and panic about her dress were much more to be expected. But ever since her attempted flight home, the intervention of the Dowager Queen, and Lori's reconciliation with Joachim, she had been on a keel so even that her family, who had arrived the week before the ceremony, were beginning to be concerned at her lack of any normal pre-wedding jitters.

But Lori didn't feel jittery. Not at all. Everything had been resolved. She had had her pre-wedding crisis already; every bride went through one, according to the Dowager, and hers had simply come earlier than usual. Mihaly had been sacked, Kristin and Katya had apologized to her profusely and explained that they had completely misunderstood the situation, the Dowager was petting and cosseting her as if she were her own daughter, and Joachim had put aside most of his urgent business with the tax haven crisis meetings to spend a good part of every day leading up to the wedding at her side, and every night in bed with her.

She had moved into the Imperial Suite, and they were leading a very cosy life together, watching box sets in the private cinema every night; they were working their way through *The Killing*, a gloomy Danish serial killer series which went on for ever, mostly in the rain, yet couldn't fail, for some reason, to cheer one up. Also, the heroine's sweater had been slashed by a knife-wielding thug and then had mysteriously knitted itself up again. Lori was endlessly amused by that, Joachim a little less so, especially when she couldn't help reminding him of it at least once an episode; she had noticed that recently she did seem to obsess about little things that didn't really matter, but that just seemed to get stuck in her head . . .

Of course, she and Joachim weren't spending every minute of every day by each other's side; that would have been suffocating. No, Lori was also absorbed by the wedding plans. The Dowager was involving her in every single aspect of the coming ceremony, every detail, particularly the guest list and seating plans, which were absolutely crucial when dealing with the highly complicated question of hierarchy for visiting royalty. Philippe was a positive mine of information, and the Dowager also had a royal etiquette expert, an old, gay Count – 'call me Bobby, dear', he had said to Lori in perfect English, kissing her hand – who had an intimate acquaintance with, apparently, every single noble family on three continents.

Still, Lori was expected to absorb a great deal of information. The wedding would effectively last for three days, with state banquets and activities before the ceremony itself; she would have to learn to recognize the major dignitaries, and she was kept busy studying photographs of them and memorizing the correct way to address each one. Count Bobby would be by her side as she greeted each new arrival, whispering in her ear; a sprightly, blue-rinsed septuagenarian, he was already fizzing with excitement at the prospect.

And she was also devoting a large amount of time to working out. Fitness, naturally, had always been a major part of her life, and since Mihaly's dismissal – it seemed to have been decided that it wasn't necessary to replace him – she had found herself in the gym, on a daily basis, with Attila. It had been a revelation that the stocky, silent bodyguard, whose sturdy physique looked like that of a classic, muscle-bound weightlifter, was actually an active practitioner of Iyengar yoga, PowerPlate and TRX, a suspension training system invented by a US Navy SEAL, where you hung from straps round your wrists or ankles, battling against the weight of your own body.

On their own, without Mihaly's charm and dimples distracting Lori, she and Attila had struck up a friendship centred on their love of working out. Attila had evolved into her personal trainer; during the time they didn't spend together, because of all her meetings, he busied himself working out new, challenging routines for them both to practise. He looped the TRX straps around Lori's ankles, got her to try agonizing combinations of planks with oblique crunches interspersed with press-ups, roped himself to her and made her try to drag him across the gym, laughing at her as she struggled with his weight.

In return, Lori had a volleyball net installed in a disused storeroom at the Schloss, and taught him to play. Attila, though extremely fit, had no 'pop', as gymnasts and volleyball players put it; he lacked the fast-twitch muscles that made jumping effortless. Lori drove him ruthlessly over the masking-tape court, taking her revenge for all the squats he made her do on the PowerPlate. Placing the ball expertly, she had him dashing from one side of the court to the other constantly, and they ended every session drained, sweaty and high on endorphins.

This, of course, meant that Lori's figure was morphing swiftly back into the strongly muscled shape of her competitive athletic days. It showed mainly in her upper back and arms, which initially had the dressmaker complaining as the pearl-encrusted lace of the dress needed to be removed and extended to fit Lori's widening frame; but one brisk, furious whisper from the Dowager silenced any further objections. Exercise clearly made Lori happy, so she must be allowed to do it as much as she wanted.

And the doctor she was seeing every week agreed with this entirely. Dr Bruschsson was the Dowager's charming, silver-haired personal physician; the Dowager had considered it might be a good idea for Lori to have a 'little visit' with him, as she had put it, the day after Lori's abortive escape attempt. Lori had been so shattered by the events of that day that she had slept till late the next morning, emerging from Joachim's suite at noon looking drained and exhausted with dark, bruised shadows under her eyes.

The Dowager had taken one look at her and suggested that Dr Bruschsson might perhaps be able to give her a vitamin B12 shot to pick her up. The latter had had her doubts, but almost immediately upon meeting Dr Bruschsson, Lori was reassured by his calm, professional demeanour and his benevolently paternal manner. She had found herself spilling out much more than she had meant to, finding the doctor a wonderfully understanding confidant. What had been supposed to be a twenty-minute check-up had lasted two hours. Dr Bruschsson had taken her pulse, drawn some blood for analysis, and given her the vitamin B12 shot plus a vial of iron supplements, to be taken morning and night. He was concerned, he said, that she might be a little anaemic, a deduction which arose from the dark circles and her pallor.

Lori had said that she thought that might be because she hadn't slept well two nights ago, and had been a bit up and down recently. Dr Bruschsson had clicked his tongue sympathetically, commented on how stressful weddings were in general, let alone when you were marrying a king, and pulled another vial of pills from his bag. A mild herbal sleeping remedy based on valerian, he said; he didn't believe in overprescribing pharmaceuticals to healthy young women in the prime of life. One before bedtime ought to set her right.

And the iron pills, plus the valerian sleeping tablets, had had the most extraordinary success. The sleeping remedy had worked that very night, and the iron pills had kicked in after a couple of days. She felt light, wonderful, relaxed; nothing seemed to bother her. She had indeed been anaemic, Dr Bruschsson confirmed when she saw him in his office for a follow-up a week later; Lori had been surprised, since she ate plenty of red meat, but, he explained, it might be a genetic issue. They could test for that later, after the wedding, if she were concerned about it.

But Lori wasn't concerned about anything at all. It was as if all her doubts had gone, any anxieties miraculously faded away. Dr Bruschsson was delighted to hear that she was enjoying working out with Attila and encouraged her to continue. He was sure, he said, that the regular training was doing her the world of good. Plus, he had another little tweak he wanted to make; a vitamin formulation for an energy boost. All natural, made up to his own formula. The Dowager herself took a version of it and look how bright and perky she was! He suggested Lori try it for a week in combination with the other pills and see how it seemed to work for her.

And adding in the vitamin supplement was an even bigger improvement. Lori couldn't quite believe how wonderful she felt. Dr Bruschsson, whom she continued to see on a weekly basis, explained that this was technically known as post-crisis euphoria; she had been through a terrible experience, where she had doubted the most important choice she would ever make in her life, and now that she had emerged on the other side, her feeling of light-headed, floating bliss was absolutely textbook. He explained it in terms of a religious crisis of faith. It was very common in accounts of saints' lives, apparently, for them to struggle with their belief in God, wrestle imaginary demons, and then, having conquered those demons, to report sensations of transcendence, positive ecstasy, because they felt so purified.

Like being born again, he said, smiling, as he sipped his tea. Of course, this wasn't at all a religious situation, but Lori should feel very reassured to know that her feelings were perfectly normal, given the significance of what she had been through, her relief in the choice that she had made.

It was hard, though, to explain this to the Makarwiczes, who were a little taken aback at this serene, almost otherworldly, incarnation of their normally down-to-earth daughter and sister. Lori, naturally, couldn't breathe a word about the Mihaly incident, nor about Katya and Kristin's appallingly misguided advice; Joachim's cousins had been strictly instructed not to breathe a word about the misadventure, and to behave with extreme decorum when they went out in the evenings with Hailey. Lori couldn't say that she had tried to run away, *would* have run away if she hadn't been stopped at Graz, and if the Dowager hadn't convinced her to return to Valtzers. She knew that it would worry them too much, which was the last thing she wanted. There was nothing to worry about, nothing at all! She felt wonderful! She had never felt better in her life!

And obviously, if she couldn't tell them what had happened, she couldn't explain Dr Bruschsson's theory of post-crisis transcendence. She could only say that she was incredibly happy and relaxed – *really* relaxed! – and that she and Joachim were living together in his suite now, which was a very good thing. And that she was really looking forward to their honeymoon in Mexico, which had the effect of distracting all of them as they burst happily into reminiscences of happy weeks spent holidaying in Cancun . . .

Besides, only a couple of days after the arrival of the Makarwiczes, the first official wedding guests arrived, an extended French ducal family, Madame la Duchesse having been a bosom friend of the Dowager Queen's back in their Swiss finishing-school days. And after that, the wedding gathered speed like a runaway train. Lori had an entire trousseau of exquisite outfits which had been carefully planned for all her official events, and the inevitable, multitudinous photo sessions for what seemed like every single glossy, upmarket, royal-approved gossip magazine in Europe: she had been assigned a dresser from the Schloss staff, whose entire job consisted in looking after her wardrobe and coordinating her hair and makeup sessions.

It was an insane whirl. She could barely catch her breath. Count Bobby guided her with great tact and discretion, the Dowager and Joachim were always by her side; Philippe made sure that her family was well looked after, seated beside Shameeka and a small group of friends from Miami, along with some carefully selected convivial, jolly, unsnobby guests. Lori longed to spend some time alone with Shameeka and the volleyball group, but somehow there was always an obstacle: Philippe or the Dowager would tell her, regretfully, that just as she thought she had an hour free to spend with her friends, there would be another official photoshoot or a diplomatic meeting with one of the crowned heads of Europe. That wasn't exactly the sort of appointment Lori could refuse, and she was constantly assured that her friends and family would and could come for long visits once she and Joachim were back from honeymoon and all the hustle and bustle of the wedding was over.

Even Shameeka couldn't help but understand that Lori's priority over this dazzling series of days had to be the scheduled meet and greets with the King and Queen of Spain, the Queen and Prince Consort of Denmark, the King and Queen of the Netherlands, the Crown Princess and Prince of Sweden, the Crown Prince and Princess of Japan, Prince Hugo of Great Britain and his princess-to-be, Chloe. Lori rapidly stopped being daunted by the famous royals she was encountering, simply because there were just so many that she soon reached overload: King, Queen, Prince, Princess just became another title for her to remember.

And as one would hope, considering their upbringings, the regal manners were universally excellent. Every royal Lori met was polite to her, and many were positively welcoming. Chloe in particular seemed lovely, and in any other circumstances Lori would have spent time getting to know her. Both of the young women were commoners marrying into royalty, both feeling their way into their new worlds and coping with the huge demands that the modern media placed on them as symbols and figureheads for their countries. They were able to talk a little at cocktail receptions and formal parties, but of course, as women, they were never seated next to each other at dinners, and what they would have wanted to say was probably not for anyone else's ears.

Philippe, however, assured her that he had secured Chloe's email address and that they would be able to get in touch after the honeymoon; Chloe had already suggested that the new King and Queen come to visit them at Kensington Palace for a few days before the insanity of her own wedding juggernaut began rolling over her and Hugo, adding wryly that she would be very grateful for any advice that Lori could give her on how to cope with it all without going insane. Lori looked so beautiful, so serene, Chloe commented enviously. She was obviously managing everything so well. Chloe would have to sit down with her and pick her brains thoroughly . . . and if Lori had any diet tips, too, Chloe would be incredibly grateful . . .

Lori had enthusiastically suggested a meeting with Dr Bruschsson; his vitamin medication had the effect of making her less hungry, as well as all the other benefits. Chloe had said that she'd fly back to Herzoslovakia if she had to: Dr Bruschsson sounded like a life-saver. And then Philippe had glided up to Lori and murmured that she needed to meet Prince Albert and Princess Charlene of Monaco, and Lori had smiled at Chloe, her tranquil, glorious smile, and been ushered off, taller than any of the other women, her blonde head moving through the crowd, Chloe staring after her in wistful envy.

The morning of her wedding, Lori awoke a few minutes before they were due to come in with her coffee and scrambled eggs. She had slept separately from Joachim, of course, in her old suite of rooms, and she looked dreamily up at the pale blue silk tester of her four-poster bed, her eyes accustoming themselves to the dark room, staring at the elaborate drapes and pleats and folds, and thinking that it looked like the sky, arranged by angels, little cupids sitting in the corners as they did on painted ceilings, pulling at the delicate fabric so it hung perfectly overhead . . .

Sitting up, propping herself on the silk pillows, she reached over to the side table. Feeling for her pill vials, she shook out her morning iron and vitamin dose and took them with some water from her bedside carafe; she found herself looking forward with real enthusiasm to those pills every morning and evening.

It was Lori's last moment of solitude as a single woman. She stretched out, feeling the pills travel down her oesophagus, settling softly in her stomach, setting her right. Balancing her correctly. Clear March morning light trickled in through the gaps in the curtains, growing stronger as the day broke fully, the sun rising; all the forecasts had predicted a sunny, rain-free day, and as Lori lay there she heard her dresser come eagerly into the sitting room beyond the bedroom, accompanied by the familiar clinking sound of a maid following with a breakfast tray.

Breakfast, shower, put on the underwear that had been selected for the dress, the tights, a robe; no need for a corset, the dress was fully boned. Hair, makeup, nail check. The dress was wheeled in on a mannequin, gasps from Lori's entire, hovering entourage accompanying its entrance, even though they had all seen it before; but it was impossible to be blasé when you were in the presence of a work of art. And frankly, Lori's Amazonian height and frame meant that her dress was also built to grand proportions. The high wooden mannequin had had to be tipped and tilted to get it through the double doors.

She was eased into it slowly, like a gigantic doll being dressed up, under the patient supervision of Frau Klertzner, for whom this was her supreme creation. It took ten minutes to pull up the antique lace pearl-beaded sleeves, to settle the bodice so that it sat perfectly symmetrically on her shoulders, across her collarbone. The dresser began the long, slow process of fastening the hundred tiny satin-covered buttons that ran down Lori's spine, slipping each one into the satin loops, one of the dressmaker's assistants holding the dress closed across Lori's back, another sweeping the train sideways, as the buttons were gradually worked into their closures.

The satin lining was cool on her skin, the dress hanging heavily on her; with all the boning, the beading, the twenty-foot, duchesse satin train, it had to weigh fifty pounds. Frau Klertzner had given herself full rein to create a truly dramatic and elaborate gown which only a woman as tall and well-made as Lori could have carried off.

The Dowager Queen – her timing, as always, immaculate – swept in just as the final buttons were being fastened, two footmen following her, two large jewellery boxes in their arms. Lori's dresser was standing on a little stool to reach her nape, two of the assistants now holding the train, staggering a little under the weight, moving it to make room for the stool. The Dowager was regal and immaculate in ankle-length brocade Carolina Herrera couture, the pale pink sash of Herzoslovakia's Order of the Golden Eagle pinned across it, glittering with diamond brooches that symbolized other honours and decorations. Her tiara had already been fixed into place earlier that morning on her back-blown, bouffant grey updo. The Dowager could have spared herself at least a couple of hours of carrying the tiara's considerable weight, but she wouldn't have dreamt of it.

'Frau Klertzner, you have outdone yourself,' she said to the little dressmaker, who bobbed a curtsey, her eyes bright with pleasure. The Dowager looked up at Lori, shaking her head in wonder.

'My dear,' she said gently, 'you have never looked so beautiful. Truly, you are a queen already.'

The footmen had placed the jewellery cases on the dressing table; when they were both opened, Frau Klertzner's assistants and Lori's dresser could not avoid further exclamations of awe.

The footmen and dressmaker were of course much too well-schooled in seeing State jewels to make any sound, and Lori herself was in a trance, steadying herself to receive the extra weight, piece by piece, of the cold, heavy, glittering jewellery with which she was gradually bedecked. It was definitely a *grande parure*: the collar, the earrings, the bracelet, and finally the tiara – the hairdresser summoned back in for a final fix and spray of Lori's smoothed-back hair.

Finally, when her various attendants had finished, she was led to the cheval mirror. Behind her, Frau Klertzner's assistants held the train, standing wide apart to spread out its full width to show her. Made to trail spectacularly down the long steps inside St Petrov's Cathedral, it was so big that she couldn't see either of the assistants in the mirror.

Lori was taken aback for a moment by the sheer grandeur of her appearance. *I look as if I'm in costume,* she thought. *Dressed as a warrior queen after a victory.* The huge tiara, with its enormous diamonds and pearls set in solid gold, added another four inches to her height; her shoes, invisible under the dress, only had one-inch heels, but that still put her over six foot three, towering over everyone else in the room, even the footmen. She was like a magnificent goddess come to earth.

'What beautiful grandchildren I will have!' the Dowager said, clasping her hands in sheer happiness, as Frau Klertzner, by her side, nodded eagerly in agreement.

I'm going to be a queen, Lori thought, staring at herself. *In a few hours, I will be a queen.*

There would be an official ceremony to crown her in the cathedral when she and Joachim returned from their honeymoon; the crown once worn by the Dowager had been resized for Lori's larger skull, extra filigree work added into the thickly encrusted framework that held an array of extraordinarily precious rubies and sapphires. But from the moment Joachim slid the simple gold ring on her finger, she would be Queen Lori of Herzoslovakia.

Queen Lori! It sounds ridiculous, doesn't it? I should have been called Maxima, like the Queen of the Netherlands. Or Sofia of Spain. Those are way more appropriate names for a queen. Lori should really be short for something longer, more ... regal. Lorinda, maybe. Queen Lorinda. No, that sounds like something out of a cartoon ...

Lori smiled at the thought. From what felt like a very long way away, she saw her mouth move in the mirror, outlined, painted a pale pink with two coats of Lancôme long-last lip stain, and then covered with a sealant that the makeup artist assured her would ensure that the colour endured right through the entire ceremony. The upwards tilt of her lips was so sweet that every woman present but the Dowager cooed in unison. Although the Dowager would never have allowed herself to make such a common noise, her own smile deepened into what a vulgar person would have called a smirk.

She gave the footmen a nod, and they promptly opened the double doors, letting in what seemed like a waiting flood of women: Lori's mother Sandy, who burst into tears the instant she saw her daughter; Hailey, Kristin and Katya, the bridesmaids, exquisitely dressed in scaled-down, champagne-coloured versions of Lori's dress; a bevy of little flower girls, the florist and his three assistants with baskets of peach rose petals ... from that moment, Lori let everything flow over her. There was no wedding planner to arrange everything; the Dowager was the ultimate wedding planner, and could be utterly relied upon to make sure that everything went without the slightest of hitches.

They were ushered from Lori's suite in a solemn procession, the Dowager leading the way, Lori following next, and her train, metres behind her, carried by the three bridesmaids, wearing gloves, of course, so that nothing should mark the perfect sheen of the white fabric. Lori had already practised walking in her wedding shoes, and she glided like a swan along the corridor and down the imposing central oak staircase. The entire staff of the Schloss had gathered in the hallway to watch her descend, every face turned up to her wide-eyed in near-worship at the sight of her. Her father and brother, waiting at the bottom of the stairs, both swallowed hard at the sight of their small-town girl transformed into a glittering, glossy queen-to-be, wearing a king's ransom of jewels as if she were born to them.

Lori laid her hand on her father's arm as he turned and walked her out of the Schloss to the waiting carriage. Hailey, Kristin and Katya had also been practising carrying her train, and they moved behind her with smooth precision, manoeuvring its huge oval sweep, photographers documenting every turn, a whole bank of cameras massed outside as they left the Schloss. Lori stepped up into the carriage, her train carefully folded around her and placed on a special velvet pad before the footmen closed the doors. It seemed as if the whole population of Herzoslovakia had turned out to line the streets of the carriage route, waving not only Herzoslovakian flags but US ones too, which made Bob Makarwicz comment appreciatively on how welcome this whole country was making his daughter.

Lori smiled again, but she didn't say a word. She was utterly composed, sealed like an egg in its shell, perfect and smooth, as she looked out of the carriage window – sadly, March in Herzoslovakia was too breezy for an open conveyance – and waved her gloved hand to the massed, cheering crowds, who called her name and blew kisses as they saw her face. It was only a short ride down the hill to St Petrov's

Cathedral, its famous stained-glass windows glistening in the sunshine, striking gleams of ruby, sapphire, emerald and gold down its grey stone façade. Lori was helped out of the carriage by her father and one of the footmen, and stood there patiently as her train was eased out of its folds by the bridesmaids working busily behind her. The Dowager swept towards her, took Lori's hands in hers, and said softly:

'Herzoslovakia has been waiting a long time for you, my new daughter. Welcome to our family and our hearts.'

Bob Makarwicz gulped and reached for his pocket handkerchief; the camera flashes increased at the sight of the bride's father wiping away tears. Screams of 'Lori!' 'Lori!' echoed around the outside of the ancient cathedral, rising up into the blue sky. Television cameras whirred, antennae and disks atop ranks of vans parked across the other side of the cathedral square; it wasn't just the entire population of Herzoslovakia, Lori realized, but hordes of international visitors who had come to see this spectacle. And of course, the world's media, which loved nothing more than a royal wedding.

The Dowager let go of Lori's hands, and nodded at her, smiling like a cat that had had an entire bowlful of the richest, fullest Jersey cream. Leading Sandy Makarwicz, she proceeded up the wide stone stairs of the cathedral; behind her came the flower girls and boys, clad in peach satin.

And then it was time. As they had practised, Lori took five slow steps forward on her father's arm, paused for a final train check, and then proceeded, her perfect posture drawing sighs of appreciation from the spectators. On each stone stair tread, she took a tiny pause, absolutely sure of her timing, her father following her lead, until she was framed in the high arched doorway.

Joachim cut a small figure at the other end of the long red carpet, his deep burgundy uniform, sashed in white, heavily decorated on the left breast with a bevy of ceremonial medals. He looked, if not actually handsome, then extremely distinguished.

Every face in the aisles was turned to her, but Lori was focused straight ahead, seeing the Dowager and her mother walk slowly to their seats right at the front, the flower girls and boys drawing soft oohs and aahs as they passed, and then, like a ripple on water, the indrawn breaths of everyone seeing her in her wedding finery for the first time. The Dowager had been very much against Lori wearing a veil: with a face that beautiful, she had pronounced, it would be a crime to cover it. Lori had been relieved at the time, as a veil would have been even more extra weight for her to carry, and the tiara itself was already cutting into her temples. She would have dark red marks when she finally took it off.

But she realized now why brides wore a veil. It protected them from the pressure of knowing how hard people were staring; out of the corners of her eyes, she could see every face swivelled greedily in her direction. But she was used to being a cynosure from her long years of playing competitive sport in skimpy clothing, and that helped to keep her features still, her gaze clear, her chin high. The stares felt physically weighted, as heavy as the satin and lace dress, as the tiara clamped around her skull, the collar around her neck, the earrings at her lobes.

Step, join, stop. Step, join, stop. That was why you walked like this, too, to give you a framework, something to concentrate on as everyone ate you alive with their stares. Step, join, stop. Step, join, stop. Past each aisle, each carved wood divider hung and decorated with woven silk ribbons in burgundy and white, the colours of the Herzoslovakian royal house. Concentrating on the physical demands of keeping her back straight, her head high, her steps even, her gaze level on the decorated altar behind the Patriarch of the Herzoslovakian Orthodox Church, who was waiting solemnly to conduct the marriage ceremony, she reached her husband-to-be.

There was no bouquet to hand over; they had experimented with various arrangements, but the unanimous conclusion was that it would have detracted from the effect of the fabulous jewels, the precious lace and sleek outline of the dress. Bouquets, the Dowager had added knowingly, often served to hide a bride's pregnancy or imperfect figure; since Lori had, in the Dowager's opinion, not a single physical flaw, there was no need to add to perfection. Her father took her hand for a moment in his grasp, squeezed it hard, and placed it in Joachim's, stepping back to his son's side. And there she was, in front of the altar, the silver-bearded Patriarch before them, a gold-bound Bible in his hands, nodding gravely at her and her fiancé as he prepared to join them in matrimony.

It was a long, elaborate, complicated ceremony, but athletes were well used to ceremonies, and Lori was a good student; she understood, by now, a lot of the Herzoslovakian words and she and Joachim had rehearsed the key moments. They kneeled and stood and kneeled again; their hands were bound with ribbon; ribboned circlets were held over their heads, and then removed; the ribbons linking their palms were unwound and added to the circlets, weaving them together into one. The rings were brought forward and blessed. Lori and Joachim rose to their feet for the last time.

There were television cameras rigged through the cathedral, capturing every moment of the ritual. So alert observers began to notice that the colour was slowly draining from Lori's face, until, by the time she stood again, it was as pale as the lace of her dress, as the pearls sewn heavily onto it. Experienced royal journalists commented on the length of the ceremony, the weight of her dress and tiara, speculated on the lack of air circulation in St Petrov's Cathedral, started to voice their concern that she might be about to faint. By the time Joachim slid the ring onto her finger, repeating the vows, Lori was as white as paper. The only colour in her face was the blue of her eyes and the pink of her lip stain. She took up Joachim's ring from the velvet cushion and began to repeat her own vows after the Patriarch's prompts.

And then it happened. Tears started to slide down her face. Lori was not even aware of the phenomenon at first; she only knew that she felt a little calmer suddenly, that something had released inside her. Her voice was clear, though quiet, but she had been assured that the microphones were very sensitive, that she didn't need to speak any louder than normal, and her words seemed to be coming out fine, as they had during the various responses the Herzoslovakian Orthodox ceremony required them to make. But her face began to feel cooler, as if there was a draught blowing through the cathedral, even though the flames in the huge silver candelabras on the altar were as steady as ever. Gradually, she realized that tears were pouring slowly down her cheeks.

Lori had no idea what to do. She had no handkerchief; she couldn't interrupt the ceremony. And besides, the tears felt strangely pleasant. It was only when she began to slide the ring onto Joachim's finger, turning towards him, and he caught sight of her face that she realized how much she was crying.

Because Joachim looked appalled. Absolutely appalled. He grimaced at her briefly, mouthing something she didn't understand; as the ring slid up to the base of his finger, and he said: 'I do,' she glanced at the Patriarch and saw that he, too, had a panicked look in his dark eyes.

Her face was icy cold now. She couldn't help putting up a hand to her cheek and her fingers came away almost dripping wet. No one in the cathedral, of course, had any idea that Lori was crying steadily and silently, a sheet of tears now streaming down her face: her back was to them. But everyone viewing her on television, millions of viewers throughout the world, was now gripped by the spectacle. Women who had been watching by themselves yelled to their husbands and boyfriends to get in here *now* and see what was happening; parties that had been thrown by royalists around the globe fell silent, every guest's eyes glued to the screen; and the entire, enormous community of Facebook, Twitter, and every other social media network began to buzz frantically.

Joachim was fumbling in his breast pocket, pulling out a handkerchief, handing it to Lori. She dabbed at her face, drawing muffled exclamations from the congregation in the cathedral, who only now realized what was going on. With a poorly concealed grimace, the Patriarch took the bride and groom's hands, brought them together, folded his own hands briefly around the clasp with a last blessing, and then gestured at them to turn around and face the aisle.

The joined circlet was in his hand now, held above their heads from his higher station on the altar step. The two ends of the white ribbon dangled down, the symbolism simple and clear: two rings joining the new couple, on their hands and above their heads. Organ music swelled. It was the culmination of the entire ceremony, the moment at which the new husband and wife were presented to the world, when the emphasis shifted from the private vows to the public acknowledgement of them.

And the public acknowledgement in the cathedral was, frankly, horror. Lori's makeup hadn't run; the makeup artist knew her job much better than that. But it was obvious that her face was running with tears, while simultaneously maintaining the same otherworldly, angelic expression which she had been wearing when she had made her entrance.

That was the real indication that something wasn't right. If Lori had been crying in happiness, clinging to her new husband, beaming up at him through her tears, that would have been quite a different story; married women around the world would have shed some tears of their own, hugged their partners, remembering the emotion of their own ceremony. But this was more surreal. Joachim was visibly uncomfortable, not knowing how to react, and Lori was simply standing there, not looking at him, her hand resting limply in his, dabbing at her face with the handkerchief as the tears continued to fall. She looked entirely disconnected from her surroundings, her beautiful blue eyes fixed on a distant horizon, as if she were seeing a vision invisible to anyone else.

Whispers ran through the cathedral. Even the best bred of the guests couldn't refrain from turning to their companions and commenting under their breath on the bride's extraordinarily detached expression. A gossip columnist would comment later that day that Queen Lori looked like a Christian martyr about to be thrown to the lions. Joachim, breaking protocol, shuffled closer to his bride, looking into her face, hissing: 'Are you all right?' to which Lori returned no answer. The Dowager and Lori's parents all stared, appalled, at the spectacle the new Queen presented and the fact that Joachim seemed to be unable to reassure her in any way.

The organ music changed into a triumphal march, the cue for them to process from the cathedral, and Lori recognized it instantly. Like a programmed robot, she began to move down the steps, Joachim a split-second behind her, catching up swiftly, their hands still linked. The flower girls and boys, prompted by their parents, dashed quickly out in front of the bride and groom, baskets of peach rose petals in their hands, scattering them up into the air, giggling adorably, a pretty picture that would normally have had the congregation cooing in appreciation.

But instead, there was a shocked silence. Lori was moving as smoothly and gracefully as ever, like a swan gliding on a lake, her eyes fixed now on the huge cathedral doors, which were swinging open; Joachim was darting nervous stares around him, assessing how much damage had been done, meeting his mother's eyes for a long, painful moment as he passed . . .

The huge crowd outside had been watching the entire ceremony on giant television screens, and were agog to see Queen Lori emerge onto the cathedral steps, to judge how she looked in person. Although they broke into cheers and applause as the children ran out, tossing their last handfuls from their baskets, and Joachim and Lori followed into the cloud of rose petals, the noise was much less heartfelt and enthusiastic than it had been when the bride entered St Petrov's. Joachim raised their linked hands, showing off the rings, which provoked a further surge of claps and flag-waving.

But every single one of the spectators present knew that things were very wrong. Something had happened during the ceremony: the bride was as stunningly beautiful as ever, but much too eerily serene about the tears drying on her cheeks to possibly be considered happy, and the groom looked as if he were making a huge effort not to turn to her, shake her and tell her to pull herself together and smile for the avidly watching cameras.

In the end, it was an anchor from KNYI, the local TV station from the Makarwiczes' home town of Dorchester, New York, who summed up best how Lori looked.

'Jeez, what have they done to our girl over there in Yurup?' she asked in a shocked tone. 'Remember her up on that podium, taking bronze for the US, looking like she ruled the world?'

KNYI flashed to a picture of Lori and Shameeka, clasping hands above their heads, tanned and lithe, huge smiles of triumph on their faces, medals flashing round their necks. The contrast with the image of Lori at her wedding was nothing short of shocking.

'And now she looks – I'm just going to go ahead and say it, Alicia,' the anchor said, shaking her head. 'She looks like a *zombie*.'

In Morocco, watching the transmission at the Tarhouna Palace with Rahim and a visiting Margaret, Belinda clutched her lover in absolute horror.

'Oh God, Rahim,' she said, 'I *knew* I should have tried to see her and said something! Look at her – they've got her on tranquillizers and antidepressants! I recognize that blank stare – I saw it in the mirror for five years. Why didn't I *do* anything? I knew about Joachim and his prostitutes, and she clearly didn't, poor thing! She thought it was a love match, just like I did! Oh, *why* did I let you both talk me out of it?'

'Belinda, it wasn't safe,' Rahim said as firmly as he could. 'It wasn't safe then, and it isn't now. It was incredible luck that no one realized who you were when you went to London, which I was *completely* against, as you know—'

'This Lori has a family to look after her,' Margaret added. 'She doesn't need you – she's a grown woman making her own decisions – she's an Olympic athlete, for goodness' sake . . .'

But Margaret's voice was feeble, and tailed off completely as Belinda grabbed the remote control and paused on the close-up of Lori in floods of tears as she said her vows. It was being streamed in an almost constant loop on rolling news stations, who were naturally over the moon at this incredible piece of luck. Not only were there not one, but two royal weddings this year, but both involved photogenic young brides and good-looking bridegrooms who were either kings, or in line to inherit the throne; that was more than enough for the news media to consider 2013 a truly blessed year.

No one would have dared to hope, however, for a twist this shocking. Herzoslovakian officials had called in favours, greased the necessary palms, managed to lower a boom of silence over everyone involved with Lori's flight to Graz, from the hotel to the heliport to the passport officials. The media had never got so much as a whiff of trouble in paradise between the King of Herzoslovakia and his bride-to-be.

But here it was. Lori's beautiful face, framed in the opulent diamond and pearl tiara and collar, stared out at Belinda, who, of course, was absolutely right about what she saw in Lori's otherworldly expression, the detachment in her blue eyes. The medication Belinda had been on over twenty years before was naturally less sophisticated, but the basic principles were exactly the same: to keep both women as close to Stepford wives as possible.

Dr Bruschsson, in collaboration with the Dowager, had maintained Lori on a cocktail of Diazepam, for anxiety, and Sertraline, an antidepressant, ever since she had been convinced to return from Graz, tinkering with the dose to achieve a perfect combination, keeping her calm and floating in a relaxed state while still able to carry out everything she had to do, barely aware of any internal or external agitation.

And for good measure, an Ambien every night to put her to sleep.

Naturally, the plan had been to gradually ease Lori off the pills when she returned from honeymoon, telling her that the 'vitamin deficiencies' Dr Bruschsson had pretended to diagnose had now been balanced by the supplements. Since the whole reason that Joachim had married Lori was to produce heirs to the Herzoslovakian throne, Lori becoming pregnant would then be paramount, and conceiving a baby while on the combination of prescription drugs that were keeping her so sedate was definitely not medically advised.

However, it had certainly not been expected that Lori's real feelings would break through during the ceremony. The pills had kept her calm even through her outrush of tears, but they had also prevented her from showing any emotion during her crying jag, which was the most suspicious aspect of all.

'If she'd only broken down properly,' Margaret said, articulating this problem with her usual acuteness. 'He could have put his arm around her – she could have clung to him – they could have passed it off as what the Yanks would call shock and awe.'

She winced as she looked at the screen.

'I mean, she has no background, does she? Must be a terrible shock, to come from absolutely nowhere and suddenly become Queen of Herzoslovakia. Enough to make you go quite wonky for a while. *Not*,' she added firmly, 'that I'm defending anyone who can't keep a stiff upper lip in public. It's a terribly bad show. But I agree with Lumps. They've got her on something, no question. Her eyes look as glazed as a china bowl.'

'She looks like a beautiful, lonely statue,' Rahim said quietly, staring at Lori's face, blown up to giant size, 'A man can't kiss and hug and reassure a statue. You can see that he doesn't have the faintest idea what to do.'

'Because he doesn't love her,' Belinda said passionately. 'He never did.'

'That's how you looked, when I met you,' Rahim said to her, stroking her hair. 'Like a beautiful, lonely statue. You were on all sorts of pills too. Do you remember? That party in Sardinia on Abramovich's yacht? I thought you had the saddest eyes of any woman I had ever seen in my life. All I wanted to do was make you happy again.'

'And you did,' Belinda said fervently. 'You did.'

'In the past tense,' Rahim said, wincing.

'Oh, darling—' Belinda twisted in his arms, tilting her head to look into his eyes. 'I just can't see that poor girl and not feel somehow responsible . . .'

Her lover pushed her away and stood up, folding his arms over his chest. He was wearing an embroidered linen *gandoura*, a short, open-necked robe, traditional lounging wear for Moroccan men; it came to just below his knees, and under it he wore loose linen trousers, his feet in leather sandals. His dress might be informal, but his stance was not, nor was his expression. His thick dark brows were drawn together, his thicker dark moustache bristled above his full, pursed lips.

'We've been safe all these years, Hana,' he said to her, his voice surprisingly tender considering how deeply he was frowning. 'Safe here, and happy. No one suspected anything, no one came after us. It has been a sadness to both of us that you cannot see your children, and I regret that more deeply than I can say, but it was not of our making. And when you wanted to see Hugo and the girl he is going to marry, I understood. I was reluctant to see you go, because I was afraid for you, but I understood. *This* girl, however—'

He shot out one arm and pointed at the screen, a dramatic gesture worthy of any screen diva.

' – *this* girl is not your family! You did not give birth to her! As Margaret so wisely and sensibly said, she has a family of her own to take care of her!'

'Yes, and look what a good job they're doing!'

Belinda, too, gestured at the screen, at Lori's glazed eyes and tear-wet face. She stared pleadingly up at her lover.

'Rahim, he's just using her to knock out a couple of heirs! She *has* to escape before she gets pregnant! Once that happens, he'll have her exactly where he wants her – completely trapped. He'll be able to use the children to keep her under his thumb, doing whatever he wants. She won't be able to take them with her if – *when* – she wants a divorce. My God, it isn't even her country! At least with me, I was in Britain! I had a house at Kensington Palace, I had Hugo and Sophie living with me, my friends, my own *language*! What on earth is she going to do? He'll tie her to that tiny little country for ever, where she'll always be a stranger – how will she ever manage to leave? She's *worse* off than me!'

Belinda was almost panting with fervour. She looked from Margaret to Rahim, her hazel eyes wide.

'I can't watch this and not try to do something about it,' she said. 'Don't you see that?'

'No!' Rahim said angrily. 'No, I don't! Not at all! You're risking everything, Hana! Already I was so worried about you travelling to London, and now – what, you want to go to *Herzoslovakia*?'

Belinda bit her lip.

'It's not like we can invite her here,' she said.

'Oh my *God*! No! Over my dead body! Hana, I mean it.' Rahim's brows knitted together into one emphatic black line. 'You cannot do this. I forbid it. Do you hear me? I forbid it!'

Margaret, having never seen Rahim in a temper before, looked with great concern at her friend, all too aware of how Belinda had responded when Oliver had thrown his fit of fury at Buckingham Palace, how distressed Belinda had been living with her husband's rages for many years. But she was instantly reassured when she saw Belinda's reaction. She was simply staring at Rahim, her eyes still wide, but no trace of fear or distress at his explosion. Rahim, clearly, was not Oliver, and Belinda had no problem with him shouting or getting angry, no fear that he might start hurling candelabras or worse.

'Rahim, I feel that it's my responsibility,' Belinda said quietly to her lover. 'I can't just sit still and see another young woman go through what happened to me. It's like history repeating itself.'

'And *I* can't sit still and watch you put yourself in danger!' Rahim said, which had Lady Margaret nodding vigorously in agreement. 'Hana, if you do this, I can't support you. I can't take this – the fear when you're away. He tried to kill you! And if he finds out that you're alive, he will try to kill you again! This is the truth – no exaggeration!'

'You must admit, Lumps, when we saw him at Buck House, he was more frightening than ever,' Margaret said to her friend. 'I wouldn't put anything past him.'

Belinda shivered. 'But don't you see?' she said bravely. 'If I do nothing now, then maybe this Lori will end up exactly where I am! No, *worse*! It was a million-to-one chance that I found Rahim, and that he had this wonderful palace where we could live together, safely. That he had enough money and power to protect me.'

She reached out her hand to her lover, who was still glowering at her, his arms folded.

'This Lori isn't going to be that lucky,' she said softly. 'She needs help. Everything's stacked against her, and that's not fair.'

'*Lucky!*' Rahim's moustache bristled even more. 'Hana, this is a fortress, not a palace. A fortress against the world. All I could give you was the most luxurious prison I could build you. And it's not enough, is it? It's not enough for you! This is the day I was always terrified would come.'

He looked down at Belinda's outstretched hand, and didn't extend his own to take it.

'You gave up your children,' he said sadly.

'Not for you, Rahim!' she said swiftly, panicking now. 'Not for you! It wasn't a choice between you and them! It was either someone working for Oliver slipping me pills so I overdosed, or escaping to save my life—'

'And it's not enough,' he repeated. 'You want to rescue this girl so she doesn't end up where you are now. In prison.'

Rahim swallowed, his Adam's apple bobbing above the open neck of his gold-embroidered robe. Belinda started to say something, but he cut her off with a slice of his hand through the air.

'You want to throw our life away, potentially, for a woman you don't even *know*,' he said, devastatingly. '*Our* life, Hana, not just yours. I chose to live here with you. I gave up many things, many possibilities, to do that. And yet we only talk about *your* loss. If you leave here to go to Herzoslovakia – if they realize who you are, if they finish what they started – you will leave me alone, without a partner. Without the love of my life. Think about that.'

He turned on his heel and strode from the room, both women looking after him.

'He's very impressive,' Margaret said quietly to Belinda. 'And you know, he does have an unarguable point, Lumps. He's in this with you for the long haul.'

Belinda sank her head into her hands, burying her fingers deep into the dyed blonde hair.

'Oh God,' she moaned. 'I know, I know! He's absolutely right. I was bloody lucky to get away with going to London without getting caught. I shouldn't risk anything again for a *very* long time.'

'If *ever*,' Lady Margaret said, very concerned. 'Honestly, I thought it was a bit much when he said he forbade you, but now I want to say *exactly* the same thing.'

Her voice tailed off as she watched Belinda raise her head again, her mascara smeared from having just rubbed her eyes, and stare at the giant screen in front of them.

'You know what I was like those last couple of years, Squashy, when I was stuffed full of pills?' Belinda said, hypnotized by Lori's exquisite, frozen face. 'I was a zombie. Just like her. That poor thing. They've turned her into a bloody zombie.'

Lori

'Champagne with guava nectar?' the concierge asked, smiling at Lori and Joachim as they were ushered inside the elegant little reception of the Casitas Royale. It was a glass-fronted bungalow, deliciously perfumed, and the glass of champagne they were each handed was scented too, the guava delicate and fragrant.

'And would you like a cinnamon aromatherapy neck wrap?' was the concierge's next question, to which Lori nodded an enthusiastic assent. This honeymoon destination was proving to be even more luxurious than she had anticipated. Looking nervously at Joachim, who was *not* in a good mood, she was hugely relieved that he was, at least, accepting the champagne with a polite smile for the concierge, and nodding at the offer of the neck wrap.

They had arrived at the main hotel, the El Dorado, in a limousine which had collected them from Cancun airport and whisked them here in barely half an hour: they had been met beneath the smart white pillars of the El Dorado by a charming butler called Elizabeth who had offered them fresh, scented towels to wipe their travel-stained hands, escorted them to a smart gold golf cart, and driven them through the hotel grounds to the Casitas section, Attila and Vassily, Joachim's bodyguard, following in a second cart. This was the smaller, even more exclusive part of the resort, no building higher than two storeys, everything intimate and personal with full butler service.

It was ten at night, a warm, tropical breeze rustling the palm trees, waking Lori up after her long sleep on the private plane; she had literally boarded, strapped herself into her seat, reclined it when the steward told her she could, and promptly passed out. But the fresh air, blowing through her hair as Elizabeth expertly whipped the golf cart around the curves of the path, and the damp towel which Lori was holding to the back of her neck, were waking her up, making her feel more alive than she had in weeks. It was like being back in Miami: the tropical night, the sound of the waves washing against the shore, the palm trees. Her heart rose. This was the perfect honeymoon destination, the reason she had wanted so badly to come to Mexico. Here she and Joachim could relax, come down from all the stress and tension of the wedding; they were here for a fortnight, plenty of time to recharge their batteries.

He's still tense and cross with me about the crying, she knew, sneaking a glance sideways at the stern profile of her husband – her *husband*! – who was staring straight ahead as the cart wound its way through the resort, seeming not to be affected at all by the beauty of their surroundings. *But he'll calm down soon. Everything else went fine. And I couldn't help it! It isn't like I did it deliberately!*

Everything else *had* gone fine: the aftermath of the wedding ceremony had been conducted according to plan. The return to the Schloss, waving to their subjects from the Throne Room balcony; the champagne reception for the VIP guests; and then, after having changed into their going-away outfits, King Joachim and Queen Lori's emergence for a last farewell before climbing into the helicopter waiting in the courtyard of the Schloss to take them off to their private jet: it had all been as precise as clockwork. Lori had followed along with every step of the very well-organized day as obediently as she had dressed that morning, gone to the cathedral and said her vows; she was even able to assure her concerned family that she was absolutely fine, had just been overwhelmed by the sheer pomp and circumstance that came with being the cynosure of all eyes at a royal wedding.

It helped, of course, that after a swift, panicked consultation with Dr Bruschsson, the Dowager had quietly given Lori another couple of antidepressants at the Schloss, 'more supplements to help with your nerves'. Lori had swallowed them dutifully, retouched her makeup, and put on her pale blue Jil Sander dress, the perfect foil for the coloured diamond earrings and necklace that Joachim had given her. Joachim had changed into a dark suit, his silk tie pigeon's egg blue, echoing the crepe of Lori's sheath. The private plane was stocked with cashmere pyjamas, silk/wool robes and sleeping socks for Lori and Joachim to change into while travelling, but their official exit, of course, had to be regally smart.

Lori looked wonderful at her new husband's side, and he handed her up into the helicopter with charming courtliness. The Herzoslovakian populace and the TV spectators were to some degree reassured by her Sertraline-and-champagne-fuelled smile as she waved goodbye to them through the window: the blades whirred, the helicopter rose into the air, and the last of her official duties was completed. For the next fortnight, she and Joachim, together with two of his body-guards, plus Attila, would be staying in the El Dorado Casitas

Royale, one of the most luxurious resorts on Mexico's Mayan Riviera.

Lori herself had chosen the Casitas, after much discussion with Philippe. For some reason she had rejected all his suggestions of luxury villas in which she and Joachim could be almost completely alone together. She had felt drawn to the idea of a five-star-plus resort with other people around, sports and activities she could join, women to meet at the spa, maybe, who she could chat with over cocktails by one of the many pools. Joachim had left the decision entirely to her, and she had overridden Philippe's objections; he had originally been dubious about the idea of a King and Queen rubbing shoulders so closely with commoners on their honeymoon, even incognito. Lori, however, had pointed out that with Joachim trying to retain Herzoslovakia's tax-haven status, being able to put out a press release after the honeymoon to show that the new King and Queen had stayed incognito in a destination that one of their subjects might have chosen would be an extremely positive PR move.

This had been a stroke of genius. Philippe's eyes had flashed excitedly behind his glasses; he had proclaimed *Mademoiselle* to be inspired, superb, and told both Joachim and the Dowager that Lori had truly excellent populist instincts.

Incognito was the key, of course. As the concierge asked for their passports, a smartly dressed man in a cream two-piece safari outfit trimmed in orange came forward, bent to whisper something to her, and, as she nodded and slipped away, he took her place, leaning across the desk to shake Lori's and then Joachim's hand.

'I am Juan Carlos, the manager here at the Casitas Royale,' he said, his voice soft, his dark eyes full of charm and intelligence. 'Allow me to handle your check-in personally, Mr and Mrs Guttman.'

He smiled with infinite discretion as he took the passports from Joachim. Philippe had discussed the situation with the hotel management and received absolute assurances from them that, during their stay, not a word would be breathed about their true identities: afterwards, a joint press release would be issued with the approval of both sides. Lori and Joachim had been booked in as a very wealthy German businessman and his wife, and the hotel had completely understood their need to take a room for their bodyguards adjoining the Presidential Suite, in which Lori and Joachim would be staying. The word honeymoon would not be officially mentioned, but the management was organizing the new couple a raft of romantic activities and tours to the Mayan Riviera's principal attractions.

Lori was hoping that they wouldn't be recognized; she rarely had been, even post-Olympic success. Her blonde, blue-eyed prettiness, her height and her slimness, meant that people tended to think she was an actress or model rather than an athlete. She'd lost count of the times she'd been told she looked like Charlize Theron's younger sister, for instance. By day, she'd pretty much always wear a baseball cap and sunglasses; by night, she would let her hair curl up as it did naturally, and wear floaty, pretty, printed sarong-type dresses to go out to dinner. She was pretty sure that she'd look so different from Joachim of Herzoslovakia's groomed, sleek-haired fiancée, whom the world was used to seeing in fitted chic designer dresses and lavish jewellery, that no one would associate the casually clad Lori on the beach with the former.

Besides, Philippe's done a very good job of convincing everyone we're on honeymoon on a Greek island in absolute secrecy, she thought happily. *I'm so glad we're not! This place looks*

*gorgeous already, and there'll be so much more to do here than
on a Greek island . . .*

'May I place your neck wrap, Mrs Guttman?' the concierge
asked, and Lori sighed in pleasure as the heated, scented
aromatherapy wrap settled over her shoulders, the perfume
of cinnamon and chocolate floating around her. Even Joachim
made a quiet grunt of pleasure as his was placed around his
neck.

Juan Carlos was clicking away at the iPad on the desk as
Lori and Joachim sipped their champagne. She dared to smile
at her husband, hold up her glass to clink to his, and after a
moment he responded, but with barely a smile in return.

'You will be very tired from your long flight,' Juan Carlos
said, pushing back his chair and standing up. 'Everything has
been taken care of – the check-in is complete, and Elizabeth
has been unpacking your suitcases. We have champagne and
canapés waiting for you in your suite. Allow me to escort you.'

Out from the scented air conditioning to the warm, moist
night air; another loop along the under-lit paths, down to the
palm-fringed sea shore; past a white and glass restaurant,
glowing gold from the subtle lighting.

'This is D'Italia,' Juan Carlos said over his shoulder as he
navigated the cart smoothly around it. 'Our Italian restaurant. I would be happy to make a booking for you tonight, if
you would like? Or, as guests in the Presidential Suite, you
are able to order food from any of the restaurants in the
hotel. All the menus are available on your TV.'

'Italian sounds lovely,' Lori said excitedly. 'And I could go
out. I think I have my second wind. Joachim, what do you—'

'I will go to bed,' Joachim said, shutting that down. 'I am
tired. But we can order food, certainly.'

The golf cart swooped under an overhang, up an incline,
and came to a halt; Lori was out at the same time as Juan

Carlos, Joachim following as the manager went up the wooden staircase to the first-floor entrance, unlocked the door to their suite and held it open.

'Please,' he said, gesturing to them to go in. Lori walked in and promptly gasped in delight at the beauty of the suite. She was in a wide living room, a very smart kitchen area to her right with a gleaming LG fridge and Lavazza coffee maker, and before her, wraparound glass walls, lights glinting beyond then on what looked like a wide balcony area that stretched out over the beach. The room itself was decorated with perfect taste, subtle colours, a dining area with pale suede chairs and a dark wood table, a Bose sound system on a console table. As she walked in further, she saw the open-plan bedroom, its huge, dark wood bed with crisp white sheets and suede bolsters, an equally huge round suede pouffe at its base.

'Around here,' Juan Carlos said, indicating that Lori should walk round the bed, past a glass table on which was an ice bucket with a bottle of Moët resting in it and the most exquisite chocolate sculpture she had ever seen in her life, 'is the Jacuzzi and the outdoor swimming pool . . .'

'Oh wow,' Lori sighed. The swimming pool, gently illuminated with underwater lighting, was a perfect circle floating above the ground; the Jacuzzi, big enough for two, was already filled with foamy water on which floated rose petals in the shape of a heart.

'We do not refer to the honeymoon at all,' Juan Carlos said, smiling at her and Joachim, 'because we are being discreet. But of course we are here to make your stay as romantic as possible. You will have a day and night butler, twenty-four seven, who will be happy to book you a candlelight dinner on the beach. Or we can bring you lunches and dinners from any of the many restaurants, as I explained. Let me show you your terrace, where you can be as private and romantic as you would like . . .'

He slid open the doors by the Jacuzzi, and they walked around the wraparound balcony, past the pool, which overlooked the horseshoe-shaped Casitas section below; at its centre was an oval swimming pool surrounded by a little river which looped around the private pools of the suites below. Palm trees were planted at intervals, strings of coloured LED lights wrapped around their bases for gentle lighting, and behind the big swimming pool was a wide thatched area with a swim-up bar.

'Casitas means "little houses",' Juan Carlos explained, seeing Lori take in the scene. 'So here, you are in the most exclusive area of all, the last set of casitas on the beach. Each has its own pool, and there are many hammocks and loungers, beach beds – it will never be crowded. But of course—' they followed him around the balcony, to see him smiling as he indicated where to look – 'you have your own hammock here, your own day bed . . .'

Lori took in the double hammock, white fringe dripping from it onto the wooden balcony, a huge day bed beyond upholstered in white towelling, piled with silk pillows, set under the thatched roof of the terrace for shade.

'Oh, it's *beautiful*!' she exclaimed happily – the glass of guava nectar champagne had definitely perked her up. Reaching for Joachim's hand, she took it impulsively. 'Isn't it lovely, honey? Aren't you happy?'

Her husband nodded as they walked down a spur of the balcony built out over the beach; the sound of the waves pounding on the beach was louder now, a pulsing, steady beat. Lori looked down at the white foam just a few metres below, breaking onto the pale sand, and felt her heart fill up with happiness at the beauty with which she was surrounded.

'This is where we can serve your private meals,' Juan Carlos said, as they stepped onto a square wooden terrace, framed by a balustrade, hung with white muslin curtains and topped with a small thatched turreted roof; it held a table and chairs, and was lit with flickering candles, the posts of the terrace wrapped with golden glowing LED lights. It was magical, enchanting, and Lori pulled her husband across it to a flight of steps leading down to the beach, pausing there at the top, her fingers wrapped through his, staring at the sea.

'So yes, this is your private beach access,' Juan Carlos informed them, 'and below is your beach cabana, reserved for your exclusive use. Of course, you may use whatever you want to in the whole of the resort, but this area is only for you.' He gestured around him. 'This is essential, naturally, in your circumstances. And I assure you, we are very honoured to have you staying here, Your Royal Highnesses, but absolute discretion as to your identities is as important to us as it is to you. Only I, the owner of the hotel, and two of my most trusted managers are aware of the situation. You will forgive us no longer using your titles – you will be Mr and Mrs Guttman to the staff, who understand that you are VIPs, but no more than that.'

Juan Carlos had chosen his moment perfectly: they were out on the promontory of the dining area, with no one on the beach below to overhear. Joachim nodded briskly in appreciation of the manager's tact, and dropped Lori's hand, walking back towards the suite.

'I'm hungry,' he said bluntly.

In the living room, Elizabeth, smart in the butler's uniform of white shirt, black tie, grey waistcoat and black trousers, was waiting to greet the 'Guttmans', proffering them each another glass of champagne. Juan Carlos nodded in approval.

'I have unpacked everything,' she said. 'Would you like me to show you where it is?'

Joachim looked at Lori: clearly, this was her job. She followed Elizabeth through into the walk-in wardrobe – really, it was a full dressing room – and Elizabeth showed her the marble bathroom, the wet room and the outdoor shower, beaming at Lori's gasp of approval as she stepped outside into the humid Mexican air once more and realized that she could shower al fresco. A beaten-bronze water fixture, which Elizabeth told her was modelled after the shape of the coconut palm tree roots, was fixed high in the air, the shower surrounded by tumbled stone walls, the starry night sky above providing a velvety roof.

'Anything you would like, please just call our number,' Elizabeth said as they returned to the living room. 'It is by your bedside table. Ask for me, or Pablo, or Liliana – we are your team around the clock.'

'This is *so* lovely,' Lori said with obvious sincerely. 'I know we'll have a wonderful hon— holiday here.'

'You can ring for anything you would like, but you have a full bar.' Elizabeth opened the doors of a wooden cupboard to show a dizzying array of bottles and glasses. 'And also a minibar in the kitchen. We thought you would like something to eat after your journey . . .'

She indicated the dining table, on which had been placed a huge fruit bowl and a cheese plate that was more like a sculpture, artistically carved shards of hard cheese in the centre, softer ones scooped and moulded below it. Beside it was an arrangement of quesadillas to eat with the cheese, stacked with architectural precision in layers, each in its own folded napkin.

'I hate to mess it up,' Lori said happily, her stomach rumbling, 'but I will.'

'Mr Guttman would like some dinner from D'Italia,' Juan Carlos said to Elizabeth. 'The asparagus and truffle risotto, and then the chocolate surprise with Baileys ice cream.'

'Of course,' Elizabeth said, nodding. 'Mrs Guttman, would you like to look at the menus?' She indicated the TV screen, where the menu for D'Italia was showing.

'You know,' Lori said, 'I'm looking at those quesadillas and thinking how long it's been since I've had Mexican food.' She grinned at the Casitas staff. 'And I've been watching my weight for ages for my—' She bit her tongue. '*Anyway*, you know what I'd love? A big plate of quesadillas. Chicken, cheese—'

'Lobster?' Elizabeth suggested.

'Oh, yeah! That too! With guacamole and sour cream and pico di gallo and – oh, *everything*. All the trimmings. Is there beer in the fridge? Mexican beer?'

'Of course,' Elizabeth said, smiling. 'And Evian and Perrier water too – we have imported water for the VIP guests. There is Häagen-Dazs ice cream in the freezer,' she added proudly. '*And* popcorn you can make in the microwave.'

'Yummy!' Lori beamed. 'You've thought of everything.'

'We will leave you now to relax,' Juan Carlos said, taking her hand, looking as if he were about to kiss it and then thinking better of it and shaking it instead. 'I hope you will be very happy here with us at the Casitas. Tomorrow, Pablo, who is the day butler, will come by and talk about the excursions and dinners we have planned for you, and I will give you a tour myself of the resort if you would like. But now I am sure, you would like to be alone.'

'Dinner will arrive in half an hour,' Elizabeth said, following him to the door. 'Please ring me if there is anything else you need.'

'Another bottle of champagne,' Joachim said, and she nodded as she closed the door behind her.

Lori took in a deep breath, put down her glass, crossed to her new husband and hugged him.

'I'm sorry about crying,' she said. 'I know it made you upset.'

'It made me *humiliated*,' Joachim corrected her, putting his hands on her arms and pushing her back. 'It is all anyone is talking about.'

'How do you—'

'There was WiFi on the plane,' he said coldly. 'While you were asleep and snoring, I connected with the world. Believe me, you have done a great deal of damage to Herzoslovakia.'

'Oh, *Joachim*—'

He strode across the room, up into the bedroom area, to the glass table on which the bottle of Moët was tilted in the ice bucket. Refilling his glass, he said over his shoulder:

'I am very tired, Lori. It has been a long and difficult day. *I* was not sleeping and snoring for most of the flight. I was awake, emailing Philippe, discussing how best to present your tears to the media. Hopefully they will be forgotten soon. It is very good that we are away and no one knows where. But all I want to do is have a shower, eat some dinner and go to sleep.'

'There's an outdoor shower,' Lori said, her lower lip trembling: but she wouldn't cry any more, she *wouldn't*, especially as it had been her stupid tears that had got them into this mess to begin with. 'It's really lovely. You can shower under the stars.'

Joachim made a dismissive sound and disappeared in the direction of the bathroom area. Lori stared after him, common sense telling her not to follow him, to hope that he would feel better after he had freshened up. Disconsolately, she pushed open the door to the terrace and stepped outside, walking over to the day bed, slumping down on it. It was a full mattress, as comfortable as any bed she had ever slept on, and the pillows, which she piled up behind her back, were exactly the right combination of yielding and firm. She drank some more champagne, her head spinning, watching the waves through the fine muslin curtain.

I'll sit down with him in the morning, she thought. *I'll apologize, explain that I don't know what came over me. I have been feeling weird recently, I suppose. Sort of like I'm drifting through things. Maybe it's the supplements? Maybe I need less, now that Dr Bruschsson's got me all balanced out?*

I didn't cry like that deliberately. I couldn't help it – the tears just came out. People get emotional at weddings! Especially their own! I'm sure Joachim will realize that when he's calmer – he's jet-lagged now, he's bound to be a bit cranky—

She looked through the glass doors to the bedroom to see if her husband had emerged from the shower. The blue water of the swimming pool caught her eye, and the idea to take a dip popped into her head, utterly compelling. In a few minutes, she had dashed into the walk-in wardrobe, stripped off her clothes, pulled on a Melissa Odabash beige snakeskin print bikini and padded across the bedroom to the door that led to the pool. She sat down, dangling her feet into the water, feeling the delicious contrast of the night-cooled water on her calves and feet, the warm evening air on her body; slowly, she slipped in, making herself immerse her head too, taking a couple of strokes which brought her to the other side of the little round private pool.

Propping her arms on the edge, she floated, kicking her legs behind her, looking down on the horseshoe shape of the Casitas below. A couple walked arm in arm along the path, talking and laughing in lowered voices. A golf cart ticked past, carrying another couple of guests driven by a butler. In a circular tiled whirlpool by the main swimming pool, another couple embraced, bubbles rising around them from the jets, a single dark shadow as they kissed, their arms wrapped around each other. She thought she could see yet another couple, lying in a hammock by the pool, the huge white-knotted shape easily big enough for two, the dangling fringes making shadows on the grass below as they rocked slowly from side to side.

Glowing, gentle golden light spilled from some of the Casitas suites, their occupants probably lying out on their day beds, or having a last drink before turning in, watching the shadows of the leaves against their fluttering muslin curtains, listening to the steady, humming break of the waves against the pale sands, the breeze rustling the palm trees. Her scalp was wonderfully cool, her wet hair plastered to her scalp like a soothing poultice; she reached up, smoothing it fully back, feeling water drip deliciously down the back of her neck.

This is absolute paradise, Lori thought. *Particularly for couples on honeymoon. Joachim will wake up tomorrow and we'll have a new start. A new day.*

We're going to have the most wonderful honeymoon ever.

Considering how much Joachim had complained about his new wife snoring on the plane trip to Cancun, he had no leg to stand on the next morning; Lori was awoken at the crack of dawn by a series of rumbling, thunderous, snorting burbles that sounded more like a wallowing hippopotamus than a sleeping human.

I don't remember him snoring like this before! she thought, and then realized that this was the first night she had spent with Joachim that she hadn't taken the valerian sleeping pills. Yesterday evening she had completely forgotten about them; she'd been so relaxed by the dip in the pool and so full of delicious lobster quesadilla and Moët that she'd climbed into the huge, comfortable bed and gone out like a light.

Maybe he always snored, and the valerian just knocked me out so much that I didn't notice?

Lori pushed back the covers and slipped out of bed, hoping that her husband's bubbling snorts were due to a combination of jet lag and the entire bottle of champagne that he had consumed the night before at impressive speed. He had forked up his risotto and chocolate pudding, washing every bite down with Moët, and then retired to bed with his iPad, mumbling about being very tired and needing to relax.

Lori had tried to coax him into the pool with her to no avail. She had resigned herself to their first night together being unromantic: *after all*, she told herself, *I bet practically no honeymoon couples actually have fantastic sex and tell each other how much they love each other and fall asleep in each other's arms the night of their wedding. I mean, weddings are really, really stressful.*

She had high hopes for this morning, though, and thought she had slept enough; the full immersion in the cool water of the pool, followed by a long outdoor shower, scented with the bright, fresh Bulgari green tea shower gel provided by the Casitas, had worked wonders. She glanced down at Joachim, lying on his back, his mouth open as he breathed heavily through it, and decided to let him sleep. Going into the wardrobe area, she pulled on exercise clothes – a sports bra, Zoca strappy top, short shorts and trainers – took her iPod from her travel bag, and, thinking that the closing of the heavy suite door might wake Joachim, slipped one of the key cards into the zip pocket at the back of her shorts and made her exit through the doors onto the terrace.

The contrast between the light air conditioning and overhead fan inside the suite, and the moist, salt-tinged, warm sea air outside was as invigorating as it had been the night before.

The sunshine was already bright, the sky a clear cloudless blue; Lori put on her sunglasses. Her head was clear, and she was ready for a run on the beach. She was just heading down the steps from the terrace when she saw a solid, black-clad figure sitting on the low wall that was the boundary between the main path and the beach itself; it rose on spotting her, and she recognized Attila at once.

'Hey!' She waved at him, a delighted smile breaking over her face. 'I thought I'd go for a run – want to join?'

'I have already run,' Attila said, grinning back at her as she came quickly up to him. The dark curls that grew low on his forehead were a little damp with sweat, the hollow of his throat, where his gold chain always hung, equally moist. He wore a tank top and a loose pair of exercise shorts; it was hard to imagine that anything but loose shorts would have fit over his enormous, weightlifter's thighs. 'But I will go again with you if you want, even though it is already almost lunchtime. I wait a long time to see if you want to run.'

'Almost lunchtime! You're kidding!' She looked again at her iPod. 'Oh, you're such a liar! It isn't even eight yet!'

She whacked him across his huge, muscled shoulder, putting her considerable strength behind it but failing to shift him in the slightest. It was a game of theirs, had started when she accidentally grazed him with a hand weight and he hadn't even registered it, and it had become a running joke between them that Attila, built low to the ground and solid as a piling, was utterly impervious to any attempt Lori might make to shift his balance.

'Where is the King?' Attila asked, looking up to the suite, seeing that all the curtains were still closed.

'Ssh! He's still asleep,' Lori said, looking around her but seeing no one close by. 'And don't call him that. Call him Mr Guttman.'

'Okay,' Attila said equably. 'Sorry.'

'No worries! So, what's our route?'

She lifted her leg and put the sole of the foot high on Attila's chest, between his massive pectorals, a stretching routine that they were so familiar with it was automatic now. Attila held her raised foot in place as Lori bent over its ankle, gripping it with both hands, pulling her torso to lie flat along her leg, feeling the stretch right from the sole of the foot on the ground, up the hamstring, into her glutes and along to the hamstring of the lifted leg. She held it for thirty seconds, then straightened up, lowered her leg and lifted the other one onto his torso.

'I'm going to get you all sandy,' she said apologetically.

Attila's enormous shoulders rose and fell.

'I dust it off,' he said simply.

'You're going to need sunblock,' Lori said, bending over, doing lunges for extra calf stretching. 'You're really white.'

'Bulgarians are white,' Attila agreed.

'Well, do you have sunblock? You're going to get burned to pieces.' Lori straightened up.

Attila's dark eyes flickered, caught out.

'Attila! I *told* you! It's going to be, like, forty degrees every day here!' she said crossly.

'I stay in the shade,' Attila muttered.

'Oh, for God's sake, it's boiling already! We're in the tropics! We'll get you some later,' she said firmly. 'And I don't want any macho bullshit about it not being manly. No one looks manly with a peeling nose.'

'*I* look manly even if—' Attila started, but Lori had already taken off, sprinting across the sand. It had been months since she had run on sand, back home in Miami, and she had forgotten both how much she loved it and how hard it was. The resistance in beach running was huge, the sand sucking the runner down with each step; it was harder than running steps. After only a short while, she slowed to a jog, her breath coming fast, her heart racing. Attila caught her up, his big thighs pounding along in a steady rhythm, his breath as even as his pace.

'This is *so* beautiful,' she panted, looking at the beach cabanas as they passed, a long line of dark wooden double four-poster beds hung with muslin curtains drifting in the sea breeze, their mattresses covered with beige faux-leather, perfect for sandy bodies to lounge on. Bolsters and cushions in the same fabric were stacked enticingly at the head, and the cabanas' wooden roofs meant that their occupants could shelter there happily from a brief tropical rain shower. Beyond the beach, the Casitas were a series of curving suites surrounding their central pools, each with a sign identifying its horseshoe: Lori gradually worked out that they were names of birds. *Gaviotas, Flamingos, Albatros, Pelicanos*: seagulls, flamingos, albatrosses, pelicans. Attila turned, heading up onto the beachside path, and she followed.

'We can't run all down the beach,' he said. 'There is no straight path. We cut back after this.'

A golf cart, driven by a butler, passed: the driver said '*Hola!*' cheerfully to them, and Lori echoed it back with a smile and a wave.

'You speak Spanish?' Attila said. Lori knew him well enough to be familiar with his dry sense of humour, and she reached out to slap his arm.

'You can't live in Miami without learning some Spanish,' she said. 'Tons of Cubans. "*Hola*" means hello. You should say it too, it's polite. Ooh, nice bar!'

It was on their left, set back from the path, a very smart, simple structure, elegant marble tiles, with low leather benches and tables beside it; it looked like a chic lounge bar in Miami or Los Angeles. They passed under an arch, into the main hotel section, past what looked like a deep rock pool carved into the beach – 'Salt water,' Attila informed her – and a wooden pier, built out far into the sea, little chairs and tables arranged invitingly along its length, and dropped back onto the sand again. The sun was in their faces, and Lori was warming up nicely. People were already coming out onto the beach, sunning themselves on the loungers or curling up in a cabana, but there was a sense of infinite spaciousness, infinite availability.

'You know what's really nice?' Lori said. 'It doesn't look like anyone's coming out early to put their towels down. Grab a spot.'

'Like the Germans on holiday,' Attila said, amused. 'You are pretending to be German now, you should do that.'

Lori giggled. 'I'll tell Joachim,' she said. 'He'll think that's funny.'

'Everything is okay?' Attila asked.

He had phrased it tactfully enough that Lori could choose how to answer, but she knew exactly what he meant. And she had implicit confidence in Attila; there was something about working out so closely, so often, that built not just a physical trust but a mental one too. You relied on each other, you knew each other's strengths and weaknesses. You talked, too, back and forth; Lori and Attila had fallen into an easy, teasing banter, but there was a deeper level to their communication too. Lori didn't know how much of the Mihaly situation Attila had been privy to, but she had gradually been aware that Attila had little time for Mihaly as a person. Attila considered Mihaly a lightweight, building his body for show rather than function. Attila, like Lori, took his training extremely seriously. It was a bond between them.

Anything she said to Attila, she was aware, would go no further. It never had, and it never would. She didn't feel the need to choose her words too carefully as she said:

'The K— uh, my *husband* isn't too happy about me crying so much yesterday. Apparently the media focused on it way too much.'

'People cry at weddings,' Attila said neutrally.

They had reached the end of the El Dorado's beach, a wall running up from the waterline to indicate the boundary; they stretched briefly against it in tandem as Lori said:

'I barely even *remember* it. I mean, I don't even know what I was crying about. I felt really out of it.'

Attila, who had wedged one calf flat on the wall and was pushing back against it, the massive quadriceps muscle at the front of his thigh bulging in four different places at once, took his time to respond. Eventually he said:

'The medication Dr Bruschsson gives you . . . maybe it is a little too strong? Sometimes I think it makes you sleepy.'

'Not so much sleepy,' Lori said, pushing into the wall doing calf stretches, 'but sometimes a bit dozy.'

'Dozy isn't like sleepy?'

They changed legs in unison, the stone wall already sun-warm under Lori's palms. She didn't know how Attila could bear to press his calf so hard into the rough stone, but he had a ridiculously high pain tolerance; she had never seen him in any kind of physical distress, no matter how hard he pushed himself.

'No, it means—' She considered. 'Out of it. A bit spacey.'

'Like your head is in space,' he said, his other thigh bulging. He rolled his shoulders back and forth. 'Yes, that's it. Spacey.' He put his foot down. 'We run again.'

They started jogging back along the beach, the sun beating down pleasantly on their shoulders.

'I think I'm probably in balance now,' Lori said, casting a glance sideways at him to see if he agreed. 'You know, my iron levels and everything. I slept last night without the valerian. I think I'm going to wean myself off them. I was so stressed before the wedding, but I feel better now, in this lovely sunshine. And I've never really liked taking pills.'

'You won at the Olympics with no pills,' Attila said, looking straight ahead.

They fell silent for a while, their feet hitting the sand in identical rhythm. A woman sitting on a lounger gave them a thumbs-up and yelled 'Good for you!' as they passed her, and Lori grinned back at her: a fellow American. Her fellow countrymen and women were so open compared to Europeans, so happy shouting out to strangers. Clearly the baseball cap and glasses were a good disguise, too – *plus, no one would think that the new Queen of Herzoslovakia would be out jogging the first morning of her honeymoon with her bodyguard, rather than her husband. So, you know, there's that . . .*

'There are two gyms here,' Attila said as they hit the path again. 'I check them out this morning. Okay equipment and some Swiss balls. And I bring TRX straps.' He grinned at her. 'We can hang them under your terrace. Work out there.'

'Oh *no*! I thought I'd have two weeks off from TRX!' Lori lamented.

'Hey.' His shoulders rose and fell. 'It is your hon— *holiday*. You can do what you like.'

'Oh my God, don't you *dare* go passive-aggressive on me!'

She shoved at him again, her hand landing on his surprisingly narrow waist. Attila made the grunting, humphing noise that meant he was amused; she had taught him 'passive-aggressive' weeks ago. They jogged towards the Casitas, Lori noticing some wooden structures built on stilts, like open rooms at a first-storey level above the beach: small signs at the base of the steps up read 'Sky Massage'.

'Cool,' Lori said. 'I wonder if they do sports massage?'

'Mexicans are very strong,' Attila said approvingly; this was his biggest compliment. 'They probably do good massage.'

'I'll check out the spa,' Lori said. 'They must do some deep tissue work.'

'The gym is in the spa,' Attila said. 'I can show you later. They have a hydrotherapy pool there too. All different jets for the massage.' He nodded seriously. 'That is *very* good. Very professional.'

'You got up early!' Lori commented. 'You've been all over.'

'We share a room,' Attila said a little glumly. 'Vassily is big, and he snores.'

Lori bit her tongue, hard, to stop herself exclaiming that Joachim had snored too last night.

'Is everything okay?' she asked. 'Apart from the snoring.'

'Wonderful,' Attila said. 'We have Mexican food last night in a restaurant back by the hotel. Vassily had three margaritas. He keeps saying this is the best holiday ever.'

He rolled his eyes.

'I tell him, this is not a holiday,' he said. 'But he laughs at me.'

'Well, Attila, you can relax a bit. There's nothing really for you guys to *do*,' Lori said frankly. 'I mean, there's security all around the resort.'

'Shh!' Attila said cheerfully. 'Don't say that, please! I like it here very much.'

She grinned.

'Sorry. But don't worry – Joachim wouldn't dream of sending you home.'

Joachim's sense of self-importance as a European monarch would not have permitted him to acknowledge that he might actually not need a bodyguard in a gated, secure holiday resort.

'Hey, it's good that we are here,' Attila said more seriously. 'You never know what happens. Plus, you go on trips outside the resort. We must be there for those.'

'That's true,' Lori admitted.

They had reached the last horseshoe of the Casitas now, Flamingos, and were coming up to the Presidential Suite; they circled the beach below, checking to see if Joachim were up, but all the curtains were still tightly drawn.

'I guess I'll have some breakfast,' Lori said. 'Want to join me? Did you eat already?'

'I find somewhere very nice already,' Attila said. 'Health-food. I show you. We can walk back to cool down.'

The resort was dotted, clearly, with charming restaurants and bars: Elizabeth had given them a leaflet last night, a guide to all the various places to eat and drink. Attila had made use of it to identify Las Olas, an open-air bar with a beach view that served wraps, shakes, coffee and salads; Lori giggled over the names of the various shakes.

'Look, Attila,' she said, scanning the menu. 'Should I have a *Poderoso*? "Powerful"? Banana, chocolate, granola and milk?'

Attila, a health-food obsessive, looked genuinely horrified.

'Like ice cream for breakfast!' he said, shaking his head so vigorously that drops of sweat from his tight curls flew from side to side.

'Or they have an *Afrodisíaco*,' Lori continued. 'That's actually the healthiest option – orange juice and spinach—'

'*El señor*, he take the *Afrodisíaco* this morning,' their waitress said, giggling: Attila turned bright red.

'I have it for breakfast,' he muttered. 'It's good.'

Lori ordered in halting Spanish, an *Afrodisíaco*, a tropical fruit salad with yoghurt and maple syrup, and a cappuccino. Attila joined her in the coffee and fruit order: he barely drank, didn't smoke, and didn't eat processed foods or dairy, apart from the cappuccinos that were his one indulgence. They sat in happy silence, waiting for their food. Lori's chair faced the sea, and Attila was on her right, so they both had a view; they watched holidaymakers strolling past, seagulls soaring in formation overhead, and the waves crashing against the series of artificial reefs built out into the water. Post-exercise, endorphins pumping through her blood, Lori felt calmer than she had in ages. The worst was behind her now, the stress of the weeks leading up to the ceremony. It was all over. She was married and could embark on her new life.

'I love that no one here knows who we are,' she heard herself saying. 'It's like two weeks out of time. Joachim and I can just hang out and be by ourselves and not have any pomp and ceremony around us. We really needed this.'

She propped her elbows on the wooden table and stared at the waves, the extraordinary aquamarine and emerald sea, shading into deeper sapphire further from the coastline.

'I could sit by the beach all day,' she said dreamily. 'I didn't realize how much I missed it.'

'Miami is like this?' Attila asked.

'No!' She laughed. 'Miami's great, but it's *way* more crowded and there's always a party going on. But you can drive down to the Keys – the Florida Keys – in a couple of hours, and find somewhere really pretty and quiet. Or, you know, hop on a flight to the Caribbean.' She nodded decisively. 'I'm going to need a winter sun holiday somewhere every year from now on.'

The waitress arrived, and Lori sat back to make room for the food; she gasped in happiness at the fruit plate in particular, an arrangement of sliced mango, papaya and pineapple, the colours of the freshly picked tropical fruit as vivid as neon, the orange and yellow and vermilion bright as paint.

'This is what it's supposed to taste like,' she said, forking up a piece of mango and sighing with happiness as the creamy, freshly picked fruit melted on her tongue. 'That's why I don't like eating mango in Europe. It never tastes good. Not like this.' She pulled a face. 'Boy, I *really* didn't realize how much I missed the sunshine and the beach and the tropics over in Europe.'

'It is very nice here,' Attila said, tactfully ignoring the fact that Lori had, just yesterday, committed herself to spending the rest of her life in a mountainous Eastern European monarchy.

They finished their meal and strolled back to the Presidential Suite, Lori commenting on the way on two gigantic backgammon and chess sets, the board tiles set into the ground, the oversized moulded resin chess pieces as high as her waist.

'I must tell Joachim about this,' she said. 'He loves board games. Maybe he could teach me chess while we're here.'

Vassily was sitting outside the room he shared with Attila, a swim-up room with an infinity pool; steps from the pool led down into what the resort called the lazy river, a loop that wound under several little bridges and into the main swimming pool. Inhabitants could slip into the river, swim or walk along it, and reach the swim-up bar in the pool; if, of course, they chose to make that effort, rather than to have their pool butler bring their drinks.

Vassily, looking very relaxed, was wearing sunglasses and Speedos and reading *USA Today*. Lori was very keen to see the reaction of the guests, who were mainly American and British, as they gradually woke up and took in the spectacle of large, hairy, near-naked Vassily, his private parts barely contained in the minimal bright red briefs. She was willing to bet that this would be the only pair of Speedos in the entire Casitas.

Vassily waved happily on seeing Lori and Attila and pointed up to the Presidential Suite, tilting his head and putting both hands beneath it in the universal symbol for sleep. Lori couldn't wait to shower any longer, though; her workout clothes were clammy and sticking to her. She headed up the stairs to the suite, slipped in the key card and opened the door cautiously, not wanting to wake Joachim; it had been a long day yesterday, and he definitely needed his sleep.

The room was dark and chilly from the air conditioning. She tiptoed through the living room and into the bedroom, where she was very surprised to see her husband sitting up in bed, still in his pyjamas. In one hand was a slab of cheese, the plate from last night set on the coverlet beside him; the other hand was angling his iPad, propped on his lap, so that the screen cast an eerie reflection on the lower part of his face.

'You're awake!' she exclaimed. 'We all thought you were still sleeping.'

'You all?' Joachim repeated, without looking up from the screen.

'Me and Attila and Vassily,' she said, walking round to his side of the bed and bending down to kiss him. Disconcertingly, Joachim did not turn his head to meet her lips; she ended up planting an awkward kiss on the side of his scalp.

'It's a glorious day out there,' she said, beginning to get nervous. 'Shall I draw the curtains?'

'Not yet,' he said, still focused on the screen. 'I have a headache.'

'Oh no! Um, shall I make you some coffee? There's the Lavazza machine in the kitchen. I could do you an espresso?'

Joachim shrugged, which Lori decided to take as a yes. She went into the kitchen area, all cherrywood and marble, switched on the machine, found the ground coffee and cups and made a double espresso. She pulled out a bottle of cold water – the imported Evian Elizabeth had mentioned – from the fridge, took a tray from the dining table, arranged some grapes and apples and plums from the fruit bowl on a plate, and carried the whole thing back into the bedroom.

'Here you go,' she said, placing it next to him on the big bed. 'Hopefully coffee and hydration will help with the headache . . .'

Her voice tailed off; Joachim was still not looking up from the screen. She pushed the tray further towards him and sat down on the coverlet, gingerly, as she was aware how clammy and sweat-drenched her shorts were.

'You're still cross with me, aren't you?' she said unhappily. 'You're punishing me for crying yesterday.'

'I have a headache,' he repeated, frowning.

'Well, maybe looking at that screen isn't the best thing for you, then,' Lori said, a little impatiently. 'Or eating cheese.'

She uncapped the water bottle and handed it to him; her husband deigned to take it and drink some.

'It's really lovely out,' she said. 'You could sit on the day bed, or the hammock, and be in the shade, but still see the sea . . . I'm sure the fresh air would help with your headache . . .'

Again, she tailed off, because Joachim clearly wasn't listening; he was tapping away at the screen of his iPad.

'Coffee?' she said, handing him the cup. He took that too, and sipped at it: *I should just shut up and give him things to eat and drink*, she thought gloomily. She took a long breath and heard it come out in a deep sigh that was entirely involuntary.

'I need to go shower,' she said, standing up; in the doorway, she looked back, hoping that Joachim would be doing something, *anything*, rather than staring at his screen. But no, the espresso cup in one hand, the saucer balanced on his lap, he was sipping while scrolling down with his thumb. Sighing again, she went into the dressing room, stripped off her sticky workout clothes, and padded naked to the outdoor shower. Joachim could have caught a view of his wife's superbly fit body as she went, but he was oblivious to the sight, too concentrated on the illuminated rectangle in front of him to even put down his cup in its saucer: he reached out and fumbled it onto the tray, tilting it and spilling the last drops onto the cheese.

Under the shower, Lori took a series of longer, deeper breaths.

Just focus on this for now, she told herself. *How lovely to be standing outside, naked, water pouring down on you, looking up at the blue sky and the birds flying past*. On the stone shelves built into the shower the hotel toiletries were lined up, all scented with the same delicate green tea Bulgari perfume, and Lori slathered her hair and body in them, staying in the shower as long as she could, washing herself again and again. She realized eventually that she was hiding out there, avoiding dealing with her husband, and that awareness propelled her, finally, reluctantly, to turn off the cascading water and wrap herself in a towel that was really generous enough to be called a bath sheet.

But in the marble and stone bathroom, she found herself taking for ever to dry herself off, apply sun cream, work Kerastase protective lotion through her hair, dump her icky damp workout gear into a laundry bag for the maid, and choose a Vix halterneck bikini from the pile that she had brought, a bamboo print one. Not white yet – that was for the second week here, when she'd developed enough of a tan to carry it off.

And suddenly, at the thought of a second week here, she felt her heart sink.

Why on earth am I feeling like this? she thought, pausing to stare at herself in the mirror, her hands stopping at the back of her neck, where they had been tying the narrow, gold-bead-trimmed straps. *I'm loving being here! They'll have to drag me away from this place kicking and screaming . . .*

In answer, the image of her husband popped straight into her head, as he was right now; lying in bed, food piled around him, curtains drawn to block out the glorious, enviably beautiful, world-class view outside.

Oh, he won't stay in bed for ever, she told herself bravely. *He's just cross with me, he feels I made a bit of a idiot of him crying like that because the press was all over it* – she hadn't dared to look at any of the media coverage, which she was sure was the right decision – *and he had a really long day yesterday, he didn't sleep on the plane much, he has a headache . . .*

She picked up a short silk Matthew Williamson cover-up and pulled it on, dropping some sun cream into her beach bag. Sunglasses on her head, flip-flops on her feet, a straw cowboy hat in her hand. Applied tinted Elizabeth Arden Eight Hour lip protectant, picked up the beach bag. Stared at herself in the mirror once more. No reason to stay in the dressing room any longer, with a beautiful golden day outside by the beach waiting for her, a cabana to lie in, a private pool to float on.

No, scrap the pool. How weird would it be to float in our pool and look over at the drawn curtains, knowing my husband's behind them, lying in the gloom, reading God knows what on his damn iPad?

The surge of anger at that thought propelled her out into the hallway and to the threshold of the bedroom. It was like a dull thud against her ribcage, an invisible punch, to see that Joachim didn't seem to have moved at all since she had left the room.

Actually, that's not true, Lori thought with a twist of rare irony. *He's been eating more of the cheese. There are Gouda crumbs all down the front of his pyjamas.*

'I'm going out to the beach,' she said, a last effort. 'Why don't you come too? You could bring the iPad and lie in a hammock . . .'

Joachim shook his head. She sagged, helpless. If he had voiced whatever anger to her he was feeling, they could have had a fight, talked it out, got through it and out the other side; but this passive refusal to engage, to acknowledge anything but his wish to be left alone in the dark, was as impossible to engage with as it would have been to wrestle Jello.

'Joachim,' she said in a very small voice, 'are you regretting getting married?'

That provoked much more of a reaction than she had expected. To her surprise, his head shot up, turned to look at her, his blue eyes bulging, a cream cheese smear on his lower lip.

'No!' he said crossly. 'No! Of course not! My God! No!'

'Well, that's . . .'

Loving? Reassuring? Good to know? Lori couldn't decide how to finish the sentence. And in any case, Joachim was already looking back at the iPad, his fingers tapping at the screen, which was now emitting odd noises, beeps and notifications.

'What are you reading?' Lori asked, curious about the sounds.

'I'm going through various media alerts Philippe is sending me,' he said, his eyes back on the screen. 'And catching up on all the business that I put aside before the wedding to spend time with you. The new tax set-up. Concessions from the G-20 summit. It's going to take quite a while.'

There was clearly no point arguing with him; nothing would change his mind. The best thing to do, she decided, was to give him his head space now, let him decompress from all the pressures of the wedding in his own way, which was clearly what was happening. Let him go into what her mother would have called his 'man-cave', and greet him with a smile when he eventually got over his sulk and decided to emerge into the sunshine.

We've got a whole fortnight, she told herself. *So what if he goes into a grump on the first day? You mustn't make a mountain out of a molehill. No one has the perfect honeymoon or the perfect marriage.*

Hopefully, he'll be over it by tonight, and we can go for a nice dinner. Maybe at the Italian restaurant? It looks stunning, and he certainly hoovered up that risotto . . .

She was closing the suite door behind her, trying her best to stay positive, when she saw a male butler, instantly recognizable from the smart uniform, climbing from a golf cart and heading towards the steps of the Presidential Suite.

'*Hola!*' said the butler, smiling at her. 'Mrs Guttman?'

'*Hola,*' Lori said, plastering a cheerful smile on her face. '*Si, soy Señora Guttman.*'

'*Muy bien! Habla español!*'

'*Poquito,*' she said. *A little bit.* She wasn't up to pulling out her Spanish so soon after that miserable encounter with her husband of less than a day.

'Okay, we speak English? I am Pablo. It is a real pleasure to meet you.'

He shook her hand, smiling; like Juan Carlos and Elizabeth, he radiated charm and intelligence, and his appearance was immaculate.

'Is this a good time?' he asked, looking at her cover-up, her beach bag. 'I see you are going maybe to sit in the sunshine?'

'No, it's fine,' Lori said, eagerly grasping at this distraction, someone to talk to. 'Is this about—'

'Organizing some trips for you!' Pablo said enthusiastically. 'Your secretary has said you want to visit the temples of Chichen Itza and Tulum, and there is a really beautiful lagoon that you can combine with a Tulum excursion. We also thought you might like to hear about our various gourmet wine-tasting dinners that we could book you into— we have a very exciting partnership now with Kendall-Jackson wines—' He looked up at the suite. 'Would you like to go inside? Or maybe sit on your terrace? I have a folder of information to show you. Is Mr Guttman—'

'He has jet lag,' Lori said, which for all she knew was true. 'But I can look at everything and make some decisions. Um, why don't we go and sit by the main pool? They have tables there in the shade, by the bar, and we could spread out everything there.'

They strolled across the grass, past some cabanas placed at spacious intervals around the pool area, past the big round Jacuzzi that Lori had seen a couple in the night before. There were more loungers, each with a rolled-up towel placed invitingly at its head, and as they rounded the pool, crossing the lazy river by one of the little bridges, Lori saw that there was a high arched fountain flowing into the pool, jets shooting up against a striking copper background.

'This is so beautiful,' she said to him, trying to cheer herself up. 'And there's so much *space*. I mean, I thought it would be busier. More crowded.'

Pablo smiled complacently, his black eyes flashing.

'We are almost at full capacity,' he said proudly. 'But each of the suites has its loungers, and patio, and then we calculate there are at least four spaces for every guest. So there is never a problem. Anywhere the guest wants to go, they will always find a hammock, a cabana, whatever they want.' He gestured at the line of cabanas and loungers beyond the pool, along the beach. 'We like to be generous,' he added. 'Plus, of course, you are in the most exclusive section of the Casitas. This pool is only for the use of people who stay in this section. So you have the best of the best.'

They sat down at a table under the high thatched roof of the sprawling bar. To one side was a gigantic wooden Jenga game, waist-high: Lori wondered if Joachim might be coaxed out to come and play that with her. Her eyes flickered up to her suite, whose curtains were still drawn. Up there, Joachim was lying in bed in the dark in some kind of self-imposed retreat from all of this loveliness, the best of the best . . .

The barman, seeing Pablo take a seat with a guest, climbed nimbly up the steps to ground level; the bar itself was sunken to allow people in the pool to swim up to it and sit waist-high on the tiled stools below the surface of the water.

'*Hola, señora*,' he said, coming over, smart in his orange uniform. 'A drink for you?'

Lori was about to say no: it wasn't even lunchtime yet. Then she glanced up once more at the drawn curtains of the Presidential Suite, heaved a sigh, and said:

'Sure, why not? I'll have a daiquiri, please.'

*   *   *

Five days later, Lori had repeated those words more times that she could count. Actually, she had switched to Spanish: '*Un daiquiri, por favor.*' And then, '*Si, gracias, uno mas.*' The pool bar opened around ten, and closed at five, and some of the Casitas guests happily lounged around it for the whole seven hours, or lay on the beach, letting the beach butler replenish their cocktails and bring them ice cream. And the most hardcore pool bunny of all was Vassily, who was blissfully relishing the fact that his job seemed to consist of lying out in the sunshine, watching a door that barely ever opened, raising his empty glass to the barman whenever the latter made a circuit.

Vassily had discovered something called a Miami Vice, which Lori hadn't ever seen in the eponymous city: it was bi-coloured, served in a tapered glass as long as Lori's forearm, raspberry below and frothy white above. Coconut was involved, though Lori had never found out what constituted the pink layer. She didn't even want to think about how many calories were in just one Miami Vice, and Vassily drank them like water. Attila teased him about them mercilessly, especially after a waiter told Vassily that a Miami Vice was '*para una mujer*', 'for a woman'; but Vassily was confident enough in his sexuality to stick with his preferred drink.

And certainly, Vassily was cutting such a swath through the female guests at the Casitas that he had no need to feel any insecurity about his masculinity. It was not just his Speedos that had caught their attention; it was also Vassily's habit of doing showy press-ups on the beach while wearing them. He wasn't as handsome as Mihaly – barely anyone could have been – but he was tall, with an impressively muscled body he loved to show off, and, when not doing press-ups, stretched out on a lounger by the main pool, he liked to prop a long, ice-sweaty glass of Miami Vice suggestively on his lower abs. Attila had told Lori that Vassily and a bleached-blonde American woman whose husband was a margarita-soused mess by mid-afternoon were beginning to absent themselves from the poolside at the same time suspiciously often.

And why shouldn't he have some fun? Lori thought. *At least someone is.*

Vassily was scarcely neglecting his duties: he had been barely called upon to perform his job at all, since Joachim was still hardly emerging from the suite. Lori's new husband had made it out of the suite as far as the terrace, and was mostly now occupying either the day bed or the hammock, his iPad always in his hand. By night it charged, its screen flickering eerily on his bedside table, by day it was his constant companion. As far as Lori was aware, Joachim had not even dipped a toe in the sea yet, though he had cooled off in the circular pool a few times.

She had put her foot down when, on the first full day, Joachim had announced that he didn't want to leave the suite for dinner, but have it served there. On hearing this information, Lori had become as hysterical as she ever got. She had *not*, she almost screamed, come on *honeymoon* expecting her husband never to leave the damn suite and come out to dinner with her. If he were going to stay in all day, he could damn well at least join her for dinner in one of the many lovely restaurants. She wanted to dress up, to go out; she hadn't brought tons of pretty outfits just to hole up in the suite, even on their stunning terrace. And she knew damn well that if they ate dinner in their rooms, Joachim would be snatching glances at his iPad the whole damn time.

Faced with this unexpected resistance, and taken aback both by Lori's raised voice and repeated use of 'damn', a word she had been brought up to consider full-on swearing,

Joachim had given in. So every night, Lori had donned a different dress, put on perfume, applied golden Lancôme body oil to her arms and legs, and Pablo, Elizabeth, or Liliana, the other butler in the rotation, would arrive in the gold golf cart to take them to whichever restaurant they had chosen.

They drank champagne cocktails in Bellini's, the elegant lounge bar above D'Italia, listening to live jazz music, and martinis on the balcony of the Martini Lounge at the main hotel. They ate sushi and bamboo-basket-steamed mahi-mahi and wok-fried beef tenderloin tips with peanuts and hot pepper sauce in Kampai, the stunning Asian restaurant with a soaring roof and huge golden Buddha on a plinth in the centre. They demolished the rice, hibiscus and guava crème brûlée at Rincón Mexicano, so good that Joachim promptly ordered another. And they took a crazily eccentric 'tour through Europe' at Fuentes Culinary Theatre, a glass-framed building in which a miked-up chef at a kitchen station 'cooked' a five-course meal of European-themed food whose main course was a 'deconstructed cottage pie' in a martini glass: giant screens showed every detail of his prep, while the sommelier's wine pairings complemented every course.

As VIPs in the 'best of the best' section, Lori and Joachim naturally had the best table in every restaurant. No one fawned over to them; the service was utterly, supremely professional. But they were treated with the finest of kid gloves, and Joachim, always conscious of his own elevated status, enjoyed both the high standards of the food, the wine and the service so much that after that first fight, Lori didn't have to pitch any more fits to make him agree to join her for dinner out.

Plus, she found herself thinking, *the variety of restaurants gives us stuff to talk about*. Because the easy conversations she and Joachim had shared before getting married seemed, frankly, to have fallen off a cliff. Gone were the times when he would ask her about herself, her family, her sporting career, seeming so interested in everything she had to say, matching her stories with ones of his own. Now, it felt as if he had heard everything he needed to hear and said everything he wanted to say. Without mutual friends to gossip about, workplaces from which to report back, or the films and box sets they had watched in the Schloss cinema to talk over, subjects of conversation were much thinner on the ground.

If Joachim had been joining Lori at her daily workouts, exploring the resort with her on the bicycles provided for their use, there would have been more than plenty for them to do; there was table tennis, the giant Jenga, chess and backgammon sets Lori had noticed before, plus a rolling schedule of activities by the big swimming pool in the El Dorado section. Tequila tastings, towel-folding classes, yoga, aquarobics, darts. The resort had not only horses, but camels to ride; Pablo and Elizabeth had taken Lori and Attila on a tour of the huge greenhouses behind the tennis courts that grew produce not just for the El Dorado but for other hotels along the coast, picking peppers and tomatoes from the vines, mint and basil from huge pots for them to taste, enjoying their guests' exclamations of delight at the fresh, spicy tastes.

But Lori had given up telling Joachim what she had done that day; his disinterest was so obvious it was like a slap in the face. The dinners, at least, provided a subject of discussion that carried them through in the evenings. And no fellow guest at dinner ever seemed to recognize them – *probably*, Lori thought a little darkly, *because we don't exactly look like a blissed-out honeymoon couple. More like people who've been married for years and don't have much left to say to each other.*

As Lori slipped out of the suite at five-thirty the next morning, wearing a silk sweater over her shorts and top, taking care not to wake Joachim, she was grimly aware that the best evening out she and her new husband had had so far was the night before, at Fuentes. *Because they gave us the viewing table, which meant we sat side by side so we had a great view of the chef and the big screens – no wonder they call it 'culinary theatre! – and the chef was so busy talking that Joachim and I could just sit and watch and not have to make awkward conversation.*

Liliana, waiting at the bottom of the steps in the golf cart, looked as fresh and pretty as ever, the eyeliner round her big dark eyes perfect and unsmudged, despite the fact that she was just finishing the night butler shift. Attila was already in the cart, wearing dark jeans and a T-shirt; he had told Lori once that he never wore light-coloured trousers, as they made his thighs look ridiculously large.

'Did you not bring a sweater?' Lori said to him, smiling at Liliana as she climbed into the cart. 'It'll be chilly till the sun comes up.'

Attila gave one of his shrugs. It was like watching a weight bar rise and fall.

'I don't feel cold,' he said efficiently.

'Mr Guttman is still not well?' Liliana asked, pressing the Drive pedal. The golf cart whirred down onto the beach path. 'It is such a shame! To miss Chichen Itza!'

'I know,' Lori agreed, rolling her eyes; she could allow herself that, since Liliana's back was to her.

'He seemed fine last night,' Liliana lamented. 'We were so happy to hear you liked Fuentes! I thought—'

'He's having some issues with the, um, sun,' Lori said, resolutely avoiding looking at Attila. 'Headaches. His, um, eyes are better in the evening.'

Liliana clicked her tongue sympathetically.

'We can find a doctor,' she offered. 'I would be very happy to arrange that for him.'

'Thank you, Liliana,' Lori said, trying not to imagine how poorly Joachim would respond to the suggestion of a doctor's visit. 'I'll tell him. He says he'll just ring for anything he wants today.'

Liliana expertly piloted the little cart up past the spa.

'You and Mr Guttman have your sunset Sky Massage ritual this evening,' she reminded Lori. 'He will be all right for that, I hope.'

'I hope so too,' Lori said grimly. 'It's, you know, *sunset*, so hopefully he'll be okay.'

The golf cart was gliding up the back road which led to the main hotel reception. The sun was not yet visible, but a faint glow was infusing the landscape, a pale pink tinge to the horizon spreading slowly into the misty violet sky. Birds were beginning to wake up and sing to each other from the trees; no one else was up apart from a few groundsmen sweeping up loose palm fronds and fallen coconuts. It had been recommended that they leave early in the morning, to see Chichen Itza before the crowds arrived and the heat of the day began to bear down. Lori had known that Joachim would baulk at the early start, but Chichen Itza, after all, was one of the new seven wonders of the world; she hadn't seriously thought that he would simply refuse to go.

And he was sneaky about it, too, she thought resentfully. She was trying so hard not to get cross, to give him his space, to avoid becoming so angry at his almost complete refusal to spend any time with her; but how could you not be resentful when your husband sat all the way through dinner with you, waited to get back to your suite, and then announced while you were brushing your teeth, so that you couldn't immediately say anything because you had an electric toothbrush in your mouth, that he'd decided he didn't want to get up at the crack of dawn and that you should just go with

your bodyguard along on the trip the next day if you were
still keen to go?

Keen to go? There was no way she was visiting the Yucatan
without going to Chichen Itza, with its world-famous pyramid! And Joachim had not only been aware of how excited
she was to go, but that, because she needed to go to sleep as
soon as possible for a very early start, she would be unable to
make a prolonged fuss about it. *As I would have done, if he'd
had the balls to tell me over dinner,* she thought angrily. *I can
see at least that Joachim's a good politician. He's got an excellent
grasp of tactics.*

Liliana had pulled up in front of the hotel, next to a smart
white minivan whose driver was standing by the open door.
Beside him was a stocky, handsome man who Liliana introduced as Alejandro, their guide. He shook their hands,
expressed surprise at their party only being composed of two,
rather than four people, and indicated that they should be on
their way.

Lori had decided that the only way for her to enjoy the
day would be to put aside any wish that her husband was
there beside her. Joachim would often be away on business,
she told herself, and she would have to travel too without
him on official engagements; she needed to see this excursion
in that light, not feel that it was ruined because Joachim
wasn't there to share it with. It was over two hours' drive to
Chichen Itza, and she put on her sunglasses, curled up on the
back seat and closed her eyes, dozing off,: *when I wake up,* she
told herself firmly, *all I'm going to think about is how lucky I
am to have a private tour of something this special.*

Fortunately, the ancient Mayan-Toltec pyramid, with its
carved god Kukulkan, the winged serpent, slithering down
the side of the north-facing staircase, was so impressive that
it quite distracted Lori from any gloomy reflections about

her husband's continuing self-isolation. It was a glorious day, the morning sunshine streaming down the grey stone, flooding onto the velvety green grass, and as the three of them approached the pyramid, they had it almost completely to themselves. Alejandro explained the history behind the construction: with a long stick, he traced diagrams in the sand, showing how the pyramid had been designed to reflect Mayan calculations about the calendar, including the famous fact that, at the spring and autumn equinoxes, the light of the setting sun, flooding through triangular chinks cut below the carved body of Kukulkan, made it look as if the serpent's body was rippling sinuously down the staircase.

To Lori's surprise, Attila was riveted by all of this, asking a whole series of questions to which Alejandro responded with great enthusiasm. Mathematics, however, had never been her strong point; her volleyball scholarship had enabled her to skate through the compulsory classes at college. No one gave a damn about the grade point average of a sports player. She wandered around the temple instead, taking photographs, and only returned when Attila yelled to her that they were going to look at a ball court.

'This you understand,' he said teasingly to her as she joined them. 'Throwing balls. The men finish the difficult talk now.'

'God, you're so *rude*!'

She faked a high kick at his bottom as Alejandro led them through the huge, imposing ball court, the Skull Platform, and the extraordinary half-ruin of the Temple of the Warriors, dazzling, fascinating words falling from his mouth, telling stories of virgin sacrifices, hearts cut from chests in the Kukulkan pyramid and carried, still beating, to the Temple of the Warriors so that it could be burnt and placed on the statue of Chac Mool. All speculation, Alejandro said sadly: the

Spanish conquistadors had destroyed so much of the culture and documentation of the Mayans and Toltecs that it was impossible to do more than guess at the significance of so many of their beautiful buildings. At the Observatory Temple, where Alejandro and Attila launched once more into excited discussion of the way the windows and doors might have been located in order for the Mayans to observe the heavens—

'Particularly,' Alejandro said, winking at Lori, 'the path of the planet Venus. The beautiful goddess of love.'

She smiled politely, but her head was spinning, so full of history and partly ruined beauty, sadness for a lost civilization – and awareness, too, of the sacrificed virgins and the skulls of their slain enemies, impaled on poles, displayed on platforms. She had reached an overload, and was glad when Alejandro announced that it was time for lunch, packed them back into the van and drove them to a restaurant beside a *cenote*, a natural sinkhole deep in the limestone bedrock, in which he suggested they take a dip before eating.

'The water is very heavy, though,' he warned. 'Very full of minerals. You must be careful not to tire yourselves out – they say you need to be twice as strong to swim in this water.'

Attila and Lori promptly looked at each other and burst out laughing, rather offending Alejandro. They had brought swimsuits, as instructed, and walked down the long flight of steps to the *cenote*, towels wrapped around their waists. Attila was still, modestly, keeping his T-shirt on until he got in the water. Not having any idea what to expect, they gasped in amazement when they reached the bottom and saw the green-blue water, glowing in the sunlight trickling down through the grotto opening above, great trails of vegetation dangling down like ropes, fifty feet long and not even touching the surface of the wide pool below. It was like swimming at the bottom of a huge stone well.

'Race you in!' Lori said, dropping her towel, running to the raw edge and diving in, the cold shock of the water delicious on her overheated skin. She emerged, pushing her hair out of her face, treading water, vaguely aware that she needed to work a little harder than usual to swim, but so physically fit that it scarcely mattered to her.

Attila, much more precise than her, had folded his own towel, put it on one of the wooden shelves and was now picking up and folding her own. It was the first time Lori had seen him in a swimsuit; he considered himself to be on duty all the time he was with her at the Casitas, and insisted, despite her telling him he was being silly, on wearing a T-shirt and shorts at all times.

So now her jaw dropped as she watched him pulling off his T-shirt in that way that only straight men did, reaching back to the nape of his neck to grab the collar, yanking it forward and over his head in one movement, revealing his near-naked body. Lori was far out in the water, and most of the other tourists, less strong swimmers who had doubtless been warned not to exhaust themselves, were holding onto the sides, so she had a clear view of the stir Attila's physique created. Every single swimmer's head jerked back to stare avidly up at him.

Attila, however, was quite unaware of their attention. He bent to put his neatly folded T-shirt on top of their towels, his hamstrings bulging, the back of his calves like fists, his high, tight buttocks fully covered by his 1930s-style black swimming trunks, but their outline as firm and perfectly rounded as half-melons. He turned, his abs a sculpted eight-pack rippling down from his equally sculpted pectorals, his biceps and triceps all as individually defined as an anatomy drawing. Above his huge thighs, the knot of his genitals under the black fabric was another fist;

Lori ducked her face into the water for a second, conscious of staring.

She came up to hear a woman hiss: 'Jesus, Mary and Joseph! *Look* at him!' as two gay men swam past her from the other side of the *cenote*, heading as fast as they could to get a better view of the god-like new arrival.

'*Not* Mexican,' one of them was saying, his strokes swift. 'Not with that divine curly hair.'

'And too white,' the other one agreed. 'Not that I'm complaining. *So* nice to have a change! *Definitely* a big cock – *very* hefty, I'd say.'

Attila had spotted Lori: raising a hand to her, he strode down to the edge and dove in neatly, his body a tight heavy arrow cleaving the water.

One of the gay men cast an envious look at Lori.

'Ugh, he's hers,' he said to his friend. 'Lucky bitch.'

Lori sank her face into the water again, utterly mortified. Underwater, she watched Attila swim up to her, the black curls plastered to his forehead, his black eyes bright with enjoyment.

'This is *very* nice,' he said, as she came up for air.

Despite her embarrassment, Lori couldn't help giggling.

'What?' he said. 'I say it wrong?'

'No – it's just that I think that's the most enthusiastic thing I've ever heard you say,' she said, smiling.

'I like to swim,' he said, effortlessly treading water, his huge, boulder-like shoulders breaking the surface. 'And this is beautiful. I did not know about places like this.'

'Me neither.'

'You feel the special water?' he asked, grinning.

'After jogging down the beach every day? You're kidding! My legs are super-strong now.'

'Good,' he said approvingly.

Every single person in the *cenote* was staring at them: Attila was the only one who didn't realize what a stir his physique had created. Overwhelmed, Lori started to swim towards the part of the pool where the rays of sunshine that penetrated through the grotto hit the water, turning it palest green, the sunlight bright as fire. She turned over to float on her back in the glow, arms wide, legs together, making a cross with her body, her eyes almost closed against the dazzling light, warm gold above her, cool water below, her arms circling slowly to keep her afloat.

Eventually, she raised her head, dropped her legs, treading water again. Attila was nowhere to be seen; she swivelled, looking for him, and after twenty seconds saw his unmistakable head pop up from the centre of the pool; his curls were so springy that the weight of water couldn't flatten them for more than a moment. He raised a hand to her.

'I try to see how deep I can go!' he called. 'It is *cold* down there.'

'I bet.'

Lori started to swim towards the wooden steps. She went to get the towels, wrapping herself in one, shaking out her hair; she told herself not to look back at the pool, but she couldn't help it. Attila had just reached the edge: he didn't need the steps. Hands flat on the stone, he flexed his arms and lifted his big body from the water as easily as if he weren't fifteen stone of solid bone and muscle. Water streamed from his big deltoids, flowed down his pectorals and over his tight small nipples. It was like watching a big jungle animal ripple up out of the pool; he stood in one single, fluid motion, his thighs flexing easily with the effort, the section of his quads just above his knees, what bodybuilders call the 'teardrop muscle', bulging out in full relief.

Everyone was riveted. Even the Mayan teenagers who rented out towels and life jackets, who had been sitting in a group up on their stone viewing area, chatting amongst themselves with no interest in the tourists whatsoever, were now openly gawping at Attila as he walked towards Lori and caught the towel that she threw at him. She debated telling him that he was the focus of every pair of eyes but decided against it.

However, as it turned out, word had spread. By the time they had headed back upstairs, changed, and walked to the open-air restaurant where they would have a buffet lunch, Alejandro, seated at one of the long tables drinking a beer, looked amused as they put down their plates, laden with pulled pork and black bean stew. The swimming had definitely worked up an appetite.

'I hear you are like Arnold Schwarzenegger,' Alejandro said to Attila, who was politely holding the chair for Lori. 'All the Mayan boys are saying so.'

Attila frowned.

'It is good to be strong,' he said, 'but it is even more important to be flexible. The bodybuilder is not usually flexible.'

'They mean it as a compliment,' Lori said, knowing that the only aspect on which Attila might be remotely sensitive was the suggestion that he weightlifted for show, not for function.

'Most definitely,' Alejandro said, nodding. He raised his hand to call a waiter. 'You want some beer?'

Attila's expression, as he looked at Alejandro's glass, was positively wistful.

'It would be nice, after the swim. But I must not drink on duty,' he said regretfully.

'On duty?' Alejandro looked, confused, from Lori to Attila. 'I thought—'

Lori jumped in swiftly before Alejandro came out with an assumption that would embarrass both her and Attila beyond endurance.

'Attila's my trainer,' she said quickly.

'Oh!' Alejandro was still confused. 'But today, you are not training, correct? You can have a beer!'

'*Dos cervezas,*' Lori said firmly to the waiter. 'He's right, Attila, have a damn beer for once.'

It came out sharper than she had intended. Not the way someone talks to her trainer. *But then, who brings their trainer on a day out like this?* Alejandro, sensing that it would be best to change the subject, launched into a description of the Spanish colonial town, Valladolid, which they would visit on their way back to the El Dorado, and when the beer came, Lori and Attila both sank theirs in a minute flat.

Alcohol, mercifully, smoothed the awkward edges, and the stew soaked up the beer. Valladolid was very pretty, and they found a coffee shop next to the Spanish church where Alejandro told them about the town's long history and Lori bought a round of iced coffees, whipped with cream, drizzled in chocolate, which they all drank with gratitude for the caffeine and the cold shock of the ice in the now scorching afternoon sun. And then, as they piled back into the van and headed back to the hotel, Alejandro, with a mischievous smile, leaned over the back of his seat by the driver and said:

'So, remember that you stopped for a photo when we arrived at the *cenote*?'

It took them a moment; then Lori nodded. A couple of Mayan kids had been stopping the tourists in groups to pose, and she and Attila had duly done so. She had forgotten all about it till now. Alejandro reached into his leather satchel and produced a glass bottle, the flattened, hip-flask shape perfect for the oversized label that was affixed to the front; he handed it to Lori, who exclaimed as she looked at it. A green and yellow border, echoing the green liquid inside, framed a large colour photograph of her and Attila, smiling for the camera, sunglasses propped on their heads. She was slightly taller than him, but there was not a hint of insecurity in his expression; they looked like a couple of fit, happy holidaymakers. A couple, in short.

'It's a traditional local drink,' Alejandro was saying. 'Mezcal, honey and aniseed. The herbs give it the green colour.'

Lori handed it to Attila, not knowing what to say.

'Very nice,' he said. 'Thank you.'

'You can try it later,' Alejandro said. 'It's good as a *digestivo*, to drink after dinner.'

But we don't have dinner together. Lori had an image of her sitting in their terrace dining area with Joachim, returned from a meal out at one of the restaurants, candles flickering on the table, Attila coming up the stairs from the beach as Lori poured the delicate green liqueur into three little dessert glasses. Or of her walking down the same stairs, bottle in one hand, two glasses in the other, to meet Attila on the beach, curling up in one of the cabanas and sipping by moonlight as the waves broke gently on the sand.

Both pictures were equally implausible. She shoved both of them out of her mind, said a polite 'thank you' to Alejandro, and added something about closing her eyes for the drive back; putting on her sunglasses, she leaned back against the seat and tried to snooze. Attila and Alejandro returned to the subject of the Mayan calendar, and their deep voices, talking about thirteen- and twenty-day weeks, the fact that Chichen Itza's pyramid had three hundred and sixty-five steps, one for each day of the year, fifty-two panels, one for each week, bored her into a doze that lasted until the van came to a halt outside the gateway to the El Dorado and a pith-helmeted security guard put his face to the van window to check the number of people inside.

Elizabeth was waiting for them at the reception; the hotel staff always made their ability to coordinate with their VIP guests' return and meet them in one of the golf carts look effortless. They thanked Alejandro, Lori tipped him and the driver, and Elizabeth whisked them back to the Casitas, reminding Lori that she and Joachim had their sunset massage scheduled for six that evening.

Joachim was out on the day bed, a series of odd swishing sounds coming from his iPad. Lori put her head out onto the terrace, said that she was having a lie-down and that he should be ready to walk over to the spa at a quarter to six; head down to the screen, he mumbled a perfunctory question as to whether she had had a nice time. Lori couldn't even bring herself to say yes. Attila had taken the bottle of Mezcal liqueur, which was lucky; if Lori had been carrying it, she might even have thrown it at her husband, screamed that she had been photographed on her lovely day out with her damn bodyguard and not Joachim. She was dying to literally shove it in his face and yell: *'What's wrong with this picture?'*

She stripped her clothes off, set her phone alarm and crawled into bed in the dark, air-conditioned room, the fan turning slowly overhead, white noise that failed to soothe her. She could balance on all fours on a Swiss ball, stand on one foot on a vibrating PowerPlate and catch a heavy medicine ball that Attila was throwing at her, do a handstand. And yet, lying on the huge, king-size bed, she was so disoriented she might have been tumbling endlessly through the air, like the medicine ball: bouncing back and forth, never settling.

That image bounced through her dreams, the weighted, rubbery texture of the ball, dimpled to avoid it slipping through sweaty hands, the blue swooshes on the black background. It made her dizzy, disoriented, and she woke up, despite the cool of the room, feeling sweaty and hot. It was twenty to six, and, when she pulled on a short Heidi Klein cover-up and once more slid open the terrace door, Joachim did not seem to have moved; the sounds coming from the iPad were beeps as well as swishes now.

'We have to get going,' she said.

'Mmn,' her husband said, not looking up from the tablet. 'I can't leave this, I'm afraid. I'm at a very critical juncture.'

'Of *what*?' Snapping to life, Lori lunged across the terrace towards him. 'We're, what, seven hours behind Herzoslovakia, right?' She calculated in her head. 'It's nearly six p.m. here – that means it's one in the morning there! What the *hell* can be going on back home that's this damn urgent?'

She actually grabbed for the iPad. Joachim wrenched it away from her, holding it defensively behind him.

'Matters of state!' he said furiously, his eyes darting back and forth, not meeting hers. 'Very important matters of state! I am busy writing important documents for Philippe to present in my absence.'

'You know what, Joachim? I have a hard time believing that! You never *look* like you're writing! You're *tapping*, or pulling things around, but you never look like you're writing!'

Lori stood over the day bed, hands on her hips, staring down at her husband, unable to believe that, after refusing to accompany her to Chichen Itza today, he was now bowing out of their couple's massage appointment. Her head was so tight it felt as if it were about to explode.

'I'm checking documents – complicated tax relief forms, very detailed proposals for bank privacy laws – I have to restructure many legal set-ups, move paragraphs around, do edits—'

Joachim's voice was rising, his light blue eyes bulging slightly as he gained momentum. Lori let him list everything he could think of that he might be doing for work, until he had run down to silence, the iPad still protectively nestled behind him, out of her reach. Then she said sadly:

'Joachim, this is awful. But I just don't believe you.'

'You should trust me,' Joachim snapped. 'I am your husband.'

'A *husband*,' she said, 'on *honeymoon*, would get up off that damn bed and come get a massage with his wife.'

Joachim bit his lip. The iPad made an urgent whirring noise, almost like a bell ringing.

'I need to finish this . . .' he said, sounding almost whiny. 'It's very important . . .'

'Fine,' she snapped, not trusting herself to say one more word; if she did, she thought she would start screaming, throw herself on him, wrestle the damn tablet from his hands and smash it to smithereens against one of the wooden balcony struts. She worked out every day, she was an Olympic champion; she was absolutely sure that she could physically overpower Joachim and grab the iPad. Her hands were twitching with the impulse to do it; she could see the glass shards scattering, hear them breaking, feel the impact of the plastic casing as it cracked to pieces.

She was breathing as fast as if she had run a race as she turned and walked away from her recumbent husband along the balcony that led to the beach stairs. Her feet were bare; she had meant to put on flip-flops, but she honestly thought that if she went back into the suite she would leave a trail of damage and destruction in her wake. There were so many things to break in there. She envisaged taking the glasses from the bar, where they were all neatly lined up by height; champagne, red wine, white wine, highball, lowball, shot glasses; actually, *not* picking them up one by one, but sweeping them onto the tiles with one long swipe of her arm, watching them all shatter in unison . . .

Attila and Vassily were waiting below the steps that led up to the main suite door, ready to escort their respective charges to the spa. At the sight of Lori, storming up from the beach, barefoot, hair unbrushed, mouth set tight with anger, they exchanged a brief glance of concern.

'He's not coming,' she said to Vassily, who dropped his gaze to the ground to avoid meeting her eyes.

Lori didn't stop; she kept walking, past the two men, aware that Attila was falling into step behind her. Vassily, she thought bitterly, could safely sneak off and go find his married woman; it was an hour after the beach bar had closed, which meant that her husband was doubtless passed out sleeping off his afternoon drinking. Joachim wouldn't stir from the day bed. And it was ridiculous to expect Vassily to sit around all day in this security-protected resort, watching a man lie on a bed on a balcony.

Why shouldn't Vassily have some fun? God knows, no one else is!

'You have no shoes,' Attila said, catching up with her. 'You want me to go back and get some for you?'

'No,' Lori said with unusual curtness. The stone path was rough under her bare feet, but not painful; and even if it had been, she wouldn't have cared. To increase the distance between herself and her husband she would have walked over glass. And the spa wasn't far, just a couple of curves around the back of two of the Casitas horseshoes, a sculptural white building whose entrance jutted like a promontory into a V in the road, with a flowing water feature in front of it over which the path extended like a rising bridge.

Its sophistication was wasted on Lori, however; she was blinded to the elegance of the soaring lime and mandarin lobby, the subtle perfume from the diffusers placed in niches

around the walls, the charming smile of the woman greeting
her with a cool fragranced towel.

'Do you have a spa service booked?' the receptionist asked,
looking at Lori's cover-up, her bare feet. Lori and Attila were
in here almost every day, as the gym was located at the back
of the spa, but obviously, Lori was not dressed for a
workout.

'Yes,' Lori managed not to snap. 'I think Liliana made the
booking. In the name of Guttman.'

'Oh yes! Of course! You have the very special Sky
Massage!' The receptionist beamed, as excited as if she were
about to have a sunset massage herself. 'Please, let me take
you into the changing rooms.' She beckoned a young man in
the same two-piece beige tunic and trousers that she was
wearing. 'Rodrigo will take Mr Guttman.'

Lori opened her mouth, about to say that Attila wasn't
Joachim, that her husband would not be joining her. But
then she closed it again. The massage was already booked;
why shouldn't Attila benefit from it? If Joachim was too
damn lazy to get off his ass and walk over to the spa to be
pampered, why should a perfectly good treatment go to
waste? And, of course, the staff here had seen her and Attila
in here every day, working out at the gym – it was a natural
assumption that they were a couple.

She shrugged at Attila, indicating that she didn't care
enough to make a fuss about the misunderstanding. His
shaggy black eyebrows shot up, disappearing in the heavy
cluster of curls over his forehead, but he duly obeyed, following in Rodrigo's wake. Lori was guided through to the
women's changing rooms, past the stunning copper wall
down which water flowed in a constant stream to a black
pool below, providing a calming background murmur. She
undressed, put her dress and underwear in a locker, donned

the ankle-length robe and slid on the rubber sandals; it spoke volumes of the attention to detail of the El Dorado that even these were luxurious, moulded around the foot and with soft massaging spines beneath the balls of the feet.

Emerging back into the lobby, she saw Attila standing by the front door in a matching robe and rubber sandals.

'Well, you said before that you wanted a massage!' she said to him, trying to smile, to make something positive out of the mess that was her current situation.

'Yes,' Attila said, looking uncharacteristically insecure, 'but—'

'Felipe is waiting outside for you!' the receptionist said, opening the glass door for them and standing back to gesture them through.

Lori and Attila stepped out onto the sloping walkway to see a woman and a man in white, orange-bordered uniforms, both holding bowls: the woman's, of carved wood, held rose petals, while the man's was black volcanic lava stone, a long trail of grey smoke rising from it and wreathing around his serious, concentrated face. He nodded solemnly at Lori and Attila and turned, walking down towards the beach; the woman, smiling, indicated that they should follow him. They passed the low Casitas buildings, reached the sand, and Lori headed for the smooth wooden steps that led up to the Sky Massage suite, an open-air room with two massage tables in it, close to the water's edge. She could see two more massage therapists waiting up there.

'No, we go to the beach first, for the ritual,' the woman said, and Lori and Attila exchanged confused looks. Lori had just assumed that Liliana had booked her and Joachim in for a couple's massage; she had no idea about any associated ceremony. She knew it was going to be four hands each, and had assumed that was the special aspect of the massage that the receptionist had meant; this was taking her completely by surprise.

Felipe was putting down the bowl by the water's edge, the grey smoke still rising up in whirls now, billowed and eddied by the sea breeze. It smelt of incense but also of herbs, a fresh clean edge to the scent: later Liliana told Lori that basil, rosemary and lemongrass had been pounded up in the bowl. Felipe came towards Lori and Attila, grave and concentrated, reached down, took Lori's right hand and Attila's left, raised them up and linked them together.

Wait. This isn't right. Lori looked, panicking, at Attila, but he was staring straight ahead, his eyes fixed on the far horizon, at the warm rose-gold sinking sun. The breeze lifted his heavy dark curls, and she saw him, suddenly, as a Greek statue, sculpted from a massive marble block, a famous warrior or wrestler who had completed mythical feats.

'We purify the union,' Felipe said, picking up a sheaf of bay leaves from beside the bowl and running them slowly up the side of Lori's body, gently touching her with the tips of the leaves; it was as if he were outlining her shape in the air. 'This is the lady's side, the heart side. We cleanse away bad thoughts, sad feelings. We make it strong.'

The leaves rustled as Felipe raised them over her head, his dark eyes serious, his concentration and belief in the ritual he was performing hypnotic. Lori stared at him, mesmerized by him and his words, utterly taken aback by what she and Attila had stumbled into; her hand, resting in Attila's huge one, felt tingling, electric with nerve endings.

'The man's side is abundance,' Felipe said, running the leaves around Attila's outline. 'Strength.' He moved behind them, rustling the sheaf at their shoulders. 'We cleanse the back, so bad spirits cannot come in the night. So you are protected.'

The waves were lapping on the sand in front of them, and the woman had picked up a rain stick and was tilting it slowly back and forth, the seeds inside falling in a slow steady shower. The sun was slipping behind the horizon now, deep blood-red streaks reaching along the distant waterline, the sky glowing pink and blue and gold.

Felipe moved in front of Lori and Attila again, the sheaf of bay leaves reaching over their heads.

'The head is the sun,' he said. 'Crow chakra. It brings energy from the heaven.' The leaves lowered to their clasped hands. 'The joined hands are love,' he continued. 'The union is purified so the love can be strong.'

Attila's hand jerked under Lori's. She had no idea what to do: stopping this ritual in the middle, after they had let Felipe get this far, would be horribly rude. *Worse than rude: you couldn't break off a shamanic ceremony once it was under way, surely! It would be incredibly bad luck.* Lori looked down at Attila's hand, his wide stubby fingers wrapped round hers, and couldn't find any way to speak out, to tell Felipe that there had been a mistake and that the man whose hand she was holding was not her husband, that her husband hadn't even bothered to join her . . .

The image of Joachim on the day bed, tapping at the iPad, filled her with such rage that she literally saw red; the last rays of the disappearing sun were no more crimson than the blood that momentarily obscured her vision. She realized that her fingers had clamped around Attila's, crushing them so tightly that it couldn't be mistaken, by him at least, for an affectionate squeeze. Before her wedding, Lori hadn't even realized that she was capable of this much anger. But the frustration, the sense that somehow she had been terribly tricked and cheated by her husband, rose in her like a tidal wave, and for a moment she was actually scared of herself, of the violent impulse she felt towards Joachim.

Her eyes closed, and she swayed a little. Attila's hand steadied her, his forearm tensing as he braced against her weight. She heard Felipe say something as if from a very long distance away, and when she opened her eyes again, the sun had sunk completely, the light that infused the sky was fading softly, and Felipe was holding out a bowl to her and Attila, his face sober and focused, seeming to absorb and understand the feelings that were flooding through her. She glanced down at the bowl, seeing that it was the wooden one full of rose petals.

'Now,' Felipe said, 'you throw away the rose petals, into the sea. All bad things, bad thoughts, are in the petals. You throw them into the water and the water will purify the bad things. And when they leave your hand, your body and spirit are renewed.'

He handed the bowl to them. Attila took it with his free hand and, as Felipe stepped back, gesturing, Attila guided Lori towards the water's edge. Silently, they took handfuls of the petals and scattered them into the waves, bright dots of pink and fuchsia and scarlet tumbling and fluttering into the white foam, dancing in the sea breeze. Lori could not look at Attila; his presence beside her was so monumental that to meet his eyes would have been overwhelming.

Forget the whole couples part, she told herself desperately. *Just leave all that bit out and focus on the renewal thing. This is actually exactly what you need. Things with Joachim, obviously, are beyond messed up. You have to work out what's going on with him, why he's MIA on your honeymoon. Deal with the fact that this marriage may be doomed before it's even really started.*

Lori picked up the last handful of petals, held them over the lapping sea, took a deep breath and let the petals and the breath out at the same moment, a long exhale of release, consciously allowing herself to think what had been on her mind for days. That she might need to cut her losses. That her marriage to Joachim, if it kept on this way, would turn out to be a complete disaster.

Her hand hung there in the air, empty, open, and she stood and watched and did not pull it back until every last rose petal was bathed in salt water, rolled over and under by the waves, the red and pink drops flowing out to sea. Her heart was pounding fast, but her head, for the first time since her wedding day, felt steady and calm. It felt as if she had been in a trance for a long time, moving through a cloud, blind to where she was going, and now that cloud had lifted, and she could see things clearly.

Attila was looking at her, she knew. Assessing how she was doing, whether she needed him to stay close, if she were going to waver on her feet again; she gave a short little shake of her head, reassuring him, making an effort to breathe evenly, slowly, as they turned around to face Felipe once more. He took the bowl from them and handed it to the woman. Then he bent down and picked up a huge white shell from the sand, holding it up to show Lori and Attila.

'The medicine leaves represent earth, the physical body,' he said. 'The rain stick and the sea are water. The *copal* that burns is fire, in a bowl made of *jicara*, from the volcano, which gives fire. The incense is the air. And the conch shell represents the god. When you make the music with the conch, you call the god, to come into you and bring the very good energy from the sun.'

He looked from Lori to Attila, waiting to make sure they understood all of this. Then he placed the conch to his mouth and blew, a low, trumpeting sound that was indeed like a summons: he turned and walked away from them, up the

beach, the conch calling them to follow, up the wooden ramp
that led to the Sky Massage suite, its white curtains moving
softly in the sea breeze, twilight behind them deepening
blue. Two other massage therapists in white uniforms waited,
hands clasped in front of them, behind the twin massage
tables.

'Now you are new people,' Felipe said, placing the conch
on a low shelf. He smiled at them. 'You are royal together, the
King and Queen.'

Lori almost jumped out of her skin. Frantically, she glanced
from side to side, looking at everyone in the massage suite,
judging their reaction to the last few words: the masseurs and
Felipe all looked as quiet and professional as ever. Attila's
black eyes flickered as she met them briefly, telling her that
Felipe's choice of words was just a coincidence, that no one
was aware of Lori's true identity as Queen of Herzoslovakia.

Don't think about that. My God. Queen of Herzoslovakia!
Don't think about that, or you'll get into a panic again!

'This will be a very strong massage,' Felipe continued.
'With four hands each, we change your energy and make it
new and positive.'

Attila grunted appreciatively as the masseurs came
forward, holding up towels behind which they could both
remove their robes and lie down on the tables. As an athlete,
Lori was completely used to being naked in front of physical
therapists; the spa had offered an optional little paper thong,
but Lori never used those. They got in the way of a really
good working-over.

So it wasn't her own nakedness that was on the forefront
of her mind, but Attila's. She heard his robe being taken from
him and hung up, she heard the creak as he climbed onto the
table and lay there face down. She knew that Attila, as
comfortable with his body as she was with hers, wouldn't

have put on the thong either. She knew that, like her, he would be stretched out on the white towel without a stitch of clothing on.

Which is totally normal, she told herself firmly. *Thank God that ritual's over, and we'll never talk about it again. It was beyond embarrassing to be mistaken for a couple, but I got something positive out of it – that bit where I threw the rose petals felt really cleansing—*

A soft grunt was pushed from her as the towel that had been stretched over her shoulders was folded back, and two pairs of hands settled on her upper back, strong thumbs and fingers tracing around her shoulder blades. Lori relaxed almost completely, her head sinking into the white leather face-rest as oil was smoothed into her skin and every kink in the body was pummelled and worked out. Her eyes were closed; she concentrated on her breathing, on synchronizing it with the strokes of the hands down her back.

But then, gradually, she became aware that she was picturing an image with every breath she took. Everything that they were doing to her was also being done to Attila. As they dug into her lower back, rocking and easing it, finding the knots, knuckling them loose, Felipe and the other masseur would be doing the same to Attila. Every part of her that they exposed by folding back the towel would also be exposed on Attila: his wide, powerful back, his narrow waist, his high, rounded glutes, his thighs . . .

Lori bit her lip and tried not to wriggle. She was in a haze of what she told herself firmly was confusion: she opened her eyes and stared at the floorboards, watching the daylight slowly fade away, the wood darkening to near-black and then glowing softly as lamps were turned on. a masseur told her in a muted voice to turn over, and she pushed up, swivelling to lie on her back, more towels held up for privacy, not allowing herself to even try to snatch a glance at Attila doing the same thing, but hearing his heavy body move on the table, his shoulders settle down, his buttocks, the front of his body fully exposed before they laid the towels over him . . .

Lori bit her lip hard as she lay back. She had to close her eyes now, couldn't keep them open with four hands on her scalp, stretching her neck, sliding under her shoulders, fingers digging in to work out every vertebra, ease her spine as long as it could reach. For a moment the utter pleasure of it distracted her completely, and then she was back imagining the masseurs working on Attila, the sheer effort it would be to burrow under his huge deltoids, to take the full weight of them, to feel them firm and solid and strong . . .

This is just because I haven't had sex with Joachim since we got married, she insisted to herself, as cold slices of cucumber were placed on her eyes, her head wrapped in a damp, cool towel. She sighed at the relief, her overheated skull gratefully relaxing; she hadn't realized how hot her scalp was feeling until the chilled towel was folded around it. Lori focused on the coldness seeping through to her hair, her skin, the icy sensation of the cucumber on her eyelids: it was exactly what she needed to counteract her previous train of thought. *A cold shock. Perfect.*

When it was unwrapped at last, after they had finished the massage, she almost exclaimed in protest. She could have lain there for hours more, cooling down her head, her eyes, calming herself, trying to feel that delicious cool spreading through every one of her limbs; the cucumber slices were peeled off, she was gently encouraged to sit up, given her robe, her arms guided into the sleeves as her eyes, blinking at the light, gradually, reluctantly, opened again.

She was sitting on the edge of the table, her robe wrapped around her, facing Attila, who was in the same position. For a moment, her gaze dropped below the knotted tie at his waist, seeing a gap as the towelling fabric fell away from one ponderous, muscled thigh, a darkness at the top of it from which, after a second, she dragged away her eyes by main force, turning in exaggerated gratitude to take a porcelain cup of green tea with lemon which Felipe was handing to her with a smile.

I must look really dazed. Beyond trippy. But I just had an amazing four-hand massage – anyone would look trippy after that—

'Oh, thank you!' she said, her voice sounding too loud in the quiet as she was handed a plate of orange and cucumber slices, peeled and overlapping. The vivid arrangement on the white plate was bright enough in itself to wake her a little more from the trance into which the massage had put her. She ate some orange, sweet and sharp, finishing her tea, pretending to herself that there was not another, large, hulking person in close proximity to her, also drinking tea and eating orange slices, that she couldn't see his big hand, his wide hairy forearm, reaching for the plate that was being held between them.

I can't see him, she told herself. *I can't see him. He isn't here.*

She kept saying that as they handed back their cups, thanking everyone, as they slid their sandals on and walked back to the spa. Felipe was leading their little procession, for which Lori was devoutly grateful; she was so dazed, even after the tea and the fruit, that she would have stumbled around for hours in the dusk if she had been left to her own devices. Even the tactful, diffuse lighting of the spa felt too bright; Felipe indicated that they sit down on a sofa at the entrance, brought them chilled glasses of champagne, gave them each a little blue drawstring bag of pretty translucent stones, as a memento. He said something else about the stones as well, their significance, but by that time Lori's head was spinning with the effects of the alcohol, which she seemed to have polished off in a matter of seconds.

She stood up, hearing herself say that she wanted to go back to her room, that she was very relaxed, and would it be okay if she went in her robe and picked up her clothes later? Felipe said, 'Of course', which was pretty much what everyone at the Casitas said to any request that she had ever made to them, and she thanked him and headed for the door, one of the massage therapists opening it for her, and Lori thanked her, stepping out again into the soft silky evening air, very aware that beside her was the person whose existence she was busy denying. Their sandals slapped lightly against the stone pathway in unison, their white robes making it easy for the occasional driver of a golf cart to see them and swerve to give them room. The moonlight, the uplighters and the golden glow from the Italian restaurant as they passed it all cast their shadows out darkly, the fronds of the palm trees playing back and forth overhead as they rounded D'Italia, taking the last stretch of path back to the Presidential Suite.

Lori had the key card in the pocket of her robe. She pulled it out as she started up the staircase, knowing that Attila was following her, his tread light for such a solid man. The door clicked open, and Lori glanced out onto the terrace; yes, there was Joachim, a dark shape far in the corner, curled on his day bed, the iPad flickering in his hands, a cocktail propped on the table beside him. She pressed the button to draw the curtains and turned away from the diminishing view, through the living room into the bedroom, through the dressing room, into the bathroom, opening the glass door that led to the outside shower, dropping her robe on the floor and walking through. Keeping moving, not thinking about what was happening, what she was doing.

What they were doing. Because behind her, Attila was still following: she turned on the shower full blast, water pouring down and crashing onto the stone floor, and tipped back her head, looking up at the sliver of moon, the dark sky overhead, thinking:

If I don't turn round, this won't happen. If I take one step forward, into the shower, if I keep pretending he's not here, he'll walk away. I don't know how I can be so sure of that, but I am.

It's my choice.

She turned around. Attila was standing in the doorway, staring at her, his eyes black as coal, his hands at the tie of his robe: she swallowed, feeling as if she were choking down a lump as big as a fist as he unfastened the belt, shrugged the robe off his huge shoulders, stepped towards her as it was falling, caught her and pulled her towards him and kissed her almost all in the same movement, his tongue deep in her mouth, his great arms flexing as he picked her up, off her feet, and backed her into the cascading water. One arm around his neck, clinging on tightly, her legs wrapping round his waist, her other hand reached down for the big cock that she had seen for one heartstopping moment, swollen and swaying as he took a stride towards her; her hand closed around it, directed it, her pelvis tilted and her eyes closed as, with the greatest relief she'd ever felt in her life, she felt Attila's cock drive right up inside her.

Lori had been wet ever since she realized he was lying next to her, naked, on the next massage table. She had even been nervous that she might actually drip a little on the towel beneath her, she was so turned on. And what she had been wanting, if she were honest with herself, ever since she had seen him at the *cenote*, ever since that switch had flicked that took him from great friend to a man with a body so extraordinary she hadn't been able to stop thinking about it ever since, had happened in one thrust. His tongue in her mouth in one breath, his cock burying itself inside her in the next.

She moaned, both arms round his neck now, rocking herself back and forth, the water pounding down on their heads as his hands cupped her buttocks, his fingers digging into her wet skin, and he caught her rhythm. His wet pubic hairs rubbed coarsely against her with each deep tilt of his hips, and she rubbed herself against him furiously, completely lost to anything but fucking him now, drawing his lower lip into her mouth, sucking on it, her teeth making a little imprint on him, blind, her eyes squeezed shut so she could focus even better on the orgasm that was about to hit her in three, two, one—

It felt like her entire body was spasming around his. Her heels drummed a violent tattoo on his buttocks and thighs, as if she were physically fighting him, attacking him, forcing the orgasm from him to match her own; he fought back, clutching her even tighter, pushing her further under the shower, pumping his hips up again and again, his grip on her painful as he struggled to keep hold under the pounding of the water pouring down on both their bodies. Her bottom bumped against the stone wall and the reverberation on his cock sent her into another, even more blinding orgasm. She gasped, knowing that she couldn't make any louder sound than that, found his mouth again with hers, let her breath out into his as she came again, sitting down harder, pushing down even more on his cock, feeling it bounce against her cervix, wanting this to last for ever but also, even more, to feel him coming inside her—

Oh God no, we can't, what am I thinking? What am I thinking!

But to her shame, she did nothing to stop it, nothing to pull back or pound his shoulders or signal anything that told him that he couldn't come inside her. The truth was that she wanted him to, desperately, had lost any ability to control herself, and it was Attila, retaining some grain of common sense, who wrenched himself out of her, pushing her legs down so her feet hit the ground, and then shoving her back to the wall again, his body tight against hers, his cock sandwiched between them, pumping hot come against her flat muscled stomach, slamming his mouth on hers, making her open her lips wide to take his groan of release as she had wailed her own orgasm into his mouth.

They stood like that, wedged under the shower, their bodies dripping wet, Attila rocking slowly against her with the last of his orgasm, his hands planted on the wall, either side of her shoulders, his hips glued to hers. Lori's arms were still wrapped around his neck. Slowly, her eyes flickered open, her wet lashes peeling off her cheeks: she looked at him, their eyes level, their lips parting. Attila, in the immediate aftermath of a long pent-up orgasm, looked stunned, literally, his eyes blurry, as if someone had hit him over the head and shoved him into her arms.

Lori's hands rose, stroking his short black ringlets, feeling how thick they were with the water weighing them down, her groin, plastered to his, vibrating against the equally thick dark cluster of coils pressing roughly into it. Her thumbs caressed his forehead, pushing back the hair, lifting it, moving it back so that she could see his face, for the first time, without the heavy mass of curls hanging over it. His hairline was square and well-shaped. Water dripped down his face in rivulets; he looked much younger like this.

Not vulnerable, though, Lori thought with a smile. *That's the cliché, isn't it, when you see someone all wet? Younger and more vulnerable?* But it was inconceivable to her that Attila's solid, sturdy face could ever look helpless. Poleaxed, yes:

vulnerable, no. *He should cut his hair,* she thought. *It would really suit him.*

Still pushing back his hair, she leaned forward and kissed him gently on his water-wet lips.

Oh God, I love him, Lori realized suddenly. *I don't just want to fuck his brains out. I'm in love with him.*

Which means I'm in even worse a mess than I thought.

Buckingham Palace

'And what *particularly* attracts you to working in a Royal Household, Garry?' purred Martin Frensham, the Buckingham Palace major-domo, propping his elbows on his leather-topped desk and smiling salaciously at the lean, muscled young man in a cheap, ill-fitting suit sitting awkwardly in front of it. Very insecure in the lavish surroundings of the Palace, Garry Wilson, the candidate for liveried helper in the Royal Mews stables, had perched his bottom on the edge of the chair and was twisting his fingers together nervously in his lap. If he had had a cap, he would have wrung it.

'I'm covering a maternity leave right now for a groom where I am, sir,' Garry mumbled. 'She'll be back in a month or so, and then I'll be out on my ear. Mr de Vere knows someone at the Royal Mews, and I've always wanted to work in London.'

'Ah yes, Mr de Vere,' Martin commented, smiling slyly at one of the head butlers, a well-built, handsome man in his late thirties who was sitting in with him on the interview. 'He's been a *very* good source for coachmen and grooms for us over the years, hasn't he, Simon?'

'An exceptional source, I'd say,' Simon agreed gravely.

Garry's eyes lit up, and he sat up straighter.

'Mr de Vere said that I could train up as a coachman,' he said eagerly. 'There's not much call for that in racing stables, but I'm a dab hand with the reins on a horse and cart, and I know *all* the royal coaches. You can test me. I have pictures of all of 'em.'

'Well, I *say*,' Simon said teasingly, as Martin made a big show of consulting the papers spread out in front of him. 'Pictures of *all* of the coaches. Which is your favourite, young Garry?'

Garry, aware that he was being mocked, ducked his head.

'You'll think I'm going to say the Gold State Coach or something,' he muttered, 'cos it's so historic. And gold. But it's postilion-ridden now, and not very manoeuvrable. I'd actually really like to drive one of the barouches. That's quite a challenge, I've heard. Light and flexible, only one pair. And—'

'Now, you're aware you'd be living on site?' Simon continued, cutting through this tedious stream of information. 'Because, as you know, we have accommodation for the grooms and coachmen and the chauffeurs above the carriage houses and the stables. The Mews is in the Palace grounds, as you probably know. It's, um, *very* convenient for the Palace . . .'

'*Very* convenient!' Martin agreed, smiling at Simon. 'Just a hop, skip and a jump across the grounds! Ooh, here it is.'

He was holding up a letter.

'Your recommendation from Mr de Vere. I understand that, as well as your ability with horses, you have some very particular skills that Mr de Vere suggests we test out.' He winked at Simon. 'You know, one of the job requirements for Liveried Helper is cleaning and maintaining the harnesses . . .'

At the wink, Simon had stood up; he crossed the room to the door, turning the key in the lock, as Martin continued:

'Mr Carey and I would like to see what hands-on abilities you have in, um, belt-buckle-opening and pipe-cleaning,' Martin smirked, as Simon let out a loud snigger. 'What?' Martin said crossly to him. 'Belt buckles! They're like harnesses!'

He turned back to Garry.

'Mr de Vere speaks *very* highly of your abilities in this area,' he said to the young man. 'And if we're impressed, we'll not only pass your application on to the Chief Equerry, who runs the Royal Mews, but we'll consider you for what I might describe as an auxiliary position here at the Palace, servicing—'

Simon coughed significantly.

'Well, all in good time,' Martin said. 'Let's get you past the practical exam first, shall we?'

Garry's brow was crinkled up, his handsome face confused, his thick eyebrows drawing together as he asked anxiously:

'Excuse me, Mr Frensham – I don't mean to be thick or anything, but Mr de Vere – well, he said you'd want me to – and I *think* that's what you mean, but I don't want to give offence – are you saying I should—'

'Christ, stop talking, come over here and suck my cock, you little slut!' Simon interrupted, sitting back down in his chair and spreading his legs.

Eagerly, Garry jumped up, relief flooding his features at having read the mood of the meeting correctly. Kneeling down in front of Simon, he unbuckled the butler's belt, unbuttoned his trousers, unzipped his fly and expertly extracted Simon's tumescing penis from the slit in his silk boxers. Hawking, he spat a wet, sticky trail along the vein that stood out along the underside of Simon's cock, worked it in with his lips, wrapped his hand around the base, bent his head to the tip and began, with a steady twisting action of his wrist, to do exactly what Simon had specified.

Martin watched with great approval, nodding as Garry's head bobbed up and down in Simon's lap. For years they had interviewed young men together, young men who were specifically recommended to them by certain extremely reliable sources. Among these were a maître d' at a five-star London hotel, a furniture restorer, a French polisher, the head of a luxury car sales firm in the West End, and Mr de Vere, who owned a racing stables in Cheltenham.

The need for personal references was of the highest importance, and not simply because Martin and Simon were naturally keen to avoid any accusations of sexual harassment. These interviews had a dual-purpose function, as the carefully selected young men were also being considered for a much more important role in the Royal Household, one which would not interfere in any way with the duties for which they had been hired; the requirements of their jobs, after all, were entirely during the daytime, while the other tasks they might be called upon to execute – and for which they would receive a hefty cash bonus – were usually performed after dark.

'Well?' Martin asked, seeing Simon's face grow redder and redder, a vein to match the one on his penis popping out on his forehead. 'Verdict so far?'

'Sucks like a Dyson,' Simon panted.

'Excellent,' Martin said contentedly, scanning the de Vere letter one more time. 'He does mention a strong desire to give full satisfaction in any position to which young Garry may be assigned . . .'

The phone on his desk rang, and Martin reached for it just as Simon coughed, grunted, sputtered and, gripping the arms of his chair, shot into Garry's mouth with a loud 'Ugh!' of satisfaction.

'Martin Frensham?' Martin said, his tone as smooth as ever. 'Oh yes, hello, David, any news? What?' He laughed. 'Oh, that was just Simon. We're conducting an interview for, er, a new liveried helper for the Mews . . . mmm . . . Yes . . . No, *very* satisfactory, according to Simon . . . well, perhaps, David. If you have good news. I have a very exclusive little soirée coming up in my rooms, and I might just be persuaded to extend an invitation to you . . .'

He looked over at Garry, who was sitting back on his haunches and wiping his mouth.

'Oh, six foot two, eyes of blue, just like the song . . . I'd *definitely* say one for Him at this rate . . . mmn . . . oh, you know what He's like, a year maximum then He's on to fresh meat . . . well, Simon and I know all about *that*, don't we, dear?'

Martin exchanged a knowing roll of the eyes with Simon, who was wiping off his cock with a monogrammed silk handkerchief.

'So tell me *everything*,' Martin continued.

Garry looked at him, head tilted in an unspoken question: Martin nodded briskly and pointed at his lap, scooching his chair back from the desk to give Garry room to kneel in front of him. Garry promptly obeyed, not bothering to get up. On hands and knees, he quickly moved in front of Martin, unbuckling the latter's belt, opening his trouser fly, extracting Martin's very minimal penis and, with a display of excellent manners that definitely deserved the glowing reference he had received from Mr de Vere, ducking over it as enthusiastically as if it had been Simon's much larger and more satisfying one.

'Oh my *God*!' Martin said as his chipolata-sized penis disappeared in one gulp into Garry's mouth: very tactfully, Garry omitted the fist grasp entirely, as the comparison between his little finger and Martin's penis would not have been flattering to the latter. Martin's exclamation had been so loud that, concerned that he had done something wrong, Garry's head tilted up to Martin's, eyes wide in a question. His lips were pursed as tightly around Martin's cock as if he were an oboe player sucking on a reed.

'No, not you!' Martin said to him impatiently. 'You carry on! Yes, sorry, David, just multitasking here.'

Simon, tucking back his detumescing penis into his boxers again, tittered at this.

'Oh my *God*!' Martin exclaimed again at what he had just heard from David.

Garry, duly warned, continued sucking without interruption of service this time.

'*David!* This is – I *thought* so, I bloody well *thought* so! I'd know her anywhere! That little *bitch*! Well, I say "little", but she wasn't exactly *small*, was she? Turn her over, she's almost like the real thing, as He used to say . . .'

Simon, buckling up his belt, nodded in agreement.

'As soon as I saw her walk into the sitting room, I *knew* there was something familiar about her! You know why, David? *She knew exactly where she was*. There was Lady Margaret burbling on to make the point that her *secretary* had never been to Buck House before, blah blah blah – *God*, I loathe that bossy old muff-diver! And her mother was even worse. Snobby old bitch.' Martin paused for breath. 'So *anyway*, there was Lady M practically bending over backwards to reassure her, but that *secretary* just walked into the Belgian Suite and didn't even look around at the portraits! She didn't give one glance around the room! Who *does* that? Hold on, David, just a sec—'

He put down the cordless phone, grabbed Garry's shaven head, thrust his chipolata still further between Garry's lips, shut his eyes, groaned loudly, and trembled.

'Uh! Uh! Yes! Uh!' he grunted. Opening his eyes, he drew in a long, deep breath, exhaled equally thoroughly, nodded in approval at Garry, and picked up the phone again. Garry, swallowing, ducked his head as Martin's penis slid out of his mouth like a small pink slug, and turned his face discreetly to the side so that he could massage his mouth, which was cramped from having to purse his lips so tightly.

'Well, *exactly*!' Gary resumed his conversation, invigorated by his orgasm. 'No one walks into that *fabulous* room and doesn't wander round to have a gawp! I don't care if you're the Obamas or Queen Lori of Herzoslovakia – oh, I *know*, that poor sobbing tart, did you *hear* what he gets up to in Berlin? Ooh, wait till I tell you *that* one! Anyway, back to our sheep, as they say in France—'

He listened intently.

'Oh, *that's* where she is! No *wonder* no one saw hide nor hair of her for years! I must say, that wasn't stupid of her – first thing she ever did that wasn't stupid – oh, I know, silly bitch, why not just keep her mouth shut, do what she wanted and be the fucking Queen? It's not like He would have bothered her ever again! God, I'd snap that offer up in a heartbeat! . . . mmn . . . mmn . . . *Oh*,' he said after a while, with absolute certainty. 'She'll be back. Believe me, she'll be back. She didn't get what she wanted, did she? Oh no. I know her. Just seeing Hugo and the Commoner won't have been enough. She didn't even see Sophie. She was always a huge drama queen – I *know*, dear, the *irony*! God knows what she had planned, but it wasn't Him coming in and throwing the most appalling tantrum – oh, it was awful. You should have seen it. He's not getting any better with the years, you know. He threw *all* His toys out of the pram!'

Garry was backing away, standing up, wiping his mouth with a tissue from the box on the desk. He looked an inquiry at Simon, who smiled at him and mouthed:

'You can go now.'

Garry raised his eyebrows.

'Yes, yes, you got the job, you stupid slut! Now off you go!' Simon hissed, flapping his hands at the young man. As the door closed behind Garry, Simon stood up and took the chair Garry had been occupying, pulling it up at Martin's desk.

'And that screech she gave!' Martin was saying. 'Well, I'd been wondering before why Blondie was pretending she hadn't been here before, but I can't say I cared much. But as soon as she screamed, I knew! God knows, we've *all* heard that scream before!'

Simon nodded vigorously in agreement. Martin glanced at him.

'Oh, you know who's here? Simon! He was there when the whole thing kicked off, of course! He was giving Simon a seeing-to when that silly mare wandered in and got her knickers in a twist and then pissed all over the floor!'

'It's called your waters breaking, Martin,' Simon corrected him, wanting to be fair. 'It's not like she actually wee'd on the Turkish carpet.'

'Whatever you call it, it was never the same again!' Martin snapped. 'David? Look, you keep your contact at the airport in Morocco well-greased, all right? Hah! Yes, that too! Ooh, I can't *wait* to get back to Marrakech! I want to know as soon as she's on the move again. Because she will be, trust me. She'll be trying to come back. *Especially* if Lady M's there with her. It's the wedding. I *know* her. She was always *very* attached to the children, that was a huge part of the problem . . . mmn . . . mmn . . . yes, well, day or night, you let me know. You've got my mobile – yes. Thanks, David. Great job. Send me the bills and I'll run them through the black accounts as always. Thanks.'

He put down the phone and stared at Simon, his eyes bugging out.

'*Well!*' he said. 'I *knew* it! Wait till you hear this – she must have faked her death in that avalanche and sodded off to fuck Prince Rahim up in the hills in Morocco! Lucky cow,' he added enviously. 'He's *very* attractive. *Love* the moustache. *Very* manly.'

'I always thought she found out,' Simon said, sitting back. 'You know. About the whole . . . idea.'

'Oh, call a spade a spade! The overdose plan!' Martin said impatiently. 'Well, it certainly explains the avalanche – so soon after the divorce. I always thought that was *very* interesting timing.'

'I don't think she'd have said anything,' Simon observed, not meeting Martin's eyes now. 'She just wanted to get out and bring up the children.'

'But she couldn't be trusted to keep her mouth shut!' Martin said angrily. 'Honestly, why didn't she just stay put? He wasn't bothering her any more, was He? But no, she had to push for a divorce, and things got messy, and she was too much of a risk!' He took a deep breath. 'You *know* what a loose cannon she was, Simon! No matter what she might have promised, she simply couldn't be trusted. I mean, it came down from on high – it wasn't *my* decision – but I have to say, I agreed with it.'

'She didn't know what she was getting into in the first place,' Simon pointed out. 'He should have picked someone who did.'

'Oh, we've been over this, Simon! Old news! It's what we have to do *now* that matters!' Martin drummed his manicured fingertips on the leather of the desk. 'I have to take this higher. David's watching the airport – we'll know when Prince Rahim charters another plane. That's the only way to get her crossing borders – the checks for private planes are almost non-existent. But we have to stay on top of this. *Especially* with the wedding coming up.'

He fixed Simon with a gimlet stare.

'You see that, don't you? We can't have her just running around, causing even more havoc! Talking to Hugo and Sophie, God forbid, spilling the beans! You *remember* what she was like when she was married to Him, don't you? She just got worse and worse until she had no self-control at all!' He shook his head. 'It's so much to take in,' he said. 'I'm in shock, to be honest with you. Absolute shock. I mean, I *love* to be right, but in this case—'

Martin sucked in his breath through his teeth.

'I'll need to schedule a *very* discreet meeting,' he said. 'Work out a plan of campaign.'

He picked up a Mont Blanc pen, uncapped it, pulled a leather-bound notepad towards him, and started doodling on it, his brow furrowed in calculation.

'I wonder if we can warn her off?' he pondered. 'Give her a right old scare that keeps her permanently penned up in her Moroccan shag pad? But now she's made it out of there already, had the nerve to walk in *here*, for fuck's sake . . .' He gestured around him with the pen. 'Honestly, Simon? A threat may not be enough. Worst case scenario – we're going to have to make sure she doesn't get near the children again. By any means necessary.'

He sniggered.

'Get me!' he added. 'I sound just like a Bond villain!'

Lori

They didn't say a word; there was nothing to be said. They picked up their robes and put them on, Lori unable to prevent herself from staring at the wonder that was Attila's naked body. Even as he belted his robe around his waist, she was marvelling at the ripple of his shoulders, the leanness of his hips. He slipped on his sandals and she watched the flex of his calves, the glimpse of one thigh as the robe, straining to contain the width of both of them, fell open. He turned and she watched his back fill the doorframe as he left, closing the door of the suite behind him quietly. And then she crossed the living room, slid open the glass door to the terrace, stepped out and stood in the dusk, looking down at her husband.

He didn't even look up. She was as sure as she could be that he had no idea of what she had just done with her body-guard, though, to be honest, she wasn't actually sure if she cared whether her husband knew or not.

'Joachim?' she said, hearing with surprise how calm her voice sounded. 'This isn't working.'

'What do you mean?' he said abstractedly, as he put his

thumb and index finger on the screen and pulled them together.

'Our marriage, Joachim. It isn't working.'

Oh, the relief. It was like dropping her robe and turning to look at Attila, naked, that pure, clean moment where you told the truth and everything else simply fell away.

Her husband clicked his tongue impatiently, looked at her over the top of the iPad, and said:

'It's fine. You're a queen, aren't you? You've got what you wanted.'

Lori's eyebrows shot up. She rocked back slightly on her heels. This was not at all what she had expected.

'*You're* okay with this?' she asked, staring at him. 'Not talking at all, not having sex? I thought you were as unhappy about it as I was! I thought you'd realized we'd made a terrible mistake – or you were angry because I cried at the wedding and embarrassed you—'

'I *was* angry about that,' Joachim said, frowning at the memory. '*Very* angry.'

'Well . . .' Lori didn't even know how to continue. 'So if you're angry with me – so angry that you barely even want to talk to me on our honeymoon, spend time with me – this isn't a marriage, is it? I don't know *what* this is, but it isn't a marriage!'

Joachim heaved a sigh, propping the screen of his iPad against his stomach.

'Ow!' he promptly exclaimed, pulling it away again. 'Hot!'

'I'm not surprised,' Lori said. 'I wouldn't be surprised if it burst into flames, frankly.'

Joachim ignored this comment as he placed the tablet down on the day bed.

'This is an arrangement,' he said, sighing as he looked up at his wife. 'A convenient, happy arrangement. You are the

Queen of Herzoslovakia! I chose you, out of all the other women who wanted so badly to be a queen! So, enjoy it. Do what you want, go where you want, as long as you are sensible.' He shrugged. 'But mostly, you *are* sensible. My mother agrees.'

Lori's legs felt weak, but she had an instinctive aversion to sitting on the day bed next to Joachim. She reached for the huge hammock which was slung from one side of the terrace to the other, pulled it down and sat in its centre, her feet propped on the floor to stop her rocking back and forth.

'Your mother agrees,' she repeated flatly.

'When you ran away to Austria, she had some doubts,' Joachim said, sitting up straighter and pushing some pillows behind his back for extra support. 'But there is the engagement – we do not want to break it. And she blames Mihaly, she says he tried with you much too early. Also Katya and Kristin. They handle things all wrong, she says. She is very cross with all of them.'

Lori stared at him, her mouth open.

'So she calmed you down,' he said. 'No scandal. That is very important. We must not have scandal. She says, after the wedding you can talk to Lori, explain how things are. She will settle down to it.'

'And how *are* things, Joachim?'

Lori felt as if someone else were speaking for her, as if she were floating above her body. She had not been under the illusion, as the days of her honeymoon moved past without her husband showing any interest in her, that this had been a love match on Joachim's side. But this calculating, clinical detachment was not what she had expected, and she was finding it very hard to process.

If she were honest with herself – and she was trying, very hard, to be honest with herself now, finally – she had to admit that she had always been aware that there had been a distinct lack of passion between her and Joachim. She had been dazzled by him, or maybe, more truthfully, by his status, his manners, the extraordinary world that he had invited her to join. She had been on an incredible high after her triumph at the Olympics, and Joachim's courtship of her had been so associated for her with that once-in-a-lifetime moment; from Olympic medallist to the fiancée of a king, all in a few months, it had been a sustained, magical trajectory, derailed only when Mihaly's pass at her had crashed her into a wall.

'How *are* things?' she repeated.

'Things are . . .' Joachim considered. 'I needed a wife. A nice wife, good, respectable, with no scandal. Who looks good in photographs. When I tell my mother I meet you at the Olympics, she looks at pictures of you and she is very excited. You are an athlete, strong and healthy. She says you will look beautiful in all the Herzoslovakian crown jewels. And she is right.' He nodded approvingly at Lori. 'You *do* look very beautiful.'

He seemed to expect his wife to be flattered by this compliment, leaving a pause for her to say so; since she just stared at him blankly, he continued.

'She says you will make beautiful children, too. And be a very good mother. She says she can tell.'

Lori's eyes, to her own surprise, pricked with tears at this. She was more than ready to settle down and start having children; Joachim's proposal had come at the perfect time for her, when she was at the pinnacle of her career, with nowhere to go but down. She had always meant to continue to work, of course, had planned to coach in her sport, but the prospect of helping Joachim in his role as King of Herzoslovakia, of learning a new language, moving to a new country, taking on a new challenge, had been dizzyingly exciting.

I got totally conned, she thought now. *I thought he was picking me, not just because he loved me, but because he thought I'd be a good queen. Because he could see that I'd throw myself into Herzoslovakian life, study the culture, talk to the international press, really try to make myself a part of his country.*

But all he wanted was a tall blonde who'd look good in a tiara and pop out more of the same.

'Did you care about me at all?' she asked in a small voice. 'Ever?'

Joachim shook his head impatiently and flapped his hands at her as if pushing the entire question away.

'But you *lied* to me,' she said, pathetically now. 'You didn't say it was a business deal. You told me you loved me, and I thought you meant it.'

'My mother said—'

'Jesus!' Lori jumped up, not the easiest thing to do from a hammock. 'Can you *try* not to say that any more? What do *you* think? You're the one that lied to me, not your mother! *You're* the one that told me you loved me!'

She paused.

'Well, your mother lied to me too,' she added slowly, as that sank in. 'A whole lot.'

This annoyed Joachim, enough to make him snap at her:

'This is all completely pointless! There is no . . .' He looked for another word in English, failed to find it, and went on, sounding even crosser: '*point* to this! What's done is done! We are married now, and that is that! When we—'

'I want a divorce,' Lori interrupted. 'I made a terrible mistake.'

The words were like heavy stones dropped one by one onto the floor of the terrace; once more, Lori felt that relief of telling the truth, as if she had been physically carrying those stones around with her and had finally let them go. She thought that Joachim would look more shocked than he did at her blunt statement of intent; she had not turned the lights on inside the suite, but the LED ribbons wound round the posts of the terrace, the recessed overhead lighting, were arranged to illuminate the day bed for its occupants' convenience, and Lori could see Joachim's face perfectly clearly. To her great surprise, however, instead of surprise, or concern, his expression seemed positively triumphant.

'You cannot get a divorce,' her husband said, settling back on the day bed with an unpleasant smile. 'It will not be a good idea for you at all. Or, more importantly, your family.'

'My—'

His first words had made Lori think, crazily, that there was some weird statute that said that Herzoslovakian royalty weren't allowed to divorce; *but that can't be possible. It's Europe, not Saudi Arabia or some country where women don't have rights.* But the mention of her family was like a punch in the stomach.

'I own their mortgages,' Joachim said succinctly. 'And their personal loans. And the savings fund they have for your grandmother in the nursing home. If you divorce me, they will lose everything. Did you know that your father had his hours cut at work? The branch office where your sister works is on the verge of being shut down, did you know that too? If you divorce me, they will lose everything.'

'People will know!' Lori said, her voice trembling. She sank back into the hammock again. 'I'll tell everyone, the media – they'll listen to me – people will know how vindictive you're being if you try to do that—'

'Pah,' Joachim said contemptuously. 'Do you not know anything about the situation with mortgages in your country? They are packaged and sold as if they were commodities to buy and trade, swapped between invest-ment banks and hedge funds so many times that to call it in – that's how you say it, I think – no one will ever know where the order comes from. The local bank decides, they don't say to your father "This is why". He is behind with his payments, he is trying to re-negotiate, like everyone else in America right now. Your sister too. And then the bank says, "No, we don't negotiate, we take your house." You have the money to pay for their houses, their loans? They have no cars now but the ones I give them, and those are in my name too.'

Lori dug her nails into her palms.

'I'll sell my jewellery,' she said, thinking fast. 'The diamonds you gave me. Those must be worth—'

But Joachim was laughing, a chillingly unpleasant sound. Lori realized that she must never have heard his true laugh before.

'Oh yes!' he agreed. 'They are worth a great deal of money! But they are not yours to sell, silly woman. I put them round your neck, I tell you how beautiful you look, the photogra-phers take pictures, everyone is happy, but the parure is owned by the Royal Family! It is part of the state jewels! You didn't really think I would give you that to *own*, to take away if you try to leave?'

He shook his head in amusement at her utter naïveté. Lori felt the blood rush to her face in a blend of anger and humiliation.

'And if you try to divorce me, the press will not report anything you say,' he continued. 'Believe me, the head of state of a very successful tax haven is *extremely* well connected. The media will very much enjoy the story I give them, that you had an affair with Mihaly before we got married, that I find this out and that *I* decide, very sadly, to divorce *you*. There will be no sympathy for you at all.'

'I – but *I* said no to *him*—'

'Ah, but in the photographs of you kissing him in your room at the hotel, you look *very* willing!' Joachim said. 'He is lying on top of you, he takes off your top, we see your breasts, he undoes your jeans – we have photographs of it all.' He smiled salaciously. 'Very sexy.'

Lori had the vivid sensation of being caught in quicksand, sucked further and further down into a bottomless morass. The realization of how profoundly she had been set up by Joachim and the Dowager Queen was only now dawning on her.

'But people will know you took the photographs—' she started.

'People will look at Mihaly and you on a fur rug in front of the fire, drinking wine and taking your clothes off,' her husband said brutally, 'and they will maybe masturbate, or pass the photos to other people, or call you a dirty whore. Maybe we say that Mihaly takes them, secretly, for black-mail, and then I find out. But no one will blame your poor fiancé who you cheated on with your bodyguard!'

Lori flinched at this.

'They will be sorry for me,' Joachim continued trium-phantly. 'They will say you are marrying me for money and status, not because you love me. And *then* we will get divorced, and your family will have no homes, and the media will chase you everywhere, and I will not have to marry again, and the next heir to Herzoslovakia will be one of Katya or Kristin's sons, because my mother will make them get married, not me any more, and that will make me very happy because I never wanted to get married at all. To anyone. So yes.'

He threw his hands wide.

'Please. Divorce me.'

Lori realized she was shaking her head in disbelief. Joachim misunderstood the gesture.

'Okay, don't,' he said. 'That is easier for you. If you don't divorce me, things are much nicer for you and your family. You stay Queen of Herzoslovakia and no one ever sees the photographs of you and Mihaly. You have an heir to the throne – two children, you have two, but one must be a boy – and after that, if you want to separate or even divorce, that's okay. I pay off all your family's debts, I give them money, I give you a settlement. You sign a confidentiality agreement, no one sees the pictures of you, because you are the mother of my children. You see the children whenever you want. Or,' he added, brightening, 'if you want to stay living in Herzoslovakia, you can have a castle and live there with the children. That would be perfect.'

Lori stared at him.

'Do you really think,' she said, 'that after this I would ever *dream* of letting you have sex with me again?'

'Oh, no!' Joachim looked positively disgusted at the idea. 'No, we don't have to do that! We can have IVF. My mother says that's best, because you can control the gender of the baby. Two boys would be good, but I only insist on the first boy. After that, if you want a girl, that's okay too.'

He picked up the iPad, obviously considering that he had said everything necessary.

'We can start that as soon as you are ready,' he said, looking down at the screen. 'The sooner the better, I think. We have to stay here for the rest of the honeymoon. It would look strange to go back early. But as soon as you want when we are back home, Dr Bruschsson knows a specialist who can do the IVF and the—' he clicked his fingers, looking for the right word – 'the sperm selection to make a boy. Obviously we must be very discreet about that, no one must know.'

He touched something on the screen, immersed in it once again.

'You can't take the pills though,' he said absently. 'My mother says you can't get pregnant when you take the pills.'

'The vitamin supplements?' Lori almost whispered; as soon as the words came out of her mouth, she knew how stupid she had been.

Joachim burst out laughing.

'Yes, the "vitamin supplements",' he said, rolling his eyes. 'The "vitamin supplements" that my mother and Dr Bruschsson give you too many of so that you cry at the wedding! I should not be cross with you,' he added kindly. 'My mother says that really, it is her and Dr Bruschsson's fault. They make mistakes with the dose, give you too many pills.'

He shifted on the day bed.

'I need to go to the toilet,' he said thoughtfully, clambering off the mattress and heading into the living room.

The lights switched on as he crossed it and disappeared into the bathroom area: Lori stared after him, her jaw dropped, still shaking in disbelief. Only gradually did she think that she must look like an insane nodding dog. Only after that did she realize that Joachim had, for the first time on their honeymoon, left her alone with his iPad.

She got up, walked over to the day bed, picked up the tablet, looked at the screen. A message in its centre flashed:

Carcassonne
It's Your Turn! With
GrampyG, CallMeLaura,
Electryone, numb3r_6 and Rolandhh!

Lori didn't know what she'd been expecting. Porn? Sport? Gambling? But not . . . she clicked on the message and watched the display on the screen change to a series of what looked like tiles, decorated with rivers, castles, towns in the process of being built . . . not a *board game.*

She thumbed through the other open windows, slowly taking in what Joachim had been doing almost every waking hour of the last few days. Playing Lost Cities, Ticket to Ride, Shadows Over Camelot, something called Battle of the Bulge which she eventually realized was a war game. One called Seven Wonders, which she found particularly ironic, considering that Joachim could have visited an actual seventh wonder, Chichen Itza, and had opted to lie here playing the game instead. Going on BoardGeek message boards, discussing FAQs and tactics and strategy. Looking up board gaming conventions in Essen, Germany, and Lancaster, Pennsylvania, which his 'friends' GrampyG, Electryone, numb3r_6, Rolandhh and CallMeLaura were pressing him to attend.

As pastimes went, it was nothing to be ashamed of. That was the oddest, weirdest thing of all: that Joachim had a perfectly respectable hobby, not a deep dark creepy secret.

I thought it would be something awful, Lori realized. *Something really bad and nasty that he would be ashamed of people finding out. Some reason that he had to get married. But . . . board games?*

This is all he wants to do all day. Sit up here on a terrace and play Carcassonne and Ticket To Ride online. He never wanted a wife at all. I was always, purely and simply, a means to an end.

Lori put down the iPad and stood up, walking slowly along the balcony, past the dining terrace, down the stairs to the beach. She had no idea what she was doing, where she was going, just that she couldn't stay in the space that she shared with her husband; once she felt the sand under her feet, she kept walking until the seawater was lapping at her toes. She stood there for a long time, staring out to sea, watching the dark waves, the stars in the sky, not really thinking anything; she wasn't ready yet. Such a volume of information had been thrown at her she was struggling just to absorb everything that Joachim had said.

The water was cool and eventually she turned around, her feet icy. She had the idea to curl up in the beach cabana, look out at the waves. And then she realized that there was a dark shape already in the cabana, which was reserved for the use of the Presidential Suite occupants only. There was only one person who it could be, and she picked up the hem of her robe so that she could walk faster, faster, faster, until she was running over the sand to him.

Attila stood up as she came towards him, catching her in his arms, taking her considerable, muscled weight without the slightest hint of effort. He hugged her, tightly, and over his shoulder she saw that on the cabana mattress, folded neatly, was the cover-up she had left at the spa, and on top of it, the bottle of mescal liqueur with their photographs on it; he had brought both back for her.

There was nothing to say, not then, at least. She didn't know how much Attila had heard, or how much he had guessed as a silent observer all those long weeks at Schloss Hafenhoffer. They were below the balcony onto which Joachim could be heard returning from the toilet, his steps as heavy as the contented sigh he made as he sank down onto the mattress, presumably from relief that his annoying wife had taken herself off somewhere and wasn't going to bother him. They listened as he picked up his iPad, resumed his game of Carcassonne with the beeping or swishing sounds which, Lori now realized, were indications that it was his turn, or the noise it made when he moved a tile.

She pushed Attila down gently to the cabana mattress, and curled up there next to him, picking up the bottle and unscrewing the top. The liqueur was sweet and tasted of aniseed, with a strong, honeyed kick to it. They passed it back and forward, sipping slowly, the Queen and her bodyguard in matching robes, wrapped silently in each other's arms, looking out at the night sea, as up above them, the King of Herzoslovakia played endless games of strategy with people he had never met and probably never would.

Chloe

'Darling? Darling, what's wrong?'

Sleepily, Chloe rolled over and put a hand on her fiancé's shoulder. His back was to her, the outline of his sleeping body a dark blur; her sleep-glued eyes took a while to adjust to the dim light of their bedroom. Beneath her hand Hugo was positively trembling, rocking back and forth. He was moaning softly as if he were trying to talk in his sleep, or maybe cry; his panting breaths sounded almost like sobs.

This was completely unlike Hugo, who usually slept as soundly as a little boy after a big day out. Chloe had noticed he had seemed restless over the last few weeks, ever since they had got back from Ibiza; she had asked him if he was bothered by anything that had happened on that trip, assuming that the revelation that his sister had been involved in an orgy would be enough to make any brother feel understandably distressed.

Hugo, however, had assured Chloe that he was okay. The one thing he had asked Chloe and Lauren was whether Sophie and Toby had had sex, and they'd swiftly reassured him that no, they hadn't; Hugo had confessed that he was really relieved, as Toby was practically a brother to him and Sophie, so Hugo would have been totally creeped out by hearing that they'd got together. After that piece of good news, he said, he was pretty much okay, but he never wanted to think about it again and he'd be very grateful if Chloe didn't mention it to him. Chloe had promised that she wouldn't, and they had dealt with it by pretending nothing had happened at all, which dovetailed neatly with the story that the Palace press officers were busy diffusing to the media. Just a pleasant Ibiza house party, chaperoned, as it were, by a respectably engaged couple to whom no whiff of scandal had ever attached. Nothing to see here, please move along.

So Chloe couldn't imagine what was making her fiancé's dreams so fraught. She was beginning to worry that Hugo was having doubts as the wedding approached; he seemed perfectly fine during daytime hours, happily taking an interest in all the multifarious and complicated procedures of organizing a royal wedding to the degree that Lady Margaret had told Chloe firmly that she was a jolly lucky young woman to have a fiancé who actually bothered to drop into a floral arrangement meeting.

But maybe he's just doing a really good job of hiding his feelings – Hugo's so polite. Maybe he's having cold feet about getting married, but he's repressing that, so it's coming out in his nightmares . . .

That thought made Chloe shudder harder than Hugo's shoulder was trembling beneath her hand. The mere idea of her wedding being called off – of her life as the rejected fiancée of the second in line to the British throne – was literally unimaginable. She would have to leave the country, change her name, have plastic surgery. There would be nowhere that humiliation wouldn't follow her. She might as well just kill herself now and spare herself decades of pain ... but her parents, too, would be utterly humiliated, and what was she going to do about that?

Chloe! Stop it! Pull yourself together!

Over Hugo's head, she could see the luminous face of the bedside clock, her eyes now focused enough to read the display: three twenty-seven. *You're just having a night-time freakout. No one ever has positive thoughts at this time of the night. Wake up Hugo, because you won't go back to sleep anyway with him making this amount of noise, and find out what on earth's going on with him so you can set your mind at rest ... it's probably nothing ...*

But when Hugo was shaken awake – more roughly than Chloe had meant, because her nerves were so on edge – what he blurted out to her, his voice heavy with sleep and suppressed tears, was not at all what she had been expecting.

'I keep dreaming about Mummy,' he said, rolling over to face her. His breath was sour, but Chloe didn't turn her head away. Instead, she reached out and stroked his hair.

'*Really?*' she said, feeling a mixture of relief that Hugo's dreams didn't seem to involve him leaving her at the altar, and sadness for him that he had lost Belinda when he was so young. 'Oh, darling ...'

'I don't know why it's happening,' Hugo said, rolling over to face her, his voice inexpressibly sad. 'I used to dream about her all the time – Sophie and I both did, even though she didn't remember Mummy that well. We'd go into each other's rooms and bunk up together after we had the dreams. Nanny never made a fuss about it. But, you know, the dreams gradually stopped as I got a bit older. It's not that I don't think about her – of course I do, especially with us getting married.'

Chloe's body relaxed at these last, reassuring words. *See? You won't need to get a nose job, change your name and move to Siberia.* Her hand stroked Hugo's cheek; she leaned forward, feeling for his lips with hers, kissing him gently.

'But now I'm having exactly the same dreams I had when I was little,' Hugo continued. 'I remember how she smelt – you know, her perfume – her voice, everything. It's all come back to me like a flash. Isn't that weird, Chlo? That I'm remembering all that as well? It's like something happened to have all those things about Mummy just pop right back into my head. I keep remembering her and Father fighting – well, mostly her, to be honest. He'd lock himself in his rooms and she'd bang on the door and scream and scream. I can even *hear* her screaming.'

He shivered, a convulsion that passed through his whole body.

'Actually, Chlo, that's the main thing I'm hearing. Isn't that awful? The strongest memory I have right now of Mummy is her screaming at Father. It's horrible.'

There wasn't anything for Chloe to say, nothing that would reassure her poor, grieving fiancé. What could you say to someone who was haunted by the sound of his dead mother's cries of misery? She turned over, pushing her back towards him, felt for his arm and pulled it, heavy and limp, over her waist, wrapping her arms around it, spooning him in the way she knew he found so comforting.

'We're not them,' she said. 'We won't be like that. We'll be happy and we'll never, ever fight.'

This managed to extract a small laugh from Hugo.

'Never *ever*,' he said, kissing the back of her head, his hand reaching for hers. 'Not about *anything*.'

With relief, she heard his breathing become deeper, regular, a sign that he was drifting back to sleep again. Her own eyes shut, her breathing slowed; she was taken aback when he said sleepily, his mouth close to her ear:

'It's not the wedding, Chlo. That's not why I'm thinking about Mummy suddenly. It's something else. I'm sure of it.'

'What?' she mumbled.

'I don't know. But it's *something*. Something set me off . . .' Hugo was mumbling now. 'I just need to work out what it is and then I won't have the dreams any more . . . not the sad ones . . .'

'Okaydarlingloveyounightnight . . .'

Chloe was almost snoring, sleep was hitting her so hard. But behind her unconscious body, her fiancé was still awake, his eyes closed but his brain, like the drum of a washing machine, turning over and over the question of what had caused him now, after all these years, to relive such vivid and particular memories of his dead mother.

Lori had finally crept back up to the Presidential Suite as dawn was breaking, but she had not been able to face crawling into bed beside her husband. She didn't think she would ever be able to sleep in the same bed as him again. Mercifully, the day bed out on the terrace was very comfortable, and there were spare blankets in one of the cupboards; she had wrapped herself up, put on an eye mask and managed to snatch a few hours of much needed sleep until the gentle whirr of golf carts below, the clink of breakfast trays being carried into suites, and the cries of sea birds circling overhead brought her back once more to consciousness.

For one long lovely moment, all she remembered was the last thing to happen the night before – or rather, that morning. Kissing Attila, endless soft lingering kisses, their lips tasting deliciously of the honeyed liqueur, drunk from the bottle which carried their smiling picture. Lying next to each other in a constant state of arousal, his cock hard, a warm wetness between her legs, pressing against each other but by mutual, unspoken agreement, not touching each other below the waist, because there was nowhere for them to go that they could be private, and the Queen and the bodyguard could not, possibly, go so far as to have sex in a cabana directly below the suite in which the King was sleeping.

Smelling Attila's body, his hot strong scent, burying her nose in his throat, her hands below the folds of his robe, learning the outline of his upper body, his amazing musculature, by feel in the darkness. Flicking his surprisingly tiny nipples, set like a pair of metal studs on the rigid, hubcap swells of his pectorals, hearing him hiss with pleasure and push his stiff cock against her leg, which in turn made her gasp with longing to have it slide effortlessly inside her. Closing her eyes in bliss at the feel of his big hand stroking her breasts, learning the feel of her contours just as she was discovering his, each of them pulling away when the physical sensations became too much for them, when one or the other knew that if they kept going they would pull their robes away, be fucking silently in an instant. He was hard as a rock, she was as wet as the sea that lapped in rhythm just a few metres from where they were lying; it would take no time at all, barely a second.

But they couldn't. It was bad enough that they were even doing this, but the cabana was not visible from the beach path, tucked away as it was in the shelter of the overhanging suite above, and the muslin curtains on either side gave some privacy. Still, someone could conceivably walk along the water's edge and see them, and hopefully, if they were just making out, they would have time to pull away from each other.

If they went any further than this, however, they would lose control completely. There was no need even to say it; they both knew. Hadn't they already fucked in the shower with Joachim outside on the balcony? Remembering that, as she licked and tugged and softly sank her teeth into Attila's lips, made Lori drag herself away from him multiple times, sit up and take another sip of liqueur, re-wrap her crumpled robe around her to cover her breasts, stare at the faint white crests of the waves beating on the reef beyond, catch her breath and let the fierce pumping of her heart slow down enough so that she resisted the impulse to throw herself on top of him, tilt her hips and drive down onto him with everything she had . . .

It was like the longest, sweetest, teenage makeout session ever, she thought now, staring up at the thatched roof of the terrace. *Only when I was a teenager making out with boys, I kept having to shove their hands away when they got too touchy-feely. But with Attila* – and Lori felt a hot, warm rush of excitement heat her entire body as she merely thought his name to herself – *with Attila we both knew we shouldn't, we couldn't, not out in the open like that . . . Oh God, I need to come so badly!*

The curtains of the suite were still closed. Joachim was a late riser. And no one, none of the butlers, would dream of invading their privacy by coming up the terrace stairs unless specifically invited to do so; they would ring the doorbell of the suite, announcing their presence, giving its occupants the chance to admit them or ask them to come back later. So Lori's hand, already under the blankets, parted the folds of her robe, parted her own folds, and slid up inside her, finding herself already wet just from the memory of Attila.

Dragging her damp fingers down to her clitoris, she came almost instantly, again and again, completely silent, her teeth firmly clamped in her lower lip to remind herself not to make a sound, not a squeak. Her body was so ready, so frustrated, that only the liqueur last night had enabled her to sleep at all, and all that sexual energy stoked by Attila had been churning in the pit of her stomach, so hot it burst immediately into flame as soon as her fingers found the right spot. Over and over she orgasmed, and all she thought, the solitary word in her head, was Attila's name, repeating on a long loop with every buck and spasm of her pelvis against her swiftly working hand.

She stopped only when her fingernail began to cut a little into her soft damp flesh and she knew that if she kept going it would start to hurt. Slipping her hand reluctantly from between her legs, she drew in a long, calming breath, feeling her heart racing, her chest heaving with pleasure and the need for outward self-control; her teeth let go their grip on her lower lip, her eyes fluttered fully open, and she stretched out her limbs with a long, sinuous action, feeling every muscle, every tendon, lengthen in anticipation of the day to come.

And then she turned her head to look once more at the closed curtains of the suite and the full realisation of her predicament hit her as if the thatched roof had tumbled on her head. Extreme sexual desire was such a powerful distraction that it hadn't been until she had thoroughly taken care of it that she could even acknowledge anything else. Now, lying there, staring at the glass walls behind which her husband lay, possibly sleeping still, possibly propped up in bed playing Seven Wonders or Puerto Rico with GrampyG and CallMeLaura, she slowly absorbed what an utter mess her life had become.

She had married a man she didn't love, because at the moment of doubt, when she had tried to run away to America and clear her head, his evil scheming mother had roped her back in and fed her a bunch of drugs and a pack of lies. And he had lied to her too, of course he had, from the very beginning, feeding her a line that any girl would have fallen for, any girl who liked him and wanted to get married and settle down and was over the moon that a solid man – a king to boot! – was ready to commit, to put a ring on her finger and start a family with her.

I told myself that I didn't feel that instant snap of attraction to Joachim precisely because he was more serious, such an ideal husband, she realized. *I told myself that it would build with time, that I liked having sex with him and that it would get stronger as the years went on, as we grew to love each other more and more in our marriage. I told myself that it wasn't some crazy thing that would burn so brightly it burned itself out, that it was a good sign that we weren't tearing each other's clothes off constantly. That a husband was different from a lover, and that what I was feeling was what a wife feels for her husband.*

I really told myself a lot of crap, didn't I? Was it because I was so desperate to marry a king?

Lori considered this, trying to be hard on herself, to take her share of the blame for the horrendous situation in which she was now stuck. But she kept coming back to her attempted flight and the fact that she had been reeled in, not just by fast talking, but by being conned into taking drugs which had altered her state of mind so much that the coherent, reasoned decision to put on her wedding dress and walk down the aisle had not been hers to make.

And then, even worse, as she thought about the pills, she had an awful, almost irresistible compulsion to go into the bathroom right now and pop the daytime dose that had been normal to her back in Herzoslovakia. Recovery from jet lag, followed by sunshine and sea air, had made her head feel so clear that she hadn't been taking them: ever since that brief discussion with Attila, jogging on the beach in the sunshine that first morning, the vials had remained on the bathroom shelf, untouched.

No, she told herself firmly. *That's not why you didn't feel you needed the pills. It's because you were spending almost the whole of every day with Attila.*

Because for the last few days you've been falling in love with your bodyguard. Or maybe you've been falling for him even before that, but you were too drugged up to realize.

While your husband won't let you divorce him until you give him two kids, the first of which has to be a boy.

That last thought jerked her up to sitting. She shoved the blankets off her and stood up, fighting the sudden craving to take that pill, calm herself down, use it to balance out her panic at being trapped.

What do I do? Stick it out till I have the kids he wants, till my family's safe, then divorce him and stay in Herzoslovakia with them? Keeping Attila on the side as my lover? Maybe he could come and live with me and the kids in the castle that Joachim's going to provide for me, post-divorce, so that I can raise his children with minimal disruption to his busy online games-playing schedule . . .

She pushed open the glass door, crossed the living room, stepped into the bedroom, Joachim's slumped body and heavy breathing indicating that he was still fast asleep. The maid had neatly arranged the yellow vials with all of Lori's toiletries on the long marble shelf that ran the length of the bathroom. In the centre of the shelf was a beautifully presented display, a flower vase with all the pale green Bulgari toiletries circled around it, and below it, two white face towels that had been embroidered with the gold sun and white palm logo of the resort, its name in silver. Lori stared at herself in the mirror behind the vase, taking a long breath in: and then, quickly, before she could change her mind, before she could be tempted, she took both plastic vials into the toilet, uncapped them, and poured the contents in a clattering white stream into the bowl, flushing it over and over until the last pill had disappeared from sight.

There was no way that Joachim would agree to head back from Mexico early, she was already aware. It would cause undue comment in Herzoslovakia if its King and Queen cut their honeymoon short. The Dowager would definitely not approve, and Lori was beginning to realize what a very important part the Dowager's opinion played in Joachim's decision-making.

So I might as well make the best of it, she thought bravely. *I'm going to do everything I planned for the rest of the stay, go on all the excursions that Pablo and Liliana and Elizabeth have organized for us. And damn it, if my husband won't come, I'm taking my bodyguard with me on every single one.*

The private butlers at the Casitas doubtless found it very strange that, for the second half of the Guttmans' stay at their resort, Mr Guttman no longer even bothered to accompany his beautiful wife out for dinner; the couple were never seen with each other. But then, one of the Guttmans' bodyguards had taken Mr Guttman's place on the special, romantic, Sky Massage ritual that had been designed to celebrate their bond as a married couple, so after that, frankly, all bets were probably off . . .

Mr Guttman remained in his suite, ordering in meals and drinks, while Mrs Guttman, together with the bodyguard, went to Tulum, where they marvelled at the beautiful ruins, situated so spectacularly on the edge of a cliff overlooking a sea which, if possible, was even more turquoise and cerulean than the waters which lapped at the sands of the resort. They strolled through the walled gardens in which the ruins were set, descended to the white beach below, took most of their clothes off and frolicked. As Lori had seen at the *cenote*, Attila's physique drew so much attention that there was comparatively little left for her. She wore huge sunglasses, which she never took off, even while swimming, tousled her hair to hang in short salt-curling locks around her face, and was confident that no one was recognizing her or seeing her as anything but the tall blonde girlfriend of the man with the most amazing muscle definition anyone had ever seen.

And when, after Tulum, their driver took them to Xel-Ha, a huge lagoon further along the peninsula, it was just the same. As long as Attila's clothes were off, no one bothered to do anything but give Lori a cursory glance. They snorkelled in the lagoon, ziplined, and raced each other along a rope balance, feet on one rope, hands reaching overhead to hold a second one for balance; Lori shot along it so fast that Attila, seeing that she was clearly going to beat his time, grabbed the top rope and, with a couple of rippling flexes of his shoulders, sent her tipping into the water, diving in straight afterwards and allowing her to duck him by way of revenge. They walked to the top of the river, jumped off cliffs, and, having burned off enough energy, corralled a two-person tube float and floated down into the lagoon again, mooring it at a pier and finishing their day out at an open bar where they drank margaritas and watched the fish shoals move swiftly through the blue water.

They went back to the El Dorado and had dinner outdoors at Jojo's, a fish restaurant on the beach which Joachim had disdained as not being formal enough for him, but Lori loved. Their waiter Innocencio made her a grasshopper out of toothpicks and palm fronds and brought them 'Coco Tropicals' for dessert, huge cocktails made with vodka, coffee liqueur, coconut cream and milk, so good that even Attila drank some and pronounced it delicious. And then they walked back to the Casitas, declining the waiting Liliana's offer of a ride in the golf cart. Attila saw Lori to the door of the suite: she went in, changed into her robe, sat quietly for twenty minutes and then descended to the beach cabana to meet her lover, with whom she lay till dawn, returning to the day bed and its pile of blankets when the sun began to rise.

Her lover, however, with whom she wasn't making love. They simply couldn't find anywhere that they could be alone safely. They couldn't go to the room Attila shared with Vassily, and though Lori had racked her brains for any other ideas, she had come up empty. The physical tension was almost unbearable; they worked out like demons, filled their days with activities, to try to distract themselves as much as possible. They toured the resort stables, went riding, played tennis, were taken on a special tour by Juan Carlos, the Casitas manager, who showed them the two crocodiles called Pancho and Maria, who floated happily in the swamp behind the hotel, and took them round a villa in the resort which belonged to a famous Mexican singer who had built a private theatre inside, scorched his initials into the grass and collected life-size mannequins dressed in exquisite traditional costumes.

They even drove to another hotel, the Sensatori, to sit at the VIP table in a wraparound glass wine cellar and eat a twenty-six-course molecular gastronomy dinner at a restaurant called Le Chique, which started with cucumber gin and tonics squirted into their glasses from a siphon, red chocolate 'cherries' filled with Campari, and puffs filled with iced margaritas washed down with liquid olives in white china spoons. Attila had never experienced anything like it before, and Lori honestly thought that if she hadn't been in love with him up till then, she would have fallen for him that night. Bravely, he tried every new bizarre and fantastical concoction, his blunt features contorting themselves in a whole series of endearingly boyish expressions at the extraordinary textures and tastes. He was so enthusiastic that the chef actually brought out an extra plate, a roll of avocado wrapped around lobster tartare which brought moans of appreciation from both of them.

'Also,' Attila said to Lori afterwards, as they lay, cradled in each other's arms, in the beach cabana, 'if we eat so much, we don't want to make sex. This is the first night I don't have my dick hard for you all the time. Maybe we eat too much food every night, get fat, don't make sex. Then we feel better.'

Lori giggled.

'I never thought I'd hear you say you want to get fat!' she said, reaching back to stroke his stomach, still as corrugated as an iron roof.

'Only for you,' he said, lifting her hair and kissing the back of her neck, making her shiver. 'Only for you I even say this joke. Love makes men crazy.'

They knew they were in love by now, but they had not officially said the three simple words to each other that would have been the ultimate acknowledgement. Lori sensed that once the words were uttered, something would break in the precarious arrangement of tensions that was holding the situation in some sort of manageable stasis; she wasn't thinking one more day ahead than the next, couldn't bear to imagine what her life would be like when they stepped off the helicopter in Valtzers. She was clinging to these last few days with Attila as if they were a life raft in choppy seas, and now, imagining what was waiting for her back in Herzoslovakia, she shivered as if a cold wind had blown over them instead of the soft, salt-scented night breeze.

'Will you ... be with me when we go back?' she asked now. 'I don't know what's going to happen. I'm so scared, and

I don't have any idea what I'm going to do. But I don't think I can cope unless you're there too.'

She laughed grimly.

'They're fine with me having a lover,' she added. 'We won't need to worry about that. The Dowager will be happy I've sorted myself out so efficiently.'

She felt Attila nod his head behind her.

'She tries to give you her own man,' he said, equally grim. 'She is very nice and friendly to share him with you.'

'*What?*' Lori jerked round to look at him, though the darkness meant that she could barely see his expression. 'You mean that—'

'She and Mihaly, yes,' Attila said. 'Mihaly and anyone who pays him. He is a whore. Countess Katya and Countess Kristin, they often share him for a night.'

Lori's breath got stuck in her throat at this revelation. She could only be devoutly grateful that she had never had sex with Mihaly, but even the memory of him kissing her breasts, trying to undo her jeans, made her feel revolted. The idea that her mother-in-law not only shared her lover with her nieces, but had effectively offered him to her daughter-in-law too, made her want to retch.

What sort of family is this? God, to think I was embarrassed by the way my folks dressed when they arrived in Herzoslovakia, that I worried about them not knowing how to behave! When all the time, the Dowager and Katya and Kristin were having sex with the same guy – and Katya and Kristin at the same time! *They're sisters!*

'Katya and Kristin said that things were different in Europe,' she said slowly. 'More *flexible*. I didn't think that meant they had sex together! Oh, and the Dowager, the morning after I tried to run away, telling me how much she disapproved of them, and that she was so pleased I was a good girl! That old *hypocrite* – when she was having sex with Mihaly herself all the time! He was never a bodyguard at all, was he?'

Attila shook his head.

'They put him there because it is a natural way for you to meet him, see if you like him,' he said. 'He made me insane. He is the worst bodyguard in the world, he does everything wrong. I try to tell him but he just laughs and tells me I should do my job and he will do his.'

'Which was to seduce me,' Lori said bitterly.

'I hate to watch it,' Attila said. 'I hate to watch him smile and joke with you. We are not all like that in Europe, I prom- ise you. Some of us are serious.' His arms tightened around her. 'Some of us want to have just one woman for our whole lives. Some of us have waited very long to have sex because they wanted only to do it with one woman for our whole lives. To make it as special as it should be.'

This jerked Lori right out of her self-loathing for having, even temporarily, fallen for Mihaly's well-practised charms.

'You're not saying you were a *virgin*?' she exclaimed incredulously. 'No *way* was that your first time!'

She could actually feel Attila smile.

'Not my first time,' he said gravely. 'But only my second woman.'

'Your *second* woman?' Lori was almost as incredulous as before.

'I have a girlfriend before, in Bulgaria. We break up two years ago when I come to Herzoslovakia.'

'Two years ago? You haven't had sex for two years? You really don't – I mean, you seem like you've done this a *lot* . . .'

'I think about it a lot, yes,' Attila said, even more gravely. 'A *lot*.' He tapped his head with his index finger. 'But to me, sex is special. Very important. I wait for as long as I need to wait to find the right woman.'

'Oh . . .' Lori bent to kiss the huge arm wrapped round her. 'And I didn't,' she said, wretchedly torn between the intense happiness that Attila's words had given her, and the mess in which she was caught. 'I didn't wait. I got swept off my feet, I know, but that's not enough of an excuse.'

'If you didn't meet the King, I would never have met you,' Attila said simply. 'So I am happy for that. And after you try to go away, they give you pills and lie to you to make you stay. So you should not blame yourself.'

Lori drew in a deep breath and let it out again in an audible exhalation; Attila had said exactly the right thing.

'You *will* stay with me when we go back to Herzoslovakia, won't you?' she said pleadingly, suddenly realizing that he hadn't answered her question.

'I stay with you for ever,' he said even more simply. 'If you want me to.'

'I do,' Lori said, without even having to think about it, hugging him even more tightly.

Those are the same words I said to Joachim ten days ago, she thought with great irony. *Only this time, I mean them.*

So here I am: I've found true love, barely a week after my wedding, with a man who isn't my husband. Who'll stick by me as I go back to my husband's country and have two babies with him . . .

Lori realized that she was shaking her head slowly in disbelief. She was happier than she had ever been, truly, profoundly, happy; and yet she was facing a future which would tie her to a man she hated for the rest of her life, and the prospect of bearing his children instead of those of the man she loved.

They didn't say another word. The last ones they had spoken to each other had said it all. They sat there, in each other's arms, watching the dark sea wash against the paler sands, and gradually they fell asleep together, cheek to cheek, Lori's blonde hair twining into Attila's tight dark curls, their chests rising and falling in unison.

Buckingham Palace

'KING MEETS STRIPPERS!' Martin read gleefully from his desktop screen. 'I must say, they've managed to wring *maximum* sauce out of that one, haven't they?'

'I thought the old dears were visiting a chocolate factory somewhere up North yesterday?' Simon said, sipping tea. 'Don't tell me Stevie slipped out somewhere later to be naughty?'

Martin rolled his eyes theatrically.

'As *if*. Those days are over, thank the Lord. No, they were indeed at a chocolate factory, and two other old dears used to work in what they called a stripping room – cutting strips of chocolate for something or other.'

Martin swung round the screen to show Simon: a big colour photograph of King Stephen, tall and imposing, exuding authority and charm, in an impeccable navy suit and the silk ascot which only he could pull off, its impeccably folded knot fastened with a pearl stick pin. His hair, still enviably thick, was silver-grey and brushed back *en brosse*. In his eighties, he still towered over the other people in the picture, two elderly women in hard white hats over protective hairnets and white factory coats.

They were smiling up at him, dazzled by his famous charisma; his wife, plump little Queen Alexandra, standing beside him in a neatly tailored Hardy Amies pale green suit, was, as usual, overshadowed by him. Her hat matched her suit, trimmed with the same white grosgrain that edged her suit lapels, her thinning white hair neatly drawn back under it, and her calm blue eyes, as always in public, looking up at the face of her handsome husband.

'Peacock and peahen,' Martin said, cruel but fair. 'Poor thing'd have to wear a vinyl catsuit to get any attention while Stevie's working his charm offensive.'

Simon sniggered at this piece of *lèse-majesté*.

'Martin, you are *awful*,' he said, glancing behind him to make sure that the door to Martin's office was firmly closed.

'So *these* two told him they used to work in the stripping room, and *he* said that sounded rather racy, and the glory and the wonder that is our tabloid press managed to extract this headline out of the exchange,' Martin said, swinging the screen back again. 'They really are very good, aren't they, the tabs?'

'Marvellous,' Simon said languidly. 'Stevie won't like that, though. He doesn't like the naughty talk.'

'No need to tell him about it,' Martin said, shrugging. 'Believe me, the press office knows better. He never watches the telly apart from the racing, and he doesn't even know how to work a computer.'

'*Queenie* will see it, though,' Simon pointed out. 'She keeps an eye on everything.'

'And she won't tell him either, dear,' Martin assured him. 'Trust me, she knows better than that. She's *all* about keeping the peace. Little Missy Not-So-Dead would have done well to take a leaf out of her book, frankly.'

'Talking of which . . .' Simon set down his teacup.

'Well, *yes*!' Martin's eyes glittered madly. 'And here we are! *Sooo* . . .' He leaned forward, steepling his fingers on the desk. 'We can't get near her inside that fortress, of course. Rahim practically owns the air they breathe in that part of Morocco. But now one *knows* she's alive and kicking, it really just is too much of a risk to let her go on that way, isn't it? I've consulted on it, of course, and word has come down from on high. She *has* to go.'

Simon stared at him, his face contorting with concern.

'*Really?*' he said. 'I mean, she hasn't actually . . . I mean, she came here and didn't do anything . . . didn't say anything to the press . . . is she really that much of a risk?'

'But now she's dipped her toe in the water and she thinks she's got away with it!' Martin said, eyes flashing even more. 'She doesn't realize that I spotted her! Don't you *see*, Simon – now she'll get more confident! She'll come back again and she'll want to talk to her children! Believe me, I know *exactly* what she's up to, how her mind works. I *know* her, don't I? I recognized her when no one else did, not even Him!'

He stood up and paced across the room to the exquisitely inlaid wooden globe resting on a gilded statue of a winged naked young man, kneeling to hold the globe on his back. Martin lifted the hinged lid, revealing a polished brass inset that held bottles at its centre with glasses ranged in a circle around them. Setting two cut-glass tumblers on the wide lip, he poured in generous slugs of Plymouth gin and then added a dash of Angostura bitters to each of them. Taking a slim silver spoon, he swirled the contents of the glasses with an expert turn of the wrist to mix the bitters through the spirit.

'Pink gin?' he said to Simon, carrying them back.

Though phrased like it, this wasn't really a question. Simon was already reaching for a couple of embossed leather coasters, placing them in front of Martin and himself.

'Ta, I'm sure,' he said in an exaggerated Cockney accent; he had wiped his own Brummie one years ago, replacing it with the RP posh necessary to climb the ladder at the Palace.

'You do see, don't you, Simon?' Martin took a long drink from his glass. 'You do see that she just can't be allowed to come back here and cause any more havoc? You remember what she was like before! Roaming the halls, strung out on all sorts of medication, howling like a banshee!'

'She never knew what she was getting into,' Simon said, looking down at his glass of delicate pink liquid which was almost entirely neat gin, watching the last few tiny drops of scarlet bitters dissolve. 'It sent her a bit doolally. I'll never forget her face when she walked in on me and Him.'

'Silly bitch,' Martin said contemptuously. 'What *did* she think she was doing? Separate bedrooms exist for a *reason*. Look at Hugo and his common little girlfriend, snuggling up like the bourgeois little couple that they are, tucking each other in every night, probably wearing matching pyjamas as they sip their tea and watch – ugh, I don't know, *Top Gear*. Or *Location, Location, Location*.' He shuddered. 'Royalty really has gone to the dogs,' he said. 'No glamour in the younger generation.'

Simon winced. 'Harsh,' he said, sipping some gin; he wasn't as able to down it as swiftly as Martin. 'That's really a bit harsh, Martin. *Location, Location, Location?*'

'Oh, please, they're *prematurely aged*,' Martin said with great hauteur.

Simon decided that discretion was the better part of valour. No point observing that at least Hugo and Chloe actually seemed to be compatible, in love, committed to each other – all extremely useful qualities in a marriage that would be conducted to a very large degree in the public eye, and ones that Oliver and Belinda's marriage had signally lacked.

'So . . .' he said, still not meeting Martin's eye. 'You're really – they're really—'

'Oh, there's a team in place,' Martin assured him. 'My contact at the airport is going to ring as soon as there's a *whisper* about Rahim chartering a plane. Once she leaves that fortress, she's easy prey.'

Simon looked up at him now, concern written all over his face.

'It's just that—'

'Oh God yes!' Martin nodded furiously. 'Absolutely! They can't possibly leave her body around to be identified. Rahim'll have nothing to lose after she's dead – he'll be all too ready to make a *huge* uproar if he thinks *we* had anything to do with it!'

He set down his glass and ticked points off on his fingers.

'Believe me, they know (a) the body has to disappear or blow up so they can't trace her DNA. Plane explosion, ideally, though security's *much* tighter at airports nowadays. That avalanche set-up was inspired, I have to admit.'

He sniffed.

'The stupid bitch didn't come up with that *herself*, I can tell you. *Any*way, (a) no body, and (b) it has to look like a hundred per cent, bona fide accident. No comeback on us. If Rahim gets so much as a wink of a clue that the British Secret Service are involved, we're fucked up the arse harder than a twink in the backroom of a hardcore bear club.'

Simon, sipping more gin, coughed it back into the glass at this vivid analogy.

'Don't mince your words for me,' he muttered.

'So we're on the same page?' Martin said, reaching over the desk to clink his glass against Simon's; his pink gin had almost completely vanished by now. 'You agree, Simon, don't you? She simply can't be allowed to endanger everything. We've protected Him all these years. And let's face it, we're just finishing what we started decades ago.'

Simon nodded.

'Absolutely,' he said, raising his glass to Martin. 'You're right. You always are.'

Martin smirked triumphantly at this.

'*Too* kind,' he purred, as Simon downed the rest of his gin in one long gulp and put his glass down on the coaster.

'I agree, Martin,' he said with great firmness. 'It's time to finish it.'

Lori

The bedroom was dark, and that was just how Lori wanted it – if she could be said to actually 'want' anything at the moment, which was debatable. Three days had passed since they had returned from Mexico. She was so depressed that she had slept for eighteen hours straight every night, and this morning she couldn't even get up. Attempts made by various members of staff to bring her breakfast this morning, to offer her anything she might want, had all been rebuffed: Lori had simply pulled pillows over her head and passed out again every time.

Their return to Herzoslovakia had not been a happy one. If the Dowager had been expecting her son to maintain the pretence, during the honeymoon, that he had married Lori for love, she had been very disappointed by the sight of the King and Queen stepping down from the helicopter in the Schloss courtyard, their expressions as rigid at their bodies. Lori had even managed a brief smile for the waiting mass of photographers corralled behind two steel wings of security fence on either side of the sweeping stone entrance steps. The Dowager was waiting at the top of the stairs, magnificently coiffed as usual, a choker made of grey pearls as large as marbles around her neck, set off by her pale pink twinset and tweed skirt, the perfect outfit for the doting mother welcoming the newlywed lovebirds back home to the family castle.

She was about to stretch out her hands to both of them, but the sight of their faces warned her that things had gone badly wrong, and she was quick-witted enough to avoid the gesture; luckily, because Lori would certainly not have taken hers. The contrast between Lori, golden-tanned, glowing with health and beauty, and Joachim, possibly the only honeymooner ever to return from Mexico more pasty-faced than he had been when he left, was marked, and the Dowager, glancing from one to the other, had to use all her considerable powers of self-control to avoid wincing.

Lori didn't cut her mother-in-law dead. She was too nice, too well brought up, to be able to manage that kind of gesture in public. But she neither held out her hand to the Dowager nor kissed her powdered cheeks; she merely ducked her head at her with an awkward little jerk, kept walking into the Schloss, went up to the rooms that she had occupied before moving into Joachim's, and stayed there.

Literally. She had not left them in three days.

The first night she had dressed for dinner, dismissed her maid, and sat down in a pale blue velvet armchair for what was supposed to have been a short, five-minute pause while she readied her nerves for a meal spent in a cosy threesome with her husband and his mother. However, when the five minutes were up she went on sitting there. A footman came to advise her that the King and the Dowager Queen were having an aperitif in the Green Salon and would like her to join them: Lori didn't reply. She couldn't. She had no idea what to say.

The footman had gone away to report, nervously, that the Queen seemed to be not only stuck to her armchair, but also mute. After his disappearance, Lori had dimly expected, through the haze of her confusion, that her husband would storm up angrily to see her; instead, twenty minutes later, the footman returned carrying a tray, silver domes over the dinner plates, a glass of champagne and a bottle of Riesling accompanying it, the footman murmuring that the King and Dowager Queen completely understood that Her Royal Highness was tired and jet-lagged and hoped she would take all the rest she needed.

It had been clever of them, or rather of the Dowager, who was – Lori was more sure than ever – the directing power behind the Herzoslovakian throne: letting Lori make her own decision to stay in her suite, giving her the sense that she had some power, that her wishes were being considered. Lori had no appetite, but she drank the champagne and picked listlessly at some pâté, and when the footman came to take the tray away again, she told him that she might be having her meals in her room for a while. He was too well-trained to show, even by the flicker of an eyebrow, that he found this strange behaviour for a new bride; he simply nodded as he lifted the heavy tray, and the next morning, her breakfast duly arrived.

Then, mid-morning, Dr Bruschsson was announced. It was not a pleasant meeting for him: in reply to whatever he said, Lori just kept repeating in a dull voice that she wanted him to go away. She had got up and dressed that morning, had not yet progressed to being unwilling to even get out of bed, but she was like the zombie she had been on the day of her wedding even without his cocktail of drugs. And when he pulled out some vials from his bag and placed them on the table in front of her, she reached over and knocked them off in one swipe.

Lori's physical strength, even in her extreme depression, meant that the vials went flying right across the room, smashing into the curtains of the bed. One hit the post and the lid burst open; Dr Bruschsson had to go down on his hands and knees to collect as many of the loose pills as he could, obeying Lori's command to get all that crap out of her room.

Lori's next visitor had been the Dowager, accompanied by a footman with a tea tray. She had sat down opposite Lori, poured tea, and said a lot of soothing things which Lori had done her best to tune out as much as possible. Lori was, frankly, frightened of the Dowager. Her mother-in-law had manipulated Lori perfectly to date, and Lori had no experience in confronting an opponent as ruthless, skilled and unscrupulous as this one. Lori had the very strong sense that if she engaged with the Dowager, she would come off worse.

So Lori tuned out her mother-in-law's words as much as she could, didn't drink the tea, didn't say a thing. The Dowager eventually left, shaking her head sadly, saying that she and Joachim would give Lori all the time she needed to settle in to the adjustment of being married, that she understood that it was a very big change; a new country, a new language. They would cancel her official engagements, make sure she didn't have demands put on her as she settled into her future in Herzoslovakia.

That was what they called the 'takeaway' back home in America, the key message of a talk. The clear, unequivocal statement that Lori could sulk as much as she wanted, but should give up any expectations that eventually she would be let off the contract she had made with Joachim. She would stay in Herzoslovakia long enough to have two children before she could have any hope at all of a divorce that wouldn't leave her family bankrupt and homeless. After the

Dowager left, Lori got up slowly, took her clothes off and climbed into bed. She hadn't showered since her return to her new country, and she was beginning to smell less than fresh: but she didn't care.

What does it matter? What does any of it matter? She didn't have a plan of any kind. Her brain didn't seem to be working properly, could only manage to say 'no' to anything she definitely knew she didn't want. Like Dr Bruschsson's pills, or seeing her husband, who had tried the day before to come in and talk to her only to retreat very fast under the barrage of bed pillows she was throwing at his head. It seemed that even a clinically depressed ex-volleyball champion didn't lose her aim, even under extreme circumstances: Joachim took two square, decorative silk pillows full to the face with such force that he reeled back under the assault.

Dr Bruschsson's pills.

Now that those words had popped into Lori's head, she couldn't, somehow, dismiss them again. She was remembering the sight of that white plastic lid popping off the yellow vial on impact with the blue silk-wrapped post of the canopy bed, the white pills scattering everywhere. And she was wondering whether Dr Bruschsson had managed to retrieve every single one of them.

They went everywhere . . . some of them might have got caught in the folds of the draperies and been there ever since . . .

No maid had dared to come into Lori's rooms since she had returned to them; any pill that had ended up in the bed curtains was still there.

It wouldn't be going back on them if there were one or two left, and I took them. I wouldn't get any more. I wouldn't ask Dr Bruschsson for any more. But I just feel so awful, and I know I won't go back to sleep for ages – thank God I'm passing out so long every night, but now there's the whole rest of the day to get

*through, and I honestly am beginning to feel like throwing myself
off the balcony* . . .

That was the first time that she had consciously thought of
– not suicide, she couldn't say the word – but of – well, what
else would she call it? She'd meant it jokingly, but it hadn't
felt funny, not at all, and the longer she lay there, the more
panicky she felt. Pulling back the covers, she swung herself
out of bed and her feet took her to the canopy post at the far
corner of the bed without any conscious intention. She
reached out, giving a sharp pull at the blue silk wrapped
around it, and sure enough, a little shower of pills tumbled
out of the folds onto the matching coverlet.

Five of them. Round white ones, which meant they were
the daytime ones; the nighttime ones had been small
lozenges, pointed at each end. And the daytime ones were
exactly what Lori wanted. They were the ones that made
her feel calmer, easier, as if things didn't matter so much
any more. Before she knew it she was sweeping them all
into her hand, walking into the bathroom, reaching for a
water glass.

She looked at herself in the mirror. The golden tan, the
blonde hair, the blue eyes, all gave her an initial appearance
of health; but, despite the huge amount that she had been
sleeping, her eyes were set in dark hollows, and her cheeks
were sunken from barely eating for the last few days, her
collarbone more prominent.

Her skin was greasy after not washing for seventy-two
hours, and the pills were sweaty in her hand now. She glanced
down at them, struggling with powerful conflicting impulses.
No matter how much she told herself that she could just
take these and stop when they were done, not ask for more,
she had the horrible suspicion that she might be lying to
herself.

But I just thought about jumping off the balcony! And it almost felt like a relief – a huge relief—

Lori put down the pills so that she could turn on the tap, fill the glass.

But I won't be able to take these if I get pregnant! When I get pregnant, because I have to get pregnant – it's my only way out—

The water glass fell from her hand and smashed in the sink. Lori dropped too, folding over herself, almost crashing to the bathroom floor. She wrapped her arms around her knees, her head sinking down, and rocked herself in a hopeless attempt at comfort, moaning dully with misery at the trap in which she was caught. That was how Attila found her half an hour later.

'Lori!'

She heard and felt him all at once, his huge arms lifting her effortlessly, carrying her out of the bathroom and back into the bedroom, putting her down on the bed, unfolding her tightly curled body into his arms, taking her hands to examine her palms.

'I saw the broken glass in the sink,' he said. 'You cut yourself?'

'No,' she said, her voice a little rusty from days of disuse. 'I just dropped the glass.'

'And the pills – I saw the pills—' He was trying to sound calm, but she heard the suppressed panic in his voice.

'I didn't take them!' she said. 'I was going to, and then . . .'

Then I thought about getting pregnant, and I couldn't stand up any more . . .

'I wash them away, *now*,' he said decisively, suiting the action to the word and returning swiftly. She leaned against him, overwhelmingly grateful for the warmth of his wide chest, the reassuringly familiar feel of his gold chain, the scent of his skin; it was as if they had been a couple for years, not just a few days.

'I wait for you to ring me,' he said, sounding sad. 'I wait, and they tell me you are in your room, you don't want to see no one, and I think, she will want to see me. But I can't say, the Queen will want to see me because she loves me! They say you are depressed, I can't say I will make her feel better! And I think, in Mexico we say we can be together, but then we come back here and we realize it is impossible . . .'

'I feel so weird about it all,' Lori muttered, her voice muffled against his chest. 'This is—' she could barely get the words out, they sounded so ridiculous – 'this is my husband's castle, he lives here with his mother – I'm just not the kind of person who can sleep with my lover with my husband and his mother under the same roof! This is so messed up!'

He nodded vigorously, his curls brushing against her forehead.

'Lori, I don't just come here to see you,' he said urgently. 'I come to tell you that people are here to visit you. No one wants to come to tell you, because this morning you tell everyone to go away. And I hear about it and go to say that I will do it. They are very grateful,' he added with a hint of irony. 'Everyone is scared of you now. The doctor says you are very angry, and the King has a mark on his face. We hear you threw cushions at him and he told the Dowager that one of the zips cut him.' He grinned. 'I like to hear this.'

Heart racing, Lori pulled back to look at him; all she had taken in was that people were here to visit her.

'My family?' she said excitedly.

But as soon as she said the words she knew her hope was in vain. Attila wouldn't have said 'people' to describe them; his English was better than that.

'No.' He shook his head. 'It is a lady from England, with her secretary. A famous lady – or no, not famous, that is the wrong word. Like royal. She acts like a queen. Like she is the equal of the Dowager. And her secretary is an Arab lady, in black robes. No one sees Arabs in Herzoslovakia, so everyone is very interested to see the lady in robes.'

'I have no idea who that is,' Lori said, staring at him blankly. 'I don't know anyone English – I mean, I met people at the Olympics, but no one royal who would come to visit me. It's not *Chloe*, is it? You know, who's engaged to Prince Hugo?'

'No, she is much more old,' Attila said. 'Like a—' he searched for the right way to say it – 'grown-up lady. She seems scary, but her eyes are kind.'

Lori shook her head, still baffled.

'I don't want to see anyone,' she started, but Attila raised a hand to stop her.

'This lady you should see,' he said with utter seriousness. 'I feel it.' He pounded his chest with his clenched fist, a blow that would have rocked a lesser man. 'She wants to help.'

'But—'

Lori cut off as Attila stood up, took her hands and pulled her to her feet, walking her to the bathroom.

'You shower,' he said. 'I put the pills down the sink and now I take the broken glass away so the maid does not cut herself.' He had placed all the pieces on a towel, which he folded carefully by the corners and picked up. 'And I go to tell the lady you will see her. I bring her to your sitting room. I can't stay, because if I am here when you get into the shower . . .'

Their eyes met, and Lori felt her body waking up again after the days of depression, feeling once again like the person she'd been in Mexico. The person who had realized she was in love with Attila, who wanted to spend her life with him. Who had to believe that there was a way out of this horrendous situation: that just because she couldn't picture her escape now didn't mean that it didn't exist. That her only choices weren't pills or the balcony.

And as soon as she started to soap herself she felt her spirits begin to rise. There was something so basic about feeling her hair squeak clean as she rinsed off the shampoo, about the grease rolling off her, the fresh scent of her body wash, that made it impossible to be quite as depressed. By the time she had dressed and dried her hair, she even felt reasonable enough to spray on some Elizabeth Arden Pretty; makeup was beyond her, but then she barely wore it anyway. Taking a deep breath, she headed towards the door that led to the sitting room. She had no idea who the 'lady' could be, but she knew that Attila was waiting there for her, and that was enough to make her open the door and walk through.

What greeted her on the other side was definitely surreal. Rising to their feet – of course, she was a queen now, they had to stand – were two women, one immaculately dressed in a smart trouser suit and what the Dowager would have described as 'good jewellery', the other, much taller, draped in a black burkha – or was it a niqab? – which hid everything but her face. And since her face was mostly concealed behind big, slightly tinted glasses, even that was barely visible. The two of them looked so incongruous together, such a clash of different cultures, that Lori found herself paralyzed for a moment in the doorway.

Attila, standing by the far wall, bodyguard-style, gestured at her to keep moving, and she obeyed; as she came into the room, the Western-dressed woman stepped briskly towards her and, to Lori's great surprise, took her hands.

'Your Majesty,' she said, in a motherly way. 'My name is Lady Margaret McArdle, and I know this will sound terribly strange, but my friend and I are here to help you. I think, if you'll forgive me, that you've got yourself into an awful mess, and you need some help, don't you?'

Lori promptly burst into scalding hot tears of relief. It took ten minutes before she calmed down, and when she finally managed to mop her eyes and draw some deep breaths, she was sitting on the sofa with Lady Margaret and her secretary on each side of her, stroking her shoulders reassuringly and telling her that everything was going to be all right.

'I must say,' Lady Margaret said, sotto voce, to her secretary, 'you *know* the doubts I had about this! But we did absolutely the right thing in coming. Look at the state of her – poor little thing.'

This must have been the only time in her adult life that anyone had ever referred to Lori as little; that idea actually made her smile, a tiny, wan, pathetic smile, but it was instantly noticed by both women.

'Right, she's ready for tea,' Lady Margaret said briskly, pouring some from a tray on the table in front of them. 'Nice and strong, with plenty of sugar. Here, drink it all.'

She handed Lori the cup and saucer.

'And after you've had that, we're going to tell you *all* about a rather cunning plan we've hatched to get you out of here. If, of course, you want to get out. Oh, Lord, no! Don't start crying again!'

'Lori, don't cry,' Attila said firmly, going over and shutting the bedroom door to ensure their privacy. 'You listen to her, okay?'

Lady Margaret glanced over at Attila, her eyebrows soaring at the phenomenon of the Queen of Herzoslovakia's bodyguard not only calling his sovereign by her first name, but telling her what to do into the bargain.

'Attila's my – we're in love,' Lori said, gulping down the tears and then some tea. 'Ugh,' she added in parentheses.

'It really helps,' the secretary assured her in a soft voice. 'You need the sugar. Do keep drinking.'

It was the first time the woman in the black robes had spoken, and Lori, even in her state of high emotion, couldn't help being intrigued by her accent, which was unmistakably English, and her manner, which was just as authoritative as Lady Margaret's. She kept drinking the tea as both the secretary and Lady Margaret looked back and forth from Attila to Lori, absorbing this surprising piece of information.

'It's wonderful that you have someone here for you,' the secretary said with great kindness, smiling at Attila. 'Would you like to join us?'

She gestured at the sofa opposite.

'No, thank you,' he said politely. 'I work now, I do not sit down.'

But he came forward to stand behind the sofa, becoming part of the group.

'Your Majesty,' Lady Margaret began, seeing that Lori was making progress with the tea, 'do you want to tell us your situation? We have a fairly good idea, but perhaps you'd like to give us an outline?' She cleared her throat. 'We understand that you haven't left your rooms since you got back from your honeymoon. We don't mean to be intrusive, but we can't help being aware that—'

Lori had nothing to lose by telling them everything, nothing to lose at all. What did it matter if this was a bizarre set-up organized by her husband and his mother, unlikely though that seemed? Joachim and the Dowager knew exactly how she felt anyway – what could these two women report back to them that was new information? Even the fact that she was in love with Attila would scarcely ruffle their feathers, since they had already tried to set her up with one lover already.

So it came pouring out. Everything. The excellent pretence Joachim had made of being in love with her, the whirlwind courtship, the oddness of his not wanting to have sex with her before marriage, the seduction attempt by Mihaly, her flight to Graz, the Dowager bringing her back, Dr Bruschsson and his little white pills, her drugged-up state as she walked down the aisle, the revelations that Joachim had made on their honeymoon . . .

The two women were perfect listeners; they drank tea, refilled Lori's cup, nodded and made soft little murmurs of sympathy at appropriate moments. She noticed, too, that they did not look remotely shocked at any of the revelations. Neither the fact that Joachim was effectively blackmailing her to stay in the marriage and have children, nor that the Dowager had proposed sharing her lover with her daughter-in-law, drew anything more from them than nods and pats of empathy on her arm that encouraged her to keep going. They were extraordinarily unshockable, something that couldn't help surprising Lori, even through the twists and turns of her story. And by the time she finished, the questions that had been nagging at her with increasing strength finally popped out. Setting down her empty cup, she blurted out:

'Who *are* you? Why are you here? And what did you mean when you said you could help me?'

Lady Margaret and the secretary looked at each other.

'Show or tell?' Lady Margaret asked.

The secretary smiled.

'Show first, I think,' she said. 'That'll reassure her.'

Lady Margaret reached down into her capacious leather handbag and pulled out a tablet computer, setting it on the coffee table.

'We have some photos to show you,' she said to Lori. 'I didn't want to print them out, because even with a private plane, you never know if someone might take it into their head to look through your things. But no Customs officer ever makes you open your computer and turn it on . . .'

She booted it up and waited for it to load.

'We're going to show you some rather explicit photographs,' the secretary said to Lori. 'Brace yourself.'

'I have no idea what—' Lori began, and then the first image popped up on the screen, and she clapped both hands to her mouth in instinctive reaction, a squeal escaping her. Attila came round behind her swiftly to see what she was looking at, and even his professional training didn't prevent him from letting out a deep snigger. Lori's husband was spread-eagled naked on the tiles of a bathroom, and a very large, voluptuous and equally naked woman, her skin as rich and dark as his was white and pasty, was hovering over him.

Or rather, her bottom was. She was gripping firmly onto a bar set into the wall so that she could squat down over his face and drench him in a way that, judging by the ecstatic smile that could just be made out below the stream, was very much hitting the spot for him. Further down the shot could be seen another large, bare, dark bottom, aiming over Joachim's crotch; he certainly didn't do things by halves.

'I hope those rails are strong,' Attila said, deadpan. 'If it breaks and they fall on him, it will be bad. They will break his nose at least. And his cock.'

'Oh, he's hilarious!' the secretary exclaimed, laughing. 'Lori – may I call you Lori?'

The Queen of Herzoslovakia nodded her assent, unable to take her eyes off the screen. She reached out and scrolled through a couple more photographs as the secretary said:

'Lori, you realize that this means—'

'I can go,' Lori said quietly. 'I can go and he can't stop me. He can't blackmail me to stay.'

These photographs were the ultimate leverage against Joachim; with them in Lori's possession, she could force her husband to bury the compromising ones of her and Mihaly forever, make him pay off her family's mortgages and ensure that he no longer had any hold over her.

'Exactly,' said Lady Margaret simply. 'My dear, you're free.'

Lori shook her head slowly. In a way, she was more confused than ever. Attila's hands rested on her shoulders, huge and warm and comforting, a solid, silent reminder that she was free, not only to do as she chose, but to be with him.

'But I can't trust this unless you tell me who you are,' she said. 'Why you've taken this trouble. I mean, if these pictures aren't real – if I can't take them to Joachim and use them to make him divorce me right away – I think it would be the cruellest thing that I can possibly imagine!'

She was amazed that she had managed to express herself so well, so clearly; her voice was shaking with desperation, pleading with them to convince her that they were everything they had said that they were; friends, not foes. Lady Margaret was nodding vigorously, but her gaze was fixed squarely on the face of her secretary, and Lori turned to look at the latter, taken aback to see that she was removing her tinted glasses and putting them on the table, unpinning the grips that held the black fabric around her face, pulling it back so that the hood lay on her shoulders.

'You probably won't recognize me,' the secretary said quietly.

'I had the weirdest thought,' Lori said, frowning, 'but you *can't* be – no, that's *crazy*—'

'I used to be Princess Belinda,' the secretary said in a low voice. 'You see, you can trust me. I have *much* more to lose than you here.'

'But you're *dead*!'

Impulsively, Lori leaned forward to squint at the woman's face. She had barely been born when Belinda died in the avalanche, but of course she knew what Belinda looked like: everyone in the world was familiar with that iconic face, perhaps even more so because she had died at the height of her fame and beauty. *If it's her, she looks wonderful*, Lori thought, staring at the woman. *A little different – and older, of course – but wonderful*.

'I had some plastic surgery,' the woman said. 'And I'm wearing contact lenses. Which is absolutely miserable when you've got tinted glasses on too, but I can't be too careful.'

'It's all true,' Lady Margaret chimed in. 'I was her greatest friend, and I didn't know that she was alive until a few weeks ago. Lumpy, tell them the story or they'll think that we're both barking.'

As Attila moved swiftly to check the doors to the bedroom and the hall, making sure that no one was eavesdropping, the woman in the burkha began to talk. Almost immediately Lori realized that she believed every word she was hearing. Partly because of how much Belinda's story echoed Lori's own; being tricked into marriage with someone she thought loved her, only to find out it had all been a lie. And after the trouble that the Herzoslovakian royal family had gone to in order to make sure that Lori didn't up sticks and leave, Lori had no difficulty in believing that Prince Oliver might have decided that his ex-wife, now that she had given him the requisite two heirs, might be too much of a loose cannon, now that she was single again, to be allowed to roam the world possibly dropping the information that Oliver had always preferred the company of his footmen or grooms to that of his wife . . .

'I couldn't see it happening again to another woman,' Belinda said simply. 'Even though Rahim is so angry with me for leaving. I don't know if he'll even be there when I get back. But I saw you at your wedding, crying like that, and I just *knew* they had you on tons of pills. I remembered that feeling so vividly, I couldn't get it out of my mind. So I pretty much begged Rahim to see if he could get some photographic evidence of Joachim's, um, tendencies—'

'You *knew* about him?' Lori said, wide-eyed.

'Oh my dear, *everyone* in Europe knows about him!' Lady Margaret said, pulling a face. 'Well, everyone in the *gratin*! We've all been gossiping about it for donkey's years! That's why he needed a nice fresh American girl with no connections to, er, our circle, and why he wanted to get married so terribly quickly, before you went to a party, say, and someone got drunk and spilled the beans to you . . .'

'I feel so *stupid*,' Lori said, sinking her face into her hands. 'I feel like such an *idiot* . . .'

'Oh, you and me both!' Belinda patted her leg. 'We can form a little support group after this is all over. Ex-Wives of Creepy Royals, Very Much Anonymous!'

That made Lori laugh; she dropped her hands again.

'I can't *wait* for this all to be over,' she said in heartfelt tones.

Behind her, something buzzed. Attila's hands left her shoulders; he stepped back, pulled his phone from his pocket, and crossed the room to answer it. Lady Margaret said:

'Well, this has been *such* a satisfactory outcome! We did the right thing coming here – I'm *so* grateful it hasn't been a wasted errand. And Lumpy's risked a great deal coming to help you. Now we can zip the photos over to you and pop back on the plane again. It's quite a trip – nearly four hours and then the helicopter – we'll be more than ready for dinner and bed by the time we get back to Morocco – thank *goodness* I have gin on the plane . . .'

But Attila had finished his first call, dialled another number and was talking urgently on the phone now, a fast stream of Herzoslovakian, clipped and fast. He looked over at the three women, holding up a hand to signal them to wait, before finishing the conversation. Then he strode back to the sofa and said:

'There is bad news. I am very sorry. I have just heard, there are men from the British Secret Service at the Graz airport. They say they are maintenance for a plane next to yours, but a person from Graz security recognizes one of them from a long time ago, from an operation they were both part of. So they know they are not maintenance. They are suspicious, and they watch and see that the men try to go close to your plane.'

Belinda let out a gasp of horror.

'They were prevented,' Attila said quickly. 'They do not touch the plane. But they have good IDs and they show them and do not get arrested, so they leave. I have told the heliport here in Valtzers that no one must go near your helicopter. And you must leave at once. I have friends who will escort you to the helicopter and then in Graz, the friend of mine from security will make sure that it is all good. But you must also make sure that in Morocco—'

'I'll ring Rahim straight away,' Belinda said, the blood draining from her face. 'My God, he'll be so angry! This was his worst nightmare!'

'I have an idea for this,' Attila said calmly, as Lori stared up at him, taken aback; she had never seen this side of him before, had, honestly, perceived him much more as a personal trainer than a real bodyguard. Suddenly seeing him swing into action was extremely impressive. 'It is you they look for,' he said to Belinda. 'That is right?'

She nodded.

'So when they realize that it is not you in these clothes, these Arab clothes, you are safe and nothing happens to you

Rebecca Chance

or to the lady.' He glanced at Lady Margaret. 'You get back to Morocco, nice and safe. And they go away.'

'But—' Belinda began, but Lori had already realized what he was saying, had jumped up and run into her bedroom to collect a few essential things: her passport, any money she had, her phone.

'I'm going to pretend to be you!' she called over her shoulder. 'Get it? We're the same height – in that burkha and your glasses I can leave here as you and no one will realize. I'll take the helicopter to Graz—'

'—and then she'll show her face. No offence, Lumpy darling,' Lady Margaret said, 'but she's twenty years younger than you—'

'No need to say any more!' Belinda said, wincing. 'But what about you, Lori – what if they recognize you?'

'Once in Graz, they can't make me come back,' Lori said grimly, coming back into the room with a small handbag. 'I'll walk through the private airstrip part of the airport with your glasses off to make it totally clear I'm not you. You barely show your passport on private planes – they just do a really fast glance at the photo, they don't even look at the name. I won't ping up on their radar like I did before when I tried to go through normal border security.' She looked at Belinda. 'And Attila will take good care of you,' she said with absolute conviction.

'I drive you to stay with friends of mine,' Attila said to Belinda. 'In Bulgaria. It is not far, just half a day. We stay there till this Rahim sends a plane for you. In my country you will be safe, I promise. I was in the secret forces there. I know many people I trust, many eyes that watch.'

'Rahim will organize something straight away,' Belinda said. 'By tomorrow morning, I'm sure. And you'll come to Morocco, of course, Attila!'

Attila grinned.

'Once I help the Queen run away,' he said, 'I go wherever she goes.'

'Oh, how romantic!' Lady Margaret said approvingly. 'Right, we have a plan! Lumpy, take that burkha off and give it to Lori – and the glasses—'

'You have passport?' Attila asked Belinda. 'Bulgaria is not in Schengen countries, we have border controls . . .'

'Yes, Rahim made sure of that,' Belinda said. 'Lumpy has a passport in the name of Hana – that's what they call her now – with all the right stamps.'

'Good! Then we all go, now! You two first,' Attila said to Lady Margaret and Lori, who was already pulling on her disguise. 'We wait for half an hour, then I take "Hana" out the staff way. No one will even look to see where I am – with the Queen in her room, there is nothing for me to do. We lock the door, and no one will come in here for a long time.'

He grimaced.

'They say to let you be quiet, so you come to realize that you have no choice,' he said to Lori.

She hoicked up the fabric that was draped heavily over her limbs, ran to him as best she could, took his face in her hands and kissed him hard on the mouth, the big tinted glasses sliding askew as she did so.

'I love you so much, Attila Vankov,' she said with the utmost seriousness. 'So much.'

'I see you in Morocco,' he said, taking her hands, squeezing them for a long moment before pushing her away again. 'I see you in Morocco and then you never leave me again.'

'I promise!'

Lady Margaret grabbed Lori's arm and pulled her towards the door.

'Walk slowly in that thing, dear,' she advised. 'It's very trippy-up-y. Hana nearly took a header already getting out of the helicopter. Head up, chin forward. Pretend you're in your wedding dress. Or actually, on second thought, maybe not . . .'

Lori stifled a laugh as she settled the glasses firmly on her nose.

'Oh,' she said, 'believe me, *this* time I'll have a smile on my face every step of the way!'

Chloe

'Do you want to try the melatonin again?' Chloe said hopefully to Hugo, whose legs, stretched out in front of him, were jiggling nervously. Up and down, up and down, restless, uneasy movements. It had been like this for weeks now, ever since the dreams about his dead mother had begun; as bedtime began to approach, he became increasingly tense, almost fretful that he would fall asleep only to wake up in the middle of the night, screaming his head off as he saw her being buried by an avalanche over and over again.

'No, I don't like it,' her fiancé said, eyes fixed on the television screen, where *A Question Of Sport* was playing. Martin Frensham would definitely have sneered at that, and at the mugs of camomile tea sitting on the coffee table. 'It made me dream of giant squid,' he added. 'It was really weird.'

'But you *didn't wake up*,' Chloe said, trying to keep her voice calm. The melatonin had been ordered by Lauren from America; apparently it was a natural sleep aid, which was all that Hugo would consent to take. Proper sleeping pills, it turned out, were things that 'one didn't do', according to Hugo, which had had the effect of making Chloe grind her teeth even harder than she had when she had found out that Hugo and Sophie had never had any kind of counselling after their mother's death. One didn't 'do' that in the Royal Family, apparently. One just left one's children to climb into bed with each other and cry themselves to sleep after their beloved mother had died in a terrifying accident.

No wonder Hugo's having nightmares now, she thought in savage fury at Oliver, who seemed to have alternated between utter neglect and bullying for their entire childhood. *And no wonder Sophie turned out such a nasty little wild child.*

Despite this new understanding, Chloe could never imagine ever being close to Sophie; the best she could hope for was an uncordial truce. After she and Lauren had viewed the footage of Sophie and Minty's epic misbehaviour in Ibiza, neither of the two aristocratic girls had dared to do any more than cast the occasional sidelong sulky glance in Chloe and Lauren's direction, and if they ever stepped out of line in the future, it would take just the smallest comment to snap them back into watching their manners. Lauren had made it clear to both of them that she had her ear to the ground and would know if they circulated any more nasty nicknames for Chloe; so far they had been as good as gold.

Which probably means they're picking on some other poor cow, Chloe thought ruefully. *But there's nothing I can do about that.*

Still, the revelation that Sophie and Hugo had had no help at all in dealing with their mother's death at such a young age had truly shocked Chloe. Even Lauren, who was tough as old boots, had admitted that Sophie deserved to be cut some slack for that.

'I'll stop giving Soph a hard time,' she'd said earlier that evening, as she and Chloe placed four M&S scampi and chip dinners in the microwave. 'Fair dos.'

'Giving her a hard time?' Chloe shut the door and set the timer. 'What do you mean?'

Lauren grinned evilly, raised two fingers to her mouth in a 'V' and flickered her tongue through the split.

'Been going on about the lady-loving stuff to her and Minty,' she said nonchalantly. 'Seems to wind 'em up for some reason. Sod knows why, after their double-act sex show in Ibiza. But I'll call it a day now, unless they fuck with us again. You know, if you think of a poor little two-year-old crying for her mum, it takes a bit of the fun out of it.'

'Oi! Gels! Where's our dinner!' Dave had yelled from the living room. 'Chop chop! We're bleeding starving!'

'Any more of that,' Lauren had said, carrying the tartar sauce and ketchup through to the living room, her voice stern but her eyes sparkling with happiness, 'and you'll get a squirt of both of these right in the face! You know what they say, eh, Chlo?' she added. 'Turnabout's fair play! Bout time *he* got squirted in the face without a warning to close his bloody eyes first!'

'Lauren! God, you're a filthy bird!' Dave said happily. 'In front of Hugo, too!'

Hugo could be heard sniggering at this.

'Please,' he said to Dave 'have you *met* my cousin? After growing up with Toby, I'm pretty much unshockable.'

Lauren and Dave, now officially a couple, were spending more and more time socializing with Chloe and Hugo. Dave was off-duty on these evenings, of course, and he and Hugo had struck up one of those swift, easy male friendships where they watched sport, drank beer and grunted friendly insults at each other. Chloe's fingers were crossed very tightly that Lauren and Dave stayed together; she and Hugo didn't have very many couples to hang out with where she got on with both parties. Hugo had a few established pairs of friends, but, nice as they were, it was hard for Chloe to truly feel part of the *gratin*. They had so many in-jokes and nicknames that she felt like an intruder when she tried to join in with them. It was easier to go downwards in the social ranking rather than up, and Hugo thoroughly enjoyed Lauren and Dave's unpretentious, down-to-earth personalities and quick wits.

They relax him, Chloe thought now, looking sideways at her fiancé. *He was laughing and joking and bantering when they were here. And now they've gone and we've cleared up dinner, he's all tense again. Oh, sod it! I was so hoping that a nice evening with Lauren and Dave watching* White Chicks *would get him happy and relaxed and ready for bed ... and it did, but now he's wound up again ...*

It was an unhappy revelation that sometimes the person you loved was actually more able to relax in the company of friends – when alone with their fiancée, they reverted to the tense, nervy state they had been in before the friends arrived. Because now she was watching Hugo's legs going again, the sure sign of a sleep-interrupted night ahead.

'When you took the melatonin, though,' Chloe repeated, 'even if you dreamed about giant squid, you didn't wake up. Which is better than, um, waking up.'

Waking up screaming your mother's name, she wanted to add.

'The squid were really awful,' Hugo said, shivering. 'Their tentacles kept wrapping around me.'

'But you *didn't wake up*!' Chloe said, hearing with horror how irritable she sounded. 'And we both actually got a full night's sleep! And with everything we've got to do over the next few months, Hugo, we *have* to get our rest! God,' she added miserably. 'I sound like I'm middle-aged already. But, you know, the paps're photographing us all the time, and if we look knackered and grumpy, they'll write that we're not getting on.'

'Oh no!' Hugo looked horribly guilty. 'I know you get the worst of all that stuff . . .' He turned to hug her. 'Do you want me to sleep in the spare room? That way I can toss and turn and get up if I need to without waking you.'

'No, I don't!' Chloe said miserably, hugging him back. 'I didn't get engaged to sleep apart from my man! I like snuggling, I like you spooning me, I like waking up with you when you have a morning stiffie, and that hasn't happened since . . . oh, Hugo, *please* will you go and see a doctor and get a prescription for some sleeping pills?'

'Father would go *mad* if he knew I was taking anything,' Hugo said, actually trembling with nerves at the mere idea. 'I can't even *imagine* what he'd say.'

Chloe bit her tongue. Actually bit it.

So that's it, she thought savagely. *That's the whole bloody problem – it all comes back to Oliver in the end! He's neglected and messed up his kids all their life, and it's still going on now* . . .

The intercom by the door buzzed.

'Must be Lauren,' Chloe said, kissing Hugo on the cheek and getting up to answer it. 'She's always leaving something behind.'

But when she put the handset back in the cradle and walked back down the corridor, she looked genuinely taken aback.

'What is it?' Hugo said, swivelling round to look at her over the top of the sofa.

'It's Lady Margaret,' she said, frowning in puzzlement.

'What – *now*?' Hugo looked at the swan-necked mahogany grandfather clock against the wall. 'It's eleven-thirty!'

'I *know*! Put the kettle on, there's a love. We might as well make more tea.'

'Are you joking? Lady M will've been on the gin for hours!' Hugo stood up.

'*I* want more tea, okay?' Chloe positively barked now. 'You can get her gin *after* you get me my tea!'

Usually, she would have tried to pull herself together, to show the stiff upper lip so prized by the British upper classes. But Hugo's refusal to take sleeping pills, and the reason for it, the shame he would feel if his father ever found out that he was still mourning his mother, was shredding her nerves so much that she just couldn't both keep calm and carry on.

Really, she thought grimly, *I should handle this how the upper classes would – drink so many G&Ts that I just pass out every night and don't even notice Hugo thrashing around as if he were a giant squid himself! But I'm not going to do that. I'm going to fight for him, I refuse to give up—*

A tap on the door signalled Lady Margaret's arrival. Chloe opened the door to see a footman standing there with a distinctly odd expression on his face.

'Lady Margaret, Miss Rose,' he said. 'And, er, her secretary.'

What on earth is she doing bringing her secretary round here so late in the evening?

But when the footman stepped back, ushering in Lady Margaret and the secretary, Chloe was even more baffled. And understanding of the footman's odd grimace. Because the secretary – who might, from her height and build, have been the same woman as before, the one who had screamed at Oliver's tantrum – was draped from head to toe in a black burkha, her face almost completely concealed behind big glasses.

'Do come in,' Chloe said feebly, leading the way into the living room. 'Um, would you like a drink?'

'I'd start pouring ones for everyone,' Lady Margaret said, her voice so odd that Chloe stared at her, genuinely worried now.

'What *is* it?' she said, seeing that Lady Margaret's face was white as a sheet.

Behind her, the woman in the burkha took off her glasses and put them on the console table, her hand shaking so much that the frames rattled on the polished wood. She reached up and unpinned the fabric of the burkha, pulling the whole thing off over her head, and Chloe saw that it was indeed the same woman as before; the slim, elegant figure, the beautiful posture. She wasn't looking at Chloe; her entire focus was on Hugo, dutifully coming back from the kitchen with Chloe's tea. He glanced from Lady Margaret to the secretary, frowning in confusion.

'Hugo?' she said, in a soft, frightened voice. 'Hugo . . .'

The sight of her had merely puzzled Hugo: the sound of her voice, however, made him gasp and drop the mug of tea. Chloe shrieked. The mug fell to the carpet, and Hugo jumped back instinctively, the boiling water spilling in front of him, just a few drops landing harmlessly on the top of his mono-grammed slippers.

'*Mummy?*' he said, in a tone that Chloe had never heard before. It sent a shiver right down her spine.

'*Hugo!*' The woman reached out her hands to Hugo. 'I'm so sorry – I'm so very, very sorry—'

Tears were pouring down both of their faces. Hugo was bright red; the woman had a livid pink flush rising up the open V-neck of her silk sweater.

'Oh—' Hugo said, staring at her as if hypnotized. 'I remember you getting all pink like that when you were angry with Father . . .'

'Oh God, is *that* what you remember?' The woman's voice was thick with tears.

'I remember what you sang when you put me to bed,' he said slowly. 'Go to sleep, little baby Hugo . . .'

Her mouth moved, saying the words along with him. She took a step towards him, and suddenly they were in each other's arms, sobbing loudly, rough harsh cries, sobs dragged right up from the bottom of their hearts. Chloe watched, dumbfounded, her legs weak, unable to believe what she had to be seeing.

'You smell just the same!' Hugo was sobbing. 'I remember that too, *so* much . . . the smell of your scent . . . oh, *Mummy*, I missed you so much!'

Chloe realized that she was shaking her head, unable to believe the sight of Hugo hugging his mother, come back somehow, miraculously, from the grave. Lady Margaret crossed the room, taking Chloe's hand, her own eyes red with the effort of not crying herself.

'It's true,' she said gruffly. 'This is Belinda. Back from the dead, as it were.'

'Hugo's been dreaming about her,' Chloe managed to say through numb lips. 'It started after you brought her to the Palace. He must have recognized her somehow.'

'My God,' Lady Margaret said. 'We really thought she'd get away with it. What a pair of idiots we were.'

'It wasn't how she looked,' Chloe mumbled. 'It was the scream. It must have been when she screamed. He's been hearing it in his dreams ever since.'

'Well, he wasn't the only one to spot her. They're on her trail,' Lady Margaret said grimly. 'MI6. Tried to sabotage our plane once already. That's why we're here. Nowhere to hide any more. Thought it was best to bite the bullet, as you might say.'

Chloe felt as if her head might be about to explode.

'I don't understand *any* of this!' she said, sounding frantic.

'Oh, darling—'

Belinda pulled back from her long-abandoned son. By now their faces looked like pieces of meat, raw and red and wet with tears, but their eyes, shining like stars, were positively rapturous. This was what emotion looked like, Chloe thought, true love, true passion: it was so beautiful to look at that she felt her own heart swell with the weight of it, with the sheer, almost religious ecstasy that she saw in Hugo's eyes.

'Chloe – I so wanted to meet you—' Her mother-in-law's voice was faint, overwhelmed. 'I'm so happy to meet the girl who loves my son . . .'

She reached out an arm to Chloe, who found herself walking into their embrace, hugging her fiancé and his mother, a sensation of incredible rightness enfolding her along with the hug. This was Hugo's mother, no question about it, no matter how completely bizarre and incomprehensible all of it seemed. And his body, pressing next to Chloe's, was now utterly relaxed, almost limp with utter relief, the absolute opposite to how it had felt just half an hour ago, wound up and taut as a spring next to her on the sofa.

Before his mother came back from the dead.

At the drinks cabinet, Lady Margaret poured herself several fingers of neat gin and downed the whole lot in one gulp, bound and determined not to break down herself. She was the only one who hadn't. Chloe was crying too, wrapped tightly in the arms of her fiancé and his mother, overwhelmed, like them, with happiness. Because she felt, for the first time ever, that Hugo truly had some sort of family.

Buckingham Palace

'They want to do *what*, exactly, Frensham?'

King Stephen turned his leonine head from one side of the Throne Room to the other, taking in the extreme majesty of its décor with considerable satisfaction. It was as if the designer had been specifically briefed to use only the most regal of golds and reds. Every chair, even the small ones placed against the walls, was gilded, every swag of fabric was red velvet, held back with gold tassels. The walls were red silk brocade, the white of the high moulded ceiling so heavily inlaid with gold that it dazzled the eyes, the huge chandeliers gleaming golden glass; a proscenium arch supported by a pair of winged figures of victory holding garlands above them was so thickly encrusted with gilt that it looked like solid metal.

It was in the Throne Room that King Stephen always felt happiest. No one could take him as seriously as he took himself: his sense of his regal status even extended to a genuine, secret belief that his ascendancy to the British throne was literally God-given, that the initials SR had always been destined to be embroidered in gold thread on the back of his own, unique throne chair, upon which his eyes alighted now with the same extreme entitlement as they had the first time he saw it. Beside it was another throne the same size, whose initials, AR, were also equally as large as his; as always, he frowned slightly at this. His wife, Alexandra, was, after all, merely a consort, not regal in her own right. It rather offended his sense of correctness that her initials were not, perhaps, just a little smaller, to signify this. And perhaps the chair could have been a little smaller too . . .

Frensham coughed.

'They want to make it, er, a *chillax room*, sir, to use Prince Hugo's modern term,' he said very apologetically. 'Somewhere for the younger guests at the after-wedding party to sit and relax between dancing in the ballroom. The idea is to install a small bar, and have a disc jockey playing, er, relaxing music. One would bring in armchairs, small tables, some sofas perhaps . . .'

Martin's voice trailed off under his sovereign's withering stare.

'I've never heard anything so bloody stupid in my life!' the King barked. 'A *bar*? In the Throne Room?'

'Just basic drinks, Your Majesty,' Martin assured him. 'No cocktail shakers or, er, shots.'

Stephen didn't even dignify this with a comment. By his side, Queen Alexandra, a small, dumpy figure beside her statuesque, looming husband, shot Martin a swift, disapproving glance.

'Coffee too, I imagine,' she suggested. 'They'll certainly need coffee.'

'Oh, absolutely, Your Majesty,' Martin was swift to agree.

'There you go, Stephen,' his wife said. 'Coffee, and perhaps some simple drinks. Of course, it's your decision, as always. But I can't help feeling that it might be nice to actually *use* the room – one rarely does, apart from investitures and the occasional state reception . . .'

'I suppose not,' he said gruffly.

'And it really is the epitome of the British monarchy, isn't it? I always love to see visitors come in and pause for a moment in absolute awe . . .'

Queen Alexandra was extremely familiar with the interior of the Throne Room, but she turned slowly in a circle, her small bright eyes taking it in once more, in a gesture that she knew her husband would appreciate as a silent homage to the regal scarlet and gold décor.

'Hmm,' King Stephen said, stroking his chin. 'I do see what you mean. As our grandson marries – which is obviously one of the most significant events to happen in this country for decades – the guests – and *particularly* those invited by his little commoner—' he sneered magnificently down his nose – 'would all be . . . er . . .'

He regularly started sentences like this, wanting to sound king-like, as if he naturally spoke in speeches, and then got lost in his elaborate parentheses. However, one of the many reasons that he had chosen Alexandra to be his bride over sixty years ago was that she was more than able to step in when necessary, and now he glanced at her, indicating silently that she should finish for him.

'They would all be overwhelmed,' she said sweetly. 'By the sheer majesty of their surroundings.'

'Absolutely! Absolutely!' Stephen nodded vigorously. 'And it might be a salutary reminder of *what*, exactly, she's marrying into. After all, when you think of where she comes from – or rather, *doesn't* – we certainly don't want her or any of her doubtless appalling friends getting ideas above their station—'

Queen Alexandra's eyes met Martin's for a long moment, in which they silently acknowledged the fact that Chloe's station, after all, would be Queen of England some day, with her own throne, CR embroidered on it in gold thread.

' – and we'll *also* need members of staff making sure than none of her friends start behaving in a way that undermines the dignity of their surroundings,' Stephen concluded, his chest puffing up under his tailored suit in pride at having finished such a long sentence himself.

Queen Alexandra and Martin exchanged another glance, in which flickered a definite awareness of how Sophie, Toby and their crew were regularly used to behaving.

'Oh, most definitely, Your Majesty,' Martin said deferentially. In his many years in service at Buckingham Palace, he had learnt that it was simply impossible to kowtow to Stephen too low, or to lard his speech overmuch with 'Your Majesty'. He was comparatively informal with Queen Alexandra, particularly when alone with her, but, as Martin had once said wittily to Simon, Elgar might have written the 'Pomp and Circumstance' march as the soundtrack for Stephen's entire life.

'He'd wear his State robes for a dressing gown if he could,' Martin had added. 'Mind you, I suppose I would too . . . all that lovely ermine against the skin . . .'

'I'm sure that the staff will be more than capable of discreetly dealing with anyone overstepping the boundaries, Stephen,' the Queen assured her husband. 'And of course, we'll be in our rooms.'

She smiled, the little smile that only curved her lips when she was genuinely amused; it was formed by her pressing them together, as if trying to subdue herself, so that it appeared almost like a grimace of pain.

'I can't *imagine* that anyone won't be terrified by the mere *idea* that you might be summoned in order to read the Riot Act to a misbehaving young person!' she concluded. 'Goodness, Stephen, they'd be quaking in their boots!'

The image of himself striding regally into the Throne Room as a group of awestruck party-goers jumped to their feet, babbling apologies, was so delicious that Stephen basked in it for a long, luxurious moment. The Queen nodded at Martin, a silent communication that indicated that he could consider the Throne Room's 'chillax' status officially approved.

'What's everyone up to? Some sort of conclave?'

Prince Oliver strolled into the Throne Room, paused just inside the doorway, and raised a hand to ensure his thick hair was perfectly smoothed back from his high, wide forehead. He was the spitting image of his father, forty years younger, debonair and classically handsome; Queen Alexandra gazed dotingly at her only child.

Two gorgeous peacocks and the peahen, Martin thought. *And it'll kick off in three . . . two . . . one . . . Him and the old codger are always at loggerheads.*

'We're busy with the details of planning your son's wedding!' father snapped at son. 'Something I haven't bloody noticed *you* pulling your finger out to help with!'

'Oh *please*.' Oliver smirked. 'As if I didn't know that Mama and Martin are doing all the work, *comme d'habitude*.'

This was designed to wind up his father in every way conceivable; the smirk, the perfectly accurate comment that Stephen was a poser who never actually lifted a finger to do a thing, and the culminating phrase of French. Stephen *hated* it when his son spoke French.

But then, Stephen hates everything He does anyway, Martin thought. *Always has, according to the old hands at the Palace. Ever since He was walking and talking, Stephen couldn't stand the sight of Him, they say.*

Martin, of course, was on Oliver's side, Oliver's loyal man, till death did them part. The Prince of Wales was the love of Martin's life, had been ever since Oliver had, as Martin put it himself, picked Martin out from the chorus for a starring role in Oliver's big four-poster bed. The couple of years Martin had spent on all fours on that taffeta quilt, or sprawled with his bottom propped up on a bolster, gripping one of the canopy poles so he could push back against Oliver's thrusts, had been, unequivocally, the best time of his life, the golden, halcyon days whose memories he constantly kept fresh, like an orchid he carefully nurtured.

Ever since he had set eyes on Oliver, Martin had been madly in love with him; his entire life from that moment on had been dedicated to the man he called simply Him. When Martin had grown too old for Oliver's tastes, he had cleverly taken on the role of procurer, Madame de Pompadour to Oliver's Louis XIV, cultivating his sources in order to provide Oliver with an endless stream of tight-buttocked working-class young men more than eager to climb onto the Prince of Wales's bed and call him by his title as he fucked them hard and fast. Garry, the stableboy recently interviewed for this demanding position by Martin and Simon, was the latest object of Oliver's attentions.

Garry's a lucky little bitch, Martin thought enviously. *Oh well, at least I get to watch them at it sometimes.*

Oliver could occasionally be coaxed into a highly discreet, very well-organized orgy, held at a gay establishment in Mayfair so exclusive that it didn't even have a name. Martin vetted all the participants, briefed them thoroughly in the correct etiquette for speaking to, blowing, or – if they hit the jackpot – bending over to accept the Royal cock up their behind, and for him, of course, all the hard work was justified by the reward of feasting his eyes on Oliver in action once more.

Naturally, Martin was much too well controlled to show anything but a perfectly proper, major-domo demeanour in public. Though his gaze was fixed on the object of his love, and he was shivering inside with pleasure – as he always did – at the sound of Oliver saying his name, outwardly Martin did not let his composed expression alter in any way.

'The idea, sir, is that the Throne Room will be transformed for the night of the wedding into a relaxed zone, as it were, for the younger party-goers,' Martin explained smoothly. 'Armchairs, mellow music, a bar serving coffee and perhaps some wine, all very respectful of the atmosphere, of course.'

'Oh, for goodness' sake!' Oliver said, throwing his head back and laughing in a theatrical way that annoyed his father so much that the King's teeth could almost be heard grinding. 'How very bourgeois! Wouldn't it be much more fun *not* to be respectful for once? I think they should have Jello shots and go-go dancers on the bar!'

King Stephen, his face dark red with fury, took a step towards his son, but his wife slid a small plump hand firmly onto his arm, detaining him through sheer force of will.

'Darling, you know Olly just says silly things to get attention,' she said, directing a basilisk stare at her son. 'Olly, if you haven't got anything useful to contribute—'

'Which he never bloody does!' the King snapped angrily.

' – why don't you flit away somewhere and stop annoying your father? And me,' she added, as casually as if it were a throwaway extra.

'For you, Mater, anything,' Oliver said, turning to his mother, picking up her hand and kissing it.

His father made a humphing noise. Ignoring him, Oliver started to saunter across the room, towards the ballroom, but he stopped in his tracks at the sight of a group of people entering the Throne Room.

'Hugo! Darling!' his grandmother said, beaming, as she always did, at the sight of her beloved grandson. 'And Sophie,' she added, with less enthusiasm. Her favouritism had always been marked. 'Lady Margaret, Chloe . . . and, um . . .'

Always the last on the list, Chloe noticed, trying not to be offended. *But Hugo's grandparents not liking me is the last thing I should be worried about right now.*

'Grandpa, Granny. And Father,' Hugo said, his voice cracking a little as he led his band of women to the centre of the Throne Room.

They were all huddling together for protection. Chloe was by Hugo's side, holding his hand to signal to him and his entire family that they were in this together. Behind them, Sophie had her arm tightly through Belinda's. They had all gone to find Sophie the night before; mercifully she had not only been in her apartment at Kensington Palace, across the courtyard from Hugo and Chloe, but sober to boot. Since the humiliation of Ibiza, Sophie had been making an effort not to go out every night, and drink less when she did party; her mother had found her getting ready for bed.

Sophie, with no real memories of Belinda, did not have her brother's instant epiphany, but her overwhelming excitement at her mother's miraculous return was even stronger, if possible, than Hugo's. She had reverted almost to a child-like state, sobbing and clinging to Belinda, unable to utter a coherent word for a long time; eventually, Hugo and Chloe had gone back to their rooms and left Belinda curled up in bed with Sophie, hugging each other to sleep. Chloe and Hugo had slept for ten hours straight for the first time since Belinda's scream, weeks ago, had triggered Hugo's buried memories. And they had woken up to Belinda and Sophie knocking at the door, bringing coffee and ready to plan their strategy for today.

'What's going on?' Stephen barked, looking at the group, his eyes passing over Belinda, not recognizing her; she was not wearing the burkha, and simply looked like a woman elegant enough to fit into even these royal surroundings. 'You look geared up for something, Hugo! Spit it out!'

Fuck fuck fuck fuck! Martin thought frantically, staring at Belinda. *What the fuck is going on? Why is that bitch here with Hugo and Sophie? Shit, Sophie's hanging on to her as if she couldn't stand up on her own – Shit, they know. They* know! *The cat's well and truly out of the bag! What the fuck are we going to do now?*

He didn't dare to look at King Stephen or Queen Alexandra. Instead, his eyes went to Oliver, the man he had loved with slave-like devotion for twenty years.

I didn't know this was going to happen! he tried to convey. *Please don't blame me for this . . . please forgive me . . .*

At the far end of the Throne Room, Simon, who had seen the group enter the Palace, slipped in and stood by the door, unobserved by anyone.

'I think someone here knows this already,' Hugo said, his voice still cracking, but his chin up. Chloe squeezed his hand tightly for support. 'Granny, Grandpa, you might want to sit down, though. I'm about to give you rather a shock.'

'Nonsense!' Stephen's voice boomed around the room. 'My God, what is this, amateur dramatics? I have enough of those from your father! Get on with it, Hugo!'

Hugo swallowed, his Adam's apple bobbing.

'It's about Mummy,' he said.

'You *know* I can't bear that woman's name being mentioned!' Stephen shouted. 'She did her best to drag this family into the mire—'

'She didn't! She *didn't*!'

It was Sophie screaming, cutting through her grandfather's words, something that absolutely never happened; he actually stopped in shock, staring at his granddaughter, for whom he had a soft spot.

'Mummy loved us! She loved us and she had to run away – she never wanted to leave us! Someone was trying to kill her!' Sophie blurted out.

'What on earth is she saying?' Stephen turned to his wife. 'Can you make sense of this?'

But Queen Alexandra didn't say a word. Her small, round face was like stone as she stared at the woman to whom Sophie was clinging.

Belinda had told her children and Chloe everything – everything apart from the fact that she had actually walked in on Oliver and Simon in bed together. She and Lady Margaret had debated it over and over again, but had found no way to explain Belinda's actions in faking her own death without telling the truth about Oliver's sexuality. And, as Belinda had made sure to emphasize to Hugo and Sophie, there was nothing wrong with being gay: it was the cover-up – the forcing Oliver and everyone around him to live a lie – that was the toxic part of the story.

Once arrived in Bulgaria, Belinda had decided that fleeing back to Morocco and staying holed up in the Tarhouna Palace for the rest of her life was not something she could bear. Previously, she and Rahim had been able to travel discreetly, after lying very low for the first few years. They had stayed with trusted friends of Rahim who did not know Belinda's true identity, chartered a yacht in Sardinia or returned to the island of Montecapra in the Tuscan archipelago, where they were safe from any paparazzi. But now that the British Secret Service was on her tail, Belinda was no longer safe anywhere but in the Palace. Once an attempt had been made to place a bomb on her plane, all bets were off. They could easily watch Rahim's mountain fortress, get word instantly if she left it and target her accordingly.

Not only would she die, other innocent victims would too. At the very least, the pilots of that plane, the crew, Lady Margaret, and Lori would all have been blown up in the attempt to kill Belinda. She wouldn't have been able to live with herself if anything had happened to them. And the only way that she could possibly avoid carnage was to face her would-be killer head on.

Having her daughter beside her was keeping Belinda's back straight, enabling her to do exactly that. Her eyes fixed on her ex-husband's face, she refused to tremble. In fact, she drew strength, ironically, from the fact that this was the second time she had been in his presence, and he was so oblivious that even now, even with her name mentioned, he clearly did not have the faintest idea who she was.

Martin knows, she thought, glancing at the major-domo, who met her eyes for a split-second and then looked away as fast as he could, dots of red showing on each cheek. *And so does Queen Alexandra. But the man who pretended he was in love with me, the man I had two children with – he doesn't have a clue.*

'*This* is Mummy!' Sophie yelled. '*This* is Mummy right here! She never died, she never did – *you* made her go away, Daddy! You tried to kill her and she had to run away!'

'What on *earth*?' Stephen ejaculated, as Hugo and Chloe shifted to the side so that they didn't block the King and Queen's view of Belinda and Chloe. It was the perfect location to break this news; the Throne Room was so huge that no eavesdropper lurking in one of the adjoining rooms could have heard a word of what was being said by the group gathered at its centre.

'It's true, Grandpa,' Hugo said. 'This is Mummy. She faked her own death and she's been living in the Atlas Mountains all this time.'

Stephen sputtered out a derisory laugh.

'Oh, for God's sake,' he said. 'Is this some kind of practical joke? Lady Margaret, I would think you'd know better than to get involved in this nonsense! Did *she* put you all up to this?'

He cast Chloe a brief, contemptuous glance. Beside Chloe, Hugo bridled.

'Or have you been taken in by a very cruel impersonation?' he added, the thought just occurring to him. The age creases on his forehead deepened and his brows bristled as he shoved his head forward, threateningly, at Belinda. '*You*,' he said majestically, 'if *you* have been lying to and upsetting my grandchildren, my wrath will be . . .'

His stance was formidable, but he had got tangled up in his sentence structure again, and this time his wife did not help. It was Lady Margaret who said bluffly:

'This is Belinda, all right. It's true, Your Majesty. Sounds like a fairy tale, I know. But she's been alive all this time.'

'Fairy tale! More like some bloody awful melodrama!' Oliver exclaimed. He was as white as his own shirt collar. 'I don't believe it for an instant!'

'Oh, it's me, Oliver,' Belinda said quietly. 'And I've told the children everything – well, nearly everything. I'm so sorry,' she added, and it was obvious from the sincerity of her voice that she meant it.

Her ex-husband, however, didn't even hear her apology. He had recognized her voice, and he was already lunging towards her in fury, hands outstretched, fingers crooked into claws. Sophie screamed at the top of her voice and threw herself in front of her mother; horrifyingly, Oliver knocked his daughter away, sending her sprawling to the ground. Whether he meant to throttle Belinda or just shake her like a terrier does a rat, no one would ever know, because Hugo and Martin grabbed his shoulders and hauled him back bodily just in time.

Belinda had stood her ground, but her breath was coming in ragged gasps of fear, and as soon as Oliver was pulled away she flew to Sophie, kneeling down beside her daughter, cooing to her softly. Oliver was struggling in Hugo and Martin's grip, and Simon came over, helping them keep Oliver under physical restraint.

'Oliver! Get a grip on yourself!' his mother snapped, walking over to her son, pulling back her arm and landing a resounding slap across his cheek. 'I'm going to count to three and then you're going to pull yourself together – when they let go of you, you will have yourself *under control*. One! Two! Three!'

At her nod, the men let go of Oliver, who stood there, head slumped forward, his hair falling over his face, swaying, breathing as heavily as if he had just sprinted from one end of the Throne Room to the other.

'Look, Father,' Hugo said with heroic restraint, considering that he had just seen Oliver shove his daughter to the carpet and try to assault his ex-wife, 'it's okay. We won't talk about it if you don't want to. Your private life is your business. But Mother has to be safe now. That's what we've come to tell you. No one must try to kill her any more.'

Belinda was helping Sophie to her feet. King Stephen looked over at the two of them, shaking his head.

'Is that *really*—' he started.

'Yes!' his wife said sharply, with so much venom in her usually calm voice that everyone stared at her. 'Yes, it is! The little *bitch*!'

'Oh my God! It was you, wasn't it?' Belinda said slowly, realizing the truth as she took in the sheer loathing in Queen Alexandra's tone. Belinda fixed her eyes on her ex-mother-in-law. 'I thought it was Oliver who tried to kill me before,' she continued, 'but it was *you* all along! You were always the one who pulled the strings, weren't you? How could I have been stupid enough to think *Oliver* could organize something as clever as overdosing me on my own pills?'

She looked at her ex-husband.

'Oliver's always been as subtle as a bull in a china shop when he gets angry,' she said with a shiver. 'Look what he just did – lunged at me without even thinking. That's him in a nutshell. He's about as subtle as a punch in the face. No, it wasn't Oliver at all. He couldn't possibly think of something that crafty. *You're* the real power behind the throne.'

Queen Alexandra, catching herself, moved to her husband's side.

'You're hysterical,' she said coldly. 'No one's going to take these ridiculous accusations seriously. You were always unbalanced and neurotic.'

'If I was that loony, you shouldn't have schemed to get me to marry your gay son, should you?' Belinda retorted. 'Oh, Margaret told me how you and her mother cooked up the scheme! I was a silly little idiot without any experience, desperate for someone to fall in love with me – I was the perfect sacrificial lamb, wasn't I?' She looked at Oliver. 'He was so handsome, so charming – how could I possibly know that he wasn't in love with me, not the least little bit? That he didn't even *like* girls?'

'Well!' Queen Alexandra said, the words seeming dragged out of her. 'You've certainly grown up!'

'I was this little one's age,' Belinda said, hugging her daughter. 'Young, weak, easily manipulated. And yes – I'm a grown woman now. Believe me, I'm not hysterical any more.' She met the Queen's eyes full-on before she looked back at her ex-husband. 'Oliver, tell me the truth – I thought it was you who got someone to give me an overdose. But it wasn't, was it?'

All the wind had gone out of Oliver; his hands were hanging by his sides, limp as the hair that was still tumbled over his eyes. He shook his head, silent.

Behind him, Simon's gaze was fixed on Belinda imploringly; Belinda glanced at him, recognizing him, and gave him a tiny, fleeting smile to say that she wouldn't betray the fact that it had been Simon, all those years ago, who had been tasked by Martin to kill Belinda, and who had, instead, warned her of the danger she was in. Simon, who had slipped in now to see what was going on, to try to protect Belinda if he could. Simon, who had always felt guilty about being caught in bed with Belinda's husband, causing her to go into premature labour with Hugo.

And then Belinda looked back at the Queen, her real enemy, the person to whom Martin had always been reporting; Martin, who would have done anything to keep his beloved Oliver's secret safe.

'You tried to kill me back then, and you told MI6 to put a bomb on my private plane just a few days ago,' Belinda said flatly to her ex-mother-in-law. 'That has to stop. I promise, on my life, I'll never say a word to anyone about all this, for my children's sake. I'll never let anyone know that I'm alive. I'll go on living as I have been, with utter discretion. No scandal, no rumours. Just as I've managed so well for decades. *But*—' she fixed Alexandra with a long, firm stare – 'I want to see my children. That's non-negotiable. I want them to be able to come to visit me. And, eventually, I want to meet my grandchildren.'

She smiled at Hugo and Chloe, who both went pink and smiled back.

'That's the deal,' Belinda said.

'You don't really have any choice, Your Majesties,' Lady Margaret said simply. 'Accept the status quo, and we'll all sail through this. Trust Belinda to—'

'*Trust* her? My God!' Queen Alexandra burst out. 'I'd as soon trust a nasty little—'

'*Mother*,' Oliver said, very quietly, but enough to stop her outburst. '*Stop*. You tried to *kill* her?'

'It was for *you*, Oliver!' His mother walked quickly over to him, taking his hands in her small plump ones. 'For you! To protect you! So that no one would ever find out that you were – that you were—'

'Homosexual,' Oliver finished her sentence, sounding exhausted. 'That I'm a homosexual, Mother.'

Both she and the King flinched at the words. Stephen turned away, his back to his son, his gaze fixed on the throne with SR embroidered on the back, his fists clenched. A muscle pulsed in his jaw.

'I never wanted to get married,' Oliver continued wearily. 'You *knew* I never wanted to get married. You should never have made me.'

'But you had to! We needed an heir! *You* needed—'

'I had plenty of cousins to inherit,' Oliver corrected her. 'You just couldn't bear the fact that you had a gay son, so you decided on a cover-up.' He looked at Belinda. 'I wanted to marry a girl who knew about me, who wouldn't mind,' he said. 'Someone like – well, like Margaret.'

'A lesbian,' Margaret said frankly. 'Yes, that would have been a *much* better idea all round. You could have gone the turkey-baster route. Quite a few lavender marriages did that, you know, back in the old days.'

Oliver huffed out a dry laugh.

'Exactly. But no, Mother wanted the full monty. Loving

wife, children, the lot. God, what an awful sham. An awful sham,' he repeated. 'I'm sorry, Belinda.'

'It's all right,' she said, tears of relief forming in her eyes at both the acknowledgement and the apology; she had never thought she would hear either from her ex-husband. 'It's over now.'

'Leave her alone, Mother,' Oliver said, dropping his mother's hands, and stepping away from her. 'Leave us all alone. I swear, if I hear that anything's happened to Belinda, I'll tell the world what I am. Who I am.'

'Oh my God!' The Queen's hands rose to her face, cupping her cheeks. 'Oliver, *no – please* – the *scandal—*'

'I know what you're really afraid of,' Oliver said. 'Christ, I'm tired. I don't think I've ever been this tired before in my life.'

He raised one hand and pushed back his hair; Martin made a tiny sound of relief at seeing Oliver's elegance restored.

'I know *exactly* what you're afraid of,' he reiterated, and he glanced at his father's elegantly suited back. 'Don't worry, I won't say a word. But believe me, I know. I know why Father couldn't bear the sight of me, ever. I know that certain of my *ways*, my *mannerisms*, struck far too close to home. Like looking in a mirror, wasn't it, Father?'

King Stephen, without a word, stalked as fast as a man over eighty could manage out of the Throne Room. His wife, her lips sealed tightly together, gave her son a long, agonized look and then hurried after her husband.

'I don't know what he's talking about, Stephen,' she said. 'Oliver's always been a very silly boy. No one has *any* idea what he's talking about . . .'

As her voice faded away, Oliver reached out and steadied himself, momentarily, on Martin's shoulder.

'God, I'm shattered,' he said. 'You'd think I'd feel better, wouldn't you, having got all that out at last? But I don't. I feel bloody awful. I'm going to go and lie down. Martin, come with me, will you?'

Martin, his eyes moist, nodded, his head ducked so that no one could see the ecstasy on his face at his idol's having turned to him for comfort.

'It'll be all right,' Oliver said, looking at the women and Hugo. 'Mother won't lift a finger against you now, Belinda. She's lived most of her life trying to make sure that some secrets never come out. Believe me, she'll set down all her weapons in return for me not pulling the stopper out of that bottle.' He blinked.

'I'm sorry about—'

He looked at his daughter.

'My bloody temper,' he muttered. 'I'm sorry.' He turned away. 'It hasn't been easy,' he mumbled. 'It's never been easy.'

With Martin following at his heels, he walked slowly from the Throne Room.

'I actually feel sorry for him,' Belinda said, watching him go, waiting till he was out of earshot. She shook her head in disbelief. 'I can't believe it. I'm actually saying I feel sorry for Oliver. I never thought *that* day would come.'

'It's over, Lumps,' Lady Margaret said. 'I honestly can't quite take it in yet.'

'It's a victory,' Belinda said. Her arm was round her daughter, and she stretched out her other hand to Hugo and Chloe, who came to her side. Simon started to slip out of the room, and she caught his eye for a moment, mouthing 'Thank you' to him; he blushed, flashing her a quick smile as he went.

'It's a victory,' she repeated, hugging the three young people. 'I know it is, but it feels so sad. So strange. Doesn't it? As if we won a battle, but everyone died.'

Her eyes lingered briefly on the doorway through which the King, Queen, and Prince of Wales had left; if she thought

it was ironic that they had all exited in the direction of the
Royal Closet, she kept that observation to herself.

'I need a stiff drink,' Lady Margaret muttered. 'Stiffer than
a bloody tent pole, as Mummy used to say.'

'I don't want to stay here,' Sophie said in a tiny voice.
'Let's go home, Mummy.'

'Oh, darling . . .'

Belinda smoothed her daughter's blonde hair tenderly.

'You were wonderful,' Chloe said to her fiancé as the
group turned to walk out of the Throne Room. 'Absolutely
wonderful.' She smiled at him. 'Majestic.'

He bent to kiss her swiftly.

'I couldn't have done it without you here,' he said. 'I'm so
lucky to have you, Chlo. It was even worse than we thought
it would be.'

'I know.' Chloe shuddered. 'It was horrible. But it's over
and done with, and your mother's safe. Which is the most
important thing of all.'

Belinda was ahead, with one arm round Sophie, the other
round Lady Margaret. On the threshold that led to the Green
Drawing Room, she turned to look back, a last brief glance at
the opulent red and gold Throne Room.

'You know I never thought I'd see this room again,' she
said quietly. 'I was so excited about being queen, about
having my own throne here. I'd come in here sometimes and
imagine it to console myself, when Oliver was being odder
and odder and I was getting more and more miserable. I'd tell
myself that being queen would make up for everything, and
sometimes I almost managed to convince myself it was
true . . .'

She drew in a deep breath.

'Goodness, what a long time ago that was! It feels like it all
happened to an entirely different person.'

Belinda turned away again, firmly putting the past behind her.

'Come on, everyone,' she said. 'Let's go back to KP and hole up for three days straight and stuff our faces and watch silly films and never, *ever*, talk about any of this again.'

Hand in hand, following the group of women, Hugo and Chloe walked towards the double doors of the Throne Room.

'If you're having second thoughts,' Hugo said to her rather sadly, 'I wouldn't blame you. This is a bloody fucked-up family you're marrying into.'

Chloe smiled up at him.

'I'm not marrying your family,' she said firmly, 'and I'm not marrying your title. I'm marrying *you*, Hugo.'

She leaned up to kiss him.

'And your family may be mostly fucked-up,' she assured him, 'but your mum is *totally* amazing!'

Epilogue

The full weight of summer heat had settled down over Morocco, even in the mountains, steady, relentless sunlight pouring over the rock formations like glittering cascades of gold. The Tarhouna Palace, positioned at one of the highest peaks of the High Atlas, had been built to take advantage of the *scirocco* and *chergui* winds that blow east and west over the Atlas Mountains; set well above the dust and sand of the Sahara, its many windows were designed to allow breezes to blow gently through the palace, its shaded stone courtyards trapped and held the cool.

Louvred wooden shutters had been fixed to every window to let in any waft of air while keeping out the sun. They were carved with intricate, traditionally Moroccan intaglio designs that made softly moving patterns on the two bodies intertwined on the bed in a suite high in an eastern corner of the palace. Sweat oiled their slowly moving limbs, the wide wooden blades of the overhead fan gently circulating the hot air below the tiled ceiling, salty drops trickling down their backs and stomachs, joining the dampness at their linked groins.

The steady turn of the fan blades, the trance-like music of the Orb playing softly, were almost the only sounds in the bedroom; the gasps of the lovers were almost inaudible, their heads leaning against each other's, their lips almost linked. They were trying to make their movements as small as possible, each tilt of their hips exquisitely minimal, each rub of Attila's cock inside Lori drawing a tiny moan from both of them. In the three months they had been staying at the Tarhouna Palace, they had had sex in every conceivable way possible, alone in their rooms, thick stone walls between them and the rest of the world; if they turned off the haunting music, all they would have heard were the calls of the Atlas horned larks circling the palace, riding the currents of the *chergui* winds breaking against the barrier of the mountain range.

These months had been like a honeymoon to them, as Attila had said to Lori in the first days of their time together. They had barely stirred from their rooms, utterly, blissfully, selfishly closing themselves off in an orgy of pleasure, finally relishing the fact that they didn't need to hide how they felt about each other; Belinda, very sympathetic, remembering her own sort-of-honeymoon with Rahim on Montecapra, had sent up trays of food to wait outside their door until they were ready to emerge: carafes of red local wine, flatbreads stuffed with cheese and meat, chicken salad with pomegranate, aubergine and mint, tabbouleh crunchy with fresh parsley, orange slices exotically dressed with rosewater.

They had fucked and feasted gratefully, taken long soaks in the huge mosaic sunken bath and fallen asleep to wake up and fuck and feast all over again; it had been nearly three days until they emerged from their rooms, limbs relaxed, wreathed in smiles, holding hands, unable to speak without glancing at each other, unmistakably in love and, equally unmistakably, with very little mental ability left, having spent the last seventy-two hours fucking each other's brains out. After that initial orgy, they had managed to join Belinda and Rahim for meals and swims in the pool; Lori had taken yoga lessons from Belinda, who was delighted, finally, to have someone with whom she could work out to her Pure Barre DVDs as well. Attila trained Rahim in his private gym, and the men established a solid friendship, playing billiards and dominoes, watching sport on TV. Attila was too clean-living to join Rahim in his regular after-dinner cigar, but the two men would happily sit together on one of the terraces, night after night, as content to say very little as Belinda and Lori were, chattering away over coffee, to gradually share every detail of their lives.

But that still left Lori and Attila great swathes of free time to retire to their rooms and make love. They had fallen into a gradual pattern, as most couples do, but what they enjoyed the most were these seemingly endless, sweat-soaked, almost tantric afternoon sessions where Attila's cock, once inside Lori, never pulled out, where they rocked slowly and steadily to long, drawn-out, near-simultaneous orgasms, where their bodies throbbed so much against each other, the anticipation so prolonged, that when they finally came their moans mingled, their arms wrapped round each other, their tongues in each other's mouths; with their eyes closed it was impossible in those moments to know where one ended and the other began.

Attila's legs were crossed, Lori sitting in his lap, his huge wide thighs as comfortable beneath her as a chair, her own rising and falling almost imperceptibly, his arms linked behind her propping her, allowing her to lean back and find just the right angle as she tilted back and forth, rocking herself closer and closer to release. Her hands were round his neck, pulling him to her every now and then for a series of drugging kisses; this deliberate slowing down was absolutely trippy, made her head swirl and feel as if her body were lifting off the mattress, as if she had taken a huge dose of Dr Bruschsson's pills. And then she would allow herself to grind briefly down, rub their crotches against each other, feel the extra pressure of her clitoris against his thick pubic hairs, her own wet tangle of curls scratching deliciously for extra friction, hearing him hiss out a breath and lock his big arms even tighter around her, his cock pushing fractionally higher inside her, filling her even more deeply, as they both took a tiny step closer to being unable to hold out any longer . . .

She wanted it to last for ever; she wanted to explode all over him, feel him shoot up inside her; those two contradictory sensations were held in perfect tension, like a soap bubble rising slowly up into the air, glistening with a kaleidoscope of bright evanescent colours. The pressure to move faster was becoming harder and harder to resist, but that was part of the pleasure: and, too, the fact that they literally did have all the time in the world, after those tortured weeks in Mexico, longing for each other and unable to finish what they'd started, those awful few days back in Herzoslovakia apart from each other. Now they could stay in here all day and all night, free to do anything they wanted, apart from the delicious constraints they imposed on each other, like the unspoken accord that Lori couldn't speed up, that she had to keep moving at this infinitesimal pace, rocking Attila's cock inside her, until their bodies finally took over completely . . .

They were so absorbed in each other and the music that was washing hypnotically over them like the circling of the fan above the bed, that it took Lori a while to register the tiny beeping sound she was hearing, and then, slowly, to realize that it wasn't part of the track, that it was from the bedside table. They didn't have all the time in the world after all.

'Ah, damn it,' she whispered against Attila's mouth. 'That's my alarm – I have to go keep Belinda company . . .'

Attila didn't say a word. He shifted, his arms closing fully around Lori's waist, managing to lift her despite the slippery rivulets of sweat running down their bodies now, swinging his legs with one gymnastic twist of his waist so that the soles of his feet landed on the tiled floor. He settled Lori squarely in his lap, raised his hips and started a fast series of pumps that made her scream, dig her hands into the great deltoid muscles of his back, shove her groin right up into his and lean back at a ninety-degree angle, trusting him not to let her fall. His hands clutched her buttocks, pulling them down so she was almost lying on his thighs; her hands left his back, reached out into the air, grabbed his forearms and held on for dear life as she leaned back even more, till she was almost horizontal, her thighs wrapped round his waist, his cock plunging into her again and again.

Her fingers dug into his arms, grateful for the curling hair that provided some traction, stopped her slipping; his even tighter-curling nest of hair rubbed insistently against her clitoris. This was the only way she had ever come without fingers or tongue helping her along, this gradual build-up, and now she knew that she didn't need any extra help, that these last final grinds of his groin into hers would send her fast and hard to her destination—

Ah! There it is, there it is—

She let go completely, her torso rocking as his thighs rose and fell beneath it in a long series of thrusts, his knees beating against her shoulders as he grunted and she felt his cock jerking with orgasm deep inside her. Her skin was too heated, too slick with sweat, to feel the extra heat of his ejaculation, but she relished the knowledge that he was coming inside her, that Belinda, bless her, had sorted Lori out with the Pill almost as soon as she and Attila had arrived in Morocco.

Belinda's been amazingly supportive to me. So now it's my turn to go and support her . . .

With huge reluctance, she untwined her legs from her lover's waist, pulled herself off him, their bodies separating with a wet, sucking noise, steadied herself on his lap, found the floor with her feet. She kissed him and padded off to the bathroom, showering swiftly but thoroughly, towelling and working scented geranium oil into her body to ward off the mosquitoes, returning to the bedroom to pull on a loose cotton dress and flip-flops. Attila lay sprawled on the mattress, arms flung wide, sweat glistening all over his magnificent body, his chest heaving, his penis only gradually shrinking down, lying pink and satisfied in its bed of thick black curls.

'Love you,' she said, pushing back her wet hair from her face: it would dry in five minutes in the hot desert air.

Attila merely grunted as she left the room, but she didn't need him to say it back. She had never been more confident of anything in her life than his love for her.

Lori went quickly down the stone staircase and along the corridor to the central set of rooms that Belinda and Rahim used for entertaining, which ran along the northern wing of the palace. Belinda was already ensconced in the television room on one of the big bleached linen sofas, and turned her head with a huge smile to see Lori coming in.

'It's started!' she said happily.

'I'm sorry – did I miss anything?'

'No, it goes on for ages!' Belinda said, patting the sofa next to her. 'I should know! We haven't even seen her yet.' She grinned. 'I'm just grateful you could drag yourself away from your siesta . . .'

'I'll make popcorn,' Lori said, blushing. 'And, um, get us some nice cold pomegranate juice.'

Belinda was absolutely right. Hugo and Chloe's elaborate, extended wedding went on for hours. When Lori returned from the kitchens with a bowl of popcorn, followed by Fatiha with a tray of iced pomegranate juice and chilled gold-decorated glasses, they had plenty of time to curl up, sip juice, and work their way through half the bowl of popcorn before Chloe emerged from the landau outside Westminster Abbey, took her father's hand, and stood, as both Belinda and Lori had once done, waiting for their bridesmaids to unfurl their trains.

Lauren was supervising: she was not a bridesmaid herself, so she could keep an eye from behind the scenes on every detail of the ceremony. In a strapless, calf-length black and white polka-dot dress over tulle petticoats, her hair up in a beehive with a red camellia in it that matched her suede court shoes, she was a welcome dash of retro style, and the commentators were thoroughly approving of her outfit. Beside her, Dave hovered, off-duty as her date, but always alert.

'Oh, she's so beautiful,' Belinda said fondly, watching Chloe start her slow walk up the steps of Westminster Abbey. 'And the dress looks wonderful. *Much* nicer than mine was.'

'Mine was beautiful,' Lori said with an ironic smile.

'It really was!' Belinda giggled. 'Your dress was the best thing about your entire wedding! Oh my God, and your tiara – your jewels – you looked *amazing*. Like a film star. Until you started crying, of course.'

Chloe's train pooled out behind her on the red carpet, Sophie, the chief bridesmaid, having eased it out to its full width; Sophie lifted it and proceeded after Chloe. Lauren had relented, allowing Sophie to wear a pale blue silk crepe bridesmaid's dress that suited her colouring perfectly. It had been very easy for Chloe and Lauren to soften their attitude towards Sophie, who had undergone a sea change in her personality since being reunited with her mother, not to mention the shocking confrontation in the Buckingham Palace Throne Room.

The revelation that Belinda wasn't dead, that she had risked her life to come back to Britain to see her children, had transformed Sophie from a messed-up party girl to a quiet, comparatively sober young woman who wanted nothing more than to spend as much time with her brother and his fiancée as possible. Lauren had said dryly to Chloe that this wouldn't last, that Sophie would doubtless swing back on the pendulum to somewhere more balanced, but Chloe was cautiously enjoying this new, infinitely sweeter Sophie, and hoped that at least Sophie's new-found appreciation for the bourgeois family values shared by Hugo and Chloe would last.

'Sophie looks *so* lovely in blue,' Belinda said contentedly. 'What a pretty dress, and so age-appropriate – she looks young but still smart. She and Chloe sent me loads of photos, so I knew Sophie's frock would be lovely, but I didn't get a full sense of Chloe's without the train.' She sighed. 'I do wish I could be there . . .'

Lori grimaced, unable to offer consolation. She tried irony instead.

'You know the funny thing,' she said, 'is that both of our ex-husbands are there and *we're* actually the ones who'd much rather have gone.'

'*So* true!' That put a smile back on Belinda's face. 'Men hate weddings! Look at our two hiding out next door – they're not going to watch a moment of this unless we make them. Oh, I'm *so* glad you and Attila are here, Lori.'

'Me too,' Lori said fervently. 'I need my Creepy Ex-Royal Husbands Anonymous support group just as much as you do, believe me.'

The two women exchanged a long sympathetic glance before turning back to the screen. An overhead shot showed the full aisle of the abbey, Chloe nearly at the altar, her small, white-clad, veiled figure tiny compared to the dramatic sweeping length of her train. Beside her, Geoff, very smart in full morning dress, his boutonnière a traditional white carnation, accompanied her along the last few steps, placed her hand in Hugo's, smiled at the bride and groom, and stepped back, turning to join his wife in the front pew.

Eileen, in a pale pink suit with a matching pillbox hat dyed to match, was beaming a smile as wide as the Cheshire Cat's: anyone who had bet on Eileen crying through the ceremony would have lost their money. Her daughter was marrying a lovely young man from a good family, and that was something to be over the moon about. Eileen was much more likely to cry if and when she eventually got back to Waltham Forest, checked the street party videos and discovered that, despite her meticulously detailed instructions, dozy Sheila had neglected to judge the doughnut-eating contest with the same critical precision that Eileen brought to bear on deciding whether people had a trace of sugar on their mouth or not.

Sophie, having arranged Chloe's train down the red-carpeted steps, came forward to take Chloe's bouquet from her. She, Chloe and Hugo all exchanged a swift look, a smile that spoke, momentarily, of the secret that they shared, their happiness that, if Belinda couldn't be there in person, they knew she was at least watching them all from her safe eyrie in Morocco.

'Does it bring back any memories?' Lori asked Belinda curiously.

'Not really,' Belinda said. 'It was such a long time ago. And when things started to go bad, it rather ruined all the pleasure I'd taken in my wedding and my honeymoon . . . I looked back and everything just seemed so – unreal.'

'I know *exactly* what you mean,' Lori said.

She was already divorced, had watched her now ex-husband take his seat in the Abbey, heard her name mentioned by the 'royal expert' reporter covering Hugo and Chloe's wedding:

'And that's King Joachim, *very* bravely attending after his own recent marriage ended in such disastrous circumstances . . . it was of course annulled very shortly after he and the now ex-Queen Lori returned from honeymoon. Speculation has been *rampant* for the reason behind the annulment, with the petition citing irreconcilable differences – *such* a shame, but we all remember Lori's tears at the wedding, don't we! Thank goodness, we don't anticipate any tears for Chloe, a bride so happy that we can see her beaming smile through her veil . . .'

Joachim and the Dowager, bowing to the inevitable, had decided to dissolve the marriage as swiftly as possible: an annulment actually meant that the marriage had never been consummated, something which was not appropriate for the royal expert to discuss while covering another wedding, but which, naturally, had been the subject of endless speculation in the press ever since the announcement. In a way, it had been a simple explanation to hint at: Joachim and Lori had been old-fashioned enough to wait till their honeymoon, and then sadly come to the realization that they had been wholly incompatible in the bedroom.

Much had been made of how sensible Hugo and Chloe had been to have a relationship before their wedding, to avoid rushing into it until they were sure. The speed of

Joachim and Lori's courtship had been interpreted previously as an enviable whirlwind romance, giving rise to a flood of articles in magazines and papers about love at first sight really existing, fairy-tale romances coming true. Now, however, the same lifestyle columnists the world over were just as happily writing screeds about 'marry in haste, repent at leisure'.

And Joachim now had the perfect excuse never to marry again; the scale of the disaster with Lori would mean he could resist any pressure from his mother to try once more.

Honestly, Lori thought, *he really ought to thank me* . . .

She took a handful of popcorn from the bowl on her lap and crunched a mouthful.

'Want some more?' Lori passed it to Belinda. 'Perfect fat-free snack!'

'Oh, Lori, I wish you'd stay here for ever!' Belinda said wistfully as she took it. 'It's been *so* lovely having you here. To be honest, I only realized how lonely I'd been without girlfriends once you came.'

Lori was just as grateful. The Tarhouna Palace had been the ideal refuge for her and Attila as the news of her flight spread, the perfect place to hole up. Her disguise and the speed of her departure meant that no one in the media had the slightest clue where she was, and though her poor family had had the press camped on their lawns for weeks, the media had eventually given up and moved on to another story. Lori had been Skyping the Makarwiczes constantly and was able to assure them that not only was she absolutely fine and well taken care of, but that, as part of her divorce settlement, their houses and cars were paid up and in their names.

She had taken barely anything else from Joachim, just some start-up money for the new project she was planning

– a gym in Miami, where Attila would be head trainer. They would have to face the music at that stage, of course, brace themselves for a media onslaught and for the likelihood that it would come out that Lori had met Attila while still married to Joachim. But, as Attila said pragmatically, the publicity would bring clients, and they should shrug and try to let it roll off their shoulders.

And goodness knows, Lori thought happily, *Attila has really big shoulders.*

'I haven't gone yet! And I'll be back to visit,' Lori assured her hostess. 'I promise. *We'll* be back to visit. And Sophie and Lady Margaret are coming over in a couple of days, too.'

Belinda beamed. 'Yes, for a good long stay once the wedding's over. I can't *wait*. Oh, look at them – God, I said I wouldn't cry, and I meant it, but they just look so bloody happy! And how lovely to see Hugo and Chloe actually getting it right first time, unlike the pair of us!'

The long ceremony had finally concluded, trumpets playing a fanfare as Hugo and Chloe, having signed the wedding registers, proceeded back down the nave of the Abbey. In the chapel behind the nave, Chloe's veil had been rearranged by Lauren and Sophie, and was now held back from her face by a magnificent diamond tiara. Arms linked, holding hands, Prince Hugo and Princess Chloe were flushed with happiness, their eyes sparkling as brightly as the diamonds adorning Chloe's head and earlobes.

'Rahim!' Belinda called. 'They're coming out – you *have* to see them now!'

The clicking of billiard balls, which had been heard from the room next door for the last half hour or so, finally stopped: cues clattered back into the rack and Rahim and Attila appeared, doing their best to act as if they didn't mind having to stop their game, but not succeeding.

'Just have a *look*,' Belinda said, stretching out her hand to Rahim. 'See how happy they are!'

'She's a lovely bride,' Rahim said gently. 'And they look very happy together.'

'They look absolutely over the moon!' Belinda corrected him. 'Oh, I'm *not* going to cry, I'm *not* . . .'

'She is much happier than Lori was when she got married,' Attila said, grinning widely as he sat down next to his girl-friend and took the popcorn from Belinda.

'*That's* not exactly difficult,' Lori said, kissing him enthu-siastically and popping some corn into his mouth.

'Oh, young lovers,' Belinda said, looking at them fondly. 'I remember the days when we couldn't keep our hands off each other either.'

'We don't do so badly now,' Rahim said firmly, taking a seat on the sofa beside her, putting his hand on her thigh.

'No, we don't.' Belinda put her hand over his. 'I have you, and my support group with Lori, and my daughter's coming to visit in a few days, *and* we're planning a family holiday with Hugo and Chloe as well on Montecapra late in the autumn! Oh, I'm so excited.'

She looked back at the screen, heaving a long sigh of contentment at the sight of her son marrying the woman he loved.

'You're absolutely right, darling,' she said to Rahim. 'We don't do so badly at all. And nor do Lori and Attila,' she added, smiling at their guests. 'It would have been lovely to get it right first time round, but we got our fairy-tale *second* ending, didn't we? Better late than never.'

'Attila makes me feel like a queen,' Lori said, curling up with her legs over his. 'And you live in a palace with a charm-ing prince, Belinda.' She winked at Rahim, who flourished her a little bow. 'Even if you can't go out much. But that's the thing about fairy tales, isn't it? They never tell you what happens after the wedding . . . now *that* would be a Disney film I'd like to see!'

'Oh,' Belinda said wistfully, 'I'd like to see that too. Maybe one day they'll tell *our* stories?'

She raised a glass of pomegranate juice to Lori, and, leaning over, the ex-Princess and the ex-Queen toasted each other.

'But for now, we'll just be the very exclusive Ex-Royals Anonymous group,' Belinda said, smiling. 'Which as far as I'm concerned, makes us two of the luckiest women in the world.'

Wish you were here? You could be...

Rebecca Chance, *Sunday Times* bestselling author of fabulously luxe bonkbusters, writes:

'I've travelled to 5* hotels all over the world researching my novels, but the Thomson A La Carte El Dorado Casitas Royale, on Mexico's gorgeous Mayan Riviera, took my breath away. I was lucky enough to visit earlier this year and have featured the resort in KILLER QUEENS. From the moment I arrived and was greeted at check-in with a chilled glass of champagne with guava nectar and an aromatherapy neck wrap, the glamour, luxury and pampering of the resort never ended. The Gourmet Inclusive eating options, ranging from healthy wraps to Italian haute cuisine and wickedly tempting desserts, are unbelievable, and washed down with margaritas and daiquiris in the sophisticated Martini and Bellini Bars. It was a holiday – err, research trip! – fit for a queen. Which is perfect, as a queen in my book honeymoons there and finds out that the unbelievably romantic, beachfront setting leads to all sorts of unexpected temptations!'

'To enter the competition to win an all-expenses paid, seven night stay for one very lucky couple at the El Dorado Casitas Royale courtesy of Thomson – take it from me, it truly will be the holiday of a lifetime.'

See www.pages.simonandschuster.co.uk/competitions/killerqueens